MIS...
MI...
MIRACLE BABY

BY
ANNE FRASER

HOW TO SAVE
A MARRIAGE
IN A MILLION

BY
LEONIE KNIGHT

MILLS & BOON

He sneaked another glance at her. She was still beautiful, but most of the light had gone out of her.

What had changed her from the daredevil, energetic girl she had been to this cool, almost reticent woman? Why had she stopped working? Especially when it was clear from the look on her face when she had helped during Mary's labour that being a midwife was what she was born to do. And then there was that odd look on her face when she'd held the baby in her arms. For a moment she had seemed to hesitate before she had taken the newborn. That wasn't in keeping with someone who was used to delivering babies. This Ellen was a mystery. Was she running away from something? And, if so, what?

He shook his head. Underneath the closed-off façade he was sure the Ellen he had once known still lurked, and somewhere inside him there was that same protective feeling. If Ellen was in trouble he wanted to know.

MISTLETOE, MIDWIFE... MIRACLE BABY

BY
ANNE FRASER

First published in Great Britain 2011
by Mills & Boon, an imprint of Harlequin (UK) Limited.
Harlequin (UK) Limited, Eton House, 18-24 Paradise Road,
Richmond, Surrey TW9 1SR

© Anne Fraser 2011

ISBN: 978 0 263 88613 9

Harlequin (UK) policy is to use papers that are natural, renewable and recyclable products and made from wood grown in sustainable forests. The logging and manufacturing process conform to the legal environmental regulations of the country of origin.

Printed and bound in Spain
by Blackprint CPI, Barcelona

Dear Reader

Maternity units can be special and magical places at Christmas—especially on Christmas Day, when everyone looks forward to the first Christmas baby.

However, not all pregnancies are straightforward, and some need the help and expertise of a dedicated maternity team—like midwife Ellen Nicholson and Dr Sean Jamieson—to ensure a healthy outcome for mother and baby.

And when that woman is Ellen herself, who has an illness that can be fatal in pregnancy, it's going to need more than the highly skilled maternity team—it's going to need a miracle.

I hope you enjoy Ellen and Sean's story.

Warm wishes

Anne Fraser

PS You might wish to keep a box of tissues handy!

Anne Fraser was born in Scotland, but brought up in South Africa. After she left school she returned to the birthplace of her parents, the remote Western Islands of Scotland. She left there to train as a nurse, before going on to university to study English Literature. After the birth of her first child she and her doctor husband travelled the world, working in rural Africa, Australia and Northern Canada. Anne still works in the health sector. To relax, she enjoys spending time with her family, reading, walking and travelling.

Recent titles by the same author:

DOCTOR ON THE RED CARPET
THE PLAYBOY OF HARLEY STREET
THE DOCTOR AND THE DEBUTANTE
DAREDEVIL, DOCTOR…DAD!†
MIRACLE: MARRIAGE REUNITED
SPANISH DOCTOR, PREGNANT MIDWIFE*

The Brides of Penhally Bay
†*St Piran's Hospital*

Did you know these are also available as eBooks?
Visit www.millsandboon.co.uk

CHAPTER ONE

ELLEN stopped her car at the top of the steep drive and surveyed the icy track to her grandmother's house with dismay. Even if she could navigate the car down the slope she would never be able to reverse it back up without the danger of sliding into the deep ditches on either side.

She climbed out of the driver's seat and into the bitter wind and lightly falling snow. She'd been driving solidly for over ten hours and every muscle ached from hunching over the steering wheel as she'd raced north in an attempt to beat the snow that was predicted to engulf Scotland. Huddling into her ski jacket and cursing the high heels of her leather boots, she decided to leave her large suitcases in the boot for later and to walk down the drive.

Taking a deep breath, she filled her lungs with the sharp, fresh air of the Highlands and felt some of her exhaustion and doubt slip away. She had been right to come. This is where she needed to be right now—the only place she had ever truly known as home.

The farmhouse roof peeked above the tops of evergreen pine and elder, smoke from the chimney curling into the grey afternoon sky. Ellen could already visualise Gran stoking up the fire, a batch of scones or bread rising in the oven, the kettle on the stove ever ready to make a warming cup of tea. A twist of anxiety knotted in Ellen's ribs and for a second she faltered. Was she being selfish coming back? She hadn't told Gran the true reason why she was coming to stay, only that she had been ill and needed time to get her strength back. If Gran knew the truth it would only upset her and she couldn't bear to do that to the woman who meant the world to her.

Puffing out her cheeks, Ellen swallowed hard. Her emotions were still all over the place; for a moment—a split second—she would forget, then the reality of her situation would hit her again, threatening to crush her.

Needing a few moments to compose herself, Ellen thrust her hands in her parka pockets, her eyes straying over the countryside until she picked out the Jamieson house. Memories rushed back: sitting in their large farmhouse kitchen drinking in the atmosphere of laughter and love pretending, if only for a short while, that she was part of a large and caring family. But the Jamiesons had moved away. And so had Sean. Where was he now? Gran had said that he planned to renovate the house his parents had left behind. Why? Was he planning to put down roots? Had he met someone and was preparing a home for them to share? Maybe even start a family?

Something she would never have.

Grabbing her overnight bag, she set off down the track, picking her way carefully in her three-inch-heel boots. Twice she nearly went over on her ankle, and twice she just managed to stay on her feet. Breaking a leg was the last thing she needed right now. Ellen suppressed a wave of self-pity that threatened to crush her. There was no point giving in to it. She had to look to the future—however bleak it seemed right now.

She was halfway down the drive when she became aware of a rhythmic banging noise cutting through the air. Glancing in the direction of the sound, to the side and rear of her grandmother's house, she saw a tall figure swinging an axe, making short work of splitting logs. For goodness' sake, whoever it was had to be freezing. He was wearing only a T-shirt and jeans in the sub-zero temperatures as he swung the axe over his shoulder.

There was something primitive about the way he worked, his muscles bunching with each lift of the axe, that made her pause to watch him. He seemed lost in his own world, oblivious to the snow falling around him, settling on his dark head.

Suddenly, as Ellen moved off again, her legs went completely from beneath her. She had been so intent on the figure in front of her, she'd taken her eyes off the slippery track. She yelped as she struggled to remain upright and the man turned. For a second their eyes held and then she was hitting the ground with a thump that forced the breath from her lungs. Even as she lay there, staring up at the sky, wet snow sneaking down the collar of her jacket, Ellen couldn't help thinking that there was something achingly familiar about those clear, pale eyes.

She heard footsteps crunching towards her and as she tipped her head back, squinting at the figure towering over her, the suspicion grew into certainty.

Sean!

Sean was here! Her already pumping heart beat faster. She had always wondered how she would feel when she saw him again, but in her imagination that meeting had been on neutral ground with her dressed to impress and coolly dismissive. Not in a crumpled heap at his feet after an exhausting and tense drive and looking like a wrung-out dishcloth.

Oh, damn it! And he looked even more devastatingly handsome than she remembered. Or was that because she was looking at him upside down?

Mortified, Ellen tried to get back up but in her panic her high-heeled boots couldn't get purchase on the ice. Just great! She was scrabbling around on the ground like some sort of flapping fish that had just been landed.

A hand reached down and before she knew it she was back on her feet.

'Are you okay?'

His voice still gave her goosebumps. After all this time?

Sean stood back, keeping a grip on her elbow, and whistled under his breath. 'Ellen Nicholson? If Maggie hadn't told me you were coming to stay, I would never have recognised you. You've changed.' He studied her with amusement. 'Or, then again, maybe not.'

His only-too-well-remembered grin made something in her chest squeeze. If she had changed, so had he. The last time she had seen him, and the memory made her cheeks burn, he had been tall and gangly. Somewhere along the way he had filled out. And in impressive style.

Flustered, Ellen wiped the snow off her jacket and the back of her trousers. Of course she'd changed. The last time he'd seen her she'd been a scrawny teenager with attitude and a terrible crush. Eight years later she was a grown woman with a death sentence hanging over her. Her past and present selves couldn't be more different. She had a sudden intense longing to be that old Ellen who still believed that miracles happened and that the world and life were simply waiting to give her everything she desired.

She could have done without bumping into Sean Jamieson right now. Just the sight of him had been enough to bring the memories of how she'd felt about him tumbling back. Suddenly she was that seventeen-year-old again, the one who had worshipped the ground this man had walked on.

Ellen pushed snow-dampened hair off her cheeks, trying

desperately to regain a modicum of self-assurance. 'Oh, hello, Sean. Nice to see you again.'

Wow, had that come out as gauche as it had sounded to her own ears? 'Not that I expected to see you here. I mean I thought you were away somewhere.' Great. Now she was babbling.

'Are you okay?' he asked. 'Did you hurt yourself?'

'Not at all. I'm perfectly fine, thanks.' And to prove it she took a step forward. Rather too quickly as it transpired. To her horror, she found herself once more flat on her back and staring up at the snow-darkened sky.

'I think I'll just stay down here till the snow melts,' she mumbled, mortified.

Sean bent down on his haunches next to her and grinned. The way his smile still made her insides turn to mush dismayed her.

'You could be out here for a while you know. Can I bring you anything?'

Despite her ridiculous situation and the crazy sensations ricocheting around inside her, she smiled. 'A cup of tea would be nice and perhaps a hot-water bottle.'

'Scone?'

'Mmm. Jam and cream.'

And now she was laughing along with him.

This time she held out her hand for him to pull her to her feet. It was as if the years had melted away and they were back to the way they always used to be all those years ago.

Sean kissed her lightly on her cheek and something sizzled below her skin, making her flustered all over again.

'Still getting into scrapes?' he asked, still smiling. 'Looks like some things haven't changed. Would you like me to have a look at your ankle?'

No, she damn well wouldn't. The last thing she wanted was

for him to peel off her boots. She hadn't shaved her legs for days. Heavens, what was she thinking? Unshaved legs were the least of her problems.

'What *are* you doing here?' she asked. 'I thought you were working in Glasgow, or Australia?' He should be in Glasgow. Or Australia. Yes, Australia was better. As far away from her grandmother's home as was physically possible. Aware she sounded annoyed with him, she softened her tone. 'Are you here on holiday? I mean, Gran mentioned you were going to renovate your old family home, but I suppose I thought you'd wait until the summer to get started.'

Even better. Not. Now she was letting him know that she had been thinking about him, talking about him.

His smile widened. 'Which one of your questions would you like me to answer first?'

'Take your pick!' She smiled breezily. At least she hoped that was the way it appeared to him.

'I am renovating the house but it's had to be completely gutted and is uninhabitable at the moment.' He brushed flakes of snow and mulched leaves from her jacket and it took every ounce of willpower not to jump away from his touch. 'Maggie's letting me use the old gatehouse in the meantime.'

The gatehouse? The one on the perimeter of her gran's land? The one that was barely a stone's throw from where they were standing? The knowledge dismayed Ellen. The biggest advantage of coming here to be with Gran was that she could hide herself away and not have anything to do with anyone. Damn, damn, damn. Why did Sean have to come back into her life? And now of all times?

'So you're renovating while you're home on holiday, then?' Ellen asked hopefully.

Sean looked puzzled.

'No, I'm here permanently. Or as permanently as I stay

nywhere. I plan to move into the old house as soon as it's eady.' He looked back at the pile of chopped wood in front of him. 'Your grandmother needed some logs. I had some xtras from my own delivery so I said I'd split some for her.'

Ellen shivered. It wasn't just from the cold, although the ce on her trousers was beginning to melt, seeping through er clothes and freezing her skin. It was a shock, seeing him. Almost as much of a shock as falling on her backside.

'Look,' Sean said, 'Maggie's been like a cat on a hot tin oof all morning, waiting for you. If we don't get you inside he'll come looking for you. We can catch up once you've aid hello and you're out of these wet clothes.'

As usual he was right. In that respect he hadn't changed. He was still the honorary older brother looking out for her. t was ridiculous to stay out in the cold and wet, particularly eeing as she'd recently been so ill. Not that he could or would now about that. Not ever.

He picked up her bag and, still holding on to her elbow, steered her towards the door.

A face appeared at the window and the next moment the door was swung open and her grandmother was standing here, gathering her up in her arms. Ellen inhaled the familiar sweetness of her gran's perfume and wished she could stay closeted in her soft, warm and safe embrace for ever.

'Ellen, child. You're soaked!' her grandmother said. 'Come away in to the fire and get warmed up. You too, Sean. I'll never know how you youngsters put up with being outside with hardly anything on. Don't you know you can catch your deaths? And you, Ellen, you should be taking more care. Especially after being ill.'

Her words made Ellen wince, but she forced a smile to her lips. It was wonderful to see Gran again. Even if her fussing made her want to break down and spill out the horror of these past couple of weeks. But she forced her emotions back down. She'd promised herself that she wouldn't burden Gran and she would keep that promise, however tempting the need to share her secret.

'Ill?' Sean frowned at her. 'With what, Ellen?'

Slipping off her jacket and scarf, Ellen took her time shaking them out and hanging them up on the coat hooks by the door. The last thing she needed right now was their concerned looks. Or Sean ever finding out about her illness. She didn't want people's pity or their well-meaning concern—how would she be able to carry on as normal then? But she'd have to be very careful around Sean—she knew from past experience those penetrating blue eyes of his missed very little.

She shrugged. 'Nothing really—a chest infection, that's all. I'm fine now.'

'I'll leave you two to catch up, then,' Sean replied. 'I want to get these logs finished before it gets dark.'

'Yes, thank you. Please don't let us keep you back,' Ellen said quickly. She wanted time to recover after seeing him. Time to transform herself back into the cool, calm and collected woman she wanted to be. At the very least, she still had her pride.

'Come in for a cup of tea before you go back to the gate house,' Maggie said, with a frown at Ellen.

Sean sniffed the air and grinned. 'Is that scones I can smell? In that case, I'll be back as soon as I've finished the last pile of logs. It shouldn't take me long.'

As the door closed behind him, Maggie ushered Ellen into the kitchen and the well-worn chair in front of the stove. Sean had guessed correctly and there was a tray of scones cooling on the rack on the kitchen table. The large farmhouse kitchen with the solid-fuel range was the same one that had always been there. The scrubbed pine table was the same one Ellen had sat at to have her meals during the long summer holidays. The over-stuffed sofa that she had bounced on as a child was there too, though showing signs of age, and this woman was the same one who had bandaged her knees and wiped away her tears whenever she had hurt herself. If only what had happened to her this time could be so easily sorted. Ellen felt the never-far-away tears prick behind her lids. Being here, in this house, with the only woman, apart from Sean's mother, who had ever shown her real affection was almost too much.

Ellen took a deep breath, suddenly thankful that Sean was just outside. Otherwise she had no doubt that in her tired and overwrought condition she would have given in and told her grandmother everything.

'So remind me, Ellen,' her grandmother was saying as she poured a cup of strong tea for her granddaughter, 'where is your mother now?'

Ellen wrapped icy hands around her mug. 'In the US. Lecturing. Before that she was in Australia for four months. I'm not sure when she'll be back. You know how she is.'

Maggie tutted disapprovingly. 'Leaving you on your own for Christmas! Again. I wish you had come to me. Maybe you wouldn't have got sick. You young women just don't look after yourselves properly.'

Nothing would have stopped her getting sick. It hadn't been that kind of illness.

'I didn't mind,' Ellen protested. 'I was working over Christmas. It's kind of wonderful being around to deliver babies at that time.'

It had been wonderful. There was something extra-special and magical about Christmas babies. Everyone looked forward to the first baby to be born on Christmas Day. Ellen smiled. Four babies had made their entrance on her shift. Four perfect babies, four delighted sets of parents. A stab of pain lanced through her. Last Christmas she had been sure that babies were part of her future. And then two short weeks ago that dream had come crashing down. When the consultant had given her the diagnosis, he'd told her that there was a serious risk should she fall pregnant.

'I have to tell you, Ellen, that a pregnancy could kill you,' he'd warned. 'The extra demands on your heart and circulatory system will make the condition much worse. I have to recommend that you think about being sterilised. The Pill is contraindicated in women with your condition, so it's the only sure way of preventing a pregnancy.'

The words on top of her diagnosis had crushed her. All her life she'd longed for a family. A real family where there was love and approval and laughter. Could she bear to work as a midwife again, knowing that she would never hold her own baby in her arms? She didn't know. All she could think of at the moment was the need to be with her grandmother. Like a wounded animal, she'd come looking to find shelter and comfort while she found a way to deal with the terror that filled her life.

Ellen forced herself back to the present. 'Mum will never change, Gran. We both know that.'

'Aye, but I can't help hoping that one day she'll realise what a wonderful daughter she has in you and how much she's missing out on.' Maggie sighed and touched Ellen on the shoulder. 'Maybe I'm hoping for a miracle.'

Ellen took Maggie's hand and squeezed it. 'It's okay, Gran, I accepted Mum's career would always come first a long time ago. But she's still my mother and I love her, whatever her faults. And anyway, I've got you. You've always been around for me.'

The two women shared a smile.

Ellen changed the subject. 'But tell me about you. How's

the hip?' Her grandmother's joints had been giving her trouble, but so far she had refused point blank to go to the doctor. She had told Ellen that a few aches and pains were only to be expected, given her age.

Maggie dismissed her question with a shake of her head. 'With Sean here to do the heavy stuff, I manage fine.'

Ellen suppressed a smile. Good old Gran. Never one to complain. Being with her was exactly what she needed right now.

'When did he come back? Why didn't you tell me he was here? All you said was that he was renovating his family home. You might have told me he was living in the gatehouse, and planning to stay.'

Maggie buttered a scone and placed it in front of Ellen. 'And if I'd told you, would you have come?'

The soft words stopped Ellen in mid-bite.

'What do you mean?' Ellen concentrated on her tea, avoiding her grandmother's searching look.

'Because over the last eight years, if I mentioned Sean was here on holiday, you'd suddenly change your mind about coming to stay. You may have thought you were subtle about it but, well, you weren't. I know how you felt about him when you were younger, Ellen. You were never very good at hiding your feelings. At least not from me.'

Ellen's cheeks were burning. Had her feelings really been so obvious?

'I did have a crush on him but that was a long time ago,' Ellen retorted. 'I'm a different person now and so, I imagine, is he.'

'Well, that's a shame. I think you two would make a lovely couple. That man needs someone to settle him down.'

'He must have a girlfriend, surely?' Ellen tried to ignore

the surge of pleasure she felt at the realisation that Sean wasn't married.

'Oh, he's had women. Plenty of them as far as I can tell. But none that seem to last.'

Gran looked at Ellen, a small smile playing on her lips. 'And your crush on Sean has nothing to do with the fact *you've* never had a serious relationship?'

'I've never had a serious relationship, Gran, because I've not met the right person yet. Besides, my work keeps me busy. I have friends, my hobbies, a whole life that I love...' She tailed off as it hit her again that she didn't know for how much longer she would have any of it. Whether Sean was in a relationship or not was immaterial, *she* wasn't exactly in the market for a long-term relationship. A lump was forming in her throat and she swallowed hard. 'So how long has Sean been here?'

'For someone who's not very interested, you sure ask a lot of questions!' Maggie said with a smile of satisfaction. 'Sean came back a few months ago. Took a post at the Royal Highland in the city. Said he wants to make his home here so he can be close to his beloved mountains. He's the doctor with the Mountain Rescue Team, you know.' Maggie sounded as proud as she would have been had Sean been her grandchild too.

Ellen hadn't known that Sean was working here. Although she had thought about Sean a lot since that summer eight years ago when he had kissed her, she'd never expected to see him again. In fact, as her Gran had guessed, she'd done her best to avoid him. It all seemed so silly now.

Just then the door opened with a gust of wind and Sean strode in to the kitchen. He indicated to Maggie to stay sitting and walked over to the range and helped himself to a cup of tea before grabbing a scone from the table and wolfing it down in two bites. He was clearly at home here.

'I've stacked the logs under cover and brought in a couple of baskets. Just give me a shout when you need more, Maggie.'

He eased his tall frame into a chair by the stove and eyed Ellen thoughtfully. 'I hear you're working as a midwife in London,' he said.

'I was. I mean I am. I'm taking a bit of a break for a few months.'

Sean frowned at her. 'A break? For a few months? Why?'

It was a perfectly reasonable question. Just one she didn't want to answer.

'Personal reasons,' she said tightly. She didn't owe this man any explanations.

Getting to her feet, she forced a smile. 'If you don't mind, Gran, I think I'll go upstairs and unpack. I'll bring in the rest of my bags later. I didn't want to risk not being able to get the car back out of the drive.'

Sean was on his feet almost before she'd finished speaking. 'Don't worry, I'll do that for you. Can't have you lying around in the snow again.'

He cocked an eyebrow at her and the glint in his eye sent more shock waves through her body. Damn. Was her body going to behave like this every time she was near him?

'Would you? I'd appreciate that. It's been a long day.' A wave of tiredness washed over her and she swayed slightly. Almost without seeing him move, she felt a steadying hand at her elbow. She looked up to find quizzical blue eyes staring intently into hers.

'Are you sure you're okay?' Cool fingers were surreptitiously feeling the pulse at her wrist. He frowned and glanced at Maggie, but she had turned away to stack the dishes in the sink. 'Pulse is fine.' His hand moved to her forehead. 'No temperature, but you are pale.'

'Nothing a good night's sleep won't sort out,' Ellen said brusquely.

Sean looked unconvinced but let his hands drop to his sides. 'You're probably right. I'll look in on you later.'

It was the last thing she wanted. She had the uneasy feeling nothing much escaped him, and she was far away from letting anyone know her secret. Not when she could barely acknowledge the truth to herself.

She forced another smile, hoping that this one would be more successful. 'Honestly. There is no need. Thank you anyway. Am I in my old room, Gran?'

'Yes, darling. I aired the bed for you and put on a fire so you should be cosy enough.'

'I'll make us supper when I've had a rest,' Ellen promised and on legs that felt as if they were filled with liquid rather than bones, she left the room.

'I'd better be going too, Maggie. I'll reverse Ellen's car down and bring in her bags first, though.'

'What would I do without you, Sean?'

'You'd manage fine. They don't make them as tough as you any more. And now you have Ellen for company.'

Sean saw a flicker of worry in Maggie's eyes. It wasn't there for long, but it was enough. There was something going on here that wasn't quite right.

'Is Ellen okay? She looks...different...somehow,' he asked

'It's a long time since you saw her, Sean. What? Seven years?'

'Eight.'

Not that he'd been counting. Ellen had been the pesky kid from next door who had hung around with him and his pals despite their best attempts to shake her. But, boy, she had changed. Eight years ago she had been all bones, an impish smile and red mop of wayward hair. She'd also had a disconcerting habit of getting into difficulty. If he remembered right, that last summer he'd had to fish her out of a pub when she'd got involved with some less than salubrious locals. And—the memories came thick and fast—ten years before that he'd had to jump into a stream to pull her out when she'd decided to try and mimic him and his friends as they'd used a rope to swing from one side to another. He'd had no idea she'd been following them. An hour earlier she'd been furious when he'd ordered her home and unbeknownst to him had followed at a distance. The memory made him smile. She'd been impossible, but he'd always secretly admired her courage and gumption.

But she *had* changed. Somewhere along the way she had become almost unrecognisable. Her prettiness had turned into an almost ethereal beauty. She was so pale her skin was almost translucent, and she was so slight, it seemed as if a strong blizzard would blow her away. It wasn't just that, though. There was no light in her eyes, no spark of mischief, no smile, no look as if she were about to dissolve in a fit of giggles. And apart from that, she'd seemed almost cool towards him. He was only too aware of the crush she'd had on him; their last meeting eight years ago had left him in no doubt of that. Of course he wouldn't expect her still to have feelings, but this nothingness? It wasn't what he'd expected either.

'Sean?' He suddenly became aware that Maggie was watching him curiously. He gave himself a mental shake. The mystery of Ellen, if there was one, would have to wait. He was due back at the hospital for a ward round, he still had Ellen's car to shift, and, after his earlier exertions, was in need of a shower. Ellen wasn't going anywhere for the next couple of weeks at least, so he would have plenty of time to satisfy his curiosity.

Ellen stood a little back from the window, watching as Sean expertly reversed her small car down the driveway. She wondered if he remembered the last time they had seen each other. She hoped to hell not. Her cheeks still burned every time she recalled what an idiot she'd made of herself. She had practically thrown herself at him, virtually begging him to kiss her. And he had, but then, as she'd leaned into him, wanting more, he'd gently disentangled her arms from around his neck. She remembered every second of that kiss. Before it, she'd been waiting so many years for him to notice that she'd grown up. She had dreamt so many girlish dreams of what it would be like to have Sean Jamieson kiss her. It had been her last chance. He had been going to Glasgow to complete his training and she had been going to London to start hers. What an idiot he must have thought her. How cringemakingly embarrassing, her gauche and increasingly desperate attempts to get him to notice her. Then she'd made up that stupid story and he had kissed her, and that had made her fall in love with him even more, if that was possible. When he'd removed himself from her arms, she had wanted to die from mortification. Not that he had laughed, although she was certain she'd seen laughter lurking in his eyes, or even suggested by word or gesture that he'd known how she'd felt about him, but he had been too much of a man of the world not to have noticed.

But that was a long time ago. What did it matter that once, eight years ago, she had made a fool of herself? These days it was hard to care about anything. Over these past weeks, all she'd felt was numb. Numb and frightened. So frightened

some nights she could hardly sleep. Maybe instead of coming here to Gran, she should have gone to her mother? Maybe
under these desperate circumstances Mum would have been
able to comfort her, be the mother to her she'd never been
when she was a child. Mother loved her. She just wasn't able
to invest any of her considerable energy into parenting her.
She had always known that and until now it hadn't mattered.
She'd always had Gran. Gran had more than filled any gaps
left by her mother. But Gran couldn't fix this. No one could.

Ellen's head was spinning. She had to stop thinking that
anyone could help her. She had to pull herself together. Work
out how she was going to live the rest of her life.

She looked out of the window. Sean had driven her car
down the drive and was removing her suitcases from the
boot. He disappeared from view and she could hear his deep
voice coming from downstairs. She sighed. There was something so vital and solid about him that still drew her. As a
child she'd always felt Sean was invincible and anyone in his
sphere was automatically included in that invincibility. But
she was no longer a child. And her problems were certainly
of no interest to him.

As he stepped out of the door, something made him look
up at her window. For a moment their eyes locked and everything spun into the distance. Breathless, she stepped back.
Her heart was beating like a bass drum. Why? Any feelings
for Sean Jamieson had disappeared with the girl she used to
be. And even if there was something still hidden there, she
was in no position to be even contemplating a love affair.
That part of her life was over, *finito*. Not even a remote possibility.

With a sigh, she turned away from the window and set
about finishing her unpacking.

CHAPTER TWO

A COUPLE of days later, Ellen came down to breakfast to find Sean sitting with his feet propped up on the range, munching on a bacon sandwich.

He stood up and grinned at her.

'Good morning. I'm afraid I've been taking advantage of Maggie again.'

'Wheesh now, Sean. You do more than enough for me, a wee sandwich is nothing.' Maggie turned to Ellen. 'Sean's just got back from a night on the mountains. I happen to know he doesn't keep much in that larder of his so I told him that he wasn't going home until I had fed him.'

Ellen helped herself to tea from the pot and took a slice of toast from a heaped plate. She wasn't hungry but if she didn't have something Maggie's suspicions would be aroused and she would give her no peace until she had wheedled information out of her. As it was, her grandmother had spent the past couple of days trying to tempt Ellen with home baking, complaining that women weren't meant to be so thin.

'What happened?' Ellen asked Sean.

'We had a climber with a broken leg about halfway up the mountain. We found him easily enough but the rescue 'copter couldn't land because of poor visibility. These boys take chances and they nearly came to grief trying to get a winch down, but in the end they had to back off. It took the six of us almost eight hours to get the stretcher down the mountain.'

It was all said matter-of-factly but Ellen knew that conditions must have been horrendous. It hadn't stopped snowing since she'd arrived and last night there had been strong winds too. However, looking at Sean, no one would have guessed he'd been out all night. Apart from a five o'clock shadow, which Ellen decided suited him, he looked more refreshed than she felt.

'Is the casualty going to be okay?'

'I expect the hospital will discharge him later today once they've put him in plaster,' Sean said. 'My biggest worry was hypothermia, but we managed to keep him warm enough.'

Sean stood up and stretched lazily. As he did so, his sweater rode up, revealing the dark hairs on his lower abdomen. To her dismay, Ellen felt a strange buzzing sensation go through her. Wasn't her crush on him well and truly a thing of the past and didn't she have enough on her plate without reacting to Sean Jamieson? On the other hand, after the past two weeks, when she hadn't been able to think of anything except her illness, it was a welcome relief to realise she was still functioning as part of the human race and that she could still feel *something*.

'I should go into town and get some supplies,' Sean said. 'I can see from the way your car is hidden by the snow, Ellen, that you haven't been anywhere. You could come with me if you like.'

'Thank you, but no.'

'Oh, for goodness' sake, child, you haven't been out of the house these last two days,' Maggie scolded. 'As long as you wrap up, a bit of fresh air will put some colour in those cheeks. And, besides, we do need some things from the shop.

If the snow carries on like this we may well be snowed in and I'm not sure we have enough in the larder to keep us going.'

'But Sean must be tired,' Ellen protested. 'And what about work?'

'I'm used to doing without sleep. I'm on call tonight so I have the morning off.'

'Okay, then,' she said reluctantly. She didn't want to be alone with Sean but she could hardly refuse to get some shopping for her grandmother.

Sean and her grandmother shared a look. Ellen realised she had sounded rude and ungrateful. Sean was only being polite. He wasn't to know that she didn't trust herself to spend any more time with him than was strictly necessary.

She made herself smile. 'Thanks for the offer, Sean. I really don't fancy having to dig my car out.'

'Good. I want to check up on one of my patients, though. If you don't mind, perhaps we can call in at the hospital on the way back? It's sort of on our way.'

Alarm spiralled down Ellen's spine. She didn't want to go into the hospital. She most certainly didn't want to go to the maternity ward. She simply wasn't ready yet. She forced the panic away. She could stay in the car. He couldn't make her go inside. She was getting het up over nothing.

'If you give me a couple of minutes,' she said, knowing she didn't have the energy to argue with both Sean and her grandmother, 'I'll go and change into something warmer.'

'So how long do you think you'll be staying?' Sean asked as they drove along the narrow roads made even narrower by the drifting snow piled up on either side. Her grandmother's croft house was around ten miles from the city centre and all the major supermarkets. Although there was a village within walking distance, it only stocked the basics.

Ellen looked out of the window. She had no idea how long she was going to stay. She hadn't thought that far. The need to come to her grandmother's house had been overpowering and instinctive. She had asked for and been granted three months' leave by the hospital where she worked. One day she'd have to decide what she was going to do, she certainly couldn't live with her grandmother indefinitely, at least not without working, but every time she thought about going back to her empty flat in London and the midwifery unit, a sick feeling washed over her. Perhaps she could get a job in the village? In one of the shops maybe?

'I'm not sure. A few weeks, maybe longer. I haven't made up my mind.'

The look Sean shot her was full of curiosity. She didn't want him to ask her any more questions, so she changed the subject. 'How is your family?'

'Mary and Louise moved to Ireland so my parents sold up and bought a house there. Patricia's in Australia with her husband. My mother hates not being near my siblings, especially now that they have children of their own,' Sean said. 'She and my father go out to Australia for three months every winter—they're there at the moment, in fact. My mother has six grandchildren now, so she's blissfully happy.'

'Gran told me that they'd moved to Ireland.' Mary, Louise and Patricia were Sean's sisters. Ellen wasn't surprised his parents had followed their children to Ireland. The Jamiesons had always been a close family unit. The opposite from her family in every way possible. 'It seems strange not to be going straight over to your mum's house to say hello, like I always did.'

'What about your mother?' Sean asked. 'I read articles by her in the *British Medical Journal* almost all the time. She has quite an international reputation. You must be proud of her.'

'I am,' Ellen said simply.

'And she must be proud of you.'

Ellen smiled wryly. 'I wouldn't go as far as that. Mum wasn't exactly happy when I told her I wanted to be a midwife. She thought my choice of career was second best and that with my grades I should be studying medicine. Now *that* would have made her proud.'

Sean sent her another sharp look. He wasn't to know that it was her hero-worship of him that had given her the idea to pursue a career in maternity. She'd loved hearing his stories of drama in the maternity unit when he was a trainee. But it wasn't hero worship that had kept her in the job. She knew she had found her vocation from the first moment she'd stepped onto the midwifery unit and, when she'd delivered her first baby, it had only strengthened that conviction. Now she didn't know if she would ever be able to bring herself to return to the job she had once loved and she despised the weakness in herself.

'If your mother knew you at all, she wouldn't have wasted her breath trying to persuade you to change your mind. It was obvious to everyone, apart from her, that you were a determined kid.' The smile on his face made Ellen wonder if he was remembering the time down by the river.

Before Ellen could think of a response to this, Sean's phone rang and he pulled over to answer it. Forced to listen to his side of the conversation, it only took her a few moments to realise something was wrong.

'I'll be right there,' Sean said, and disconnected. He turned to Ellen. 'I'm sorry, but the trip to the shops is going to have to wait. That was the labour ward. They've had a call from one of our patients. She's in labour but can't get to the hospital. She lives in a croft house way off the beaten track and with the recent snow, the ambulance hasn't a chance in hell of getting to the house.' He rubbed a hand across his chin. 'They've called in the RAF but they might not be able to get there in time. Besides, we're closer and this vehicle can handle most conditions.' While he was talking he had turned the car back in the direction they'd come. 'I'm afraid you're going to have to come along for the ride. Come to think of it, it's good you're here. I might need help.'

A bubble of panic rose in Ellen's chest. He had no idea what he was asking of her. How could she tell him that there was no way she could help deliver his patient's baby? She was barely holding it together as it was, how would she manage if she had to hold a baby in her arms? But what other option did she have?

She tucked her shaking hands under her thighs lest Sean notice. So this was it. Before she was ready and before she had a chance to prepare herself, she was going to have to deal with a baby.

There was no way she could refuse. Not when someone was in trouble.

'Is this her first?' she asked, pleased her voice didn't betray her anxiety. 'What's the problem?'

'Yes, it's her first. She was due to be admitted for an elective section next week. Her baby is breech. We tried to turn it around at 37 weeks, but failed. Damn. Perhaps I should have insisted that she come in earlier but she was determined to stay at home for as long as possible. On top of that, her husband works on the oil rigs and hasn't been able to get home because of the weather. To cap it all, she has an elderly mother with early Alzheimer's and she didn't want to leave her on her own for too long.'

Ellen felt a pang of sympathy. It seemed she wasn't the

only one whose life had been turned upside down. Maybe concentrating on someone else's problems was just what she needed. *Oh, God, please give her the strength to cope with the next few hours.*

'Can you ask the ward to patch us through to her? I could take some details over the phone while we're driving.' Ellen focussed her mind, trying to think ahead. A breech delivery could get complicated.

Sean did as she suggested, switching the phone to speaker, and within minutes a frightened voice came over the line.

'Dr Jamieson. Thank goodness! The nurses on the ward said you were coming to help me. Are you near? When will you get to me?'

'Marie, everything is going to be fine,' Sean said calmly. 'I hope to be with you in about ten minutes. I have a midwife in the car with me and she's going to talk to you as we drive. You don't know her but she's very experienced. Her name is Ellen.'

'Hello, Marie.' Ellen took over the call. It was good that Sean had a speaker phone. This way she wouldn't have to keep breaking off to update him and he could concentrate on navigating the icy roads. If anything, the snow had started to fall harder since they had left the house and visibility was down to a few metres. Ellen knew that they couldn't rely on the RAF helicopter being able to put down any time soon. 'Ellen here. I'm the midwife Sean was telling you about. Can you tell me how far apart your contractions are?'

'No! I don't know how to do that. All I know is that it hurts!'

'Okay. Just listen to my voice. I'm going to tell you exactly what you need to do. Every time there is a big pain and it goes away look at your watch and count the minutes until the pain comes back. Can you do that?'

'I'll try.' Marie's voice rose as another contraction hit her. Ellen looked at her watch. 'Tell me when it eases off, Marie, and I'll count with you.'

Having something to concentrate on seemed to help Marie's panic. It seemed that the contractions were four minutes apart. Not so good.

'I'm just turning in at the end of the road to your croft, Marie,' Sean said. 'Hopefully I can make it down the track. If not, we'll walk. One way or another we'll be with you in a few minutes. You just keep counting those contractions for us.'

Sure enough, as soon as they pulled up at the gate of Marie's croft it was obvious that there was no way even Sean's four-by-four would make it down the snow-covered track.

Ellen thought of the high heels she was wearing. Not so great for trudging through waist-high snow.

Sean seemed to read her mind. 'I have spare boots in the back. They may be a few sizes too big but if we have to walk they'll keep your feet warm and dry.'

A few sizes too big was optimistic. Sean was tall.

'Do we have anything with us?' Ellen asked. 'I'm assuming we might have to deliver the baby here.' She chewed on her lip. 'It's some time since I had to do a home delivery.'

Sean's answering smile was tight. 'Me too. And the answer is no. I have some surgical gloves and a very basic medical kit with some morphine in the boot that I keep in case I'm called out to a rescue, but that's it, I'm afraid. We're just going to have to do the best we can.'

It took them five minutes to walk down the drive, every minute taking Ellen closer to the delivery.

They let themselves in the door, calling out as they shrugged off their jackets. After the freezing conditions outside the house was pleasantly warm.

'I'm up here.' Marie's voice came from a room at the top of the stairs. Sean headed upstairs, taking the steps two at a time, but Ellen had noticed a frail old lady in the kitchen. Judging by the look of fear on her face, Marie's mother had no idea who they were or what they were doing there.

'Are you Marie's mum?' Ellen asked.

'Yes. But Marie's at school. What are you doing in my house?' Her voice gathered strength. 'You must leave, or I will call the police.'

No wonder Marie was reluctant to leave her mother. The old lady was clearly very confused.

'Why don't you take a seat in the living room?' Ellen suggested calmly. 'My name's Ellen and I'm a nurse. The man who went upstairs is Dr Sean Jamieson. Your daughter is going to have a baby and we're here to help her. I need to go and see how she is but if you could stay down here and listen for the phone, that would be a big help.'

The old lady's face cleared for a moment. 'Yes. Of course, silly me. Marie is having a baby. My memory isn't what it used to be, dear. Sometimes I get a bit mixed up.'

Ellen led her into the sitting room and switched the television on. Judging by the number of cushions on the chair in front of the set, and the side table laden with reading glasses and bottles of pills, this was a favourite place for the old lady. With a bit of luck the cookery programme would keep Marie's mother distracted long enough for them to deliver the baby.

Upstairs Sean was examining Marie.

'Nine centimetres dilated,' he said. 'Even if the RAF manages to land soon, and I very much doubt that they'll even be able to take off in this weather, this baby isn't going to wait.' He smiled reassuringly at Marie. 'Don't worry. Everything's going to be fine. I've delivered lots of breech births in my time and they're all doing well.'

Ellen introduced herself.

'Okay, Marie,' Ellen said. 'As Dr Jamieson said, everything is going to be just fine. I've left your mother watching television. Dr Jamieson will stay with you while I wash up. Where can I find some clean towels?'

'In the cupboard next to the bathroom,' Marie said, her words tailing off in a cry of pain.

'And scissors? Do you have a pair of kitchen scissors? We'll need them to cut the cord.'

'In the kitchen. The drawer next to the sink.'

'I'll be back as soon as I can. You just hang on in there. Try and relax between contractions. I know it's hard but it will help you conserve energy for when you start pushing.'

Ellen ran down the stairs and back to the kitchen, glancing into the sitting room on her way to check on Marie's mother. Happily she seemed to have dozed off in front of the television. Ellen put the kettle on to boil, found the kitchen scissors and scrubbed her hands. Then she placed the pan on the stove to boil the scissors. After that she ran back upstairs, found some towels and went back into the bedroom. To her dismay even the small bit of effort involved had made her breathless. It was an untimely reminder of her own medical condition. One that she didn't need right now.

Sean looked up and noticed that she was puffing as if she'd run a half marathon. 'You need to get to the gym more often.' He grinned. 'That's what happens to city girls, Marie.'

Over the top of Marie's head, he winked at her. Ellen knew he was trying to keep the mood light, but for a moment she felt like socking him.

'Contractions now coming two minutes apart,' Sean continued.

At this rate they had only minutes before it was time for

Marie to push. They exchanged a glance and Ellen found herself relaxing. Everything was going to be okay.

After she'd placed several towels underneath Marie she ran back downstairs to fetch the pan with the scissors. She'd leave them cooling in the water. That way she wouldn't have to touch them until she was ready.

Ellen placed her hands on Marie's abdomen. The contractions were regular and strong. The difficulty would be when she started to push the baby out. Sometimes with a breech delivery, the baby's head got stuck. That was the critical time. With the rest of the body and the cord outside the birth canal the baby would try to breathe but be starved of oxygen. They had to stop that from happening.

Suddenly Marie cried out. 'It's coming. Oh, God, I have to push.' She drew her legs up instinctively and Ellen could just see the first signs of the baby appearing and a greenish discharge as well. *Meconium.* Ellen looked at Sean and raised one eyebrow in silent query about whether they *should be worried.*

'Meconium is normal with breech babies.' Sean answered the unspoken question. 'Your baby is going to be here soon, Marie.'

It was good that Marie didn't know that Ellen's heart was still pounding almost as fast as her patient's. If Sean was worried at all, and he must be, he was keeping it well hidden.

'It's coming again,' Marie gasped.

'Draw up your knees, take a big breath and push hard into your bottom. Your baby is almost here now,' Ellen encouraged.

Suddenly, the baby's bottom slid into view, followed by the torso and thighs. Sean grasped the baby's trunk and turned the shoulders uppermost.

'Another push, Marie. You're doing fantastically well,' Ellen said.

Sean used his fingers to ease the baby's arms across the tiny chest, before guiding the shoulders through the birth canal.

So far so good. The baby's chest moved as it took a gasp. And again. They needed to get the rest of the baby out—and quickly.

'What's happening?' Marie asked, panic in her voice.

'We need to wait for the next contraction then you must give the biggest push of all, Marie,' Ellen said, trying to sound as calm as possible. It seemed like minutes had passed. Where had the contractions gone?

'I'll support Marie's legs, Ellen, while you deliver the baby,' Sean said. 'Just lift up baby's feet and support the chin and cheeks with your right hand and the baby will come.'

Ellen knew that Sean wasn't talking to her so much as to the mother. Ellen had attended breech births in her time, but that had always been with a full paediatric team in attendance.

Sure enough, with the next contraction the baby's face and forehead eased out and Ellen was suddenly holding the limp baby boy by the feet. Her heart hammered against her ribs. They needed to get the baby breathing. Ellen placed the tiny infant on the clean towels she had laid on the bed.

'Why isn't my baby crying? Why is he so quiet? Is he all right?' Marie was scrambling onto her elbows, desperate to see her child.

'They are often a little stunned when they come out bottom first,' Sean explained. He wiped baby's face and body vigorously with the towel then held two fingers against his tiny chest.

'Heart rate's good.' Although he smiled, Ellen could see

the tension in his eyes. 'Come on, baby, time to breathe,' he murmured under his breath.

If only they had some oxygen to give the baby. Or a neonatal face mask.

Just as Ellen began to fear the worst, the baby gave a huge gasp followed by a soft whimpering sound. Thank God! Ellen looked up at Sean, and he gave her a slow smile.

'Congratulations, Marie. You have a baby boy,' Ellen announced.

Later, after mother and baby were settled, Ellen and Sean stepped to the side to give them some time alone. Now that the adrenaline was seeping away, Ellen felt shaky.

Sean smiled at her. 'Well done. We make a good team.'

And they had.

'I'd hate to think what would have happened if we hadn't been able to get here,' she said. 'It could have had a very different outcome.'

'I guess that's why we do what we do. There's no feeling quite like delivering a healthy baby when the odds are stacked against it.'

They looked across to Marie, who was murmuring to her baby as he suckled. Under the satisfaction and pleasure Ellen felt at the sight was a deep sadness. Now that the emergency was over she allowed herself to look properly at the baby they had just delivered. He had the cutest bow lips and snub nose and a smattering of fine blond hair on his head. Tiny fingers reached out to his mother as he fed, and, as his tiny legs kicked with pleasure, Ellen's heart cracked a little.

She would never know what it was like to hold her baby in her arms. She would never feel her child's skin against hers, never know what it was like to love and be loved unconditionally. Never know the joy and the pain, and she knew there was always pain when it came to loving, of bringing up a child. She forced the thought away. There was nothing to be gained in thinking like that.

At least she'd been able to cope with seeing a baby born without breaking down. Up until this moment she hadn't been sure that she could. Now she knew that eventually she would be able to go back to being a midwife and the knowledge was a huge relief. Being able to help other women achieve what she never could, would give her life purpose again. If her time on this earth was limited, at least she was making a difference to someone else's life. It was the first step towards a future.

'I'm going to call him Sean,' Marie said, looking up from her feeding baby. 'If he'd been a girl I would have called her Ellen.'

'Great choice of name,' Sean said with a grin.

'Ideally we should take you to the hospital,' Ellen told Marie. 'But that would mean taking baby Sean into the cold as well as taking your mother with us. I'm guessing that she wouldn't cope with being left on her own? So, if you like, you could remain here and I'll stay with you.'

Marie's eyes lit up. 'Could we? My sister was going to come to be with Mum but of course, with the baby being a bit early she's not here. I did phone her as soon as I knew I was in labour and she said she'd set off as soon as she could. She lives in Glasgow so I don't know how long it will take her, or even if the roads are passable. Would you really stay with me? Don't you have somewhere else to be?'

Ellen shook her head. 'Right now there is nowhere I need or want to be more than here.'

CHAPTER THREE

THE next day, Sean came to collect her from Marie's. The snow had turned to rain through the night. The roads had been cleared and the track leading down to Marie's croft was slushy rather than icy. A couple of hours earlier, Marie's sister had arrived along with a load of shopping. Ellen was relieved that the sisters' mother seemed to recognise her. It had been a difficult night spent between the baby and the old lady, and Ellen longed for a bath and a few hours in bed. Sean told them that he had arranged for one of the midwives to come and see mother and baby the next day.

Sean admired the baby again and had a word with Marie before they left. Inside the car he looked intently at Ellen.

'You look different somehow. Tired…but different.'

'Thanks a lot, Sean. No woman likes to be told she looks tired, even if it is true. It usually means she looks terrible.'

The look Sean gave her was unfathomable. 'I don't think you could look anything but beautiful.'

A shiver ran down her spine. Was Sean beginning to see her as a grown woman at last? Why now? When it was too late?

'Why, thank you, kind sir,' she said lightly. 'But, I have to admit, I'm looking forward to a shower and change of clothes.'

'Why did you give up working as a midwife?' Sean asked

suddenly. 'Anyone can see that you love what you do. It's such a waste.'

Ellen thought rapidly. What could she tell him that would make him stop pressing her for answers she didn't have or want to give?

'I haven't given up being a midwife. I'll be going back in a while. I just wanted a break. I planned to take some time out to…' She stopped. She didn't want to explain about the aborted trip to India. That would lead to more questions she didn't want to answer. Everything seemed to lead back to her illness. '…to think about some stuff.' She changed the subject 'What about you? What are your plans? I thought someone with your reputation would be working in a large teaching hospital.'

'I like it here. I love being close to the mountains and I like being part of the Mountain Rescue Team. Living here suits me. The hospital has a first-class reputation, which is continuing to grow. They wanted someone with expertise in high-risk pregnancies to develop the service, so they asked me.'

It was as if someone had thrown ice cubes down the back of Ellen's blouse. It was ironic. For a second, but only for a second, she was tempted to ask him whether he'd ever had a patient with pulmonary hypertension. Instead, she changed the conversation.

'What about girlfriends?' Although Gran had said there wasn't one, Ellen found herself wanting to be sure. There could be someone Gran didn't know about.

Sean shot her a look. 'No one permanent. I'm happy with my life exactly how it is.'

Ellen felt a surge of relief. Which was dumb. It wasn't as if she had any aspirations as far as Sean Jamieson was concerned. It was just that she couldn't stop remembering how she'd once felt about him. She needed to remember that he wasn't the same person she had known as a child—and neither was she. Nevertheless, it felt good to have him back in her life. If being with him unsettled her, at least it was a diversion from her own morbid thoughts.

Ellen closed her eyes as a wave of tiredness washed over her. Spending the night in a chair in between checking up on baby Sean and Marie's mother hadn't been conducive to a good night's sleep. 'Wake me up when we get home,' she said, and closed her eyes.

Sean slid a glance in Ellen's direction. Home. It was funny, the way she'd said that. Almost as if they were a married couple returning to their home after a night out. And even odder that it felt right somehow.

He was going crazy. He had to be. Ellen hadn't been back in his life for much longer than a few days and already he felt as if she'd never left.

The image of her lifting her face to his to be kissed came rushing back as if it had only been eight weeks ago instead of eight years. If only she'd known how tempted he'd been back then to carry on kissing her, to take her to bed, to take up the promise in her eyes. But, thank God, at the last minute reason had come rushing back. He was older than her and so much more experienced. Not only that. He'd known that she'd thought herself in love with him and there had been no way he could take advantage of her feelings. He had been fond of her, in the way he was fond of his youngest sister, too fond to risk breaking her heart.

He smiled. His first memory of Ellen was when he had been ten and she had been five. A little girl with a round stomach and bright red curls, she had formed an instant devotion to him, following behind him and his friends whenever she could.

And so it had continued. Every year she'd arrive to stay with Maggie for the summer, and every summer she would insist on pursuing him and his pals whenever she could keep up. It had irritated the hell out of them all but he'd felt responsible for her. More often than not he would glance back, when his friends weren't looking, just to check that she hadn't hurt herself or got lost. There had been that incident by the river when she had been eight and he thirteen. If he hadn't been keeping an eye on her she could have drowned, so great had been her determination to do exactly as he'd done, even if she had been about a foot smaller and the river had covered her head when it had only come up to his armpits. He grinned as he recalled a face red with fury and mortification, small fists banging on his chest as she'd demanded to be let go. She had been a little tiger.

And so the summers had gone on. She'd hung about his house with his sisters and parents, happy to sit by the fire and listen while he and his noisy family had laughed and argued. Even then he had sensed a deep loneliness in her. He couldn't understand why she hadn't spent the summers with her mother. As she'd got older, she'd stopped following him and started spending more time with his sisters, pretending—and he didn't know how he knew this—to share their interest in make-up and clothes. Maybe it was because she'd always worn the same rolled-up jeans and thick cotton checked shirt. Come to think of it, that was the kind of clothes he'd always worn too.

There had been a gap of a couple of years when he hadn't seen her—he'd been at medical school and had spent his holidays travelling in Europe—but when she'd been sixteen he'd been back, and he'd barely recognised the coltish beauty who had turned up at his house.

He sneaked another glance at her. She was still beautiful, but most of the light had gone out of her. What had changed her from the daredevil, energetic girl she had been to this cool, almost reticent woman? Why had she stopped working? Especially when it had been clear from the look on her face when she had helped during Marie's labour that being a midwife was what she was born to do. And then there had been that odd look on her face when she'd held the baby in her arms. For a moment she had seemed to hesitate before she had taken the newborn. That wasn't in keeping with someone who was used to delivering babies. This Ellen was a mystery. Was she running away from something, and, if so, what? He shook his head. Underneath the closed-off facade he was sure the Ellen he had once known still lurked, and somewhere inside him there was that same protective feeling. If Ellen was in trouble, he wanted to know.

Later that day, once Ellen had had some sleep, Sean came by the house again.

'We never did make it to the shops. I'm going now. Would you like to join me?'

She hesitated. There was no need for them to go together now that the snow had melted.

'I'd also like to show you the hospital. There's a patient I promised to see. Come on, what do you say?'

She said no. But only on the inside. Somehow her mouth was saying yes.

The shopping was easily managed. Ellen couldn't prevent herself from glancing in Sean's basket and she wasn't altogether surprised to find a fair number of frozen microwave meals along with a reasonable helping of fruit and vegetables.

To her embarrassment Sean caught her in the act and pretended to be shocked.

'Ellen! Has no one ever told you that it's rude to stare?'

Once again, she felt fourteen years old and her cheeks reddened. Would Sean always treat her as if she were his little sister?

'And has no one told you that ready-made meals are bad for your health?' Ellen responded.

'They're only for emergencies,' Sean protested. 'I'm not much of a cook and I eat at the hospital a lot. That way I can use all my spare time to work on the house. And on my days off, Maggie usually insists that I have something with her. She's definitely where you got your obstinate streak from.'

Back in the car, Sean headed for the hospital. Ellen's curiosity got the better of her. 'Who is this patient you're going to see? What's wrong with her?'

'She's one of my gynae patients who came to see me with a large fibroid growth. Normally we would have done a hysterectomy, but she's only thirty-four and wanted children. So we agreed that we would try and shrink the fibroids. Luckily it worked and she fell pregnant almost as soon as treatment stopped. The hospital phoned to let me know she's in labour and I promised her that I would look in. Once I've seen her, I'll show you around. Last year the hospital was extended to include a special care nursery and more delivery beds. It's pretty much state of the art and I'm sure you'll find it interesting.'

Once again panic threatened to engulf Ellen. She took a deep breath to force it away. It wasn't as if she would be on duty. She wouldn't have to go into the delivery room if she didn't want to and no one would be passing her a baby to hold. Besides, if she insisted on staying in the car, Sean's curiosity would be well and truly aroused. She could see that already he was finding her behaviour strange, to say the least. And although holding Marie's baby had been difficult at first, she had coped. More than coped. The baby in her arms had been a reminder that life went on and that life and death were linked in a continuous cycle. If her time on this earth was limited, what better way to spend it than helping others into the world? Perhaps she should go back to London and her job? Keeping busy would distract her from her own problems and might even help her come to terms with what had happened. Plus, she couldn't stay with Gran for ever. Besides, from the way she kept getting goosebumps whenever she was in Sean's company, perhaps living so close to him wasn't a good idea either.

But she wasn't ready to leave. She wasn't strong enough yet to deal with whatever she had to on her own. She needed more time.

'Okay. If you're sure the midwives won't mind,' she said. 'I'd like that.'

The distinctive smell of the labour ward hit her the moment she walked in and her heart leapt. This was where she belonged. This was where she felt the most confident. The labour ward had always felt as if it was her home from home. One of the midwives came over to them as soon as she spotted Sean. But not before she gave Ellen a searching look.

'Sean. Fiona has been asking for you. She's almost fully dilated and was really hoping you'd be the one to deliver her baby.'

'Jessie, this is Ellen Nicholson,' Sean introduced Ellen. 'She's a midwife from London...and a friend.' This time there was no mistaking the acid look from the young and pretty midwife. 'I said I'd show her around, but seeing as Fiona's determined I am to deliver her baby, I wonder if you would mind showing Ellen around yourself?'

Jessie looked less than pleased. 'Sorry, Sean. No can do. We're really short-staffed. Half the ward's off with swine flu.' Jessie flashed Ellen a tight smile. Perhaps she was simply harassed, Ellen thought. She of all people knew how stressful an understaffed labour suite could be.

'I'll be fine,' Ellen said. 'If you could point me to the staff lounge, I'll keep out of your way.'

Jessie studied her thoughtfully. 'A trained midwife, eh?'

Ellen's guessed what was coming. 'I'm on leave,' she said.

'Damn,' Jessie said forcefully. 'We really could do with an extra pair of hands.' Jessie gave Sean a playful tap on the shoulder. 'You'd better get into scrubs, Sean. I'll show Ellen where she can wait and then I'll let Fiona know that you're here.'

Ellen was thumbing a magazine when the door opened and an older woman with bright blue eyes and a worried frown came into the room.

'Jessie told me I'd find you here. I'm Lena McPherson, Midwifery Manager.'

Ellen shook the extended hand wondering, but already guessing, what the woman wanted with her.

'I know you're a midwife,' Lena said. 'And Jessie did tell me that you are only here on holiday, but I did wonder if you would consider joining our bank of midwives. We're desperately short-staffed because of the flu. If we don't have enough midwives we may well have to start sending our high-risk pregnancies to Glasgow and we'd really rather not. Our mothers want to have their babies here where they know and trust us and the doctors. Any travelling is an added stress they don't need.'

Talk about coming straight to the point. And emotional

blackmail. However, perhaps this was exactly what she needed? She could work and have something to take her mind off her own problems and still have some time with her grandmother before going back to London. It would only be for a couple of months at the most.

'When would you like me to start?' Ellen said.

CHAPTER FOUR

On Saturday, Ellen got up early and, taking her coffee, wandered outside. It had snowed again overnight and the hills in the distance looked spectacular with their blankets of snow. Maybe later she would go for a walk down to the loch that was hidden in one of the hollows. Up until today she hadn't really felt up to exercising—part of her was worried that she might trigger an attack of breathlessness despite the fact that she knew she could become ill any time. Whether she exercised or not had nothing to do with it. In fact, as her physician had explained, the better physical shape she was in the better chance she would have of surviving an attack. Her consultant was right. She had two options. She could continue to feel sorry for herself and hide away or she could pick up the pieces and live every moment of her life as she'd always done—to the full. And the first step would be getting back to work. She had agreed to start on Monday and knew she had made the right decision.

Since she'd come back some of the terrible weight had begun to slip from her shoulders. Whether it was being with her beloved grandmother again, or knowing that she had the mental strength to continue with a job she loved, she didn't know.

Or maybe it had something to do with being around Sean,

a small voice whispered. Maybe being around him makes you feel brave?

As if thinking about him had made him appear, Sean stepped out of his house, holding a mug of coffee. The realisation that they liked to do the same thing in the morning made Ellen smile. Sean was wearing faded jeans and a thick, black cashmere sweater that emphasised the breadth of his chest and arms. He looked as rugged and as elemental as the mountains behind him and Ellen's stomach lurched. She still found him disturbingly sexy.

He placed his coffee on the bench outside his front door and stretched. Then he picked up the mountain bike that was propped up next to his door and hefted it over his shoulder.

Ellen walked over to him. The crunch of her boots on the hard snow made him look round. When he saw it was her he grinned broadly, his even white teeth contrasting with his weather-tanned skin, and Ellen could almost hear her heart pounding against her ribs.

'An early riser too,' he said.

Ellen glanced at her watch. Although it was just after seven, the sun had only recently lifted above the horizon.

'Time is too precious to waste lying in bed,' she said. Perhaps it was the tone of her voice more than her words but Sean looked at her sharply.

'I mean...' she added hastily. 'Who wouldn't want to make the most of a beautiful day like this?'

'I was about to head out for a cycle, but I can do that any time,' Sean said. 'How would you like to come with me for a walk up Ben Nevis instead? If you have walking boots, that is? If we leave in the next twenty minutes there's enough time to get up and back down while it's light, even if we go slowly.'

Ellen arched an eyebrow at him. 'Are you suggesting I'll keep you back?'

'Your grandmother did say you'd been unwell. And judging by your pallor, and the way you puffed up the stairs at Marie's house, it seems to me you're not fully back to normal. Come to think of it, going up Nevis is a rubbish idea. Tell you what, I know a hill that is less difficult and it has a great fish restaurant at the bottom of the trail. Why don't we try that one?' He hesitated. 'Or we could just have lunch.'

The strange thing about her illness was that it didn't necessarily get worse with exercise. However, perhaps it was better to play it safe for a few weeks longer. It was one thing deciding to live her life to the full and quite another taking foolish risks. Besides, Ellen guessed that Sean would much prefer going up a mountain at his own pace. She suspected he'd be up and down Ben Nevis in less time it would take her to walk a couple of miles.

'If you don't mind, I'll give going up any mountains a miss. I want to help Gran out today. She has a couple of cupboards she wants to clear out.'

'Why don't I take you both out to lunch, then? I happen to know Maggie likes a trip out every now and again.'

'I'll ask her,' Ellen said. 'Now shoo. Go cycle your mountain and call in on your way back. I'll have had a chance to ask Gran by then.'

Ellen watched as Sean jumped on his mud-splattered mountain bike. Then with a wave he was away. Seeing the speed with which he cycled up the snow-encrusted path confirmed her decision. A walk with Sean would be no stroll.

Why hadn't he married? It couldn't be from lack of willing women, that was for sure. Was Sean one of those men who hated the thought of being tied down? Or had he simply not met the right woman yet? Whatever the reason, she was glad he was still single. Even if he would never think of her as a potential girlfriend.

Sighing, Ellen took her coffee cup back inside and set about making pancakes. She'd always enjoyed baking. As a child, whenever she couldn't follow Sean and his gang she'd watched Maggie bake. Even now she used baking as a way to unwind and she could make scones that melted in the mouth.

As she mixed up the pancake mixture her grandmother came downstairs. As usual she was dressed in a tweed skirt with a blouse and carefully styled hair. Ellen had never seen her grandmother look less than immaculate.

'Darling, you're up!'

Ellen crossed over to kiss her grandmother's cheek, breathing in the familiar scent of lavender.

'I thought I'd make you breakfast for a change,' Ellen said. 'Why don't you sit down and let me look after you?'

Maggie did as Ellen suggested. 'Was that Sean's voice I heard?' Maggie asked.

Ellen nodded. 'Yes. He was going mountain biking. He asked me if I fancied going on a walk up Ben Nevis instead but I chickened out. It would be too much like when we were children—him striding ahead and me doing my best to follow.'

'You did rather make a nuisance of yourself when you were a wee girl,' her grandmother agreed, 'but something tells me Sean Jamieson doesn't see you the same way. Not any longer.'

Ellen was glad that the heat of the stove would go some way to account for the blush that rose to her cheeks. But to be on the safe side she turned her back on her grandmother and pretended to concentrate on her pancakes. 'Why do you say that?' Ellen asked, trying to act as if she wasn't really interested in the answer.

'Och, you know us old ladies. We like to watch you young

folks. I always knew you had a thing for Sean Jamieson and if I'm not mistaken, you still like him.'

'Liking is not the same thing as having a *thing* for someone, Gran. I've admitted I thought I was in love with him when I was a teenager but all young girls have crushes at that age.'

'Well, my dear, he seems to have noticed you now. I saw the look on his face when you were last together in my kitchen. It was as if he was seeing you for the first time. I saw that same look on my Hugh's face often enough before he worked up the courage to ask if he could court me.'

Ellen nearly dropped her spatula. She whirled around to face her grandmother. 'Now don't you go getting any ideas, Gran. I'm not looking for romance. And I'm so over Sean Jamieson.'

The twinkle in her grandmother's eyes told Ellen that Maggie wasn't convinced. However, the old lady tactfully dropped the subject.

'Careful you don't burn those, my girl,' Maggie admonished.

Ellen turned back just in the nick of time to save her pancakes.

She set them on a plate and poured hot water from the range into a teapot before setting them in front of her grandmother.

'Sean did ask if he could take us for lunch,' Ellen admitted.

'Well, what about that?' Maggie said, smiling.

'He asked both of us, so don't get any more ideas, Gran.'

'Aye, well, he's too much of a gentleman not to ask me. He knows I like my wee trips out and about.'

'So you'll come?' Ellen finished laying the table and sat down opposite her grandmother.

Maggie's smile widened. 'And play gooseberry? Of course I'm not going to come. You two go and have a lovely time.'

'Gran...' Ellen said warningly.

'I think my hip is playing up,' Maggie said, giving her side a vigorous rub to add to the lie. 'And it's still slippy out there, so I'm going to give it a miss.'

'In that case, I'll just stay with you.'

Maggie snapped her brows together. 'Now, you listen to me, Ellen. You're a young woman. For some reason you're still not married and if you're not careful you'll be left on the shelf. I couldn't think more highly of Sean if he were my own grandson. It will give me a lot of pleasure knowing that you two are out enjoying yourselves. Now maybe nothing will come of it—I was only teasing before—but he's company for you. You can't spend the rest of your time here inside with an old woman, no matter how much she enjoys your company.'

Ellen had to laugh. She had definitely made the right decision, coming here. Maggie always said exactly what she thought, and if Ellen decided to tell her the awful news about her illness, she knew Maggie wouldn't allow Ellen to give in to the self-pity that lurked below the surface.

'Okay, Gran. You win. I'll go for lunch with Sean. But I'm warning you, don't get any ideas 'cos you'll only be disappointed.'

Just after one there was a tap on the door and without waiting for a response Sean strode into the kitchen where Ellen and her grandmother were peeling vegetables for that night's dinner.

He had showered and shaved, which was just as well as Ellen had caught a glimpse of him when he'd returned from his cycle. She'd almost been unable to make out the man underneath the coating of mud. She was, however, alarmed to notice a jagged cut on his forehead.

'What happened to you?' she asked. 'Wait. Let me guess, you came off your bike.'

'Good guess,' Sean admitted. 'Happens most times. I was trying to beat my record.'

'And what would have happened if you'd knocked yourself out? You could have been lying out in the freezing cold for the rest of the day,' Ellen said. Heavens, now she sounded like his mother!

Sean shook his head. 'Can't worry about stuff like that or you'd never do anything. Anyway, are you ready for lunch? What about you, Maggie? Are you joining us?'

'Not today. But Ellen is going.' Maggie flashed Ellen a warning look daring her to change her mind. 'And don't you pretend you're not pleased to have Ellen all to yourself.'

Ellen was mortified. Gran speaking her mind to her was one thing, speaking it to Sean was quite another. What if Sean got the wrong idea? It was too embarrassing.

But Sean just grinned. 'Can't say I'm not looking forward to it.'

'I'll just grab my coat,' Ellen said, desperate to get Sean out of the room before her grandmother said anything else. What if she started going on about Ellen not being married and getting on a bit? Ellen wouldn't put it past the elderly minx.

But to her relief they managed to get out of the house and into the car without further embarrassment.

'Sorry about Gran,' Ellen said as Sean manoeuvred the car up the slippery driveway.

'I think she's great,' Sean said. 'I'd rather people said what was on their minds, wouldn't you?'

He wasn't to know it was a loaded question. She couldn't

even begin to imagine telling people what was on her mind. The sympathy and pity would be too much. The only person she had told was her flatmate and best friend, Sigi, and that had been bad enough. Sigi had been distraught and begged Ellen to call her mother, but Ellen had refused. Mum would insist on trying to manage her life from now on, and even if she did it from the best intentions, it would drive her crazy. No, she was used to sorting out her own problems, although this was off the Richter scale as far as problems went, but she would manage this too. How, she still wasn't sure.

'I gather you've agreed to work in the maternity unit as a bank midwife,' Sean said, interrupting her bleak thoughts. 'Thank you. They're really stretched at the moment. Some of the staff are having to work double shifts and it's taking its toll.'

'I don't mind,' Ellen said. 'In fact, I'm looking forward to it.'

'As soon as this weather clears up and the swine flu is over we should get back to full strength,' Sean said. 'But we are always looking for good midwives. I don't suppose you'd consider joining us on a permanent basis?'

Permanent. Now that was a word that no longer had any meaning.

'I don't think so.'

'Why not? Do you really like London so much or do you have other plans?'

'I did. I was hoping to go out to India and work for a while.' The words were out before she had considered them. Now he would want to know why she hadn't gone. Damn.

'Hey, that's a coincidence. I'm taking a three-month sabbatical over the summer to teach in Malawi.'

Ellen didn't know if she was relieved or disappointed to hear it. She strongly suspected the latter.

'What stopped you from going to India?' Sean continued.

Ellen sucked in a breath. What had stopped her? Finding out she had pulmonary hypertension. That's what. She hadn't had any symptoms. Perhaps if she had it wouldn't have come as such a shock. Part of the process of applying for a post abroad, particularly in countries with a high incidence of tuberculosis, was a chest X-ray. Ellen had gone along for hers not imagining for a moment that the result would tear her life apart. Even now she couldn't quite believe it. She kept pushing it to the back of her mind, hoping that one day she would wake up and find it was all some horrible nightmare.

'Ellen?' Sean's voice brought her back to the present.

'I…er…I caught pneumonia. I thought it was better to wait to do something like that until I was sure I was better. I already had a sabbatical from work, so I thought I would come here for a bit of a break.'

'Not running away from anything, by any chance?' Damn the man. He could still read her like a book.

'No,' she lied. 'Do I need to have a reason to take time off from work? Not everyone wants to work all the time, you know.'

'Yet you agreed to help us out at the hospital?'

'I didn't really think I could say no. Besides, it's only for a short while. I'll take time off afterwards.'

Thankfully he seemed satisfied with her answer. 'The Royal Highland sends midwives to Malawi to teach if you're looking for a placement any time.' He smiled wryly. 'Only when you've helped us out of this hole, of course.'

'Maybe I will,' Ellen said evasively. 'In the future.'

There was that word again. Future. What if she didn't have one?

'I spent some time in Pakistan,' Sean continued. 'During

the floods. It was quite a challenge, but I loved it. I'd like to go back one day—under different circumstances, of course.'

'You always were one for excitement,' Ellen said. 'Is that why you joined the Mountain Rescue Team?'

'When I'm not working I like to be on the mountains, either climbing or on my bike. And I'm a doctor so it makes sense for me to be part of the team.'

Ellen asked Sean to tell her about some of the rescues he'd been on. He spoke about them in the same matter-of-fact tone he always used but Ellen sensed he was underplaying the drama considerably. From the sound of it there were one or two situations when things might not have turned out well at all had he and his team not been there. Ellen was happy to listen while he chatted.

They pulled up outside the restaurant and Sean turned to Ellen, a quizzical look on his face.

'Is something wrong, Ellen? Something I can help with? You seem—I don't know—quieter than I remember.'

The question took her by surprise. She didn't remember Sean ever being the kind of man who picked up emotional signals. He'd always seemed too much of a man's man for that. Not that he'd been unfeeling. He had always kept an eye out for her and protected her from his friends' irritation and disdain and she'd loved him for it. The problem was, the more time she spent with Sean, the more she remembered the way she'd felt about him. And that way lay danger.

'I'm perfectly fine,' she lied. 'Now, what about that lunch?'

As Sean waited for Ellen to come back from the ladies', he couldn't shake the uneasy feeling he was getting whenever he was with her.

It wasn't just that she was quieter, he could hardly recognise the fiery child she had been, but she kept going somewhere in her head. Drifting away as if preoccupied by something or someone. Perhaps that was it. Maybe she was here to recover from a love affair? The thought made his gut clench. Suddenly he didn't like the thought of Ellen being in love. Since he'd seen her again, something had happened to his insides. It was as if he'd been waiting all his life for her to come back without realising it. Perhaps he'd been in love with her all along? Was that why no woman had ever measured up? He shook his head. That was just nuts. He hadn't thought about Ellen since the last time he'd seen her. At least, not much. Sure, he'd wondered about her every now and again. Wondered how she was getting on. Wondered if she had truly fallen in love for the first time. But those thoughts had been those of a benevolent older brother, hadn't they? But, hell, there was nothing brotherly about the way she made his heart kick whenever he saw her. There was nothing brotherly about the heat in his pelvis and there was certainly nothing brotherly about the way he kept imagining her skin under his finger-tips, her red hair cascading down her naked back, her nails raking into his skin as he made her cry out.

Damn.

This wasn't good.

And it wasn't just that he thought she was hot, hotter than any other woman he'd met, there was something about her that made him want to just hold her. And most definitely not in a brotherly way.

He studied his drink balefully. He wasn't used to feeling conflicted when it came to women. Usually it was straight-forward. He saw someone he liked, he asked them out, they spent time together and then one of them, usually him, broke it off when it seemed things were getting serious. He always made it clear before anything started that he wasn't looking to settle down and if some women thought they could change his mind, that wasn't his problem.

So what *was* the problem? If Ellen had left someone behind in London, then left was the operative word. Wasn't he just the person to make her forget? After all, it would be good for her and would make her realise that whoever had hurt her wasn't worth a single tear.

He watched as she made her way back to their table. She looked at him and smiled and for a moment he had second thoughts. But only for a moment. Nothing was going to get in the way of his mission to make Ellen realise that spending time with him was just what she needed.

CHAPTER FIVE

ON MONDAY morning, Ellen was back at the maternity unit, this time as a fully signed-up member of the team. As she'd hoped, as soon as she'd stepped into the labour ward and changed into her scrubs, she felt at home. She'd made the right decision.

Jessie seemed delighted to see her. 'Thank goodness you said yes,' she said. 'I don't know if I could have coped if they'd asked me to do another double shift.'

'It's good to be here,' Ellen said honestly. 'What do we have?'

'Five in labour, all progressing well. I know they want you to divvy up your time between here and the antenatal clinic. We expect Mrs McGregor in delivery room one to have her baby by lunchtime, so if you want to attend her, you should be able to see her through before you're due in the clinic.'

'Sounds good to me,' Ellen said.

She discussed Mrs McGregor's care to date with Jessie before introducing herself to her patient. This was Flora's second pregnancy, the first having been straightforward, and she was progressing well, already five centimetres dilated. The midwife at the admissions unit had thought the baby's heartbeat had been slow so Ellen connected Flora to the CTG monitor as a precaution. So far so good. Mrs McGregor should be holding her baby in a couple of hours.

Flora gripped Ellen's hand as another contraction tore through her. Her husband had left the room to get himself a sandwich and his absence was making Flora fret. When the contraction had passed, Ellen heard an ominous slowing of the baby's heart. She checked the monitor. Her own heart thumped as she waited for the deceleration to recover. Two minutes, two and a half minutes. Now the baby could be in distress. Slowly the baby's heart rate crawled back over 100 beats per minute. Happily Flora's husband, Jack, chose that time to return so she was able to study the tracing for a few minutes without Flora noticing.

'Could you just turn around onto your other side, please, Flora?' Ellen asked. 'I'm just going to page the doctor to ask him to have a look. I'm not altogether happy with the baby's heart rate. Now, I don't want you to get alarmed. It may be nothing, but we always like to be on the safe side.'

Using the phone by the bed, Ellen asked switchboard to page the obstetrician on call for the labour suite as a matter of urgency. She knew how quickly a tracing could go from being worrying to being life-threatening for the baby and she wasn't going to take any chances.

As she waited for the doctor to respond, she studied the tracing again. The baby's heart rate had returned to normal and the variability was normal too. But after the next contraction it dropped again. There could be a number of reasons for this, but none of them were good. If the heart rate continued to dip, it could confirm that the baby was in distress. In which case they would need to get Flora to Theatre and sectioned. Ellen did a quick internal examination to make sure that the baby's cord hadn't come down below the head.

'There is a chance we may need to deliver your baby quite

quickly. That could even mean by Caesarean section,' Ellen told Flora. 'I know it's not what you had in your birth plan but unfortunately sometimes things don't go the way we planned.'

A bit of an understatement, she thought ruefully. Last year she would never have guessed that she was facing a future without children—if she had a future at all.

She dismissed the thought. Right now Flora needed her full attention.

'But I want Jack to be with me when the baby's born,' Flora wailed. 'I don't want to go to Theatre.'

'If you have to go then there's a good chance we can give you an epidural. You know, where they make you numb from the waist down? That way you'll be awake for the baby's birth and Jack will be able to stay with you in Theatre and be there when your baby's born. But let's not get ahead of ourselves. We should wait to hear what the doctor thinks.'

At that moment the door opened and Sean came into the room. He was wearing blue scrubs and still had his mask pulled down around his neck. Ellen guessed he must have come straight from Theatre. Annoyingly her heart gave the little run of beats it always did when she saw him.

'Hello.' Sean smiled reassuringly at the frightened woman on the bed. 'I'm Dr Jamieson, one of the consultant obstetricians.' He cocked a questioning eyebrow at Ellen.

'Baby's CTG tracing has dipped a couple of times over the last ten minutes.'

Sean came to stand beside her and leaned over her shoulder to look at the tracing. Ellen was acutely aware of him and it took every ounce of willpower not to move away.

'Flora's eight centimetres dilated now,' Ellen added.

'Mrs MacGregor, Flora, I think we are going to have to help you deliver your baby. Sometimes in cases like yours, where we think the baby is in distress, we would take you to

Theatre and do a section. However, in your case, I think we will do a ventouse delivery. I'll explain everything as we go along.'

Ellen hid her surprise. Surely they'd be better off—and safer—taking Flora to Theatre? If the vacuum delivery failed, then they would have to do a section anyway and every minute lost could make all the difference to the baby's health.

Hiding her doubts behind a reassuring smile, Ellen tapped Sean on the arm. 'Dr Jamieson, could I have a word, please?'

They stepped just far enough away to be out of hearing of Flora and her husband.

'Why not take her straight to Theatre?' Ellen said. 'That's what I would do in your shoes.'

Sometimes the midwife and obstetrician disagreed about the best course of action to take and although the final decision was always up to the consultant, Ellen was used to being heard. In the London hospital where she worked most of the obstetricians took on board what she thought. She was determined her views were not going to be brushed aside. Even by Sean. Especially by Sean.

'I would take her to Theatre, if I had a choice,' Sean said. 'But I've just come from there and there isn't one available. We've had a couple of emergencies. If we hang about waiting until one does become free, we could get ourselves and our patient into difficulty. We need to set up for an assisted delivery so could you page a paediatrician? Although my guess is that they could be tied up with what is going on in Theatre too. I don't think we should rely on one appearing any time soon.'

Damn and double damn.

Sean looked Ellen in the eyes. 'How are your neonatal resus skills?' he asked quietly.

'I spent some time in the special care nursery. I'm double

qualified.' Not that she wanted to be put in a position where they had to resuscitate a baby. However, it seemed that there was little they could do about that. The sooner they delivered this baby the less chance there was that it would need to be intubated.

No sooner had they set up the trolley for delivery and positioned Flora's legs in the stirrups than she announced that she felt like pushing. Again the baby's heartbeat plummeted and Sean attached the vacuum cup to the baby's head just as another contraction was starting to build up.

'Okay, Flora, one big push now, please,' Ellen said.

With a single downward pull on the rubber handle of the ventouse, followed by a gentle upward lift, Sean delivered the baby onto Flora's tummy.

'Ellen, can you get the baby onto the resuscitaire for a check, please?' Sean asked, quickly clamping and cutting the cord. Ellen bundled up the baby girl, checked the cord pulsation and wiped her down gently with a towel. Before the baby had time to gasp Ellen gently sucked out her nose and mouth to clear any mucus, before placing an oxygen mask over the little face. The baby spluttered and grimaced from the intrusion.

'Oh, dear, you don't like that, do you, baby?' Ellen said with a smile as the baby quickly pinked up.

Sean shrugged out of his gown and grinned. 'You have a beautiful baby girl, Flora. I don't think there's anything to worry about, but the nurses will take her up to the special care nursery so she can get a thorough check-up. You'll be able to see her there as soon as you've had a rest.'

An exhausted but happy-looking Flora smiled at Sean and Ellen. 'She really is beautiful, isn't she? Just look at her! Have you ever seen anything more perfect?'

Jack took his wife's hand. He had been watching in silence. 'A daughter. I can't believe I have a daughter!'

The happiness in their eyes made Ellen's heart ache. At least if she would never know the joy of holding her baby in her arms, she could experience it second hand through her patients. It wasn't the same, of course it wasn't, but it would have to be enough. She blinked rapidly, forcing away the tears that burned the back of her eyelids. Luckily the hustle and bustle as the nurses from the special care unit came in to collect the baby gave her a few moments to collect herself.

When she looked up it was to find Sean watching her intently.

'I'll just finish writing up Mrs McGregor's notes,' he said. 'Then maybe we could grab some lunch?'

Ellen looked at her watch. She was due in the antenatal clinic in half an hour, but she should eat something if she wanted to stay alert.

'I'll join you as soon as Flora's left for the postnatal ward,' she said. 'Ten minutes?'

As Sean was so tall, it wasn't hard to find his head in the crowded staff dining room. Ellen paused in the doorway and watched him for a moment. He was eating the same way he did everything—with intense concentration. As she studied him, a shiver ran up her spine. He was so damn gorgeous and it was completely unfair that he could still make her feel like the naïve teenager of eight years before. How many nights had she spent in her room listening to love songs and dreaming of being Mrs Jamieson? The memory made her smile. She had been every schoolgirl's first-love cliché. Only it seemed that in her case those feelings had never really gone away. She understood now why the few relationships she'd had had fizzled out as soon as the boyfriend at the time had wanted more. She recognised now that subconsciously she had been comparing them to Sean and finding them lacking. None of them had ever made her feel an iota of what she'd felt for Sean eight years ago. She'd always tried to tell herself that it was unrealistic to feel like that, that it was particular to a first love and had no basis in reality. Now she wondered if she still believed it. Eight years had passed but her feelings for Sean hadn't dimmed one bit.

Which was ridiculous! It had to have something to do with what had been happening in her life over the past few weeks. Or was she really still in love with him? The thought stopped her breath.

Sean looked up and waved her over. As she approached he got to his feet.

'You okay?' he asked.

'Any reason I shouldn't be?' For a horrible moment she wondered if he had read her mind.

'We haven't exactly let you find your feet slowly,' Sean continued as they sat back down. 'A couple of nice, easy deliveries to get you acclimatised would have been good.'

Ellen grinned with relief. 'I guess it comes with the territory. Don't get me wrong, I love it when everything goes according to plan, but there's nothing quite like the feeling you get when you save a baby who might otherwise have died if you hadn't been there, is there?'

Sean grinned back and their eyes locked and held. Everything disappeared as Ellen's heart seemed to stop beating.

'Who would have guessed that little Ellen Nicholson would turn out to be one of the best midwives I've had the honour to work with?' Sean said softly.

Ellen frowned at him. 'Little Ellen Nicholson disappeared a long time ago,' she murmured.

'Something tells me she didn't,' Sean said. 'I guess she was there all along. I just wasn't seeing her.'

The silence stretched between them filled with something Ellen couldn't quite put her finger on. All she knew was that Sean was really looking at her for the first time. Her heart was pounding so hard she could hear the rush of blood in her ears. Why did Sean have to start noticing her now? When it was too late?

'I should get something to eat,' Ellen said, aware that her voice was unnaturally high. 'I have to be back for the start of the clinic in less than twenty minutes. On second thoughts...' she studied Sean's plate of fried fish and overcooked cabbage '...maybe I'll just grab a sandwich from the vending machine and take it outside. I could do with some fresh air.'

Labour ward was always kept at a temperature to be comfortable for the newborn babies, but the heat wasn't so comfortable for the staff. The windows were kept shut for the same reason, so Ellen often chose to take a sandwich and coffee outside at lunchtime to get some fresh air. But that wasn't the only reason she wanted to go outside today. She needed to get away from Sean and the way he was making her feel.

Immediately Sean pushed away his plate and got to his feet. 'Good idea. I'll come too.'

It wasn't exactly what Ellen had hoped for, but she could hardly spurn his company. Not without seeming rude.

They took their sandwiches to a bench outside the hospital. Although the temperature had risen over the past couple of days it was still below freezing and Ellen shivered.

Sean put his arm around her.

Ellen tried to shrug him off. 'What if anyone sees us, Sean?' she asked. 'We hardly want to be the subject of hospital gossip.'

'I don't give a damn what anyone thinks,' Sean said.

'But…' he slipped his arm away from around her shoulders '…if it makes you uncomfortable.'

The truth was it felt good. Too good.

'Will you have dinner with me tonight?' Sean asked.

Ellen's stomach felt as if a fairy was doing a little pirouette. She would like nothing better. What was the harm? It wasn't as if she could break Sean's heart. She was pretty sure that wasn't possible. But what about her own?

Now, there was a dilemma. What do you do when every day could be your last? Hide away, hoping for the best? Go on as you've always done? Or take a gamble and make the most of every minute, knowing that you could get hurt?

It didn't take much thinking about. She wanted to be with Sean. And for the time being it seemed he wanted to be with her.

'I'd like that,' she said simply.

CHAPTER SIX

BY THE time Sean left the hospital it was almost seven. He'd been about to leave when a patient had been brought in who needed a section. He could have left it to the on-call obstetrician, but Sean had followed this patient all through her pregnancy. She'd had two previous miscarriages and a stillbirth so was understandably anxious. As was sometimes the case there had been no explanation for her previous history, which made it worse in some ways. Passing her over to another doctor at this stage would have been unfair.

Happily the section had been straightforward and the patient had had a healthy little boy.

The way she and her husband had thanked Sean made it seem as if they believed he was totally responsible for their successful outcome. Sean knew he'd had little to do with it but if it made the couple feel happier when they tried for another baby, it could do no harm.

It always took him a little while to leave the patients and the hospital behind and he liked to use the drive home to slowly unwind before the evening. He told Ellen he'd pick her up at seven-thirty and had just about enough time to grab a shower and change. He also had to squeeze in a phone call to book a table somewhere. And not just anywhere. He wanted to blow her away. He suspected that Ellen wouldn't be impressed with the same restaurants he took other women to and for some reason he wanted to take her somewhere he had never taken another woman. He racked his brain for something different. Then he came up with it. There was a place in the heart of the countryside. It was a well-kept secret and mainly frequented by locals, a small restaurant with rooms, and those in the know came from miles to eat there, sometimes even as far away as England. But at this time of year there wouldn't be a huge demand for the tables. It was cosy with the limited number of tables set in front of an open fire. It wouldn't be easy to get to since more snow had fallen but his four-by-four was pretty good at handling most things. He smiled. Ellen would love it.

More than once Ellen had considered ringing Sean to cancel their date, but as she'd already told her grandmother she was going to dinner with Sean, she knew there was no chance that Maggie would allow her to cancel. Besides, at this late stage it would be unforgivably rude.

Nevertheless, she felt unaccountably nervous. Once—a long time ago—a date with Sean Jamieson would have been all she dreamed of, but that had been when she had still been a naïve young girl who had believed in happy ever afters. As she dressed she kept telling herself she was being ridiculous. After all, it was just dinner between two old friends and colleagues. Hadn't she told herself that she would do as she wished from now on and to hang with the consequences? What possible consequences there might be, she chose not to think about.

Why, then, was she taking such care to select just the right outfit? She had to admit she wanted to knock Sean's socks off. It still smarted that he had barely noticed that she had become a woman eight years ago and it would be good to get him to sit up and take notice. It might be childish, but it would feel good, and she could do with all the feeling good she could manage at the moment.

So in the end she selected a favourite dress in a deep blue that brought out the colour of her eyes. She loved the sensuous feel of the soft fabric against her skin and she knew that it gave her curves in all the right places.

Sean was waiting in his usual position in the kitchen when she came downstairs, next to the range with his long legs stretched out as he teased Maggie. Her grandmother was always a little giggly when Sean was around and Ellen had no difficulty seeing the assured and beautiful woman Maggie had once been. Ellen would have been happy to have half her grandmother's confidence.

Sean jumped to his feet and gave Ellen one heart-stoppingly slow look before whistling under his breath. He murmured something she couldn't quite hear but she had to admit she had got exactly the reaction she'd hoped for.

'You look beautiful, darling,' her grandmother said. 'Doesn't she, Sean?'

'Stunning,' Sean said simply, and Ellen knew he meant it. He helped her into her coat and ushered her out to the car. 'It's a bit of a drive, the place we're going to, but believe me it's worth it.'

'Might you get called out on a rescue?' Ellen asked. 'The weather's still pretty awful.'

'The good thing about the weather being this bad is that it tends to put most people off the mountains—except for the seasoned ice mountaineers. But they almost always warn us that they're on the mountain. I checked before I came to get you and as far as Control is concerned there's no one out there.'

As they drove, Ellen asked about the worst rescue Sean

had been involved in. He explained that mostly they had to retrieve people from lower down the slopes, gravity tending to make sure that people fell downwards, and that as long as they could get to them quickly, they were usually all right.

'Usually?' Ellen repeated.

Sean sighed. 'We have one fatality a year on average. Mostly those climbers are dead by the time we get to them. I've only had one who was alive when we reached him who died on the way down. That was pretty hellish. He had multiple trauma and a head wound that was probably unsalvageable. On the other hand, we've made some good saves. People who most certainly would have died from their injuries had we not reached them, and those who would have succumbed to hypothermia if they'd had to spend the night on the mountains.'

'It must feel good to know you've made a difference. I know I feel like that when we deliver a healthy baby who wouldn't have made it without our help.'

The rest of the journey passed quickly as they chatted about obstetric cases they'd both had that had caused problems but turned out okay in the end.

'I hate it when a woman comes to us and we can't get a heartbeat,' Ellen said. 'The ones where the pregnancy has seemed entirely normal—and then all of a sudden there's no baby. It seems so cruel.'

'We all hate it when that happens,' Sean said quietly.

A few minutes later they were at the restaurant and Ellen smiled in delight. It was a renovated and extended old black house with a thatched roof and thick whitewashed walls. As they stepped out of the car, the falling snow made the scene look like a picture postcard. A thick plume of smoke puffed from the chimney and the aroma of scented wood drifted across the silent night air. There were only four other cars in the car park.

Inside it was even better. The low-slung roof and large inglenook fire created a sense of cosiness, counterbalancing the formally laid tables with their white starched linen table-cloths and sparkling crystal wine glasses.

The evening passed in a blur for Ellen and later she could hardly remember what she'd eaten, except that it had been delicious. Sean was good company and knew just how to make her laugh. For the couple of hours or so it took to eat their meal she managed to forget.

In the end the waiter's shuffling feet alerted them to the fact they were the only ones left in the restaurant.

'I can't believe it's eleven already,' Ellen said as they slipped on their coats. She turned to Sean. 'Thank you for a wonderful evening.'

He sketched a mock bow. 'You are very welcome. Perhaps we could do it again? Tomorrow, for example?'

'Maybe,' Ellen said. 'We'll see.'

Outside, snow had almost completely covered Sean's ve-hicle and he frowned. 'I had no idea it was snowing quite as heavily. We'd better get going before it gets any worse.'

In contrast to the warmth of the restaurant, inside the car was freezing and Ellen huddled into her coat and shivered.

'I should have come out first and warmed the car for you,' Sean said.

'I'm okay.'

They had been driving for fifteen minutes when out of nowhere a dark shape appeared in front of them.

Sean cursed and hit the brake. The car skidded sideways before glancing off a tree and coming to rest in a ditch.

'Are you okay?' Sean said. She couldn't see his face in the

darkness, but she heard the fear in his voice. 'Ellen, Ellen, answer me!'

'I'm okay. Just a bit stunned. Was that a deer? Do you think it's okay? I can't tell if we hit it.'

'I'll go and look,' he said. 'Stay here,' he added as he opened the car door, letting in a freezing blast of wind and a flurry of snow.

Despite her shock, Ellen had to smile. Where the heck did he think she was going to go? There were no lights to be seen anywhere.

Sean disappeared into the darkness. After a few minutes he was back. He jumped back into the driver's seat and blew on his hands.

'There's no sign of the deer. I'm pretty sure we missed it or the car would be in a worse state than it is now. I'm going to try and get us out of here.' But when he turned the ignition the car coughed and refused to start. Sean hit the dashboard in frustration and tried again, repeatedly.

'No go, I'm afraid. Must have damaged something when we hit the tree.' His voice was terse and Ellen could tell he was worried. 'Look, I don't think this is the kind of night to be calling out someone to pull us out of the ditch. The driving conditions are too bad for that.' He held up his phone, moving it around. 'Besides, I can't get a signal anyway. We're too near the mountains here.'

'So what are we going to do?' Ellen asked. There was no signal on her phone either. Suddenly it didn't seem so funny any more. The restaurant was miles away and there were no lights indicating a house nearby.

'I've got my radio for the Mountain Rescue,' Sean said. 'There's always someone manning control. Not that I want them to have to come and get us. They'll never let me forget it. If I was on my own, I'd just wait until the morning and walk.'

But to his obvious frustration the team was out on a call. The volunteer manning the radio said that they had tried to reach Sean but hadn't been able to. The missing climber wasn't believed to be injured, just trapped on a ledge, but everyone who could be reached had gone to help him.

When Sean's expression darkened Ellen suspected that he hated missing out on the rescue as much as he hated being stuck. 'Could you get a message to Ellen's grandmother? Tell her that we're okay, but might not be back until morning.'

Ellen turned to look at him. 'What do you mean? Surely someone will drive along eventually? We could flag them down for a lift.'

Sean shook his head. 'There won't be any traffic along here at this time of night—not in this weather. We could stay in the car,' he said. 'However, it's likely to freeze tonight and without being able to turn the engine over we can't use the car heater. I have a blanket in the boot but even so it will be an uncomfortable night. No, I think our best bet is to head for a bothy I know of that's about half a mile away from here. It isn't much, but it does have a wood-burning stove and probably tea and coffee. Climbers and walkers use it and usually leave it well supplied. Do you think you could manage? I have a spare pair of wellies and extra socks in the boot as well as a blanket.'

'I don't think we have an option, do we?' Ellen said. 'Lead on, MacDuff.'

She felt ridiculous in her dress with Sean's boots. However, keeping her high heels on was a complete no-no. She felt like something out of a cartoon. All she needed now was a witch's hat and she'd look the part.

When she passed that on to Sean, he laughed. 'I think you

look cute,' he said. Then he grew serious again. 'I'm sorry about this, Ellen. I wanted the evening to be memorable, but not like this.'

Her heart gave a little pitter-patter at his words but he looked so pained she had to laugh. 'Forget it. Not your fault. It's an adventure. I'll pretend I'm on a trip to the Arctic circle.'

Although the bothy was only half a mile away it was heavy going. Ellen followed in Sean's footsteps, using his back as protection against the snow, which had turned to freezing rain and was driving horizontally into their faces. Ellen realised that it was just like it used to be, her traipsing after Sean, only this time it was at his invitation.

Every time they took a step they sank in the snow. About halfway there Ellen stumbled badly and fell face down in the snow, where she floundered like a turtle.

She tried to get to her feet before Sean noticed—why was he always seeing her at her worst? But he had turned around and saw her before she could do more than get onto her hands and knees.

She was unable to read his expression in the driving snow but suddenly she felt herself lifted into his arms.

'You look a little like the Snow Queen,' he murmured into her ear, his warm breath fanning her frozen cheeks. Despite their grim situation she could hear the laughter in his voice. She wasn't surprised. Beneath the man there still lurked the boy who liked getting into—and out of—difficult situations. 'It will be easier if I carry you,' he said.

Knowing that wriggling out of his arms would be a waste of energy for both of them, she snuggled against him, feeling the warmth of his body even through his sheepskin jacket. She remembered fantasising as a girl of being held like this, in different circumstances, of course, and it felt as good if not better than she'd dreamed.

A few minutes later, Sean kicked open the wooden door of the bothy and set her down on her feet. Unable to see in the pitch dark, she waited until she heard the scrape of a match followed by a satisfied sigh from Sean. Moments later he had lit a Tilly lamp and Ellen was able to see their shelter.

Not that there was much to see. A bunk bed, a pot-bellied stove, a small table and a couple of wooden, rickety-looking chairs.

At least they were out of the snow and there were some logs and kindling by the stove.

Sean took off his jacket and laid it around her shoulders. 'I'll have the fire going in a sec. There's a kettle on the table. The tap's next to the stove. Keep your fingers crossed the water hasn't frozen.'

Ellen couldn't do anything with her fingers. Along the way they had turned into lumps of ice. To make everything worse, her dress and tights were wet from where she had fallen into the snow. She began to panic. What if she got ill?

Sean quickly got the fire going and turned to her, no doubt looking for the kettle.

He took one look at her and must have realised she was too cold to move.

'The fire will get this place warm in no time,' he said. 'But you need to get out of these wet clothes.'

'And put on...?' Ellen asked through chattering teeth. But Sean was already slipping out of his shirt. Even though she was so cold she could barely think, the sight of his bare chest did something crazy to her insides.

'Take off your dress,' he ordered, slipping his jacket off her shoulders and handing her his shirt. 'It will be colder for a moment but better in the long run.'

When she hesitated he took a step towards her. 'Do you need me to help you?' he growled. Even in the dim light she could see the reflected glow from the fire in his eyes and what she saw sent a welcome warmth through her belly.

Hastily, she shook her head. 'Turn your back,' she said. Then, as he did so, using the time to fill up the kettle from the thankfully working tap, she slipped her dress over her head, followed by her saturated bra. Next, she slid her arms into his shirt, still warm from the heat of his body and smelling of wood smoke and very faintly of aftershave.

'Underwear too,' Sean said with his back still towards her. 'If they're wet?'

Did the man have eyes in the back of his head? But he was right. This was no time for false modesty. The thin material of her panties was also soaked through.

'Here, pass your clothes to me,' Sean said, reaching behind him without turning round.

Another time she might have found the sight of him hanging her lacy white undies up alongside her dress on a piece of string over the stove amusing, but right now she felt awkward, frightened and so very cold.

Having finished hanging up her wet clothes and setting the kettle on top of the stove, Sean picked up his jacket and placed it around her shoulders.

'Y-y-you keep it,' Ellen protested through cold-numbed lips. 'You must be frozen.'

'Then you'll just have to keep me warm,' he said, and pulled her down onto the lower bunk bed before fitting himself around her so that her back was against his chest. He wrapped his arms around her so tightly she could feel the length of his body along every inch of hers.

At first Ellen lay stiffly next to him but as the warmth

of his body began to chase the ice from hers, she let herself relax.

'It will warm up soon,' he said, his breath warm against her hair. 'As soon as the kettle has boiled I'll make us some tea.'

'I'm sorry,' he said after a while.

'What for? You couldn't have known this would happen.' A thought struck her and she frowned. 'You didn't plan this, did you, Sean Jamieson?'

'I might have wanted to get you on your own and in my arms—' his voice was husky '—but I would have chosen something more...roman—appropriate.'

His words made Ellen shiver. This time it wasn't from the cold.

'You know, eight years ago I would have given anything for you to say that,' Ellen said honestly.

There was a silence behind her for a moment. Sean leaned over and turned her around so she was facing him. The way he was looking at her made her stomach flutter.

'What do you mean, eight years ago?' he said.

She wasn't sure whether he was referring to her wanting him eight years ago or to the fact that her words implied she no longer wanted him. She chose to answer the first.

'You must have known I had a terrible crush on you when I was seventeen.' One thing about not knowing whether she had a future, it made it easier to cut to the chase. She no longer had the time to play games, not that she'd ever been much of a game player. Why shouldn't Sean know she'd once had a crush on him? She didn't have to say she had been head over heels in love. Her honesty didn't extend that far, and anyway it wasn't as if she still felt that way. Okay so even now he could make her melt with one look, but perhaps if she told him about how she'd felt and they laughed about it, the uncomfortable feeling that it had never gone away would vanish once and for all. It was surely worth a try. 'C'mon, be honest. I was terrible at hiding it. Especially when I tried to kiss you. Do you remember?'

'I remember.' The laughter was back in his voice. 'But when I wouldn't kiss you back you said you just wanted to practise kissing for when you kissed your real boyfriend. Do you remember that?'

Ellen knew her face must be bright red. And not because she was beginning to thaw. Every moment of that mortifying evening was burned into her memory. Gran had insisted Sean take her to the pub and order her a soft drink. Ellen hadn't known that her grandmother had put Sean up to it and had truly believed he was asking her out on a date.

He'd brought her home after an hour during which he'd been constantly glancing at his watch. Later she'd guessed he'd had a date but it hadn't crossed her love-addled brain back then. They'd stood at the door and Ellen had waited expectantly for his kiss. When it hadn't been forthcoming she'd taken matters into her own hands and stood on tiptoe and, placing her hands on either side of his face, brought his lips down to hers. At the last moment, Sean must have realised what she'd intended. He'd turned his face away so that her kiss had landed on his cheek. He'd stepped back and looked at her, his face a humiliating mixture of surprise and alarm and something else…pity.

'What are you doing, Ellen?' he'd asked, softly.

Knowing she'd completely misread the situation and trying to regain some dignity, she'd blurted the first thing that had come into her head.

'I've got a boyfriend in London. We haven't kissed yet. I thought…you…' She had trailed off. If anything, that had sounded even more ridiculous. She'd shuffled her feet and had been about to dash back inside when Sean had caught her by the arm and turned her to face him.

'And you want to practise with someone you know but don't care about in that way?' he'd asked, his voice low. Ellen had chosen to ignore the amusement that had rippled under his words.

He had tipped her chin, forcing her to look into his eyes.

'Do you still want to try?' he'd asked. Her heart had been pounding so hard she'd been barely able to breathe. Strange feelings had shot around her body and her limbs had felt heavy, languorous, as if she hadn't had the energy or the will to move them.

Unable to speak, or even breathe, she'd nodded.

Very slowly Sean had brought his mouth down to hers. She had tasted the faint tang of mint. His lips had been warm, his mouth a confusing mixture of firmness and gentleness.

Her knees had gone weak and she'd clung to him. As his kiss had deepened she'd felt a warmth flood her body. She hadn't wanted the moment ever to end.

Then his hands had been on her hips, pulling her closer, and she'd gasped as she'd felt his response against the thin material of her dress.

Confused, she'd stepped away, still breathing heavily. Sean had looked at her through half-closed eyes.

'I think you should go in now,' he'd said roughly.

Aware that something had changed between them but uncertain of what and knowing that she wanted nothing more than to step back into his arms and have him go on kissing her for the rest of her life, she'd looked at him blankly. He couldn't stop kissing her now.

But Sean had moved away and he was looking angry. Had she done something wrong? Had she shown him that she cared about him? Had he been repelled by her? She hadn't known.

All she knew had been that she had made an idiot of herself and that she felt like crying.

Spinning on her heel, she'd left him standing and rushed back inside, grateful that her grandmother hadn't been sitting up, waiting for her. She would never have been able to hide her confusion and mortification from Gran.

Coming back to the present, she realised Sean was still looking at her, a smile playing on his mouth as he waited for her answer.

'I remember,' she said honestly. 'But I lied. There was no boyfriend. I just wanted to kiss you.'

'I know,' Sean said. 'I didn't know up until I kissed you, but no woman kisses a man like that if she's in love with someone else.'

'You must have laughed at me,' Ellen said.

'No. It was a surprise. That was all. You have no idea how hard it was for me to stop kissing you. You were so young. So innocent. I was older, more experienced. I couldn't have taken advantage of what you were offering and still lived with myself.'

'You weren't that much older! Five years.'

'But too old for you. At least back then. When I realised that you had a crush on me it would have been easy to take advantage, but that's all it would have been. You were going back to London, I was going back to Glasgow. I would only have hurt you.' His arms tightened around her. 'But now, Ellen? How do you feel now?' His hand moved to the curve of her hip and she shivered. The truth was he still made her feel dizzy with longing.

She shifted in his arms until she could see his face. She looked into his eyes and what she saw there stopped her heart.

His kiss was everything she remembered. And more.

His mouth and lips were demanding a response from her,

his tongue doing things to her that she hadn't thought possible. A flash of heat spread through her body and she pressed herself into him, needing to feel every inch of him along the length of her.

For a moment he pulled his head back and looked deep into her eyes and what she saw there thrilled her. 'Well, little Ellen Nicholson, I think I'm jealous of the man who taught you to kiss like that.'

She wasn't about to tell him that it was his kiss that made her respond like that. No man had ever made her feel as if she were drowning, as if the world and its problems had just disappeared, as if all that mattered was right here, right now.

'Shut up and kiss me again,' she said. She had waited eight long years for this and wasn't going to wait any longer.

She felt his lips curve under hers as his mouth found hers again. Then he was dropping kisses on her forehead, pulling his hands through her damp hair, wrapping her face in his hands as he brought his mouth down on hers again.

The heat of the stove had warmed the room. Still kissing her, Sean's fingers were at the buttons of the shirt she was wearing. He moved his mouth to the base of her throat. Her heart was behaving so strangely, Ellen could barely breathe.

Sean undid each button, his kisses dropping lower as more of her skin was revealed.

Then the buttons were undone and he raised his head to look at her. Ellen threaded her fingers through his thick hair and pulled his head down to her breasts. When his tongue found her nipple she arched her back and smothered a cry as bolts of electricity shot through her from the top of her head to the tips of her toes.

Sean stopped what he was doing and looked at her, smiling at her response.

'I want to make love to you, Ellen. I want you more than I can remember wanting a woman.'

Suddenly, through the mist that was clouding her brain, Ellen realised what she was doing. If he carried on touching her she wouldn't be able to make herself stop. She would make love with him. And that was something she couldn't allow to happen.

She pulled away and jumped to her feet.

'No, Sean,' she cried. 'I can't.'

His eyes were on hers and his smile was puzzled.

'It's okay, Ellen,' he said quietly. 'We don't have to if you don't want to.'

'It's just that I can't,' she said.

He sat up and his eyes were shadowed in the flickering light from the Tilly lamp.

'Hey, hey. It's okay. Come and sit back down. I promise I won't touch you.'

She wasn't going to go back to the bunk. She wasn't sure she could trust herself. Instead she sat down on one of the rickety wooden chairs and bringing her knees up to her chest, hugged them to her.

'Is there someone else?' Sean asked.

She shook her head mutely. 'It's not that.'

'Then what is it?' He smiled ruefully. 'I shouldn't have rushed you. I'm sorry. That was clumsy of me.'

'Can we just leave it, Sean?' she said. 'Forget what happened?'

'I don't think I can. But I promise you, if you come back over here, I won't touch you again.' His eyes glittered in the lamplight. 'Not until you want me to.'

Ellen's teeth were chattering, but she knew it wasn't from the cold. She had so nearly let Sean make love to her. What if he hadn't brought protection? What if she had slept with him and got pregnant?

Sean got to his feet and looked at his watch. 'It's one. We should try and get some sleep. Hopefully by tomorrow I'll be able to get help. Why don't you take the bottom bunk and I'll take the top one? You have the blanket.' He held it out to her.

Ellen was torn. On the one hand she was scared that if he touched her again, he would know how much she wanted him. On the other, he would be cold if she took the only blanket.

Don't be silly, she told herself. She needed to be sensible.

'We'd be warmer if we shared one of the bunks.'

Sean's eyebrow shot up and he grinned.

'If I can trust you,' she added hastily. 'I meant what I said. I am not going to make love with you. Can you promise me that you won't...er...try anything?' Man, she sounded like a schoolgirl on her first date.

For an answer he took her by the hand and led her towards the bunk. He waited until she was lying down and then lay next to her, pulling the blanket over them both. Then Sean kissed her chastely on the forehead and, wrapping his arms around her, closed his eyes.

She listened to his rhythmic breathing and gradually felt herself relax. Her shivering subsided and she snuggled closer to the warmth of his body. Maybe just for tonight she could pretend that she was in the arms of someone who loved her.

After a surprisingly restful night's sleep, Ellen woke up to find herself alone. Still wearing Sean's shirt, she slipped out of her bunk and, testing her clothes and finding them dry, dressed quickly. She guessed Sean must have walked back to the car. Before he'd left he'd banked the fire, which was blasting heat into the small room. He had also placed a kettle of water on the stove and, finding a basin, she used the hot water to give herself a rudimentary wash. Anything more thorough would have to wait until she got back home.

Having made herself look as presentable as she could in the circumstances, Ellen looked out of the door. It must have stopped snowing before Sean had left as his footsteps were still visible. She grimaced as she looked down at her feet. She could hardly walk in these boots but it wasn't far to the car and she was damned if Sean was going to carry her again.

As she poured herself a cup of tea, the door opened and Sean burst in. He was wearing his sheepskin coat and Ellen realised his chest had to be bare underneath as she still had possession of his shirt. She thrust a mug of tea into his hands and handed him his shirt.

'Are you okay?' she asked.

'I managed to get a signal on my phone by climbing to the top of the hill. The garage is sending a recovery vehicle straight away. They should be here in the next twenty minutes. I also called Maggie to let her know you were okay.'

'What about last night's rescue? How did that go? Is the climber all right?'

'Apparently he wasn't hurt. They took him to hospital to get a once-over but he's due to be released later this morning. As I expected, I got a bit of stick about getting myself stuck.'

'I'm ready to leave whenever you are,' Ellen said. 'It's not as if there's much to pack.'

'I hope I haven't ruined your reputation.' Sean grinned. 'I'm afraid half the village will know by now that you spent the night with me and the other half will know by the end of the day.'

'And I don't suppose that anyone will think for even a second that I spent a night with you but managed to resist you?' Ellen said.

'Who cares what they think, Ellen? I learned a long time ago not to care for other people's opinions. You and I know the truth and that's what matters.'

The truth. What was that?

The trip back to the car was far easier in the daylight and without the driving snow of the night before. As Sean had promised, the recovery van was there before them. Unfortunately the car couldn't be fixed at the roadside and would have to go into the garage for repairs.

Sean and Ellen sat up front with the driver as the car was loaded onto the back of the recovery vehicle. Ellen was glad that the presence of the driver made anything more than small talk impossible. She needed some time alone to think about what had happened—correction, almost happened—between her and Sean.

Sean insisted they drop Ellen off at the top of the driveway leading to her grandmother's house before continuing on to the garage.

'Go to bed. Get some proper sleep. I'll come and see how you are when I finish at the garage,' he said.

'How will you get back here without a car?' Ellen dug in her handbag and, finding her car keys, passed them to Sean. 'Take my car. Then later, if you need to pick up your car I can drive you back into town.'

'Why, thank you, ma'am.' Sean took the keys and touched her lips lightly with his fingertips. 'Now, straight to bed with you. And apologise to Maggie for me for keeping you out all night.' The laughter was back in his voice and Ellen felt a pang. How good it would be to feel normal. To believe that whatever this was between her and Sean was the start of something and not the end. She shook her head slightly. Those kinds of thoughts were dangerous and she had to put them out of her head once and for all.

CHAPTER SEVEN

THE weeks passed quickly and spring arrived, bringing warmer and longer days. Ellen settled back into her job as a midwife easily. And if it hurt sometimes to be reminded of what she couldn't have, she managed to find some solace in the fact she was helping to bring healthy children into the world.

She saw Sean every day at work and sometimes in her grandmother's house. Occasionally he asked her out, but she always came up with some excuse, although as the weather grew warmer and the days started to lengthen, sometimes she would walk with him on the croft. They would talk about patients and his trip to Malawi. He was due to leave in June and expected to be away for three months. Often he would ask her about her life in London and although he looked curious, even pleased, when she told him she had no immediate plans to go back, he didn't try and probe too deeply.

One day, Sean came to find her in the labour suite.

'I have a patient who has been admitted to ITU. She's twenty-six weeks pregnant and is ill with swine flu. We're not sure she's going to pull through so we need to decide what to do about the pregnancy.'

Ellen frowned. 'What do you mean?'

'Why don't I bring you up to speed on the way to see her?'

Sean said, and after Ellen had let the nurse in charge know where she was going, she fell into step beside Sean.

'Mrs Gillespie is unconscious and on a respirator,' Sean explained. 'There's a chance that if we deliver the baby the mother's condition might improve.'

'In other words, sacrifice the baby for the mother? Is that the choice?' A tight band was forming around Ellen's chest.

'A twenty-eight-weeker has a chance of survival,' Sean said quietly.

'And a massively increased chance of multiple health problems.'

Sean nodded. 'That's why we haven't delivered the baby yet. We've spoken to the father about his choices and I wondered if you might have a word. Go over the options with him again. Give him another take?'

Ellen stopped in her tracks and sucked in a breath. Did Sean have any idea what he was asking of her?

'You can't ask me to do that. It's an impossible decision,' she said as Sean stopped and turned towards her. 'Why on earth didn't Mrs Gillespie take the vaccination offered to pregnant women? All this could have been easily avoided.'

'Her husband tells me that she was worried the vaccination might harm her baby. Whether you and I agree with her decision, she made it for the best possible reasons.'

'If you deliver the baby now, there is still a chance that neither mother nor baby will survive,' Ellen said. 'Is that correct?'

Sean nodded. 'It's not much of a choice, is it?'

'And why should I speak to him?'

'Because someone needs to promote the interests of the child. As doctors we want to save our patient above everything else.' He placed a hand on her shoulder. 'You're good with people, Ellen. The patients trust you. I think it would elp for Mrs Gillespie's husband to have someone else to discuss his options with. I don't want you to tell him what to do—none of us has the right to do that—all I want you to do s be another ear for him to talk to.'

Ellen digested what Sean was saying. Mr Gillespie was in a horrible position.

'Okay,' she said finally. 'Let's see if Mr Gillespie has any questions for me.'

The air of quiet efficiency in ITU always tore at Ellen's heartstrings. There were six beds, each with two nurses at the bedside and often a relative who would be waiting with an awful desperation to know whether their loved one would pull through. She averted her eyes from a mother who was weeping over her teenage son who was almost invisible under the wires snaking from every part of his body. The posture of the mother, the desperate look in her eyes as they passed, was almost too much to witness. Ellen's throat closed as dread coiled in her stomach. One day, perhaps sooner rather than later, this would be where she would end up. Who would be beside her bed? Would her mother be there, regretting that she hadn't spent enough time with her only child before it was too late? Would her father come? Ellen hadn't seen him since he'd left her mother when Ellen was five, so she doubted it.

Perhaps it was time that she told her mother? Ellen still felt fine and sometimes she would let herself hope that her diagnosis had been some horrible mistake. She was due to see her consultant in London in May for a check-up and she couldn't help but hope that he would tell her he had been wrong, or that they had found a miracle cure. But she owed it to herself, if not her parents, to let them know what was happening. She made up her mind. She would tell her mother after she'd seen the consultant again.

Then they were beside Mrs Gillespie's bed. Like the lad

in the bed two along she was hooked up to the ventilator and a series of monitors. Two nurses were bending over her. One was moistening her mouth, the other taking a blood sample from her arterial line. The husband was nowhere to be seen. Perhaps he had stepped outside for a breath of air. As the ITU nurses spoke to Sean in whispered voices, Ellen studied the woman in the bed.

If it hadn't been for the paraphernalia of the ITU Ellen would have thought the woman was asleep. Her newly moistened lips were parted and slightly turned up at the corners as if she were sleeping and dreaming pleasant thoughts.

Having finished speaking to the nurses, Sean shook his head slightly and handed Ellen Mrs Gillespie's maternity records.

Mrs Gillespie—Moira—was twenty-six and had one healthy child born two years before. Her pregnancy had been normal and no problems had been anticipated. Until she had contracted swine flu, that was.

At first she had ignored the symptoms. Her husband had taken a couple of days off work to look after their two-year-old so that his wife could rest, but on day three Moira's condition had worsened. Within half an hour she had started having difficulty breathing. The husband had called their GP, who had called an ambulance. By the time it arrived Moira had been unconscious and had had to be ventilated by the ambulance staff. That was yesterday. Moira hadn't recovered consciousness and if anything her condition had deteriorated.

Instinctively, Sean and Ellen moved out of earshot of the unconscious woman. They knew that the hearing was often the last function to go and they didn't want to take a chance Moira could hear what they were saying.

'The nurses tell me she's not responding to treatment. Her condition is continuing to deteriorate,' Sean said.

Ellen nodded and stepped back to the bed. Very gently she palpated Moira's uterus. The baby was the right size for dates and still had a healthy normal heartbeat. The mother's body was directing all its resources to protecting the child inside her. If the baby were delivered, the mother's body might redirect all its defence mechanisms to making the mother better.

'How are they?' A broken voice came from behind Ellen.

She turned around to find a man with red-rimmed eyes standing behind her.

'Mr Gillespie—Tom—this is Ellen Nicholson, one of the midwives. She's come to check on the baby. Your wife's condition is not improving. In fact, if anything it's getting worse. I know this is hard for you to hear but I thought you might find it useful to talk to Ellen about any decisions you might have to make. If you need me, I'll be at the nurses' station.' Sean pressed Tom's shoulder sympathetically, before leaving Ellen and Tom alone.

Tom smiled down at his wife.

'Isn't she beautiful?' he said almost to himself. 'The most beautiful girl in the world. We've only been married for four years. Our anniversary is in two weeks' time. We thought we had everything. Each other. Our daughter. Now this baby to complete our family. Everything Moira and I ever wanted.' He took a shuddering breath. 'Our little girl can't understand why she can't see Mummy,' he said softly. 'She keeps crying for her. I would have brought her in, but I don't want her to be frightened. I don't want her memory of her mother to be like this.' His voice broke on the last words and his shoulders started heaving.

Ellen put her arm around him and held him as he cried. Her throat was aching and tears burned behind her eyes.

'She's still with us,' she said. 'You can't give up hope.'

She waited until Tom regained some of his composure. 'How can life turn out like this?' Anger had replaced the terrible grief in his eyes. 'Moira didn't do anything to deserve this. She had a rotten childhood. She was brought up in a children's home, you know. She could have been hard and angry, but she's not. She's the kindest woman I know and the best mother a child could ask for.'

Silently Ellen passed him a glass of water and Tom took a noisy sip. She knew only too well the sense of disbelief Tom was experiencing. One day his life was going on as normal, unexciting perhaps but normal. Then the next it was all falling to pieces. She pushed the thoughts of her own illness away. All that mattered right now was this woman and her distraught husband.

'They say that they could deliver the baby by Caesarean section and then Moira might improve. She could get completely better and we could try for another baby later.' Tom looked at Ellen with anguished eyes. 'Is that what I should do? Even if it means that this baby might die? I don't know if Moira will ever forgive me for making that decision.'

'You don't have to decide right now,' Ellen said. She summoned Sean over, who had been watching them closely. 'Dr Jamieson, what will happen if we don't deliver Moira?'

'There is a possibility she could deteriorate quite quickly. But they are keeping her under close observation here. Hopefully we would have some warning.'

'What then?' Tom asked. 'What if she did get worse suddenly?' His voice was firmer now.

'We would have to deliver the baby. But every day that Moira stays alive the baby is growing and developing. So the longer we wait the better chance of survival it has. But...' Sean hesitated. 'The safest option would be to deliver your wife as soon as possible.'

'And you can tell me one hundred per cent that if you do, Moira will get better? That she'll make a full recovery?'

Sean shook his head. 'Sometimes we find that delivering the baby makes a difference. Pregnancy makes swine flu worse, which is why we recommend vaccinations, but at this stage we can't be sure. It's possible Moira would die anyway.'

A calmness descended over Tom. 'And the ITU consultants agree with you?'

'Yes.'

'But she could still get better? Without delivering the baby?'

Sean nodded. 'It's possible.'

'And if the baby is delivered now? What will that mean?'

'The baby's lungs won't be fully developed. If we can keep the baby alive and ventilate it, he, or she, will have a decent chance of survival.'

'Of survival?'

'Yes. I have to tell you that at this stage in the baby's growth, even if it survives it may have multiple health problems. Possibly even be brain damaged.'

'Not much of a choice, eh?' Tom tried a smile. 'How long do I have to make a decision?'

'As Ellen said, you don't have to make a decision right now. But you might want to consider giving us permission to section your wife should her condition deteriorate suddenly. If that happens, we may not have time to track you down. It would be better to have your signed permission in advance.'

Tom nodded. 'In that case, that's what we'll do. Show me where I sign.'

That evening, Ellen sat outside her grandmother's cottage. Spring had arrived properly and although it was still cool in the evenings, there were tulips in the garden's borders. Earlier she had dropped her grandmother at one of her friend's houses to play bridge. Images of the conversation with Tom played in her mind. Life and death inextricably linked. She'd thought she'd known that, but until now she'd never really faced the knowledge on a daily basis.

The crunch of footsteps on gravel alerted her and she looked up to find Sean standing over her. Silently she shifted along the bench so he could sit next to her.

'If you're hoping to beg dinner, you're out of luck,' she said. 'Gran is having supper with friends.'

Sean pretended to look offended. 'I can feed myself, you know. I make a mean toasted sandwich.'

Ellen laughed. She was secretly relieved Sean was there. He would distract her from her gloomy thoughts.

'Or I can go back to the hospital and eat at the canteen. It's what I usually do.'

'Or I could feed you,' Ellen said. 'C'mon, let's raid the fridge.'

They went inside and Sean settled himself in his usual chair by the fire. Ellen's heart contracted. Anyone looking in from the outside would think they were a couple.

'Omelette do?' she asked. 'There are cheese scones to go with it that I made earlier.'

'Cheese scones? You're a woman after my own heart.'

There was a silence after his words. For a moment their eyes locked and Ellen was the first to look away. Whenever she was with Sean she felt as if nothing else mattered. It had been a mistake, coming back here. She should have known the minute she had seen Sean again that she had never forgotten him. Her first love. Her only love. There was no point pretending to herself any more. She loved him. She'd always loved him and she would never stop. If only she was healthy, perhaps they would have had a chance. He must never know how she felt about him.

'How is Moira?' She changed the subject as she removed the eggs from the fridge and placed a pan on the Aga to warm. Talking about work was safer. Besides, she genuinely wanted to know.

'No change.'

She cracked several eggs into the pan. It would have to be a large omelette if it was to feed Sean.

'It's still possible both she and the baby could die, isn't it?' she said. Then, without warning, she started to cry. Her tears slid down her cheeks before hitting the stove with a hiss.

Sean was on his feet and behind her. He wrapped his arms around her and pulled her against him. He reached across and removed the pan from the heat.

As she continued to cry, he lifted her in his arms and sat back down, cradling her as if she were a baby.

She hid her face in his shirt, powerless to stop the tears. She couldn't be strong any more. She needed to grieve for what she had lost. Her future. Any chance of a child. Any chance of love.

Sean stroked her hair, murmuring soothing words.

He waited until her shuddering tears stopped.

'Do you want to talk about it?' he asked gently. 'I'm a good listener.'

She continued to hide her face, afraid to look him in the eyes. She knew if she did, her secret would come spilling out. And she wasn't ready to say the words. Not yet. Maybe never.

She struggled to sit up, but Sean's arms tightened around her, forcing her to stay where she was.

'Is it Moira? You know we'll do everything we can to bring

her and her baby through this. Have you never lost a patient before? Is that what's upsetting you?'

It was—partly. But it had also been the sudden realisation that she could really die. It hadn't really sunk in before. Somehow she had managed to pretend to herself that a mistake had been made. Up until today she had been in denial. Now she knew with absolute certainty there had been no mistake. She had an illness that could kill her at any time. Maybe not for years, but equally it could strike tomorrow, or the next day. And she desperately wanted to live.

It was easier to nod than to explain.

'I don't know if you were aware of what happened to my sister?' Sean said. 'You must have been—what—six at the time?'

All Ellen knew was that Sean had had a sister who had died when he was a child. It was only several years later that she had learned that Seonag had died in childbirth. Her grandmother hadn't known the details.

'It's why I became an obstetrician,' Sean said. 'My sister should never have died. She had pre-eclampsia, but she could have been all right if she'd agreed to have had labour induced prematurely. But she wouldn't even consider it. She had a massive stroke when she was twenty eight weeks pregnant. The baby survived—she didn't.' Although his words were clipped, almost toneless, Ellen could hear the pain in his voice.

She looked up at Sean. Until now she hadn't thought about the impact his sister's death must have had on him. She had been in London when it had happened and when she'd next come back to Inverness-shire, Sean had seemed the same as he always had. But she should have known that his sister's death would have affected him hugely. The Jamiesons had always been a close and loving family. It was why she'd spent so much time hanging around their house.

'David was raised by his dad and his grandparents on his father's side,' Sean said. 'He's seventeen now, doing well. He's even thinking of becoming a doctor.

'I haven't lost a mother in my career,' Sean continued. 'And I don't intend to. That's why I'm keeping a close eye on Moira. I've told them to page me if she shows any sign of deteriorating. I promise I'll do everything in my power to save mother and baby. Do you trust me?'

Ellen nodded. She did trust him. More than trusted him, she loved him. As simple as that. Except it wasn't simple. She didn't have a future. She had nothing to offer him.

Sean placed a finger on her chin and lifted her face to his. With his other hand he very gently wiped away the tear tracks on her cheeks. Then he lowered his head and he was kissing her.

The world was spinning as she returned his kiss. It was as if she was caught up in a vortex and was unable to do anything except cling to him as if her life depended on it.

His kiss deepened and she threaded her fingers through his thick hair, pulling him closer. He gave a muffled groan as she slipped a hand inside his shirt. She was barely aware of what she was doing. All she knew was that nothing else mattered except the here and now. She wanted Sean as she had never wanted anything before. She knew it was reckless, but if she couldn't be reckless now... She let the words tail off in her head. All she wanted was to be loved by him, just once.

She got to her feet, aware of her heart crashing against her ribs, and held her hand out to him.

He took it, a wordless question in his dark blue eyes.

'Come upstairs,' she whispered.

'Are you sure?' Sean asked.

She nodded and pulled him behind her up to her bedroom.

Inside her room she locked the door and still with her eyes fixed on his slowly undid the buttons on her blouse one by one.

His pupils dilated as he looked at her and her heart rate escalated so she was hardly able to breathe. This was what she had been waiting for all her life.

He stepped closer to her and wrapped his hands in her hair, pulling it away from her shoulders so he could see her better. She closed her eyes as she felt his hands on her throat, the roughened pads of his thumbs on her skin as he slipped the blouse off her shoulders. Then his hands were behind her and she felt a cool draught of air as he undid her bra and her breasts came free. She heard his sharp intake of breath and a rustle as he took off his own shirt. Then her bare skin was against his; the warmth of him thawing her frozen heart. She trailed her hands over his chest, exploring each ridge and muscle.

He bent his head and circled each nipple with his tongue and a moan escaped her lips. He hesitated for a moment and scared that he would stop what he was doing she pressed his head closer. Her need for him was so intense she thought she would explode. All the years of wanting and dreaming.

His hands were on the button of her skirt and she wriggled her hips to help it fall down.

As he undressed her, they were moving towards her bed.

She sat on the edge, daring to peek up at him. The only light was from the full moon shining through the open curtains of her window and she was glad of the darkness to hide her shyness.

Still in his jeans, he dropped to his knees and slowly, so slowly she thought she would scream from her need of him, he slipped her panties down. She raised her hips to help him and her body convulsed as his hands cupped her bottom, one of his fingers stroking her, finding her wetness and touching her with a mixture of unbearable gentleness and a certainty about what would give her the most pleasure.

She arched her back as she climaxed.

He paused and held her until her body stopped shuddering. Her eyes were still closed. She was scared to look at him in case he could read her eyes. Then he slipped off his jeans and underwear. Her eyes still closed, she heard a rustling and knew he must be protecting himself. Then his hands were on her again, probing and stroking until she was ready for him. Slowly, so slowly, he eased himself inside her. He moved gently as if he was scared to hurt her, but she rocked her hips against his and as his thrusting grew deeper and more urgent she felt a spiral of triumph. Somehow, instinctively, she knew what he needed and when. Once again wave upon wave of pleasure racked her body. Then they were moving together faster and faster, each in their private world of pleasure. Just before she climaxed again she opened her eyes to find his fixed on hers. Then finally, when she thought she couldn't bear it any more, they came together.

For a moment they stayed where they were and then he scooped her into his arms and laid her on the bed until they were lying close together, the length of their naked bodies pressed against each other. She wasn't shy any more. It felt natural and right to be with him. As if they had always belonged together. As if they were two parts of a whole. At least, that's how *she* felt.

Sean moved his body until he was lying on his back and her head was resting on his chest.

'When did you say Maggie would be back?' he asked, before kissing Ellen on the top of her head.

'I'm to collect her at ten,' Ellen said.

Sean looked at his watch over her head. 'Eight o'clock.'

Ellen lifted her head until she was looking up at him. He was grinning down at her.

'Who would have guessed that little Ellen Nicholson would turn out to be so wild?' he teased.

She picked up a pillow and hit him with it. Soon they were tussling on the bed and then everything turned serious again as she straddled Sean. His hands were caressing her back, running down her thighs, stroking her buttocks, and unbelievably she wanted him again.

Sean sat up, her legs still straddling him, and then got to his feet.

Supporting her with his hands, he reached down into his jeans pocket.

He cursed. 'It was lucky I had one condom as it was. I didn't expect to find us in this situation. I could go to mine, but something tells me you can't wait.'

He arched his eyebrow at her. Ellen was surprised again at how she felt no shame, no embarrassment, as he laid her on her back and spread her legs with his hands. She protested briefly as he started kissing her on the insides of her thighs, the feel of his mouth as he moved inexorably upwards driving her to the point of no return so that when he placed his mouth on her most private of places she was lost.

When she was able to think again, Sean was looking down at her smiling into her eyes.

'When did you get to be so beautiful?' he said.

Before she could think of what to say in return, Sean's mobile rang. With a word of apology he leaned over and retrieved it from the pocket of his jeans and looked at the number.

'Sorry. I have to take this,' he said. 'It's the Mountain Rescue Team.'

As he spoke to whoever was on the other end of the phone, Ellen studied him. What had they done? Where would they go from here? Should she tell him about her illness?

Sean would be heading off to Malawi in a couple of months. If she told him, would he still go? Or would he stay out of a misplaced sense of loyalty or—worse—pity?

She would rather never see him again than risk that. Why not enjoy whatever time they had left, especially as it could be the last time she had with him? But did he want to spend more time with her? Or had this been just sex for him?

Sean was pulling on his clothes, the phone tucked between his shoulder and his chin.

'I should be with you in under twenty minutes,' he said, before disconnecting.

'I'm sorry, Ellen. I'm going to have to run. There's a group of climbers stuck halfway up Ben Nevis and one of them has a suspected fractured pelvis.'

'It's okay,' she replied. 'Just go.'

Sean popped to the bathroom and Ellen got out of bed, wrapping the sheet around herself. When Sean returned he was frowning.

'I'm really sorry, sweetheart, but the condom I used seems to have split. I didn't ask, but are you on the Pill?'

His words filled her with terror. What had she been thinking? To be honest she hadn't been thinking at all. That was the problem. If she had she would never have taken the risk, even knowing that Sean was using protection. But she of all people should know that the only sure-fire way not to get pregnant was not to have sex. It was too late to think about that now.

Something in her expression must have alerted him. 'You're not on the Pill, are you?'

'No. And I can't get pregnant.' She tried to keep the panic from her voice.

'Then I think you should get hold of the morning-after pill,' Sean said. He walked back across the room, sat down next to her and hugged her. 'I'm so sorry to dump this on you and to leave it like this, but I really have to go. There's a man's life at risk.'

'It's all right,' Ellen said, although it wasn't. Not really. Waves of anxiety were washing over her. She took a deep breath. She would get the morning-after pill. Tomorrow. As soon as the surgery opened. It wasn't a big deal. In the meantime, Sean was needed.

She pushed him away gently. 'Go. I'll see to it.'

'I'm not sure when I'll be back,' he said, 'but I'll see you soon.'

CHAPTER EIGHT

As SOON as it was light, Ellen slipped downstairs, taking care not to wake her grandmother. Although it was only just after six, she had given up on trying to get back to sleep.

She poked the ashes in the grate of the elderly range and added some peat and a little kindling. She knew it wouldn't be long before the fire was roaring away.

She stepped across to the window. It was hard to believe that she had been here for two months already. The brown winter grass had given away to a lush green and there was a hint of warmth in the morning sun. Soon the tulips outside would be replaced by her grandmother's roses.

She wondered if she'd be around to see them. She might live for another few years—long enough for them to find better treatment for her condition, even a cure. It could happen. Only a year or two ago the life expectancy for someone with pulmonary hypertension was three years at best, now no one put a figure on it. All they said was that the prognosis was getting more hopeful every year.

She filled the kettle from the cold-water tap and placed it on the stove to boil. Even if she had years, it wasn't long enough.

But there was always the chance that she would work her way up the transplant list, although she knew better than to hold out too much hope for a new heart and lungs. How would it feel to have someone else's heart and lungs inside you? Especially knowing that that person had had to die in order that you had a chance of living?

She had to stop thinking like that. She should never have made love with Sean. She should never have let herself fall in love with him all over again. It only made the fact that they didn't have a future so much harder to bear.

But she could no more have stopped herself than she could have walked on water. The need to be with him, to be part of him, even if it was only for one night, had been irresistible.

She shook her head in wonder. She could have died not knowing what it was like to be loved by him.

The kettle whistled and she poured the hot water into the teapot. She had to phone for an appointment for the morning-after pill. There might only be the smallest chance she could be pregnant but it wasn't one she could allow herself to take. One thing her consultant had been very clear about was the danger of a pregnancy. Some women with PH survived but many didn't. He'd advised her to think about sterilisation, but it had been too soon to take that final, irrevocable step. And it wasn't as though she had imagined herself having sex so soon.

She poured the tea into a mug and sat down at the kitchen table. Knowing that she could never have a child had been almost as much of a blow as knowing she might die at any time. Ever since she was a teenager she had dreamed about being a mother. Maybe it was seeing Sean and his large family and the joy they shared in one another, maybe it was because she had never felt that joy, that sense of belonging in her own family, and longed to create a family of her own where her children would always know they were loved, above all else. Who knew? But she suspected it was one of the reasons she had become a midwife. She loved everything about new babies. Their total dependency, their unconditional love, the way they smelled, their tiny features—everything. It didn't mean that she didn't know that they grew up into tiring toddlers and difficult teenagers—her patients were always telling her amusing horror stories about their children—but none of that would bother her. Because she could remember so vividly what it was like to feel awkward and out of place as a child and then as a teenager, she knew she would have been a good mother.

At least she had her work. It was small compensation, but it was something.

And what about Sean? Did he plan to become a father? She doubted it. Sean was too used to doing as he pleased.

But thinking about Sean and babies was pointless. Neither were going to be part of her future. Was it even fair to carry on this relationship with Sean, however unlikely it was that she would break his heart?

On the other hand, the weather had improved, the nurses who had been off with swine flu had either returned to work or were due back soon and she would be out of a job. Perhaps then it would be time to go back to London? In the meantime, was it wrong to want what she had with Sean to carry on for a little while longer? Even if it was, did she have the strength to put an end to it? Wasn't that too much to ask of her?

He would be going away soon, but in the meantime, if she continued to see him, would she be able to stop herself from sleeping with him? She couldn't take another risk. Okay, it was unlucky what had happened last night with the condom, but even if there was the remotest possibility it could happen again, she simply couldn't take the chance. She sighed. No. It was better that she stop it right now.

Finding the number of the doctor's surgery next to the

phone book, Ellen rang and asked to be put through to one of the GPs. She explained that she needed the morning-after pill. The GP was happy to leave a prescription for Ellen to collect at the front desk, which she did on her way to work. She took another few minutes to fill the prescription at the nearest chemist and as soon as she was at the hospital she swallowed the tablets with some water.

When she made her way onto the labour ward, Sean was already there. A wave of relief flooded her. Although she knew she would have heard had the rescue not gone according to plan, it was still reassuring to know that Sean had made it safely off the mountain.

As if feeling her eyes on him, he looked up from the notes he was writing in and caught her eye. A slow grin crossed his face and her insides turned to liquid. At the same time, a wave of sadness, so intense it almost made her cry out, washed over her. She knew she had made the right decision to stop this, whatever it was, with Sean. Feeling as she did, she would never be able to resist him. And if she did go out with him and refuse to make love with him, he would want to know why.

Intensely aware of him, she forced herself to pay attention to the morning handover. There were four women in labour—all progressing well—and two who were coming up to the ward to have their pregnancies monitored as day patients.

'There is still no change with Mrs Gillespie,' Jessie said, finishing her report. 'Dr Jamieson has been up to see her. The baby is developing normally, so it's just a case of wait and see. One of us will continue to go across to ITU twice a day to monitor the baby. Any volunteers for this morning?'

'I'd like to go,' Ellen said. 'I spoke to the husband yesterday and I'd like to keep the relationship going with him. If we're not busy here, would that be okay?'

'Good idea, Ellen,' Jessie said. 'We'll be fine here for the time being, although you may be needed when our two day-patient ladies come in. But they're not due until later on this morning.'

'Why are they being monitored?' Ellen asked.

'One has diabetes and the other we are keeping an eye on for pre-eclampsia.'

'Why don't I go along to ITU now, then?' Ellen suggested. 'I suspect Tom will be there by now.'

At the door of the ward, Sean caught up with her. He lifted a stray lock of hair that had escaped from her ponytail and tucked it behind her ear. 'How are you?' he asked. 'Did you sleep okay?'

To her annoyance, Ellen felt her cheeks colour as images of her and Sean amongst the tangled sheets rose to her mind again.

'Yes,' she lied. 'I went to fetch Gran after you left and we watched TV for a while. How did the rescue go?'

'It was a fractured femur, as expected. Plus a broken pelvis. We had to arrange for a Sea King helicopter to lift the casualty off the mountain. It took a while to get the patient stabilised but we managed okay. They took him to Glasgow. I phoned an hour ago and he's doing okay. Won't be doing any climbing for a while, though.'

He bent his head and whispered in her ear. 'What about tonight? Can I see you? I hated running off like that, especially when…'

'I picked up a prescription from the surgery this morning,' Ellen said quickly. 'But, Sean, last night was…wonderful, but I don't think we should repeat it.'

Sean looked stunned. Clearly he wasn't used to being turned down.

'Why the hell not? We're good together. I can't believe last night didn't mean something to you.'

The problem was it meant too much. Not that she could tell him that.

'I need to go, Sean,' Ellen said, stepping away from him.

'We'll talk about this later,' Sean said grimly, and as Ellen walked away she felt his eyes on her.

In ITU she found Tom in almost exactly the same position as the day before, sitting next to his wife, talking to her softly while holding her hand. At the sight of the young husband, Ellen's heart splintered. If only someone could wave a magic wand and make everything all right for everyone.

'Hello, Tom.' She placed a hand on his shoulder. 'How is Moira?'

'No change, but at least she's not getting worse.'

She placed a cup of coffee she had brought with her next to him. 'Drink this,' she said. 'Then I thought we could go up to the special care nursery. When your baby is born, it is likely that he or she will be brought up there.'

'It's a wee boy,' Tom said. 'We found out at the scan.' He took a sip of the coffee. 'Thanks. Are you always so thoughtful?'

'I know what I would want if I were in your shoes,' Ellen said. 'Sometimes it's the small things we can do that help. I only wish, we all wish, we could do more.'

'Aye, well. Sometimes you're on your own,' Tom said. He finished his coffee with a gulp. 'Let's go and see this special care nursery, then.' His voice was heavy as if he had already given up hope.

'Tom,' Ellen said firmly. 'There is every chance your baby will be delivered in a reasonable condition. Dr Jamieson has given you his word that he'll do everything in his power to make it happen. You mustn't give up. Moira needs you to stay strong—for her and both your children.'

Tom shook his head before managing a tight smile. 'Okay. You're the boss.' He leaned over and kissed his wife. 'I'm just going to see the special care nursery, love. Our baby might have to go there when he's born, so I'm just checking that they are up to speed. Be good while I'm away.'

Upstairs, on the ward, Ellen introduced Tom to the nurse in charge and explained why they were there. Ellen knew that even from the nurses' station the ward would look a scary place to Tom. At least if he saw it now, he would know what to expect and wouldn't feel as overwhelmed. There were six incubators in all, four of which had tiny baby occupants. Each cot had two nurses and one had a couple of doctors and nurses all working over the baby.

Ellen passed Tom a gown and mask and helped him into them, explaining that they needed to protect the babies from any infections visitors might inadvertently bring in with them.

She took him over to one cot where the nursing staff were changing the baby's feeding tube. She stopped a couple of feet away and explained to Tom what the nurses were doing.

'When babies are born early, their lungs are often not developed enough for them to breathe on their own, so we keep them ventilated until they can manage. We have to sedate them to do this and that means we have to feed them through a tube.' She went on to explain the different machines and tubes that were attached to the baby. 'There's holes for you to put your hands through so you'll be able to touch your baby. That's important.'

Tom was taking in everything she said, nodding to show he understood.

'How long are the babies here for?' he asked.

'It depends very much on their condition when they're

born. Little Maisie, who we're looking at now, has been here for a couple of months already. She was born very prematurely—at twenty-eight weeks—but Maisie is doing well and putting on weight. She was on a respirator for the first few weeks, but as you can see, she's breathing on her own now.'

All that could be seen of little Maisie was her tiny hands and her miniature mouth and nose.

'We put hats on all the babies to help preserve their body heat but as you can see she's only wearing a nappy. That's so the nurses can observe her closely—it's another reason why the ward is so warm. Do you have any questions?'

Tom looked around. Next to a cot a mother was holding her baby, feeding it from a bottle.

'What about that baby?'

'That's Sophie. I was actually there when she was born. She was also premature. Why don't we go over and you can say hello to her mother?'

After talking to Sophie's mother, Tom seemed much happier and Ellen knew she had made the right decision, bringing him here. As they left, he turned to Ellen and took her by the hand.

'You know, for the first time I actually believe everything might turn out all right after all. Thank you, Ellen. From the bottom of my heart.'

Ellen swallowed the lump in her throat. 'It's my pleasure. Now, why don't we go back down and you can tell Moira all about it while I check her over to see how your baby is doing?'

Later that evening, Ellen was in the kitchen making bread, chatting to her grandmother while she knitted. She was unsurprised when there was knock on the door and Sean came in.

He bent over and kissed Maggie on the cheek. She gave him a wry smile in return. 'What's that for, lad? No, let me guess. You smelled the baking and thought you'd come and investigate?'

'You know me, Maggie. Never could resist home cooking, but this time you're wrong. It's Ellen I came to see.'

The old lady's eyes brightened. She picked up her knitting. 'There's a programme on the television I wanted to catch, so I'll leave you two alone, shall I?'

As she left, she winked at Ellen. Ellen had to control the impulse to beg her grandmother not to leave her alone with Sean, but she knew that would only be delaying the inevitable conversation. Sean, she suspected, was not one to give up easily if there was something he wanted.

As soon as her grandmother had left the room, Sean came up behind her and nuzzled her neck. 'You smell like all my favourite things. How about coming over to mine after supper?'

Ellen wriggled out of his grip and turned to face him.

'Not tonight, Sean.' She took a deep breath. 'Why don't you sit down?' She pointed to the chair farthest away from her. 'Over there.' If he carried on touching her, she would melt.

Sean looked bemused but did as she asked.

'I can't see you again. I mean, I can see you, obviously, we work together, but last night—that was a one-off. It can't happen again.'

Sean's puzzled frown grew deeper. 'Why not?'

'Because, Sean, I have to be honest. You and I want different things from life. You are going away soon and I will be going back to London.'

'And?'

'And there is no point in us starting something. One of us will only get hurt.'

'I think we've already started something, Ellen. But if

you're looking for promises from me, it's a little soon. Let's just enjoy what we have and see where it takes us.'

'That's just it, Sean. It's not going to take us anywhere. I'm not prepared to play the little housewife and wait patiently for you to return. Besides, I have a life in London and I'll be going back there soon.' She made herself sound steady and calm. She couldn't afford to give him any hint of how much she hated pretending.

'How do you know it's not going to go anywhere?' he asked. 'Not that I'm making any promises—but why don't we make the most of what time we have together for however long it lasts?' He was looking edgy, as if he was worried Ellen was trying to force him into some sort of commitment he wasn't ready—or able—to make.

It wasn't just that she didn't know how long it would last—the problem was that she couldn't let this continue without telling him the truth. And she didn't want to.

'No. I'm sorry, Sean. Last night should never have happened. You caught me at a low moment, that's all. Please believe me when I say that it is not what I want.'

He got to his feet, disbelief written all over his face. 'If that's what you want, Ellen. I have to respect your decision,' he said stiffly. 'Now, if you'll excuse me, I'll just say goodnight to Maggie.'

CHAPTER NINE

THE days lengthened and grew warmer as summer approached. Although the nurses who had been off had all returned, Ellen had agreed to stay for a little longer. At work Sean was friendly but never gave a hint by word or look that there had ever been anything between them. Ellen's heart ached as she counted down the days to his departure. To her secret relief, she didn't see or hear of Sean with another woman. That would have been too much.

Mrs Gillespie remained in ITU. She was now at thirty weeks and every day Tom's belief that the baby would survive grew stronger.

Maggie often asked about Sean and wondered out loud why he wasn't coming around to visit. But then she would answer her own question, remembering that in the summer Sean spent most evenings mountain biking when he wasn't working on the house. However, Ellen often caught her grandmother looking at her speculatively.

Although Ellen had spoken to her mother twice, she hadn't been able to bring herself to broach the subject of her illness over the phone.

One Saturday morning, Ellen woke up feeling nauseous. She only just made it to the bathroom before she was sick. As she sat on the bathroom floor, getting her breath back, a realisation struck her. Her period was late.

Her heart started hammering. She hadn't been paying attention because she hadn't thought for a second that after taking the morning-after pill she could get pregnant. Was the way she was feeling now due to her illness?

She forced herself to take deep, steadying breaths. The first thing to do was to get a pregnancy test. If that was negative then she had to make an appointment to see her doctor.

Her head spinning, Ellen ran out to her car and headed for the nearest pharmacy.

Sean finished writing up his notes and leaned back in his chair. He was looking forward to the weekend and a couple of days out on the mountains. Maybe then he'd be able to stop thinking about Ellen.

Damn. Why was he letting her get to him? Okay, so he wasn't used to being turned down, and he was used to being the one who ended relationships, but it wasn't just that his ego had taken a battering.

It wasn't as if he'd imagined a future with Ellen. In fact, that was part of the attraction. She would be going back to London and he was going to Malawi for three months. There was a tidiness about the fact that they both knew that, whatever the attraction was that was between them, it wasn't permanent.

But he couldn't get her out of his head. The way she had felt in his arms, the way she had looked into his eyes with a mixture of amazement and passion. He knew that she wouldn't have slept with him if she hadn't felt something.

In that case, he thought as he eased himself away from his desk, it was better this way. Better that it stop before either of them got in too deep.

Why, then, did he feel as if someone had removed a piece of his heart?

* * *

Ellen sat on the edge of the bath and stared at the double blue line. Her heart was beating so rapidly she felt nauseous. The pregnancy test was one of the new ones, the type that told you how pregnant you were, and according to it she was five weeks.

Praying it was wrong, she unwrapped the second package she had bought and did the test again. The result was the same, as she had known it would be. But she'd taken the morning-after pill. How was it possible that life could be so unfair? If it wasn't so tragic, it would be funny. Only a few weeks ago she had been going about her business and if not blissfully happy, she had been content. She'd had her work, her friends—and a future. Since then she'd been diagnosed with a fatal illness, been told that she should never have children, met Sean and fallen in love with him all over again, and now she was pregnant.

What on earth was she going to do?

Her London consultant had been perfectly clear. She might continue for years with her illness without any symptoms, but if she got pregnant there was a chance—an unacceptable chance in his opinion—that she would die. It was why he had recommended she consider sterilisation.

Instinctively her hands dropped to cradle her tummy. There was a baby inside there. No, she mustn't think of it as a baby. At five weeks it was simply a cluster of dividing cells.

Her heart stuttered. She couldn't have this baby. It was all wrong. Even if the pregnancy hadn't been life-threatening, she wasn't ready to be a mother. It wasn't as if she and Sean were together.

But deep inside there was this tiny flutter of joy that she couldn't ignore. A baby. *Her* baby.

A rush of fierce protectiveness flooded her body. Okay, she hadn't wanted to get pregnant and the thought terrified

her, but neither had she wanted to get ill. So far everything i
her life had happened almost by chance. It wasn't this baby'
fault that he or she had been conceived by accident.

Stop thinking of it as a baby, she told herself. *She couldn
be thinking even for a moment that she might keep it. Tha
was crazy.* The pregnancy could kill her and she didn't wan
to die.

She slumped and let the tears come. More than anything
right now she wanted her mum.

Her mother's voice over the line brought a lump to Ellen'
throat and for a moment she couldn't speak.

'Ellen? Are you there?' her mother asked impatiently. 'I
anything wrong? Is Gran okay?'

Ellen cleared her throat. 'Gran's fine. She's out with he
friends at the moment.'

'Good, good,' her mother said distractedly. Ellen could
hear the tapping of a keyboard in the background. No doub
her mother was writing or answering emails while she wa
on the phone. Her mother had always been the master o
multitasking. She wouldn't have got where she was—a
renowned expert in the field of genetics whose expertise and
opinions were sought all over the world—if she hadn't been
Her mother's book had caused a stir not only in the medica
world but with the lay public as well.

'I was wondering when you were coming back,' Ellen said
'I haven't seen you for so long.'

'I was going to call you and let you know. My agent ha
asked me to go from here to Asia. It's a fantastic opportu
nity to bring my work to a wider audience. It means I won'
be back until after Christmas. You don't mind, do you, dar
ling?'

It wasn't really a question.

'Actually, Mum—' Ellen started, but before she could complete her sentence her mother interrupted.

'Look, sweetie, there's someone at the door. Probably the car the studio has sent for me. Could I call you back?'

Ellen swallowed hard. 'Have you spoken to Dad recently?'

Her mother tutted impatiently. 'You know your father and I don't speak, Ellen. And don't hold out for him to get in touch with you either. He's far too wrapped up in his new wife. Look, I really have to go, but I'll call you soon. I promise. Give my love to Gran.'

And before Ellen could protest, the call was disconnected.

Ellen looked at the receiver in her hand before replacing it gently. What else had she expected? Her mother had always made it clear that she didn't really want a child, that Ellen was an inconvenience in a world where women like her mother had to be focussed and single-minded. And as for Dad, Ellen knew he cared about her, but he had never been able to play second fiddle to his wife and had left when Ellen was five. When he'd married again, he'd made it clear that his first priority was to his new wife. Mum and Dad should never have had children, Ellen realised. They simply were not cut out for it.

She swung round as her grandmother came through the front door. This elderly woman was the nearest she had to a mother. It was Gran who phoned and wrote, Gran who had come to her graduation, Gran who had looked after her during the school holidays, Gran who'd listened to her pour her heart out when the other children had teased her. It was Gran she wanted to speak to.

Her grandmother took one look at Ellen and her cheerful greeting died on her lips.

'For heaven's sake, child. What on earth's the matter? Has something happened to your mother?'

Her grandmother's face paled. Despite the fact that Ellen's mother rarely found the time to speak to her own mother, Gran loved her only child unreservedly. She'd explained to Ellen that Jacqueline couldn't help the way she was and that her lack of interest in her child and mother didn't mean she didn't love them.

'No, Gran. Mother is fine. I've just been speaking to her. She's extending her tour and won't be back until next year.'

Her grandmother's face fell for a moment, but then she smiled, even if it didn't quite reach her eyes.

'I had hoped... Never mind. You'll be spending Christmas with me, won't you?'

Ellen didn't have the heart to tell her that she had no idea where she'd be at Christmas or even if she'd be alive. Her throat was aching from the effort to stop the tears from coming.

Maggie's eyes narrowed again. 'Is it disappointment that your mother isn't coming home that's making you look so sad?' she asked. 'You know, although I love my daughter, sometimes I could cheerfully wring her neck.'

'No. It's not that. I am disappointed, but I guess I wasn't counting on her coming back for Christmas.' Ellen couldn't remember the last time she had spent Christmas with her mother. Not since she'd left home anyway. The realisation that this could be the last Christmas brought a fresh wave of self-pity. She blinked rapidly. She needed to talk to someone, but was it fair to burden her grandmother? Her fallback position had always been her best friend, Sigi, but she was in the Maldives on her honeymoon and Ellen didn't want to spoil her happiness.

Maggie stared at her intently. 'Kitchen,' she ordered, and Ellen smiled weakly. The kitchen was the place Gran always used when she wanted to get the truth out of Ellen. Kitchen and a cup of tea. If only this problem could be so easily sorted.

Still unsure of what if anything she would tell her grandmother, Ellen did as she was told and took a seat next to the stove, warming her frozen hands on the towel rail in front of the range. Her grandmother was quiet as she organised the tea.

Eventually she pulled a chair up in front of Ellen and passed her a cup of tea on a saucer. Her grandmother never used mugs.

'Spit it out, darling. I can tell ever since you got here that something's not right. You've lost your sparkle. I didn't like to probe because I hoped you would tell me when you were ready. But you haven't. So I'm going to ask you straight out. What's wrong?'

The need to talk to someone was suddenly greater than her need to protect her grandmother. Besides, she knew that now she had brought it up her grandmother wouldn't rest until she got the truth.

She decided to start at the beginning and told her grandmother everything—including the fact she thought she was pregnant with Sean's child.

As she spoke her grandmother reached out and clasped her hand. Ellen knew it was a terrible shock for the old woman.

'I don't know what to do,' Ellen said.

'My dear, dear child. I don't know what to say. Are the doctors sure? Could there be a mistake? You look so well.'

'It's one of those illnesses where you don't always get symptoms,' Ellen said. 'Sometimes the first you know about it is when you become desperately ill or can't get your breath. Not everyone has the same severity of symptoms, but the outcome is more or less the same—a shortened life.' She kept back the fact that currently six years was the average length of time people with her condition could expect to live. There was only so much her grandmother could bear.

'Does Sean know?'

'No. And I don't want him to.'

'Why ever not? Surely he's the perfect person to talk to? He's a doctor, he cares about you and, perhaps more importantly, he's the father of your child.'

'What should I tell him, Gran? That I'm pregnant, but don't know whether to continue with the pregnancy? That I don't know how long I could live? How do you think he'd react? You know him better than I do. But I'm guessing he'd insist that I put my health first and have a termination.'

'And don't you think you should, darling? Maybe in time they'll find a cure, and you could have babies then. But if...' Her grandmother's voice fractured. 'If you die there will never be any babies. And if you do go ahead with this pregnancy and, God forbid, you die, then what about the child? Who would look after it? I could try, but I'm not getting any younger, and as for your mother...I don't think you should pin your hopes in that direction.'

'I know all that, Gran. My head tells me that the only thing to do is to have the termination, but my heart...that's a different matter. It's not as if I think terminating the pregnancy is wrong, I've always believed that every woman has the right to choose based on her own circumstances, but I've always wanted children, Gran. I never made any secret of the fact and doesn't this baby have as much right to live as I do? Even though I'm only a few weeks there's this connection. I can't explain it but I love my baby already.'

Tears were rolling down her grandmother's face. 'I couldn't bear to lose you, my darling. You must see that.'

Ellen stood and hugged her grandmother. As she did so she felt her frailty and it shocked her. It was selfish to have burdened the old lady, but her grandmother was made of stern stuff and Ellen knew she would have been hurt more had she not confided in her.

'I have some time to make up my mind,' Ellen said. 'But you must promise me that you won't tell Sean—or my mother. I don't want her to cut short her trip and come rushing here. That would be unbearable. I was going to tell her but I think it was the right decision not to. At least not now. Not until I'm clearer. Now, why don't I make us some scones to have with the soup for lunch?'

The next day, Ellen was in the ward when Sean approached her.

'I was planning to go and see Mrs Gillespie in ITU. Would you like to come with me?'

Ellen hated the way they were so formal with one another. It was almost as if they were strangers. If she decided to keep the baby, she would have to tell Sean. And if she told him about the baby, she would have to tell him about her illness. It was such a mess. It didn't help that every time she saw him her heart rate went into overdrive.

'Of course. Could it wait a few minutes? I have a mother and baby I just need to see before they go up to the postnatal ward.'

When she'd finished with her patient, Ellen joined Sean again. The ITU unit was a five-minute walk from the maternity wing but just as they were about to leave, Sean's pager went off.

He looked at the number and frowned. 'It's ITU. My guess Mrs Gillespie's condition has changed.' He turned to one of the other midwives. 'Could you call ITU and let them know I'm on my way?' he said. 'C'mon, Ellen, we should sprint.'

Although it wasn't quite a sprint, Ellen had to jog to keep

up with Sean's quick strides. Even that small effort made her breathless and she felt a surge of panic. Was her pregnancy already having an effect on her lungs?

'How was Moira when you last saw her?' she managed between breaths.

'Not so good,' Sean admitted. He looked at her and frowned. 'You're a bit out of breath. You feeling okay? Perhaps you're not completely over the chest infection you had?'

'Just need more exercise,' Ellen said evasively. 'Haven't been to the gym since I got here.'

ITU was a flurry of activity when they arrived. As they'd suspected, it was Moira's bed that had been screened off and behind the curtains a number of nurses were gathered, looking concerned. An ITU consultant was shaking his head.

The senior nurse looked at Sean and her anxiety was plain to see. 'We're losing her,' she said simply. She passed Sean Moira's chart.

Sean looked at the chart and his expression turned grim. 'We need to deliver her right away,' he said.

'I'll let Theatre know,' the nurse said, moving towards the phone.

But Sean shook his head. 'There's no time. It will take theatre half an hour at least to get set up. Call the paediatricians and get them up here.' He looked towards the ITU consultant, who was also an anaesthetist. 'I'm going to section Mrs Gillespie right here. If you could keep her ventilated? Nurse, I need a pack. Ellen, I'm going to need your help.'

As the nurses gowned him and Ellen up, Sean looked around. 'Where's Tom?'

'He's at home. We're not expecting him in for an hour or so.'

'Someone get him on the phone and let him know what's happening.'

There was no need to anaesthetise Moira as she was already unconscious. The tension around the bed was almost palpable. Ellen knew Sean was taking a risk but she also knew that if there was any chance of saving Mrs Gillespie they had to get the baby delivered.

Sean was passed a scalpel and without hesitating he sliced into Moira's abdomen just above the pubic bone and horizontally. Normally the incision would be vertical, but Ellen knew that by making the incision that way Sean was increasing the chances of getting the baby out quickly.

Another cut of the scalpel and he was through the uterus. Seconds later he pulled the baby out and passed it to Ellen, who was waiting with a clean towel.

Ellen tore her eyes away from what was happening to Mrs Gillespie and concentrated on the baby. It was, as Tom had said, a little boy and although the baby was small he seemed perfect in every way.

At that moment the paediatric crash team hurtled into the ward, pulling an incubator behind them. Ellen sighed with relief as the baby took a tentative breath.

She passed the baby over to the paediatric team and turned her attention back to Moira.

There was silence in the room as everyone held their breath, watching the monitors. The next couple of minutes were critical.

Then, to everyone's relief, the monitors showed that Moira's oxygen level was rising again and her pulse stabilising.

Sean looked at Ellen from his position next to Moira and grinned. 'Not out of the woods yet, but I'm optimistic. Well done, everyone.'

There was a brief flurry as everyone in the room whispered their relief to each other. The paediatrician had attached the baby to the ventilator and he and his team rushed the baby off to the special care nursery. The next couple of hours would be critical for the baby, but Ellen was optimistic that with the right care the little boy would do well.

Ellen helped Sean as he sutured Mrs Gillespie's wound. Every minute their patient's pulse and blood pressure improved. As Sean had suspected, delivering the baby had improved Moira's condition and probably saved the young mother's life. Ellen felt a surge of satisfaction. This was what made her job worthwhile. This is why she loved doing what she did and why she couldn't see herself doing anything else.

Once Moira was stitched and stabilised, Ellen and Sean left her in the expert care of the ITU nurses and moved across to the nurses' station to write up their notes.

'How do you think Moira will do?' she asked.

'I'm confident she'll make a full recovery,' Sean said. He smiled at her again. 'You did well. It was pretty tense back there for a bit.'

'I've never seen a section outside Theatre,' Ellen admitted.

'It's not a tricky operation,' Sean said. 'But I'm glad there weren't any complications.'

At that moment Tom appeared in the doorway. He took one look at his wife's screened-off bed and paled. Ellen hurried over to reassure him.

'It's okay, Tom. Mother and baby are doing fine. Moira's condition deteriorated so Dr Jamieson had to section her. Remember we spoke about the possibility?'

Tom nodded, still looking frightened.

'As we hoped, delivering the baby improved Moira's condition. She's still being ventilated but I suspect it won't be for much longer.'

The relief in Tom's eyes was almost painful. 'Our baby?' he whispered.

'Your baby boy has been taken up to SCBU. At this stage his lungs are still under-developed so he's been taken up to the special care nursery so they can keep a close eye on him. Remember we spoke about that? I'll take you up there in a moment so you can see him. But would you like to see Moira first?'

Tom's eyes filled with tears and although he tried to speak, he couldn't. Ellen took his response for a yes and led him behind the screens.

The nurses stood back to give Tom access to his wife. Tears streaming down his cheeks, Tom took his wife's hand in his.

'You're going to be okay, sweetheart,' he whispered, 'and so is our baby. I'm going to see him now and I'll come back and let you know how he's doing.'

'If your mobile can take photos, you can take a picture of him to show Moira when she wakes up,' Ellen suggested.

Up in SCBU, Tom and Moira's baby was surrounded by doctors and nurses and for a split second Ellen's heart stopped. Had the baby deteriorated since being born? It was possible. She breathed a silent prayer and handed Tom a gown and mask. Just then one of the nurses looked up and seeing them waved them over with a smile.

'Is this Dad?' she asked, looking at Tom. 'Your baby is doing well,' she continued when he nodded. 'We're going to keep him on oxygen and monitor him for a while but we think he's going to do just fine.'

The staff parted to allow Tom to see his baby. Tears rolled down his cheeks as he looked at his child and then at Ellen.

'It's okay, Tom. You can touch him. Put your hand through this hole here and take his hand.'

Her heart felt as if it was swelling inside her chest as Tom did as she suggested and five tiny fingers gripped Tom's finger.

'Hello, son,' Tom whispered. 'Your mummy will be here to see you as soon as she can. You just get stronger until she does.'

Tom turned to Ellen. 'Thank you,' he said. 'Thank you for sticking with us. And tell the doctor I owe him. You have given me back my wife and child and I'll never forget either of you for as long as I live.' His smile was like a beacon. 'I have all my family safe again.'

Ellen left Tom with his baby and after checking up on Moira returned to the labour ward. The delighted staff had heard about what had happened and crowded around Ellen, asking for details. Sean was nowhere to be seen.

After Ellen had brought them up to date one of her colleagues thrust a cup of coffee in her hand. 'Go and relax for a few minutes. Get your breath back. You deserve it.'

When her protests that she was all right and quite ready to go back to work fell on deaf ears, Ellen did as she was told. The truth was she was more shaken by the morning's events than she cared to admit. Moira and Tom, it seemed, had their happy ever after. Soon the small family would be reunited and then they could get on with the rest of their lives.

But what about her? Could she hope for the same outcome? It was possible that she would go through her pregnancy without getting ill and have a healthy baby. Okay, so the chances were higher that she wouldn't and that the pregnancy could bring her pulmonary hypertension on with a vengeance, and if it did, neither she nor the baby would survive. But already she knew it was a chance she was going to take. Maybe she would be like Moira and be one of the lucky ones. Many people would consider it crazy but she just knew she couldn't have a termination. It simply wasn't an option for her. Already she felt fiercely protective of the baby inside her.

A wave of relief washed over her. She had made a decision. For better or for worse, although she still had a great deal to think about. Stuff that she shied away from, like who would look after the baby if it survived and she didn't?

One day at a time, Ellen told herself. One decision at a time.

CHAPTER TEN

As the weeks passed, Ellen was acutely aware of her baby growing bigger day by day. She still felt well apart from the sickness which plagued her in the mornings. Sean was friendly, although reserved, and she often looked up to find his eyes on her.

She knew she had to tell him about the pregnancy but kept finding reasons to put it off. She had no doubt that if Sean knew about her illness he would try and argue her out of having the baby and it wasn't an argument he was going to win. In a couple of weeks he'd be heading off to Malawi and he wasn't due back until the autumn. Obviously, if she managed to get through the pregnancy, he would have to know then, and it would be a shock, but it would too late for him to do anything except accept her decision.

On her weekend off she had gone back to London and officially resigned from her job. Her manager had been sorry to see her go, but understanding. Ellen had also been to see her consultant, Dr Simpson, in London. There had been no mistake. Her diagnosis was unchanged.

'Have you considered a termination?' he asked when she told him she was pregnant.

'Are you telling me that this pregnancy will kill me?'

Dr Simpson shook his head. 'No. It makes your condition

more dangerous but there's a chance that you and the baby will survive the pregnancy. It's not a gamble I'd advise you to take, though.'

Ellen looked out of the window. 'All my life I knew I would have children. Three or four of them. As soon as I knew I was pregnant this baby felt real to me. I don't know if you understand what I'm saying. I can't think of my baby as anything else than a child who deserves a shot at life.'

'Even if you might not be around to care for it?' the consultant said quietly.

Ellen took a shuddering breath. 'My decision might not be rational. My head is saying one thing, my heart another. All I know is that I cannot terminate this pregnancy as long as this baby has a chance. It may be the worst decision I ever make, but it's the only one I *can* make.'

'In that case, I have to refer you to an obstetrician up north. You're going to have to be monitored very carefully. It's possible that they will want to deliver your baby between thirty-two and thirty-six weeks depending on how you do. At the moment there's no indication that your condition is resurfacing.'

'But it is possible that I'll get through the pregnancy without getting ill? And that I could go on for years without...' She swallowed the words. She couldn't bring herself to say them.

'Without dying,' the consultant finished for her. 'Yes, it is possible, but it is more likely that you'll die prematurely. You need to be prepared for that. Make a will. Appoint guardians for your child should he or she make it and you don't. You're still on the waiting list for a heart and lungs but I'm going to have to suspend you until after you deliver—you do understand that, don't you?'

'I do. I know you think I'm being irresponsible, and I

didn't plan to get pregnant, but now I am, I'm not going to terminate the pregnancy whatever happens. So I'll just have to trust that I can get through this.'

'Although I don't agree with your decision, I admire your courage,' the doctor said. 'Now, do you have a preferred obstetrician in the Royal Highland? I know Dr Jamieson is working there and he has an excellent reputation. I can refer you to him if you like?'

'No! Not him!' Ellen said. 'I mean, I know from first-hand experience that he's very good, but...' She hesitated. 'He's the father.'

Dr Simpson's eyebrows shot up. 'And he's happy for you to continue with this pregnancy? I must say I'm surprised. Dr Jamieson, of all people, will know how risky this is for you.'

'He doesn't know,' Ellen said miserably. 'And he's not to know. Can't I see someone in London instead? I could come back here to have the baby. There's no need for anyone at the Royal Highland to know and I'd like to keep it that way.'

'It is, of course, up to you. But it will be difficult for you to keep travelling down to London for your antenatal appointments, particularly as I'm going to want to see you every couple of weeks and I suspect the obstetrician will want the same amount of contact. Perhaps you should consider moving back to London?'

The thought of leaving Inverness jolted her. It would mean leaving Gran and with Sean going she needed her grandmother's love and support even more. It seemed she had little choice. If she wanted to stay in Inverness she would have to see one of the obstetricians there and although he would be duty-bound not to tell Sean, in such a close-knit community it was always possible that her medical history would become known. However, she'd face that if and when it happened.

Keeping her pregnancy from Sean, however, was not an option. Not if she was going to be seen at the Royal Highland for her antenatal care.

'In that case, could you refer me to Dr Cassidy at the Royal Highland? But could you wait a couple of weeks? I need to tell Dr Jamieson first.' She couldn't let Sean find out from the hospital grapevine that she was having a baby. His baby.

'I think that's a good idea,' Dr Simpson agreed. 'But, please, don't wait too long to discuss it with him. I'm sure he'll want to know sooner rather than later.'

Dr Simpson was probably hoping that once Sean knew he would be able to dissuade her from going ahead with the pregnancy.

Heavens, she dreaded having to tell Sean.

Sean swivelled his chair round until he was looking out of the window. In less than a week he'd be leaving for Malawi but the thought gave him less pleasure than he'd hoped. He was still looking forward to the challenges of the three-month sabbatical where he'd help to train local doctors and nurses but some of the sheen had been tempered with the knowledge that by the time he came back Ellen might have returned to London. He kept asking her out but she continued to refuse in the same soft voice that left him no room to doubt that she meant what she said.

He could have sworn she cared for him. He was pretty sure she wouldn't have slept with him otherwise, but why wouldn't she go out with him again? Was it really because he was going away? That was the reason she had given, but he wasn't convinced. Although he couldn't promise her anything—it was far too soon for that—they could keep in touch by email and see how things went.

He was deep in thought when his colleague Dr Cassidy

tapped on his open door. Bill was close to retiring and some people thought he wasn't keeping as up to date as he should but Sean liked and respected his colleague and would trust his experience any time. Despite being the senior consultant, Bill had no problems seeking Sean's advice or discussing patients where he wanted a second opinion.

'Do you have a few minutes, Sean?' Bill asked.

'Sure. Pull up a seat.'

Sean waited until he and Bill went through the time-honoured ritual of exchanging small talk. He knew there was no point in trying to rush the older man.

Eventually Bill came to the point of his visit.

'I've had a referral from a colleague in London,' he said. 'He wants me to take over the care of one of his patients who is living here and is pregnant.'

That wasn't unusual. Patients were often referred from other cities.

'The thing is, she has rather an unusual condition complicating her pregnancy. Pulmonary hypertension. I've never looked after anyone with it before and wondered what you knew about it.'

Sean whistled. 'I've had limited experience of the condition myself,' he admitted. 'Although there was a lady with this when I trained in Glasgow. Thankfully it's pretty rare.'

'What was the outcome?' Bill asked. 'The referring letter said that pregnancy is contraindicated for this condition and although her consultant advised against it this lady went ahead and got pregnant anyway. Apparently she is planning to continue with the pregnancy, although his advice is to terminate.'

'It's a condition that is pretty nasty in itself,' Sean said, 'and pregnancy makes it worse. There is a high mortality rate. Would you like me to see her on your behalf? I'm going away in a week so I won't be able to take over her care, but I could still see her for an initial consultation if it would help.'

Bill shook his head. 'Sorry, no can do. She's a member of staff here and apparently asked for me specifically. I could ask when she comes to see me if she'd prefer to see you. I'd much rather she did. You're the one with the most experience of high-risk pregnancies in the hospital.'

'Sounds like a plan,' Sean said, getting to his feet. He was due in Theatre and as much as he liked talking to Bill Sean hated to keep his patients waiting. 'I have to go, Bill. But I'd be happy to see her any time. How many weeks is she by the way?'

'Seven, nearly eight.'

'In that case,' Sean said, 'the sooner she comes to see you, the better. This week, if possible—especially if she agrees to see me. Let me know, whatever happens.'

At the weekend, Ellen was outside, trying to keep Maggie's garden under control for her. The June sunshine was warm on her shoulders and the hills stretching into the distance were a lush green. Nearby birds twittered and sang as they hopped from branch to branch of a rowan tree.

A shadow fell across the patch of border she was weeding and she looked up to find Sean looking down at her with a strange expression on his face. He crouched by her side and silently started pulling up weeds alongside her. They worked in companionable silence for a while until Ellen's grandmother called from the doorway that she had some tea and scones and if anyone was hungry they could have tea in the garden.

'I've missed Maggie's scones,' Sean said quietly. 'But more to the point, I've missed you.'

Ellen's stomach lurched.

'Come out with me tonight, Ellen,' he said. 'I'll be leaving next week and I'd really like to spend some time with you before I go.'

'Okay,' she said, and she could see she had taken him by surprise. If she was going to tell him about the baby, this would be her last chance. 'But why don't I cook for you at your place?' She wanted privacy for this conversation.

The bemused expression on Sean's face almost made her smile. First she'd capitulated and then she'd suggested the intimacy of a dinner for two at his place. She could only imagine what was going through his head.

Gran appeared at the door, carrying a tray laden with baking and tea, and Sean jumped up to take it from her.

He carried it over to a table in the shade of the rowan tree.

Maggie sat down and chatted to Sean while Ellen poured. Ellen could tell from the sharp glances her grandmother was sending her that she was willing her to tell Sean.

'I'm making Sean dinner at his place tonight, Gran,' Ellen told her grandmother. 'I know it's your night for bridge and I was cooking anyway.'

Maggie looked at her sharply. 'I think that's a good idea, love. When are you leaving us, Sean?'

'Next week,' he said. 'But it's only for three months. I'll be back in plenty of time to get your log pile replenished for the winter.'

'Ach, you know that's not the only reason I like having you around,' Maggie protested. She hid an exaggerated yawn behind her hand. 'If you two kids don't mind I think I'll leave you to it. It's time for my afternoon nap while I catch up on my soap.'

'What shall I make for dinner?' Ellen asked. 'Is there anything you don't eat?'

Sean grinned. 'Don't you know by now that I'll pretty

much eat anything? Particularly if it doesn't come out of the hospital canteen.'

They spent a few minutes catching up on patients.

'By the way, what do you know about pregnancy and pulmonary hypertension?' Sean asked.

Ellen's heart crashed against her chest. For a moment she couldn't speak. But Sean didn't seem to have noticed. 'Dr Cassidy—Bill—came to see me last week. He's had a patient referred to him from London who has pulmonary hypertension and he wanted my opinion. I suggested he ask the patient to come to see me before I leave for Africa. Apparently she was cautioned against getting pregnant but went against the advice of her doctor and got pregnant anyway.'

Ellen's mouth was so dry she could hardly speak. 'Perhaps she didn't plan to get pregnant. These things happen. We of all people should know that.'

'Okay. I grant you that but, hell, Ellen, she should be thinking seriously about not continuing with the pregnancy. Apparently she's adamant that she's going to.'

'Then shouldn't her wishes be respected? It's not our job to make decisions for our patients, only to advise them and look after them. Take Moira, for example. Everything turned out okay in the end. Her husband could have given you the go-ahead to section her when there was no chance for the baby but he trusted in you—in us—and everything worked out.'

'It could have easily gone the other way. We could have lost Moira and the baby. Then Tom would have been bringing up his daughter on his own. I wouldn't wish that on any one. It must be difficult enough bringing up a child without being a single father. I know I couldn't cope. I can't imagine being a father as it is, let alone having sole responsibility.'

Every word chilled Ellen more and more.

'How do you know you wouldn't cope?' Ellen said. 'When we're up against it we all find hidden strength.'

Sean stretched his hands behind his neck and sighed with contentment. 'Since there's no chance I'll ever have to find out I'm not going to waste time thinking about it.'

'What about your nephew?' Ellen persisted. 'Have you never spent time with him?'

'David?' Sean said. 'No, I'm afraid I left that to my parents and my sisters. I'm not really into kids. Besides, I was moving around all over the place. I wasn't really in a position to get to know him.'

'And now?'

'He's fine with his dad.' He opened one eye and squinted at Ellen. 'Why all the interest? I have to be honest, I don't really see me with children. Not for a few years yet, at least. What about you?'

Ellen stumbled to her feet. This wasn't the way she had planned to tell him. In her head she had prepared a meal, they had eaten it while chatting about non-controversial subjects, and then over coffee she would tell him quietly but firmly that she was pregnant and what she planned to do about it.

Right now all she wanted was to put as much distance between herself and Sean's questions as she could.

But before she could move Sean reached out and took her by the arm. 'What is it, Ellen? You've gone as white as a sheet. Are you okay?'

Ellen looked at him, knowing that she couldn't delay the conversation any further. It might not be the place or the time of her choosing, but it was what she'd got.

Her legs were shaking so badly that it was a relief to sink back down into her chair. It was doubtful her legs would have carried her back to the house anyway.

'Sean...I have something to tell you,' she said. 'I was going to wait until tonight, but…well, I guess now is as good a time as any.'

'You can tell me anything,' he said. 'You know I'll keep it in complete confidence.' He was looking puzzled as he waited for her to speak. She'd seen him like this before—with patients. He never rushed them or indicated through the slightest gesture that he had somewhere else to go. It was one of the things she loved about him.

'Remember when we made love…'

'It's not something I'm likely to forget.'

Ellen blushed as he flashed his lazy smile at her. Then he frowned. Sean was sharp and no doubt was beginning to see where this conversation was going.

'You did take the morning-after pill, didn't you?'

Ellen nodded. 'I got it the very next morning and took it straight away.'

Sean's sigh of relief made what she was about to tell him a thousand times worse.

'But it didn't work, Sean. I'm pregnant.'

This time he did pale. She could almost hear his brain working as he calculated dates in his head. 'But, hell, Ellen that was weeks ago. You must be, what? Seven, eight weeks. Why didn't you tell me before?'

'Because I wasn't sure at first whether I was going to continue with the pregnancy.'

'And now?'

'I'm going to have this baby, Sean. I've made up my mind.'

'Without even discussing it with me?' His expression darkened. 'Don't you think I have a right to be involved in your decision?'

She looked Sean calmly in the eyes. 'I'm telling you now.'

He shook his head. 'When you've already made up your mind,' he said flatly.

She nodded.

'Ellen, I'm not ready to be a father. When I have a child I want it to be part of a family with two parents who love each other enough to commit the rest of their lives to being together. I care about you, Ellen, but marriage? It's too soon. We need more time together.'

'You think I should terminate the pregnancy?'

'I think you should consider it.'

'I'm not asking your permission, Sean. I don't want anything from you. Certainly not marriage. I just thought you had the right to know.' She paused. 'At least try and understand. All my life I've felt as if I'm on the outside, looking in. Whenever I was with your family I felt envious. Believe me, Sean I didn't want to get pregnant, but now that I am, I'm not going to get rid of my baby just because it isn't convenient for me or you.'

'And you think that having a baby will fill this need to be part of a family? Is that it? Do you really think that's a good enough reason to have a child? It sounds pretty selfish to me.'

Every word was like a razor blade cutting into her heart. She knew he'd be shocked, disbelieving even, but this reaction? He was looking at her as if he didn't recognise her.

'Just in case there is any doubt, Sean,' she said coldly, 'I didn't expect you to drop on your knees and propose to me. That is not why I'm having this baby and not why I'm telling you. I don't expect to play happy families with you, believe me. I've managed on my own through most of my life and I'll manage now.'

He pulled a hand through his hair. 'I'll help financially, of course.'

A wave of anger surged through her. Help her financially? Did he think money was what she wanted from him for their baby? She wasn't the love-struck teenager any more who worshipped him unconditionally, and equally he wasn't the man she thought he was. She didn't need anything from him. If she couldn't have his love she didn't want anything. She wanted to lash out and to hurt him, to make him feel some of the pain and anger she was feeling inside. She bit down on her lip to stop the words spilling out. This might be the last time she ever saw him.

'I will look after my baby myself, Sean. Now go, please.'

He opened his mouth to speak but she turned away from him and as tears blurred her vision, she walked away from the man she loved.

CHAPTER ELEVEN

A FEW days later, Ellen was standing in the early-morning air, holding her cup of coffee while leaning against the wall. Sean hadn't been near her since she'd told him about the baby and although she told herself that she expected that, she knew that deep inside she'd been hoping that he would come around and at least talk about what plans they were going to make for the baby's future. She'd seen him in the hospital but the only time he spoke to her was to talk about a patient.

He was leaving for Malawi later today. It would be hard not seeing him but she would manage. Anything was better than seeing the coolness in his eyes when he looked at her.

One of Maggie's pet lambs was looking at her hopefully. There had been four orphans that had required bottle-feeding and most of them still hoped that Ellen or Maggie's appearance by the wall meant a bottle.

'Ellen.' His voice came from behind her and she whirled around. She hadn't heard his footfalls on the thick grass. Her heart leaped. Maybe he was coming to tell her that he wasn't going. That he was staying and that somehow they would work things out. But the moment she saw his eyes she knew she had been wrong to hope.

'I'm leaving tomorrow. I wanted to apologise for the way I behaved last time we spoke. It was inexcusable. Finding out you were pregnant was a shock and it's going to take me a little time to get used to the idea of being a father, but it takes two to make a baby and I'm not going to let you do it all by yourself. Can you forgive me?'

Ellen nodded. Her throat was so tight she could barely speak.

'I can't get out of going to Malawi now but when I come back we'll make plans. Okay?'

He was going. Really going. And this could be the last time she ever saw him.

'Okay,' she said. Inside part of her was screaming, *Don't go. Stay with me. I don't know if I'm brave enough to do this on my own. I don't know if I can bear the thought that I might never see you again.* She had to bite down hard on her lip to stop the words from coming out.

He took her by the hand. 'Will you be all right? Will you write to me and let me know how the pregnancy is going?'

She forced a smile to her lips. 'Of course. Don't worry about a thing. I'll be here when you get back.'

Sean stared into her eyes. 'Promise?'

Ellen crossed her fingers behind her back. 'I promise. Now go.'

Sean removed his hands from his pocket and reached across and tipped her chin, forcing her to look him in the eyes. She blinked rapidly, determined that she wouldn't break down. At least not until she was alone.

'Please, take care, Ellen,' he said gruffly, and then he was gone, leaving her feeling as if her world had ended.

The next few weeks passed slowly. As her bump continued to grow, Ellen started to make plans should the baby be born alive but without her.

The first thing she did was start a diary. At her twelve-week scan she had asked to know the sex of the baby. It was a boy. Every night she wrote a couple of pages addressed to her son. She told him about her childhood, told him about Sean and how much she loved him and how she had always loved him. She wrote about girls and how she expected him to behave. She wrote about her mother and father and told him it wasn't their fault that they couldn't be the perfect parents. *'If I live, my darling, all I can promise you is that I will try to be a good enough mother to you. Try and love your grandparents. Try and see beyond their faults.'* She wrote everything she knew about Sean. How she had always loved him and that her son should be proud to have him as his father. And at the end of each entry she wrote, *'Just be happy. Whatever you do with your life, be happy.'*

The thing that worried her most was that she still had no clear plan about what to write in her will should the baby be left alone. She couldn't pass custody to Sean, not without speaking to him, and she still didn't know what part, if any, he planned to play in their child's life. She wasn't prepared to put her mother as a guardian—she still didn't know about the pregnancy and even if she did, she would never give up her nomadic lifestyle to accommodate a grandchild. Not when she wouldn't do it for her own child. That left Gran, who wasn't getting any younger, and Sigi. The only solution Ellen could think of was to appoint Maggie as guardian with Sigi as a fallback should anything happen to her grandmother. But she hadn't even told Sigi she was pregnant yet. She would have to do so soon.

Her grandmother kept begging Ellen to write to her mother but Ellen steadfastly refused. Perhaps it was cruel of her to deny her mother a say, but she knew that she would be horrified by the situation Ellen had managed to 'get herself into'.

The amazing thing was that, apart from the odd bout of

breathlessness, she felt so healthy. If it hadn't been for the X-ray she would never have guessed she had a life-threatening illness. She coughed. And frowned. How long had she had the cough? Four weeks at least. She tried to ignore the flicker of alarm she felt. It was just a cough.

Sean wrote to Maggie every couple of weeks. He seemed to be enjoying his time in Malawi. Gran told Ellen that he asked about her. It wasn't enough. Not nearly. He was due to return in September and Ellen wondered if she would still be here. So far she hadn't written to him. What could she say?

As winter drew closer, the days shortened and Ellen spent most evenings next to the fire, reading a book or writing in her diary while her grandmother knitted.

'It won't be long before it's Christmas,' Maggie said. The only time Maggie had been prepared to discuss the possibility that Ellen would not survive her pregnancy had been when she'd agreed to be guardian. Since then she'd refused any talk that suggested Ellen wouldn't be around in the future.

'No, Gran, not long at all. Only seventeen weeks,' Ellen teased. 'By that time I should be home with my baby.'

'You should do your Christmas shopping sooner rather than later,' Maggie advised. Then, as she realised what she'd said, her face crumpled. 'Oh, I didn't mean it that way, darling, of course I didn't. I meant that there won't be much opportunity with a baby around.' Dr Cassidy had told Ellen that the latest he was likely to leave her before he sectioned her would be a couple of weeks before Christmas.

'I know you didn't mean that I wouldn't be around, Gran. You can't keep worrying about saying the wrong thing— particularly since you're the only person I've been honest with. And you're absolutely right, once the baby is here there will be precious little time for shopping.' She closed her eyes. 'Imagine, Gran. By Christmas I'm going to have my baby.'

Her grandmother blinked furiously. 'So you will, darling.'

'I haven't much to get for Christmas,' Ellen continued. 'Something for all the ward staff, something for the babies in Special Care and something for you. I plan to post a calendar to Mum and one to Dad closer to the time. Not much of a gift but the one I have in mind has photographs from a local artist, so I think they'll enjoy it. It's kind of difficult to think of what to get people who have absolutely everything.'

'Not everything,' Maggie said quietly, her lips folded into a thin line. 'They don't know what it is to be there when they are needed, they don't know how to really give love. In fact, I would say, for all your mother's wealth and fame, she has very little. How did I manage to bring up a daughter who has so little interest in everyone else, even her own daughter?'

'You taught her to go after what she wants. You taught her to believe in herself. The same as you taught me,' Ellen said.

'But you have never forgotten about those who love you. You have never put your own needs above everyone else's.'

'Maybe that's exactly what I'm doing, Gran.' Ellen's voice broke. 'Oh, Gran, I'm so scared. I'm so scared of dying and I'm so scared of leaving my baby to grow up on his own.'

Her grandmother put her knitting down and held open her arms. Ellen went into them, seeking the comfort she had always found there. She let the tears come as she hadn't allowed herself to cry since she'd discovered she was pregnant. She cried for her own lost childhood, for Sean, for the parents who couldn't love her, but most of all she cried for her baby and her desperate worry that there would be no one there for him when he needed someone.

Her grandmother murmured soothingly as she stroked Ellen's hair. 'Have faith, my child. It's going to be all right.

I'm going to do my best to stick around as long as possible so you...' she patted Ellen's swollen stomach '...will have me to help with the baby for as long as possible. And if we're not, then you trust your friend to do her best for him, don't you?'

'I know she'll try. But one day she and Kenneth are going to have their own children. I don't want my child to feel second best.'

'What about Sean's parents? They're lovely people. They might be prepared to look after him.'

'I don't know, Gran. I don't even know what Sean has told them.' Ellen wiped her eyes and blew her nose loudly on the handkerchief Maggie passed to her. 'I rather think it's up to Sean to tell them. And he doesn't even know that I might not be around to raise our child.'

'You have to tell him, Ellen.' Her grandmother tutted. 'He has the right to know. I can't imagine that he'd stay away if he knew. I can't believe he's still in Africa even if he doesn't know the whole truth. His place should be here with you.'

'I can't blame him, Gran. This was my decision and as he said I never gave him a chance to be part of it. I should have.'

'Even if he was never going to change your mind?'

'Which is why I didn't tell him.'

Ellen gasped as the baby kicked. 'I think he's got his father's legs,' she said. And once again, she knew with absolute certainty she had done the right thing. She propped her feet up on the footrest. Her ankles were aching, probably from the weight of her pregnancy.

Suddenly Maggie leaned forward and peered at Ellen's legs.

'I know you've put on a little weight, darling, but aren't your ankles a little swollen?'

Ellen followed her grandmother's gaze to her feet. Maggie was right. Her ankles were swollen. Far too much to be simply due to her pregnancy. And her cough. Taken along with her swollen ankles, she couldn't ignore that either. Terror robbed her of her breath. It seemed as if her luck had finally run out.

Sean flopped down in his room and tried to close his eyes. The heat made it difficult to sleep at night but it wasn't just that. Every night he was kept awake by thinking about Ellen. He hadn't been able to stop thinking about her since she'd told him she was pregnant. The truth was, he hadn't been able to stop thinking about her since she'd arrived back in Inverness-shire.

He was going to be a father and the thought terrified him.

He should have stayed.

But he had made a commitment to come here. He'd been here for ten weeks with still a couple of weeks to go. Not that he was really needed. The small hospital was well organised and a team of Scottish midwives from Glasgow pretty much had the training under control. It was the local midwives and doctors who would make the difference in the long term, not the visiting doctors. The local medics were better placed to understand and deliver the antenatal care that was required. He had done his bit by teaching and supervising the medical staff's training. They had learned quickly and there was little left for him to do. It had been a satisfying few weeks and if it weren't for Ellen, he would have enjoyed every minute of it.

One of the camp orderlies came into the room. 'Letter for you, Dr Jamieson.'

Sean sat up quickly. At last a letter! Ellen hadn't kept her promise to write to him. He had sent a letter to her but had no way of knowing if she'd even received it. Post was notoriously unpredictable and slow. He'd written simply that he hoped the pregnancy was going well and that he'd see her when he got back to discuss the future. It had, he admitted, been slightly on the cool side, but he hadn't known what else he could say. He cared about her, thought she was as sexy as hell, but was he prepared to settle down? Be a husband as well as a father? No way. Not yet. He simply wasn't ready.

The writing on the envelope was unfamiliar and he felt a sudden pleasure. He'd never seen Ellen's writing before and if the small, tightly written letters weren't what he'd expected there was a lot he didn't know about the woman who was carrying his baby. He tore the letter open.

At first he was disappointed. The letter was from Maggie, not Ellen, and then, as he read on, his heart crashed against his ribs.

No! Ellen was ill. Ellen had pulmonary hypertension and was pregnant. He couldn't believe what he was reading. His Ellen was sick and he was here, on the other side of the world. He forced the panic away. He needed to get to her. Now. Before it was too late. Unless it was already too late.

He crumpled the letter.

Oh, Ellen. What have you done? Hang on, sweetheart. Please, just hold on.

CHAPTER TWELVE

ELLEN and her grandmother were tidying up before going to bed when there was a knock on the door. Ellen looked at her watch. It was after eleven. Who could possibly be coming to visit at this time? Dr Cassidy had released her from hospital after a couple of days. He had prescribed Sildenafil to keep the vessels in her lungs dilated and heparin injections to prevent thrombosis. She was feeling better. Now it was a case of wait and see. Ellen had had to stop working at the hospital and she missed the company. Most of the midwives knew about her pregnancy and her PH, although not that Sean was the father, and they fussed over her every time she attended the hospital. Ellen was grateful for their support, knowing that she would be relying on them when it was time to deliver her baby.

When she opened the door, Ellen was stunned to see Sean standing there. He wasn't expected back until next month. The blood felt as if it were draining from her body. She placed a hand on the door frame to steady herself. Sean was here. She feasted her eyes on every beloved feature.

He was tanned by the African sun but there were lines around his eyes that hadn't been there before. Her heart was beating as if she'd just completed a marathon.

'Sean! What are you doing here? I thought you were in Africa.'

'Don't keep him standing there.' Her grandmother's voice came from behind her. 'Ask him in.'

Ellen stepped back to let Sean pass her.

'How are you, lad?' her grandmother said.

'I've been better, Maggie,' he said grimly. 'I need to speak to Ellen.' His voice was tight and he looked angry.

'Don't worry about me. I was just on my way to bed.' Maggie caught Ellen's eye and gave her an almost imperceptible nod. There was something about the two bright spots of colour on her grandmother's cheeks that made Ellen wonder. 'I know you two have a lot to talk about. I'll see you both in the morning.' And with those words she beat a hasty retreat. Ellen stared after her, a suspicion beginning to form in her mind.

Sean followed Ellen into the small sitting room. Her heart still beating wildly, Ellen bent and stoked the dying embers of the fire. When she was sure she could speak normally she turned to face him.

'Why are you here, Sean?'

'Because I couldn't stay away. I was an idiot to have gone and left you alone in the first place.'

'You had made a commitment. Besides, there was nothing you could do here.'

He crossed the room and took both of her hands in his. 'How are you, Ellen?' His eyes dropped to her stomach and his voice was low. 'And the baby?'

Looking into his eyes and seeing the fear, Ellen knew. Someone, no doubt her grandmother, had told him everything.

'We're both fine,' Ellen said. 'The baby is developing normally and I'm doing okay too.'

Some of the tension left Sean's face. 'Thank God.'

'Why don't you sit, Sean?' Ellen suggested. She hid her hands behind her back to disguise their trembling from him.

'Ellen you should have told me the truth.'

'The truth, Sean?'

'That patient that Dr Cassidy asked me about before I left. The one with pulmonary hypertension. That was you, wasn't it?'

Ellen nodded. There was no point in pretending when Sean clearly knew everything.

Sean's eyes darkened even further. Ellen had never seen him look so angry. 'Do you think if I'd known you had pulmonary hypertension and were pregnant that I would have left you? Dammit, Ellen. What were you thinking? Don't you know you could die? Why didn't you tell me?'

'And what would you have said? Please sit down, Sean. I can't think with you towering over me.'

'*You* can't think?' But he did as she asked and sank down into his seat. Seconds later he was back on his feet and crouching by her side. 'I've been going crazy, trying *not* to think. I came as soon as Maggie told me you were ill. I couldn't get to a phone that worked so I've spent fifteen hours on a plane not knowing if you were alive or dead. Have you any idea what you're doing?'

'I do know what I'm letting myself in for. I know exactly what can happen. The PH could return again at any time and kill me. And the pregnancy increases the chances of that happening.'

'You have to have a termination,' Sean said. 'It's the only way. At nineteen weeks you're further on than most obstetricians would like, but in your case I think I can persuade one of my colleagues to carry out the procedure.'

'Sean, once and for all, I've no intention of terminating this pregnancy. You have to understand that.'

Sean let go of her hand and sat down in his seat again. 'Then you'll have to tell me why you're willing to risk your life for a pregnancy that was a mistake. I need to understand. If you want a baby so much, you could adopt in the future. Have you thought about that?'

Ellen half smiled. 'I don't want *any* baby, Sean. I want *this* baby. I didn't mean to get pregnant—it was the last thing on my mind when we made love. I took the morning-after pill, but it didn't work. I've always wanted a child, a family of my own, but it's not just that. I thought about ending the pregnancy, I tried to think of the baby as being just a mass of cells, but I couldn't. I love my baby, Sean, and if possible I intend to have it.'

Underneath his anger, Ellen could sense his sadness.

'You must know that even if you survive the pregnancy you could still become very ill and die up to two weeks after the baby is born. I can't let that happen.'

'I'm afraid it's not up to you, Sean.'

'And if you, God forbid, die, who is going to look after the baby?'

'I haven't worked that one out yet, Sean. I know I—we—will have to make a decision about that. If I name you on the birth certificate you will have first call on the child.' Her eyes were burning and she could hardly speak past the lump in her throat. 'Could you love our baby, Sean?' she asked.

His eyes were hooded and she couldn't read his expression. 'You're crazy, Ellen,' he said. 'If you think I'm going to stand by and watch you die, the same way my sister died, then you have made a mistake.' His voice broke. 'Please, Ellen, see Dr Cassidy. Talk it over with him. Think about terminating this pregnancy. I'm begging you.'

Was she crazy? Probably. But whatever her rational mind told her, she couldn't ignore the overriding gut instinct she had to protect her baby. But she had been so caught up with what was happening to her she hadn't considered what Sean would go through. He had lost his sister through childbirth, now he might lose her too.

Ellen didn't want to die. Not for a very long time. Neither did she want to think of her baby growing up without her, without love. Was she being selfish? Maybe. She had behaved instinctively, following her heart. She'd had nothing else to guide her.

'You're wasting your breath, Sean,' she said softly.

He gripped her by the shoulders and his eyes drilled into hers. 'Then I won't be any part of this.'

Her heart shattered. She knew now that she'd hoped that somehow, no matter how often she'd told herself she could manage, Sean would have been around for her to lean on. 'It's your decision,' she said quietly.

Slowly she got to her feet and started to collect the dishes from their tea. Just then she felt a flutter in her abdomen. It was just the tiniest movement but she knew immediately what it was. Her baby. She dropped her hand to the top of her diaphragm and gasped as the baby wriggled again.

Immediately, Sean was by her side, the anger in his face replaced with concern.

'What is it, Ellen? Do you have a pain somewhere?'

She took his hand and placed it on her abdomen. 'Feel that, Sean?'

His eyes widened as the baby moved again. 'This is our son, Sean. A moving, living, fully formed baby boy. Now will you believe me when I tell you there isn't a chance in hell that I will have a termination?'

Sean looked at her for a long, long moment. Then as if he knew there was nothing more he could say, he turned on his heel and walked out of the door.

CHAPTER THIRTEEN

SEAN pedalled his mountain bike furiously up the mountain. Sweat was pouring down his face, running in rivulets down his back, and his thighs were burning from the effort of pumping the wheels and pushing the bike against the gravity of the mountain.

How could she? How could Ellen do this to him? How could she do this to herself and her unborn child? She had taken leave of her senses. He'd been nuts to get involved with her. The minute he'd seen her again his instincts had screamed to stay well away. But he'd let lust cloud his judgement.

His lungs were screaming with the effort to take in air but he pushed on. It was easier to ignore the torment in his body than the one in his head.

Should he try to talk to Ellen again? Make her see that continuing with this pregnancy was madness?

No. There was no point. It would be a waste of time. If he hadn't known it before, he'd known it the moment she'd placed his hand on her stomach and he'd felt the baby kick.

And something had happened to him too. She was right. That was their baby inside her. Their baby growing. His son! A smile crept over his face. That was some kick!

But that baby could kill Ellen. Or die with her, and there was nothing he could do about it.

He pedalled faster. Then suddenly he brought the bike to a stop. What was he doing? How hard did he have to pedal before he left Ellen behind? There wasn't a place far enough away to do that. Wasn't it time he faced up to what was happening? He'd left Ellen when she'd told him she was pregnant and last night he'd threatened to leave her to cope on her own. What kind of man was he?

He'd always felt protective of her but that was nothing to the way he felt now. His fear and anxiety had caused him to behave like an unfeeling idiot. Shame washed over him. How could he even think of abandoning her now when she needed him more than ever? It was time he stopped thinking about himself and started thinking about her. If she was going to have this baby, and it seemed she was, then she wasn't going to do it on her own.

Sean turned and headed back downhill. What a selfish bastard he'd been. He needed to see her. Right now. He couldn't let her spend one more minute than she had already believing she was on her own.

Ellen looked up from the bench where she was sitting reading a book, while enjoying the sun. Sean was coming towards her, carrying his bike over his shoulder, a wary smile on his face.

He threw the bike on the ground and came to sit next to her. He had his hands thrust deep in his pockets. Ellen wanted to reach out, brush the lock of hair from his eyes, promise him that it would be all right, but everything in the way he held himself told her that now was not the time.

'I always seem to be saying sorry to you,' he said eventually.

'You kind of do,' Ellen said wryly. 'I suppose all this has been a bit of a mess.'

'When you told me about the pregnancy, I was shocked. It

hadn't crossed my mind that it was a possibility. Then I hear that you're ill with a potentially fatal illness that can only be made worse through pregnancy. I couldn't accept any of it. It was my sister all over again. I felt so powerless.' He smiled ruefully. 'It's not a feeling I'm used to. When my sister died I swore I would do everything I could to stop it happening to another woman and her family. But I couldn't and I can't do anything to keep you and my baby safe.'

He closed his eyes for a moment. 'In the hospital, even back in Africa, I'm always in control, but now there is nothing I can do. Except be there for you. And our child. If I was a better man I would have known that straight away. But I know it now and I'm not going to leave you again. Either of you.'

Ellen smiled tightly. 'I don't think it's altogether up to you.'

'Please, Ellen. Hear me out.'

Ellen placed her hands in her lap. Whether to hide the fact they were shaking or whether it was to stop herself from reaching out and throttling Sean, she couldn't be sure.

'Fire away.'

He turned to face her, his deep blue eyes drilling into hers. 'I've had plenty time to think and I want us to get married.'

'Go on,' Ellen said quietly. A slow burn of anger started deep in her stomach.

'It's the obvious thing to do. We can marry and that way, if anything happens to you, you'll know that the baby will be looked after.'

His words took her breath away. So he had decided how it was all going to be. The flicker of anger turned into a fire.

'There are so many things wrong with that statement, Sean, I don't know where to start.' The look of astonishment on his face gave her some satisfaction.

'First of all, I never asked you to come in and rescue me as f I was one of your victims stuck up a mountain. Secondly, I don't need rescuing. I made the decision to go ahead and have his baby, knowing and understanding the consequences of that decision. Thirdly, I don't want or need you to marry me as if I were a Victorian damsel in distress. Unless, of course, you're here to tell me you love me?' She glared at Sean. 'No? I thought not. And even if I went along with your suggestion, I'm not at all sure that I want my baby to be brought up by a father who isn't even sure that he wants him. My baby is going to be loved,' she continued, 'not merely tolerated.'

Sean's eyebrows snapped together and his expression darkened. 'You are not the only one this affects, Ellen. Do you think I want my child brought up by anyone except his immediate family?'

'Gran will look after him. And if and when she's no longer able to, my friend Sigi will. I've thought it through.'

'Clearly you haven't,' Sean snapped back. 'I love Maggie. She's a remarkable person, and someone who I'd be honoured to have in my child's life, but she's getting on. She can't play with him, she can't kick a ball, or take him mountain biking, all the things a child needs. And then when she isn't able to look after him, you're going to pass him on to a friend! When I am right here, prepared and willing to look after my child.' He lowered his voice to a whisper. 'Please don't do that to me, Ellen.'

'Do you promise me that you will love my baby? Being a parent is more than mountain biking or football. It's being there in the middle of the night, wiping snotty noses, changing nappies, sitting up at night, waiting for him to come home. It's all of those things. Can you do all that, Sean? And do it with love—not resentment?'

The look on his face told her everything she needed to

know. If Sean said he would look after their child, then he would. But did he really understand what he was promising?

'It means you won't be able to go off travelling at the drop of a hat,' she continued softly. 'Or go down to the pub or off on your bike whenever the impulse grabs you. And as for women...' the thought of another woman with Sean was almost as painful as thinking about another woman bringing up her child '...you may find that the woman you love doesn't want to take on a child. These are all things you have to consider.'

'I have considered them, Ellen. I know exactly what I'm promising. I want my child with me. I don't want to have to petition the courts to get access. I want my child to know I'm his father and that I'll always be there for him and that nobody can ever take him away. Please, Ellen, marry me. I promise I'll do my best to make you happy.'

Thoughts were tumbling around Ellen's head. She was torn. She didn't want Sean to marry her for the wrong reasons. There had to be another way.

'I could name you on the birth certificate and sign whatever I need to give you custody should anything happen to me. Isn't that enough?'

Sean knelt at her feet. 'Ellen, I find this almost unbearable to think, let alone say, but there is a chance that in the last stages of pregnancy you will become really unwell. And like Moira, the baby might have to be delivered in order to save his life.' He swallowed. 'There might not be an opportunity to put me on the birth certificate.'

Ellen knew that what he was saying was correct. But, still, to marry someone who didn't pretend to love her but whom she loved dearly would be agony. On the other hand, hadn't she sworn that she would do everything she could to protect her baby's future? If she survived the birth and after, she could release Sean while still sharing custody of the baby.

'Let me think about it, Sean. Now, please just go.'

'Don't think too long, Ellen. I'll be back tomorrow and the next day and the next. Until I get the answer we both know is right.'

Ellen talked it over with her grandmother in the morning and, after another sleepless night, made up her mind. If Sean was sure, she would marry him. As soon as she made her decision she felt as if a weight had lifted from her shoulders. Whatever happened to her, her baby would have its father and his father's family. Her child wouldn't be alone.

Having made the decision, she went over to the gatehouse to give Sean her answer.

The relief in his eyes convinced her she had made the right decision. He hadn't put the proposal to her because he'd felt he should but because he genuinely wanted to ensure his child's future.

'But,' she warned him, 'both of us should feel free to give up on the marriage at any time. Is that agreed?'

'It won't be me,' Sean said.

Ellen shook her head slightly. 'I won't marry you unless you promise me that either of us can leave the marriage after a year. I will never stop you having contact with your child whatever happens, but I need to know that either of us can walk away with no hard feelings on either side if ever one of us wants out. If you don't agree to this then I won't marry you.' Ellen knew she would never be the one to leave, but she had to make Sean believe that he was free to fall in love with someone else. However much she hated the thought, she hated the thought even more that he would feel himself bound to her through pity and duty.

Sean frowned. 'If that's what it takes, I promise.'

'Okay, then,' Ellen said. 'I'll marry you. When?'

'As soon as possible,' he said gently. The words hurt but she knew he was right. The last thing either of them should do was pretend that Ellen might not become seriously ill at any time.

'I think we have to wait fourteen days. Would you mind if it was just the two of us and Gran and one other witness? There's no point pretending that it is some sort of romantic wedding. Of course nobody except the two of us and Gran need to know the truth.'

'I never thought I'd be getting married without any of my family there,' Sean said. 'I doubt if they'll ever forgive me but I guess I can tell them that we decided on a quiet wedding because your family couldn't be here.'

'As long as you don't tell them about my illness, Sean. If I know your mother and sisters, they'd be here, supposing they had to swim across the sea, and I couldn't cope with their sympathy. Not right now. I know it's unfair of me to ask you this, but could you wait until after the baby is born to tell them everything? By all means tell them we're getting married.'

Sean looked around the gatehouse. 'I guess we should look for something bigger until I've finished renovating my house. This place is big enough for me but three of us will be a tight fit.'

'Gran wants us to move in with her. She says that she's happy to move in here if we want privacy but I've assured her that won't be an issue. I suggested I keep my room and you have the one opposite.'

She looked at him steadily, wanting to make it clear that sex was off the agenda.

'Whatever makes you happy,' Sean said simply.

CHAPTER FOURTEEN

THE wedding service at the registrar's office in Inverness town centre was not what Ellen had dreamed about when she'd imagined getting married. She had gone shopping for a new dress, but her bump meant that she felt more like a beached whale than a glamorous bride. When Sean had seen her he'd let out a low whistle. 'You look beautiful,' he said as they took their positions in front of the registrar.

And he looked heartbreakingly gorgeous in a grey suit with a white shirt and a mauve tie.

Afterwards they went for something to eat at the best restaurant in Inverness, before returning to Maggie's house. Maggie had insisted that she would spend the night with a friend.

'I know this isn't the way any of us imagined you'd be starting your married life, my dear, but this is your wedding night. The start of your future together. You won't want me around.'

Ellen felt awkward as they stepped out of the taxi. How was she going to cope alone with Sean?

Winter was well on its way and the nights were closing in earlier. Ellen went upstairs to change while Sean lit a fire in the sitting room. When she came back downstairs, he had set two glasses of champagne on the table by the fire.

'I know you're not drinking,' he said, 'but a sip of champagne won't hurt.' He raised his glass. 'To my beautiful bride.'

'Please, Sean. Let's not pretend when we are alone. At least give me that dignity. I know we have to put up a show when we're around other people, but when we're alone, can't we just be two friends, enjoying each other's company?'

Her heart was aching so much she could hardly breathe. As a young girl she had dreamed of being married to Sean, but in those dreams they had been in love. This reality was almost more than she could bear.

Ellen clinked her glass against his and forced a smile. Somehow they had to find a way of living together that wasn't awkward. 'By the way, you look pretty good yourself.' She placed her untouched glass on the table. 'If you don't mind, Sean, I think I'll go to bed. It's been a long day and I'm a little tired.'

'Are you okay? Are you feeling all right?' There was no mistaking the alarm in his eyes.

'Please don't fuss, Sean,' she said sharply. 'I couldn't bear it if you're going to treat me like some sort of invalid. All this is bad enough without that.' She softened her voice. 'If we are going to get through the next few months we have to try and forget that I could become ill, forget that I could die. I'll go along to my check-ups, of course, and we will talk about what kind of future I hope my—our—child will have, but otherwise you have to promise me that we won't talk about it. Not ever. Can you do that?'

Sean opened his mouth to speak but closed it again. Sadness washed over his face and he stepped towards her. Ellen swallowed hard and moved out of his reach. If he so much as touched her, she knew she wouldn't be able to stop herself telling him how she felt about him, about the chance she might never see her baby grow up, might never be there to kiss him better, be there to hold him if he was hurt, be there to protect him from the inevitable slights and agonies of growing up.

All she could do was keep writing her diary and trust that Sean would protect their child for them both.

'I'm going into town to do some shopping,' Ellen said. 'If I'm going to get anything for Christmas, it should be now. I'm afraid shopping for Christmas dinner will likely be up to you.'

Sean jumped to his feet. 'I'll go. Give me the list.'

The three months since their marriage had been unusual to say the least. They made an odd threesome. He, Ellen and Maggie. They hadn't even discussed where they might live in the future. Ellen had made it clear that all talk about that was off limits. In the evenings, Maggie retreated to the snug to watch television. Ellen read or wrote in the notebook she kept with her at all times, while Sean wrote papers for the *BMJ*, repaired his bike or worked on renovating his house. At the rate he was going it would be next year before the house was habitable. Would she even be around then? The thought made him feel physically sick.

At the weekends they went for short walks or out for dinner. As time had gone on, Ellen had grown quieter. Often he would catch her holding her stomach with a secret smile on her face. He watched her closely for any sign of the pulmonary hypertension, but to his relief Ellen stayed healthy. He knew, however, that that could change in a heartbeat.

Ellen shook her head. 'I want to go myself. I'm not an invalid, you know. Besides, there are some things I need to get. If everything goes the way we hope it will, I'll probably be home with the baby. It will be his first Christmas and I want it to be special.' She didn't say that it could be the only Christmas she would have with her child, if she made it to Christmas—they both knew only too well what could happen—but they were both keeping up the pretence that everything was going to be okay.

Sean's heart ached with fear and love. The thought of losing her was ripping him up inside.

'We never really celebrated Christmas in my house,' Ellen continued. 'My parents thought it was "over-commercialised and best ignored".'

Sean had often thought he'd like to throttle her parents, but never more than now.

'But I've always loved it. And, Sean, promise me that you'll always make Christmas special for the baby. An enormous tree, fairy lights, the works.'

Sean swallowed the lump in his throat. If it was tearing him up inside knowing that Ellen might never see this Christmas, let alone any others, what was it doing to her?

'You are going to be here for many Christmases,' he said with as much conviction as he could muster. 'I'm not going to let anything happen to you.'

Ellen smiled wanly. 'I plan to be around for as long as possible,' she said, picking up her coat and sliding her arms into it. 'I'll just see if Gran wants anything.'

When Ellen had left, Sean paced the house, feeling restless. These past months had been a form of torture. As he had promised Ellen, they didn't speak about what could happen. Instead they talked about their childhoods, his time in Malawi, patients, anything except what was truly on their minds.

Every day it got harder. He was trying to keep his distance, not feel anything, but it was getting more and more difficult. He didn't want to fall in love with Ellen. The situation was hard enough without that. He did love her, but it was the protective love of a brother for his sister. Not that the way he'd felt when he'd made love to her had been anything like brotherly. Was it possible to lust after someone, to want to touch them so badly it made his chest ache, without being in love? He couldn't afford to be in love with her. He couldn't stand by and watch another woman he loved die. He wouldn't.

His eyes fell on the book she wrote in every evening before bed. It was the one she had said was for their baby should anything happen to her. That was the only time she had mentioned the possibility. He picked it up, meaning to place it on the side table, but as he did so, it fell open. Although he knew it was wrong, he started reading.

Dear Baby,

I know that right now you are only a few rapidly dividing cells and that most people won't even consider you a baby, but that is what you are to me. A little boy or girl who is depending on me to protect you. I have to be honest. For a little while, I considered not having you. But it was only for a day or two. Then I started imagining you. Maybe you'd have your daddy's eyes, or my red hair (I hope for your sake you don't!!!) and I knew that I was going to keep you, even if I couldn't be around to watch you grow up. If you are reading this by yourself, you are probably at school. I wonder if you are top of your class, like your daddy, (and me) or if you are finding some subjects difficult. (Maths was never my thing although I was really good at English and Chemistry.) If you are struggling, remember to go to your daddy and ask for help. Everyone struggles at something. Even your father. His sister told me once that he wasn't very good at writing essays—too impatient. He's still restless, he likes to be busy all the time. Maybe he takes you mountain biking. If he does, make sure you wear a helmet. Heads get hurt really easily.

Sean felt as if all the air was being squeezed from his chest. He sat down and continued to read.

Dear Baby,

You're growing inside me all the time. My jeans won't button up now. Sometimes I feel fat, but mostly I'm just happy that you are getting bigger. Daddy is away in Malawi, helping the mummies there have healthy babies. He is a good man, he just doesn't know it. Sometimes mummies and daddies do and say things that they don't mean. They say things because they think it's for our own good and because they are scared we will make mistakes. My mum (your gran) was angry with me because I didn't go into medicine. She thought because I had the brains, I should be a doctor, but I wanted to be a nurse. I'm so happy I followed my heart. Follow your heart, my darling child. Always do what makes you happy. I don't know yet if you are a boy or a girl. I don't care. All I want is for you to be born healthy and for you to be happy. I'm sad to say that you won't be happy all the time. But the sad times make the happy times even better. By this time you will know what happened to me. Although it hurts me to think I might not see you, or hold you, I'm so happy that you are going to be born. I look at the birds and the sea and they seem more beautiful to me than they ever did. It is like the world has gone from black and white to Technicolor. (Ask someone what that last word means if you don't know.) I wouldn't change anything. I want you to know that.

Sean's eyes were burning and he blinked rapidly. He knew that to continue to read was like looking into Ellen's soul without her permission, but he couldn't stop. There were pages describing how she had met him, how she had hero-worshipped him—in fact, everything that she knew about his life.

I loved being around Daddy's family. You see, my mother didn't really like being a mummy. She couldn't help it. She is a very fine doctor and it is good that she travels the world teaching other doctors. I was a lonely child. Except for the time I was with my gran and in your daddy's house. His house always seemed so warm and cosy. They always seemed to be laughing and they never minded me being there. They treated me as if I belonged. As if I was part of a real family. I know that they will always love you and if you need them they will be there for you. So if you ever feel lonely, or if you have a problem and Daddy can't help, go to them. They will help you, I promise. I have to tell you, though, so that you understand, one of Daddy's sisters died when she had her baby. It doesn't happen very often, but it happened to her and maybe me. Daddy was very sad after she died and he is very worried that the same thing might happen to me. He came back from Africa today and I talked to him about you. I love him very much. I think I have loved him for as long as I can remember.

The shock jolted Sean so much he almost dropped the book. She loved him. Did she mean as a friend? Was she pretending for the baby's sake? He had to know.

Dear Baby,
Daddy and I got married today. Unfortunately our families couldn't be there, except for my gran. I do hope

*you got a chance to know her. It was a happy day. When
I saw Daddy all dressed up but looking more nervous
than I had ever seen him, I thought my heart would
burst. Two days ago, he helped rescue someone from
the mountains. Daddy is a brave man, but you mustn't
think you have to be like him. You can be whoever you
want. I know now that you are a little boy. I saw you on
the scan they give all pregnant mummies. I saw your
heart beat and I love you more than I can say. I'm so
happy right now.*

Sean's heart kicked against his ribs. She was keeping all
this inside. In many ways she sounded as lonely now as she
had been as a child. And it was his fault. He should have
made her talk to him, instead of tiptoeing around her and
the reality of what could happen to her. He jumped out of
his seat and started pacing again. He would give anything to
hold her right now, to make her believe that everything was
going to be all right. But he couldn't make it all right. There
was nothing he could do to protect his beloved Ellen. The
realisation slammed into him. Of course he loved her. No
amount of keeping his distance or pretending was going to
change that. He loved her. He would never stop loving her.
Not to the day he drew his last breath. He sat back down and
read some more. This entry was dated last night.

*Dear Baby,
    They have said that you will be born before Christ-
mas. You are going to be the best present I ever had.
This is the part that is most scary. If I become unwell,
they may need to deliver you early. I have made them
promise that they won't try to save my life at the expense of yours. Daddy isn't happy about that. When I*

told him, his face went as dark as a thundercloud (I hope you won't see that face very often!) and he argued with me. For a very long time. But I wouldn't change my mind. It is not because I want to die, I don't. I want to live very, very much, so I can be there for you when you grow up, but more than anything I feel I have to make sure you are all right. I guess lots of mummies feel this way, we can't help it. You are our babies and we have to protect you, whatever happens. Daddies are different. They don't have the baby inside them. They don't feel them move under their hearts (by the way, you had an attack of hiccups yesterday—it made me laugh) so you mustn't think he doesn't want you. He does. He is going to love you so much when you are here, I promise you. And once you are born, he will do everything to protect you, like he used to protect me when I was a child. You can trust Daddy to look out for you, always.

But I was telling you about Christmas. I imagine it already. You and me and Daddy together in our house. Christmas wasn't really celebrated in my home when I was growing up. My mummy thought it was too commercialised (another word for you to ask someone) so we didn't really have presents or a tree. My gran sent me presents, so that was nice, and we would have something special for Christmas, a duck maybe. Turkeys are too big for just two people and a waste, my mother said, but I don't care, we are going to have turkey, because that's what Christmas is about. But not just about that. Mum was right about one thing. There are lots of people who have very little and they feel worse about that at Christmas, so I want you to think about them. I don't want it to make you sad, but I really believe that doing something for other people makes us happy (don't worry if you don't understand all this now, you can re-read this bit when you are older) so if you can spare a thought for other people or, even better, do something to make them happy, then I think it will make you feel good. But celebrate Christmas, my darling. Get Daddy to find the biggest tree he can, put lots and lots of lights on it, and lots more decorations all over the house (if it makes you feel better you can think of me and know that I am looking down at you and it makes me smile). Tell him to buy a turkey. (I am going to ask Gran to teach him how to cook it just in case. I have been trying to teach him to cook other things so you won't starve, but I'm afraid, so far, Daddy is not proving to be a very good student. Remember that impatience I told you about? Well, I'm afraid he thinks cooking is a waste of time when you can get something from the shop that you can just stick in a microwave but, my darling, it doesn't taste very good and it is not healthy, so I'm afraid I have insisted that Daddy learns. We have progressed from scrambled eggs to stew at the moment and you should learn to cook too.)

Where was I? I'm afraid these days my mind wanders a little. There is so much I need to remember to tell you. Oh, yes, Christmas. And other celebrations. Like birthdays, or when something good happens. Celebrate whenever you can. Be happy whenever you can. If I have one message I want to leave you, it is that. Be happy.

For a long time after he'd finished reading, Sean sat in the chair, thinking. He'd been so caught up with his own need to protect himself he hadn't allowed himself to truly think about what it must be like for Ellen. Although she was trying not to show it, in the diary she planned to leave for their child he could almost hear her heart breaking in every word. She was a far braver and better person than he was.

And she could die.

And their child could die. Ellen was right about one thing. He cared about the baby she was carrying inside her, but if it came to choosing between the child and Ellen it would be no contest. He was angry. He didn't know who with, whether it was Ellen for risking her life, whether it was with the baby for putting Ellen's life at risk or whether it was at the world in general, and he didn't care. Ellen was wrong. He wasn't a good man. A good man couldn't blame a baby for something that was not his fault.

One thing he did know was that he had to tell Ellen how he felt about her. Before it was too late.

CHAPTER FIFTEEN

SEAN was waiting for Ellen when she returned from her shopping trip. Her eyes were lit up and she was clutching bags of shopping.

'Ellen, could you come into the sitting room, please?' Sean asked.

'Is something wrong?'

'No. I'd just like to talk to you.'

'I want to put these bags away. And it's so beautiful outside, I was hoping to go for a walk. Can we walk and talk?'

'Sure.' He was so nervous he didn't know if he was relieved or frustrated to have to put off what he had to say. He held out his hand. 'Why don't you give me the packages and I'll put them away for you?'

Ellen immediately hid them behind her back. 'Oh, no, you don't,' she said, her eyes still sparkling. 'I don't trust you not to peek. It'll only take me a few minutes to run up to my room.'

She was right not to trust him. If she knew he'd read her diary…

He watched her climb the stairs, the bulk of her pregnant stomach giving her a slight waddling gait. She had never seemed more beautiful to him.

They set off for a walk down towards the loch. It was a favourite place of Ellen's and a walk they did most days whether it was sunny or not.

The mountains were reflected in the loch like perfect mirror images. Sailboats dotted the water as fishermen stood on the banks, casting their lines. It was so still, the only sounds to be heard were the cries of the seagulls. They stopped at the bench Ellen had started to call theirs and sat in silence for a moment.

'I love it here. Will you bring our son here as often as you can? Maybe teach him to fish, or sail? I'd like to think of him being outside with you as much as possible. Just promise me you'll watch over him and not let anything happen.'

'You'll be here to watch over him yourself.'

It was the first time she had referred to the future and he knew he shouldn't interrupt.

'Our baby will be here soon,' she said. 'We've done well to get this far. At least I can be pretty confident that, whatever happens, our son will be fine.'

'I still think you should have agreed to be sectioned earlier. Why not tomorrow? The baby will do just as well.'

'We've been over this, Sean. You won't make me change my mind. The only thing that is going to bring this birth forward is if my health declines.'

Sean felt an unexpected resurgence of fury.

'Dammit, woman. Aren't you scared at all?'

'Of course I'm scared. But what option do I have? Giving in to my terror won't change anything.'

'How can you say you love me, yet even think of leaving me?' As soon as the words were out of his mouth, he regretted them. It wasn't at all how he'd intended to go about declaring himself, but he had to go on.

'Ellen, I love you. I think I fell in love with you when you were seventeen and made me kiss you. I want us to be married in the true sense. More than anything I want us to grow old together.'

Ellen frowned. He could almost see the wheels of her brain turning.

'I don't remember telling you I loved you, Sean.'

'But you do, don't you?'

'I said I don't remember telling you.' Her expression darkened. 'Wait a minute, don't tell me. You found my diary and you read it. Oh, Sean. How could you? How could you do that? I trusted you.'

'I couldn't help it,' he said. 'I didn't mean to read it, but when I saw it was open, I couldn't stop myself. I know it was despicable but I thought it was for the baby. I didn't think you would write about me in it.'

'So that's why you want us to be married properly, as you put it. You read in my dairy that I love you and you felt sorry for me.' She stood up, two bright spots of colour on her cheeks. 'Is there anything more pathetic than that? How do you think that makes me feel? That you feel sorry for me. As if it isn't bad enough that I have to put up with your pity because I might die sooner than I planned, you compound the humiliation by thinking that pretending to love me will somehow make what I'm going through easier. What an egotistical, thoughtless, untrustworthy man you are, Sean. How dare you?' She bunched her fists. 'I'm going to go home now. Don't you dare follow me, because I won't be held responsible for what I might do.'

And before he could think of the right words—any words—she had turned her back and was stomping away.

She was right to be mad with him. He was all kinds of a fool the way he had handled that. However she was wrong about one thing. He did love her, but how the hell was he going to convince her now?

When he got back to the house he went in search of Maggie. There was no sign of Ellen, but her diary had been removed from the sitting room.

He found Maggie in the kitchen, cooking up a storm. 'Are you expecting an army for dinner?' he asked, picking up a home-made sausage roll. He put it down again, realising that he had no appetite.

'I always cook when I'm worried,' Maggie said. 'I find it helps keep my mind off things.' When she turned around, Sean saw that she had been crying. 'Only I find I can cook as much as I like these days but it doesn't help. Oh, Sean, I'm so scared for Ellen. I'm so scared for all of you.'

He wrapped his arms around the older woman's shoulders. His throat was tight.

'I'm scared too,' Sean admitted. 'But it's good that she's kept well so far. You know, I don't think Ellen's frightened at all. These days she seems almost serene.' At least she had up until the past hour or so.

'You really love her. Don't you?'

'I love her more than I thought possible. All I need to do now is convince her…'

Maggie smiled. 'It's up to you to make her believe,' she said.

'That's why I have a plan.'

And Sean told Maggie exactly what he had in mind.

'So we're going to section you the day after tomorrow. I'm happy that we've managed to get you safely through the pregnancy so far. But now that the baby should be able to breathe on its own, I think waiting any longer will just be an unnecessary risk.'

Sean and Ellen were sitting in Dr Cassidy's office. It was

a novel, and not entirely welcome, experience for Sean to be on the opposite side of the desk.

'Why not today?' he asked.

'Because Wednesday is the day I think best. And Ellen agrees with me. As we've discussed, it really is up to Ellen and me, Sean. You have to stop seeing yourself as her obstetrician. You're not in a position to make unbiased decisions.'

Sean knew that Dr Cassidy was right. It didn't mean he had to like it.

'Now, as you know, Ellen, you won't be out of danger until a couple of weeks after the delivery, so we'll be keeping you and baby in hospital until then. If everything goes to plan, you and baby could be home for Christmas.'

Ellen's eyes shone. 'I can't believe that in a couple of days I'll be holding my baby.'

Sean and Dr Cassidy exchanged a glance. Although Ellen knew that it was still a very real chance she wouldn't make it, she refused to mention the possibility, although Sean knew she was still writing in her notebook.

'The baby might have to be in Special Care for a few days,' Dr Cassidy said, 'but only as a precaution.'

'I know, and I know he'll get the best care there,' Ellen said. 'I trust the staff completely.'

She turned to Sean and gave him the first smile he'd seen since the day down by the loch. 'And I trust Sean to look after our child.'

Back home, Sean made Ellen sit by the table as he made dinner. Outside the snow had begun to fall and he hoped that there would be no callout for him tonight. He'd told the team that he would be unavailable for a couple of weeks from Wednesday.

Ellen struggled out of the chair. 'I'm going upstairs to the nursery,' she said. 'I want to have one last check to see that we have everything.'

'Ellen, we couldn't fit another soft toy or piece of equipment into the room if we tried,' Sean said with a smile. But he knew that wasn't the real reason she wanted to go up to the room. Often during the night he would wake and tiptoe into the nursery to find Ellen in the rocking chair, either scribbling in her notebook or simply staring into space, a small smile on her face. He knew she was imagining the baby in her arms as she rocked. 'But you go on up while I finish in here. I'm getting to make a mean stew these days.'

After reading her diary, he had applied himself to his cooking lessons.

'I'm not going to have my child brought up on pizzas and fast food,' she'd said. It was only through these oblique references that Sean knew she was still planning for a time when she might not be around.

When she didn't return by the time he had put the casserole in the oven, he went upstairs to find her. As he'd guessed, she was sitting in the rocking chair, one of the soft toys in her arms as she stared out of the window at the falling snow.

'Dinner won't be long,' he said, and went to stand behind her. He stroked her silky hair as she rocked.

'I don't mind what he does when he grows up as long as it makes him happy,' she said. 'Set clear boundaries but don't be too hard on him.'

'What was it like for you, growing up, Ellen?' Sean asked. 'I know what it was like for you when you were here, you always seemed so happy, if lonely, but it couldn't have been good to spend so much time away from your parents.'

'Mum and Dad didn't want me to be a nurse. They thought I should follow them into medicine, become a professor at the very least. I think I was a disappointment.'

'But you stuck to your guns. You were a stubborn kid and you are an equally stubborn woman.'

'I always knew I wanted to be a nurse and not a doctor. I wanted to be more hands on.' She reached up for his hand and he wrapped his fingers around hers. 'I think having a crush on you might have influenced my decision to become a midwife but it was the right field for me. Whatever happens, I'm happy that I helped so many babies into the world. That is a legacy in itself, isn't it?'

'What about your parents? When are you going to let them know about the baby?'

'I'll phone them once I know the baby's fine. Maybe they'll come and see him.' Her voice was wistful. 'I'd like to see them. Even though my mother has never been the maternal type, and Maggie has been more of a mother to me than Mum ever was, she's still my mother and now I'm going to be a mother myself, I want her.'

'I'll phone her when the baby's born.' It was almost as much as Sean could do to stop him venting his outrage out loud at the way Ellen's mother had treated her. He didn't want Ellen to know that he'd already spoken to Mrs Nicholson and that it hadn't been the easiest conversation.

He moved around and crouched in front of Ellen. 'I promise you that I will do everything I can to make sure our child has a happy upbringing. He will see his grandparents—my parents—and his aunties and uncles as often as I can arrange it. Your parents too. I will make sure our child knows he is loved every day of his life.'

'I know you will.'

'And I love you, Ellen. I wish you could believe that, but I plan to spend the rest of our lives showing you every day how much you mean to me.'

Ellen reached out and touched him gently on the face. 'It's

okay, Sean, you don't need to pretend. It's enough right now for me to know that you will love our baby.'

Sean was a nervous wreck when Ellen was wheeled into the theatre. Although he was in scrubs and theatre mask, as he was almost every day of his life, this time he was an observer. Dr Cassidy had made it abundantly clear that if Sean tried to interfere in any way, he'd have him evicted from the theatre, respected colleague or not.

But right now all Sean wanted was for the baby to be delivered and the risk to Ellen diminished. The anaesthetist had already given Ellen an epidural back on the ward. Ellen was pale but her eyes were glowing with excitement.

As soon as Dr Cassidy was satisfied that Ellen was suitably numb from the chest down, he nodded to Sean and picked up a scalpel. Sean squeezed Ellen's hand. 'Just a few minutes, my love.'

With a last reassuring glance at Ellen, Dr Cassidy sliced through the skin to Ellen's uterus. Sean flinched even though he knew Ellen couldn't feel a thing. Moments later their baby was being passed to one of the midwives. The baby gave a howl of outrage.

'Alison and the paediatricians are just going to give him a once-over, then you can hold him for a few minutes. Then they'll take him to SCBU while they repair your wound.'

Sean was saying the words to reassure himself as much as Ellen. They both knew the procedure by heart, but this time it was different—it was their baby who was being checked over.

Then at last Alison passed the baby to Ellen. He was warmly wrapped so only his tiny face was visible. As he was placed in Ellen's arms, Sean felt a crushing sensation inside his chest. His son. His beautiful, perfect son. He hadn't thought about the baby, not really. Only in the context of Ellen and her health, but now as he gazed down on the woman he loved holding their child he felt an indescribable surge of protective love. And if he felt that, it was mirrored twofold as his wife gazed with wonder at their baby son.

'Hello, Seamus,' she whispered. 'Welcome to the world. Daddy is here too.' She smiled up at Sean with such brilliance it took his breath away. Nothing and no one was ever going to take this woman from him.

CHAPTER SIXTEEN

SEAN glanced nervously around the room. The tree was up and decorated. He'd wrapped the presents and placed them underneath. The fire was burning and appetising aromas were coming from the kitchen. Okay so he'd had help, but he'd needed everything to be perfect. In twenty minutes he was leaving for the hospital to collect his wife and child. Outside the snow had continued to fall, but even the weather had decided to behave and the temperature was just right to prevent the snow from turning to ice.

Had he forgotten anything? He didn't think so.

The past two weeks had been the most frightening of his life. He'd spent every spare moment with Ellen and their baby, getting to know his son. But when he returned home at night alone he lay awake terrified that the phone would ring, summoning him to Ellen's bedside. But the days had passed without a call. It seemed as if this time Ellen had been lucky. How long that luck would last, he didn't know, but he was grateful for every day they had together.

When he arrived at the hospital, Ellen and Seamus were dressed and waiting for him, surrounded by a group of admiring nurses. Sean knew that he would never forget their kindness to him and his small family. It had been a humbling experience, being on the other side, and the care they had all received had been faultless, as it was for every patient who came through the doors.

The sight of his baby brought a fresh wave of pride and wonder. As did the sight of his wife.

'Ready to come home?' he asked Ellen.

She sighed happily. 'You know I am. Kind though everyone's been here, I'm dying to have Seamus in his own home, with us.'

Ellen paused with her hand on the door handle of the car and smiled. There was a wreath on the front door as well as Christmas lights hung from every tree in the garden. In front of the house, in pride of place, was a snowman, complete with coal for eyes, a carrot for nose and pebbles arranged in a wide grin. Was that Maggie's hat and scarf it was wearing?

'Too much?' Sean asked anxiously.

'Perfect,' Ellen assured him, getting out of the car. The baby, wrapped up and in his car seat, looked at the lights and blinked. 'You're going to have to take plenty of photos to show him when he's older.'

Inside was even more of a surprise. She couldn't imagine how Sean had got the tree through the front door. It was the biggest she had ever seen. Luckily the dimensions of the room with its high ceiling meant it looked exactly right. Sean had wrapped holly and lights around the stairs and he set about lighting the hundreds of candles that were dotted around the house.

The ache in her throat made it difficult to speak. It must have taken him hours and he'd done all this for a baby who was far too small to appreciate any of it.

In the dining room the table was set for two with more candles and a CD of carols in the background. This was how she'd always imagined Christmas to be. Her in her home with her child and husband. The only thing that wasn't right was the husband bit. Now Sean was officially father to his son, they could divorce and he could get on with living his life without a wife he didn't love. She pushed the thought away. She refused to let anything spoil the first and possibly last Christmas the three of them would share.

'I'm going upstairs to get Seamus ready for bed. Would you like to give him his bath?'

'I guess,' Sean said. 'Unless you'd prefer to?' The thought of bathing the baby terrified him, but he was damned if he was going to show Ellen that it did.

'You have to learn how, Sean. Don't worry, I'll keep an eye on you.' Her eyes were dancing. How he loved those eyes.

Before leaving to fetch Ellen and Seamus, Sean had lit the fire in the nursery too and as Ellen undressed their child, he filled the baby bath with water and brought it into the nursery.

Ellen pronounced herself happy with the temperature of the water and passed him a naked Seamus. The baby looked up at him with such trusting eyes Sean knew he had to make a decent job of this. Even if he would have found hiking to the top of Everest easier and less frightening.

But he managed. Even if it took him three times as long as when Ellen did it and even if there was more water on the floor than left in the bath. He couldn't get over how small and fragile—and slippery—his son was.

Once Seamus was dressed in his sleep suit, Sean left Ellen to feed him. As he turned at the door and saw his wife gazing down at their child, he thought his heart would break.

Downstairs he put the finishing touches to the meal and stoked the fire. He was nervous. What if Ellen said no?

He wouldn't take no for an answer. He knew she loved him. He simply had to make her believe he loved her too.

Just when he was beginning to worry that Ellen had fallen asleep, she appeared in the doorway.

'That's him asleep. We should have a few hours before he wakes for his next feed.'

Sean crossed over and took her hands in his.

'Come and sit down by the fire. I've something I need to say to you.'

Looking curious, Ellen did as he asked.

Feeling a bit of an idiot, Sean got down on one knee by her chair.

'Ellen, my love, I want to ask you if you will spend the rest of your life with me. I love you, more than I can say. And I need you. Life without you means nothing.'

'You don't need to pretend, Sean. You have the right to your baby. I will never take that away from you.'

'For pity's sake, Ellen,' Sean said desperately. 'I'm not saying this because I think I should, or out of some misguided sense of pity. I love you. I will always love you. Will you get that into your stubborn head?'

She looked at him with steady grey eyes. Then she smiled.

'You know what? I think you do,' she said.

'And you love me?' For a horrible moment he wondered if she had fallen out of love with him. Could he really blame her? He had behaved badly. 'I know I don't deserve your love. I should never have left you. But I was angry. Furious even. I didn't know it then, but I was angry that you had made me love you and yet you were prepared to risk dying so you could have our child. It didn't seem like a fair exchange to me.'

'I understand,' she said. 'I never blamed you.'

'So will you marry me properly? At least renew our vows in front of family and friends?'

This was the moment he had planned for. Earlier he'd collected Ellen's parents from the airport—they'd be staying in a hotel close by, his family had all arrived and were settling into their hotel, as were Sigi and her husband. He'd arranged for the minister to come at about four o'clock and he'd even written the words he planned to say to Ellen.

Tonight would be their real wedding, complete with family and friends and their baby. After the service everyone would leave to give them time on their own before returning on Christmas Day in time for church followed by a full Christmas lunch prepared by his sisters and Maggie. He suppressed a grin at the thought of five strong-minded women sharing a kitchen.

'You know that I could still get ill at any time. That the threat will never go away. I know there's a small chance that I might get a new heart and lungs, but it's only the smallest chance.'

'Dammit, Ellen. I know.' He pulled his hand through his hair. 'I know it and I hate it. But I would rather spend the rest of my life knowing that what we have could be taken away at any moment than not have you in my life at all. I hate being with you but not being able to show how much I love you. I want you to be my wife in every sense of the word.'

'In that case,' she said, 'I say yes.'

Then at last she was in his arms and she was kissing him with an intensity that took his breath away.

Some time later they disentangled themselves. Sean glanced at his watch. People would start arriving soon.

As if on cue, the doorbell rang. He left Ellen checking up on the casserole and went to answer it. He recognised her mother immediately. He'd arranged for her to come first, knowing that Ellen would need some time alone with her before everyone else arrived.

As he took in the stiff-looking woman in front of him, he stifled the impulse to reach out and strangle her. How could she have stayed away when her daughter needed her? But as Dr Nicholson stepped into the light, he saw her face was pale and her grey eyes, so like Ellen's, were wide with worry.

'Where is she?' she said. 'Is she okay?'

Sean stepped outside and pulled the door behind him. Before he let Ellen's mother in he had some things he wanted to say to her.

'She's okay. And so is the baby. You'll see them both in a moment. But...' he glared down at her '...I need to ask why you didn't come before. Couldn't you tell your daughter needed you?'

'She didn't tell me she was sick,' Jacqueline replied. 'Or I would have come sooner. Of course I would.'

'She shouldn't have needed to tell you she was ill. I know she asked you to come, but you refused. What kind of mother treats her child as if she is some kind of unwelcome hindrance? You should be proud of her. Ellen has given more in the last few years than most people give in a lifetime.'

'I am proud of her. But I don't need to be lectured on my responsibilities as a mother. I've had to listen to a couple of hours of that already from my own mother. Now, I would like to see my daughter.' Jacqueline drew herself up to her full height and stared Sean directly in the eyes. He knew then that Jacqueline would never change. Ellen had been right about that. But at least she was here and Sean knew that Ellen's soft heart would forgive her mother. He had promised Ellen a perfect Christmas and if that meant putting up with the mother-in-law from hell for a couple of days then so be it.

He opened the door for her. As Jacqueline stepped in to the hall Ellen came out of the kitchen. She froze as she saw her mother and Sean read the conflicting emotions that crossed her face. Surprise, hurt, but then, last of all, happiness.

'Mum,' Ellen shouted, and flew into her mother's arms.

Over the top of Ellen's head Sean saw the tears glistening in his mother-in-law's eyes. She wasn't perfect, but at least her being here had made Ellen happy.

'Why don't you take your mother upstairs to see the baby?' Sean suggested, knowing it would give the women some time on their own before everyone else arrived.

As the guests arrived one by one, Sean tried to keep them quiet. But as the room filled up with Sigi and her husband, Sean's parents and his three sisters who had left their respective broods back at the hotel with their husbands, and of course Maggie, it became impossible to keep the noise down.

Eventually Ellen and her mother came back downstairs. Ellen looked stunned to see everyone there. After hugs and kisses had been exchanged and everyone had trooped upstairs to admire the baby, who had woken up with all the commotion, Sean herded everyone back downstairs and filled their glasses. There was still one person to arrive, but before he did, Sean had something to say.

He called for silence.

'Thank you all for coming. I know most of you would have preferred to spend Christmas back in your own homes, but it was important to Ellen and me that you should be here for our first Christmas together.'

Everyone exchanged glances.

'I can think of nowhere I'd rather be,' Sigi said, to a murmur of agreement.

Ellen studied each face in the room. 'Thank you for coming. So far this has been the perfect Christmas. I have my son and my friends and family and...' she smiled widely '...Sean, of course. Christmases don't get much better than this.'

'As you all know—except Ellen—there is another reason I've asked you here tonight.' He turned to the woman who meant the world to him.

'Ellen, I love you more than my own life. Will you repeat our marriage vows in front of these people and make me the happiest man alive?'

Ellen looked around the room. Everyone she cared for was within these four walls. And Sean had arranged it all—just for her. He loved her. She could see it in his eyes, the way he touched her, the concern and love he showered over her. By bringing all these people together, by making the house a celebration of Christmas, he had shown he understood what she needed, and she knew he couldn't have done all that if he didn't love her.

A warm glow spread through her. Right now, this Christmas Eve, she truly had everything she wanted.

'Of course, my love,' she said. 'I'd be honoured.'

EPILOGUE

Dear Baby,

I am writing this in hospital. Mummy made me promise because she couldn't do it herself.

This past year has been the happiest of my life. And the saddest. I have watched your mummy every day, scared that she would get ill and knowing there was nothing I could do to prevent it. The good thing is that I know I have made her happy. She has laughed a lot. The three of us have spent lots of time at my parents' old house, fixing it up. (At least, I was fixing it up, I wouldn't let her help, but I was glad of her company and yours, my son. I still get a great feeling when I say these words.) The house is ready. You're walking now. Boy, I never realised how fast a child who has only learned to walk can move! Your mummy has just managed to catch you in time to prevent disaster more than once. She says you have my impatience, I think you have her stubbornness. We do argue, sometimes, but we always make it up. We can never stay mad at each other for long, especially when we know every moment together is precious.

I can hardly see to write these words, because my eyes are blurring. You see, a few days ago we got a call from the hospital to say that they had a match for Mummy's heart and lungs and could we come to the hospital straight away? When you're older, I'll explain it all to you, but I'd been waiting for that phone call every day for the past year.

At first Mummy wasn't sure that she was going to have the operation, but I persuaded her. It was her best chance to live a long life, even though the operation carried risks.

Mummy wanted to write to you before we left for the hospital, but we had no time to do anything but get there as fast as we could, so that is why I am writing.

We love you and we love each other, she wanted you to know that. She said I was to tell you that having you made her happier than she thought possible, that loving me and being loved by me was the best thing that ever happened to her, and she doesn't regret one second.

It's dark in this room. The only sound is of the machines bleeping as they record how the patients are doing. The only other sound that I can hear is of your mummy's breathing.

She's sleeping now. The operation was successful and although she'll be in hospital for a little while, she'll be coming home to us, Seamus. Coming home for good.

Love,
Daddy

* * * * *

HOW TO SAVE
A MARRIAGE
IN A MILLION

BY
LEONIE KNIGHT

All the characters in this book have no existence outside the imagination of the author, and have no relation whatsoever to anyone bearing the same name or names. They are not even distantly inspired by any individual known or unknown to the author, and all the incidents are pure invention.

First published in Great Britain 2011
by Mills & Boon, an imprint of Harlequin (UK) Limited.
Harlequin (UK) Limited, Eton House, 18-24 Paradise Road,
Richmond, Surrey TW9 1SR

© Leonie Knight 2011

ISBN: 978 0 263 88613 9

Harlequin (UK) policy is to use papers that are natural, renewable and recyclable products and made from wood grown in sustainable forests. The logging and manufacturing process conform to the legal environmental regulations of the country of origin.

Printed and bound in Spain
by Blackprint CPI, Barcelona

I am a good nurse, I love the children I care for, and that's all that matters.

She repeated the affirmation in her head, but it did little to divert her attention from the unsettling whole-body warmth she was experiencing in response to Richard's touch.

'Are you all right? Have something to drink.'

Clearing her throat, she tried to restore her self-control. But Richard's eyes were firmly fixed on hers, as if he had something important to say but was uncertain how to say it.

'I'm fine now.' She took a sip of the offered drink.

He put his carton of coffee down, ran long fingers through his mane of unruly hair and cleared his own throat. He finally spoke.

'I guess it's time to talk…about you and me.'

'Yes,' she whispered, and fixed her gaze firmly on the ground.

Originally a city girl, **Leonie Knight** grew up in Perth, Western Australia. Several years ago, with her husband, two young sons and their Golden Retriever, she moved south to a small rural acreage located midway between dazzling white beaches and the magnificent jarrah forest of the Darling Scarp. Now her boys have grown and left home, and the demands of her day-job have lessened, she finds she has more time to devote to the things she loves—gardening, walking, cycling, reading, and of course writing. The fact that she spent most of her adult life working in first a suburban and then a rural general medical practice, combined with the inspiration she gets from her real-life hero, makes it only natural that the stories she writes are medical romances.

This is Leonie's second book.
Why not check out her fantastic debut?

SUDDENLY SINGLE SOPHIE

Did you know these are also available as eBooks?
Visit www.millsandboon.co.uk

Dedication
I dedicate this book to all cancer patients,
cancer survivors and their families. I also acknowledge
the devoted and caring group of doctors and nurses
who provide them with support, knowledge, hope
and light through their journey towards the goal of
recovery. They are truly an amazing group of people.

And to Claire, who had the courage and generosity
to have her head shaved.

PROLOGUE

JOANNA cradled her tiny newborn son in her arms. Just three days old and so beautiful...

Although the journey she'd travelled in the past twelve months had not exactly been a smooth one, it had been worth every moment of the anguish and uncertainty. The perfect, fragile, sleeping child she held more than made up for the shock of finding out she was pregnant at the age of nineteen, when her chances of conceiving and carrying a baby to full term had been so low.

The living, breathing evidence of her love for Richard compensated a million times over for the blackness of her mind-numbing fear when she'd begun to haemorrhage at thirty-five weeks. She'd suffered the physical and emotional pain of the emergency Caesarean section without complaint because the result was akin to a miracle. After the birth she'd been told by her obstetrician that her chance of unassisted conception was even less than before her gorgeous little boy had arrived. That didn't worry Joanna. She had everything she had ever dreamed of snuggled up against her breast.

And Richard had been there for her all the way.

She was truly blessed.

Hearing the familiar sound of soft-soled shoes on polished

vinyl, Joanna glanced towards the door of her hospital room. And she wasn't disappointed.

'Hello, you,' Richard said quietly before his gaze moved to settle on the baby…their baby.

'*Howell*, Samuel Benjamin. 2605 grams, 49cm. A precious son…'

The succinct words of the birth notice hardly did justice to the potpourri of emotions Joanna had felt—still felt—at bringing a new life into the world. It was a joy she thought she'd never experience.

Richard beamed, offering yet another extravagant bouquet of delicately scented yellow roses. He laid them, with the others, on the shelf above the compact desk. The room would be overflowing if she stayed in hospital much longer. He'd brought flowers every day since the birth and the tally now stood at three bountiful bunches.

She smiled. 'Hi,' was all she managed to say before her husband's lips covered hers and he delivered a kiss loaded with gentleness and joy. Sam's eyes opened briefly when his father ran a tentative finger gently across his little forehead. He then promptly drifted back into a peaceful sleep.

Taking a step back, Richard released a long, satisfied sigh.

'What was that for?' Joanna asked.

He hesitated a moment as if he needed the time to collect his thoughts. His voice was husky when he replied.

'You're beautiful. You've given me the gift of a perfect child and I think, at this moment, I must be the luckiest man on earth.'

He sat on the side of her bed and reached for her hand, covering it with his own before he added, 'And I love you, Joanna Howell… More than you can ever know.'

But she did know, had always known, and she knew that those simple words didn't do justice to the feelings they had for each other.

CHAPTER ONE

Eleven years later

IT was Dr Richard Howell's first day at Lady Lawler Children's Hospital and a mix of excitement, anticipation and uncertainty churned in his stomach like cement in a fully loaded mixer.

It wasn't anything to do with the job, though.

The inevitability of bumping into Joanna again after spending three years working away in the U.K. had unsettled his nerves and filled his mind with memories, not all of them pleasant.

He snapped closed the latch of his briefcase at the conclusion of the interdisciplinary meeting which was held every second Monday morning in the paediatric oncology department. He still felt jet-lagged—he'd only arrived back in Western Australia three days ago—but was sure it wouldn't take long to get back into the swing of his hectic oncology consultancy.

'Coming for lunch?' James Francis, the paediatric surgeon, asked as they left the meeting room and headed for the lift. 'The food in the doctors' dining room isn't exactly gourmet but it's far superior to the canteen.'

'Not today.' Richard had seen a notice on the pin board of

the ward reminding the staff of 'Shave or Colour for Kids' Cancer Day'. Although he wasn't sponsoring anyone he'd planned to go down and watch, with the aim of giving the participants some encouragement and handing over a donation for a very worthy cause that was close to his heart. 'And I think I'll take the stairs. I need the exercise.'

'Suit yourself.' The surgeon's voice faded as the door of the lift closed. Richard bounded down several steps at a time and took a right turn at the bottom.

He remembered the canteen from when he'd worked at Lady Lawler on his paediatric rotation as a resident. That had been thirteen years ago, before he'd met Joanna and six months before he'd received his specialist training position at the Stirling, the largest children's hospital in the state. A year later he'd met and married Joanna and she'd presented him with a beautiful son the following year. He'd thought his life was as perfect as it could ever be...until their world had been ripped apart. They'd decided to separate and he had taken up a posting in the U.K. Two years had turned into three and he'd extended his stay for the simple reason that he couldn't face coming back—and seeing his wife again.

Yes, Joanna was still his wife, though they had been separated well past the official time necessary to apply for a divorce. Joanna had never pursued the matter, though, and he'd not had the desire or opportunity to remarry. So it hadn't seemed important.

But now he was ready to lay the demons of his past to rest by somehow making up for his cruel abandonment of his wife after the heart-breaking death of their son. He wasn't sure how he was going to do it and it had been a difficult decision to make. He was home and there was no turning back.

Richard glanced around the busy hall. There were a couple of familiar faces but no one he knew well enough to sit with. The canteen hadn't changed. Same monotonous menu of sandwiches, salad and a choice of a couple of hot dishes— usually a lukewarm pasta and one of an endless number of variations of chicken and rice. He chose sandwiches and juice and then made his way to one of the few empty tables on the far side of the room.

The 'Shave and Colour' was well under way on a make-shift stage near the exit. Members of the nursing staff seemed to be the main participants.

His attention moved to one of the nurses who sat with her back to them, submitting to a complete head shave. What struck him were her incredible tresses. Her hair wasn't particularly long, but it was jet-black, thick and shiny.

This woman has guts, he thought. He couldn't think of a more powerful or personal way to show how much she cared for the children she was sacrificing a truly stunning head of hair for.

Who was she?

Richard had a sudden need to know. He wanted to meet her and tell her how impressed he was with her courage. He was intrigued, and interested in her motivation.

A few minutes later the woman on the stage turned around, grinning, her skull as smooth as a billiard ball. Her assured gaze flitted around the room as the canteen occupants clapped and cheered. She waved and smiled at people she obviously knew.

Then her eyes locked on his. The connection lasted only a few moments but it had a profound effect.

It was Joanna.

His wife.

He hardly recognised her.

She'd always had long hair, braided or swinging halfway down her back. Every time she'd gone to the hairdresser, she'd come home with different-coloured highlights and he couldn't believe he'd forgotten the magnificence of her natural hair colour.

And she'd gained weight. She wasn't plump but had healthy, rounded curves and colour in her cheeks. She also exuded a self-assurance he'd not seen in her during the eight years they'd been together.

Her appearance now reminded him of how much Sam's illness and tragic death had drained her. Now her trademark love of life had returned. He suspected she had managed to come to terms with the painful memories, as well as rid herself of any feelings she had for her estranged husband.

Her eyes were still fixed on his when her smile faded. It was if she was challenging him to pick fault with what she'd done…as if she knew he'd experienced a peculiar grief for her loss, both past and present.

The challenge was oddly exciting.

Richard's heart rate picked up a notch or two and he shook his head, trying to make sense of his jumbled thoughts. Probably jet-lag…hunger…first-day blues…

Part of what he experienced was raw, physical attraction and it took him totally by surprise. He hadn't felt like this since…

He looked away, unable to sustain contact with Joanna's unsettling gaze any longer. He attempted to finish his sandwich but it tasted like chalk and stuck in his throat as he tried to swallow.

Taking a deep breath, he decided he would go over and say hello. It wasn't as if his return would be a surprise to her. She knew he was coming back and that he would be working with her. He'd made enquiries and found out she'd added oncology nursing to her list of qualifications and that she worked on Matilda Ward here. So he needed to define the boundary between work and any remaining vestiges of their personal relationship.

As he stood Richard took his wallet out of his pocket and extracted a fifty-dollar note, but by the time he made his way over to the stage to make his donation, Joanna had disappeared, probably back to the ward and her patients. The combination of disappointment and relief left him heavy-hearted but he hoped he'd see her the following day when he officially started on the wards.

His thoughts were interrupted by his pager. He had an appointment with the hospital's medical director in ten minutes and he'd requested a reminder. He put the fifty dollars in the donation box.

It was time to file away his thoughts of the woman he'd once loved so fiercely and possessively and get back to work.

The previous week the nursing staff of Matilda Ward had had a detailed briefing about Richard Howell, the new head of the paediatric oncology unit at Lady Lawler, so Joanna had had plenty of time to prepare psychologically for his arrival. Lynne, the charge sister, had explained that, prior to a professional appointment in the U.K., he'd worked as a consultant at the Stirling Children's Hospital from the time he'd begun his specialist training about twelve years ago. Lynne understood that he was an excellent doctor and a pleasure to work with, she'd told them.

Once the practical details of his return had been discussed, the curious female staff had embarked on the predictable gossip session.

'How old is he?' one of the young nurses had asked. Their previous boss was retiring and was well into his sixties.

'Ooh, close to forty, I'd estimate,' Lynne had replied.

'Good-looking, I hope,' Karen, the play therapist who had just broken up with her boyfriend, had piped up.

Lynne had then scanned the group of inquisitive faces. 'I can't answer that one. I haven't had the pleasure of meeting him.'

'He'd have to be an improvement on old Dr Price. Is he married?' Karen had persisted.

Joanna had remained conspicuously silent during the discussion, but had felt the sudden heat of an unexpected blush at the mention of Richard's marital status. Fortunately the other women's attention had been focused firmly on Lynne, who had begun to put away the patient notes from handover. She hadn't quite finished her exposé on Dr Richard Howell, though, and the woman had glanced at Karen, who had never been shy of saying what she was thinking.

'Don't get any ideas, Karen. As far as I know, he's unattached. Separated or divorced, I heard.' She'd hesitated. 'Or at least he was when he left to go overseas.' She'd looked at the play therapist sternly. 'But I don't want your mind straying from the job. Which reminds me, that's what we all should be doing—working, not gossiping.'

Joanna had made a hurried exit and immersed herself in her work, trying not to think of the ramifications of Richard reappearing in her life. During the week before his arrival she'd tried to convince herself she would remain objective. Determined her relationship with Richard would be no different from her relationship with Dr Price, she'd devised an affirmation she'd repeated many times.

I am a good nurse, I love the children I care for and that's all that matters.

But when Joanna had scanned the room after having her head shaved and seen the tall, fair-haired man staring at her as if she had just committed a crime, her heart had done a back flip and *all that mattered* had been the connection she'd felt with a man she'd tried so hard to forget. She hadn't thought she'd see Richard until the following day when he officially commenced his clinical duties. She also thought she'd mentally prepared herself for all possible scenarios. Oh, how wrong she'd been.

Thank God she'd reverted back to her maiden name before she'd applied for the job at Lady Lawler. Even though Howell was a common name, she suspected there'd be the inevitable, light-hearted enquiries about whether she and Richard were related. She'd not told any of her colleagues the truth about her marriage and she had no plans to do so.

Seeing him again, after three and a half long years, had sent a surge of adrenaline coursing through her veins that felt like a slow-burning fuse. Her days of emotional fireworks were over, though. She'd worked hard to regain a meaningful life. She'd also realised there was no place in her future for a husband. She wouldn't run the risk of being abandoned again when the going got tough. Richard was her husband in name only. She'd put off discussing a divorce in the wild hope they might rediscover the love they had once shared in the early years of their marriage when Sam had been healthy and happy—the light of their lives. But Richard had not been able to cope with her grieving. He'd gone away and it was too late now.

I am a good nurse, I love the children I care for and that's all that matters.

The closer she came to a face-to-face meeting with Richard, the more difficult it became to convince herself, especially now his first day on the ward had finally arrived.

She opened her locker in the nurses' change rooms and replaced her casual clothes with the cheerful oncology staff uniform of coffee-coloured trousers and a crazy rainbow-patterned top. The outfit had been cleverly designed to have pockets in all the right places but bore no resemblance to the traditional dress of a nurse.

Thinking about the day ahead, she smiled as she stowed her gear in her locker. She wondered how Tye Coombs had coped with his final chemo the previous evening and whether Dylan's grandparents had arrived from the country in time to wish him a happy birthday. As she walked into Matilda Ward she was greeted by the usual bustle of the night sister gathering the day staff for the morning handover, but even their cheerful chat didn't distract her from thoughts of how she would cope with meeting Richard again. She tried her best not to appear preoccupied.

'My God, you're brave, Joanna,' Karen said as she breezed into the nursing station.

Joanna smiled. 'You mean my zero-gauge haircut?'

'Yeah, I didn't think you'd be game to do it again this year.' She ran her fingers through her own honey-brown locks, which still had the vestiges of purple glittered streaks. 'But then again, you can get away with it.' The woman studied Joanna's face for a few moments longer. 'I wish I had eyes like yours and that fine bone structure.'

Joanna laughed. 'I do it for the kids, and I don't think they notice the finer points of *bone structure*. I suspect you're just saying it to make me feel better.'

'No, I really mean it.'

The conversation was cut short by Lynne, the charge nurse for the day, summoning them all together.

'We've had a fairly quiet night and we actually have two empty beds, but I understand there's a thirteen-year-old boy coming in today for bone biopsy tomorrow,' Barbara, the night sister, began. 'And there was one new admission at about midnight. Cassie Blake's come in with a temp of

39.5 and a productive cough. Most of you know her, I think. Twelve-year-old with ALL.'

Lynne interrupted, 'Do you know what that stands for, Tracey?' She directed her question to the student nurse who had started on the ward the day before. The girl blushed.

'Acute…er…lymphoblastic leukaemia,' the girl amended.

'Well done. Sorry, Barb, go on.'

'No problem.' Barbara smiled and refocused her attention on the pile of patient folders. 'She's halfway through induction chemo as an outpatient and responding well. Chest X-ray's clear but she's on IV antibiotics and two-hourly obs. Temp's come down to 37.9 already. The physio will see her this morning and she's to have another blood count.'

Joanna became aware of the presence of a late arrival in the small nurses' station. By the hint of aftershave she knew the person was a male and he was standing directly behind her. She began to feel embarrassed that he had a full view of her recently shorn skull and as she moved sideways he leaned towards her and whispered, 'No need to move,' as casually as if he'd never met her before. 'I'm just eavesdropping.' Then he addressed the whole group.

'Don't let me interrupt, ladies…' he glanced apologetically at Grant, the only male nurse on for the shift '…and gentleman. Just thought I'd get a head start on the ward round by listening in. Hope you don't mind.'

'Of course not, Dr Howell.' Barbara beamed. 'I was just about to say that you would be seeing Cassie this morning to assess her.' She addressed the group again. 'You've all heard Dr Howell is starting his clinical duties today as medical oncologist, taking over from Dr Price.'

All eyes turned towards the man standing behind her. Joanna sensed the rush of warmth and felt certain her whole scalp was glowing. This kind of reaction was so out of character. She was embarrassing herself and behaving like a teenager.

'Thanks, Barbara, but please go on. Pretend I'm not here.'

Easier said than done, Joanna thought as she forced herself to concentrate on the remainder of the handover. It was no easy task with the man she had shared the most traumatic time of her life with standing so close she could feel his thigh touching her hip and the warmth of his breath on her neck. She didn't want to draw attention to herself by moving again, though.

Barbara was finishing. Joanna cleared her throat but her voice still sounded husky.

'What's happened to Tye?'

Barbara laughed and Joanna thought she detected a hint of a wink. 'Even the prospect of his favourite nurse on duty today couldn't keep him here. He left last night, straight after his treatment finished.' She looked around the room. 'Anything else, any questions?'

There was an impatient silence. They were all ready to embark on another busy day's work.

'Great, I'm out of here, then. Have a good day.'

Richard's aim had been to get the feel of the staff attitude, the atmosphere of the ward and a rundown on the patients from the nursing point of view before his morning ward round. He'd had no idea whether Joanna would be working a morning shift so, when he saw her in all her close-clipped glory, he mentally rearranged his schedule.

She'd blushed at the mere sound of his voice; her breathing had quickened and he'd detected the slightest trembling of her hands when he'd accidentally touched her. He'd have to make an opportunity to speak to her alone, not only to reassure her that the last thing he wanted to do was to upset her but also to offer her an olive branch and let her know he wasn't about to intrude on the life she now had…unless she wanted him to.

He leafed through the case notes while Lynne allocated patients and duties to her staff for the day.

'Joanna will be coming with us, if that's okay with you, Dr Howell?' Lynne interrupted his train of thought. He didn't look up, but gathered the files and put them on the trolley.

'Fine by me.'

'She's the only nurse who gets to know *all* the kids on the ward and their families.' She chuckled. 'And a few of their secrets they won't share with anyone else.'

Now, why didn't that surprise him?

Joanna was again looking embarrassed, as if she wasn't comfortable with compliments—an unusual personality trait in an experienced, capable and obviously respected nurse. Richard dismissed the thought that his presence was the reason and focused his attention on what the charge sister was saying.

'We'll see Cassie, our most recent admission, shall we?' Lynne said as she guided them into the small room next to the two single rooms set aside for the special care of patients with severely compromised immune systems or serious infections that might be a threat to the fragile health of other sick patients on the ward. They all dutifully rubbed sanitising gel onto their hands.

'Cassie's been isolated as a precaution until we get confirmation of the nature of her infection. With your okay, Dr Howell, we'll move her into the general ward as soon as we can.'

Joanna entered the room first and Richard noticed the girl's face light up at the sight of her. Cassie's mother, though she looked as if she'd had little sleep the previous night, also managed a smile.

Joanna held up her hand in a high-five gesture.

'Love the new look, Jo,' the twelve-year-old said with a cheeky grin as their hands touched. Both mother and child were behaving as if Richard and Lynne weren't in the room. Their attention was entirely on Joanna…and they weren't the only ones. She had transformed on entering Cassie's room: she was now confident, charismatic even and seemed to have an aura of optimism hovering around her.

'Can't have you getting all the attention on the ward. I did it purely out of jealousy,' Joanna said.

Cassie smiled and then finally acknowledged that Joanna wasn't the only one who had entered the room.

'Who's that?' she said with the typical forthrightness of the young. 'Is he the new doctor?'

'Where are your manners, Cass?' her mother said as she stood to introduce herself. 'I'm Kerry.' She extended her hand.

'Dr Richard Howell. I've taken over from Dr Price and will be looking after Cassie for the rest of her treatment.' He turned to the girl and smiled. 'Hi, Cassie. I gather you're doing well with the chemo but you've had a setback. What's happened to bring you back to hospital?'

The girl looked at her mother then began to cough. It was a rasping, throaty cough and, combined with Cassie's good spirits, he doubted she had a serious infection.

'You tell him, Mum,' she said, slightly breathless from the exertion of coughing.

'Her brother had a cold last week. Cassie caught it, just a runny nose and a bit of a dry cough and I thought she was getting over it. She's in the middle of the cycle so I thought her neutrophils would be coming up and she'd be okay. But then last night—'

Cassie interrupted. 'I got a fever and started coughing some gunk.'

'And you know the rules about coming in—'

'If I feel sick and my temperature goes over 38 degrees. But it's come down, hasn't it, Jo? When can I go home?'

Richard looked at the chart. Her temperature had steadily and rapidly decreased since she'd commenced antibiotics and the last reading was just above normal.

Joanna looked at him for confirmation, with those huge brown eyes that he used to be able to read like a book. Not now, though. The window to her thoughts had the shutters jammed closed.

'You're right. It was close to normal when night staff checked an hour ago. It's all good news but I need to examine you.' He glanced at Kerry for approval and she nodded.

After checking Cassie's pulse, throat, ears and chest, the only thing he could find was a slightly inflamed throat, consistent with a viral infection.

'She's had a sputum and urine sent off?' he asked Lynne, but Joanna answered.

'And blood cultures. We should get microscopy back today but culture probably won't be until tomorrow.'

'Okay. Things are looking good, young lady, but we have to be sure we're giving you the right antibiotics. We'll get some results back today, including your blood count, but I'd like you to stay in until tomorrow when we'll have all the tests back and can be absolutely sure you're on the mend.'

Cassie frowned and her mother had a look of resignation as if she was expecting it. Neither spoke.

'I'll come and tell you the results as soon as they come through,' he added. 'And you can be moved to the main ward.'

'Thank you, Dr Howell.' It was Cassie's mother who spoke.

'Okay. And if you have any problems, I'm happy to see you and talk, answer any questions you might have.'

Lynne headed towards the door, a not-so-subtle indication she thought they'd spent long enough with their first patient, but Cassie had hold of Joanna's hand and was pulling her close. She made an attempt to whisper but it was obvious the girl wanted Richard to hear every word of what she was confiding to the nurse.

'You're right, Jo,' she said in a loud whisper. 'He *is* gorgeous, and much nicer than Dr Price.'

Richard couldn't help the tiniest smile that twitched on his lips.

Joanna had described him as gorgeous!

Certainly not a word he would use but it was the first glimmer of hope that the rock-hard shell she'd built to shield her emotions from him before they'd finally split up might have weakened with the passage of time.

'Sorry about that,' she said, averting her eyes and seeming to lose all composure. He couldn't work her out—confident and efficient one minute, quiet and uncertain the next. But he had little time to ponder her behaviour further.

'Where to now?' he asked, and dutifully followed Lynne as she introduced him to the rest of the patients and their relatives. Though it took nearly two hours to complete, he appreciated the sense of not being hurried, of being able to take the time needed to answer parents' questions and get to know the children, their problems and fears as well as their interests and pleasures.

And Joanna always seemed to know the right thing to say, to break the ice with a taciturn parent, persuade a retiring child to open up or a frightened teenager to express what they really felt. Richard was impressed. It was definitely two hours well spent.

When they'd finished seeing the last patient, a baby with an adrenal neuroblastoma recovering from surgery, Lynne excused herself, saying she had some administrative work to do before a teaching commitment with the student nurses.

'If you could take an early tea break, Joanna, can you take charge while I'm away?'

'No problem.' Joanna tidied the folders on the trolley. 'Is there anything else I can do for you, Dr Howell?' she said politely.

Yes, there was, and he decided to risk asking.

'Can I join you for your break, Sister Raven?'

Her eyebrows shot up at his use of her maiden name and the tormented look in her eyes asked why. The truth was he wanted to spend more time with her, alone, away from the distractions of the ward. He wanted to find out how she felt about him, but he certainly wasn't about to admit his motives.

'All right. I'll be ready in about five minutes.' Then she quickly walked away.

He stood watching till she was out of sight.

CHAPTER TWO

THE ward round with Richard had been an ordeal and Joanna knew she should have had more control. But she'd felt self-conscious. For no logical reason, she'd thought she had to prove she was a capable nurse; to show the man she had once been so dependent on that she'd managed to do something worthwhile with her life, something that didn't hinge on her being the perfect wife and mother.

On reflection she realised she'd been trying too hard. That realisation hadn't stopped her going into panic mode when he'd asked to accompany her on her break.

After the ward round finished she headed to the ladies' and glanced at the mirror. She looked no better or worse than usual but needed a moment to herself before going back. She took a couple of deep breaths.

A moment later, Tracey burst in and looked at her curiously.

'Are you all right? You look a bit flushed.'

'I'm fine. I worked a few extra hours yesterday and I feel tired, that's all.'

Without expecting a reply, Joanna left the restroom and hurried back to the main part of the ward, not wanting to keep Richard waiting. As she rounded the corner she saw him leaning up against the counter, all long legs, broad shoulders and sandy-coloured hair that seemed to have a mission to create its own style. He was deep in conversation with the pharmacist and looked up when she arrived.

'I won't be a minute,' he said with a friendly smile and then resumed his conversation.

How could he be so blasé when *her* emotions were in such turmoil?

She busied herself by checking through a bundle of test results that had recently arrived.

'Are you ready?' He stood looking over her shoulder and she could feel his warm breath on her neck. As she straightened up and turned he paused for a moment, dangerously close to her, eyes searching hers as if for the answer to an unspoken question, before he stepped back.

'You can finish what you're doing. I don't mind.'

'No, it can wait. I have to be back by ten because Lynne has—'

'A teaching session,' he interrupted with a smile. 'Where were you planning to go on your break?'

'To the canteen, if that's okay with you?'

The expression on his face changed. The relaxed cheerfulness and downright charm he'd spread through the ward by the bucketload that morning vanished in the time it took Joanna to replace the pile of reports in the 'in' basket.

'I was hoping for somewhere more private.' Richard loosened his tie and then cleared his throat, the only indication he wasn't as calm as he made out. 'You must realise we need to talk, and the sooner the better. If we're to work together...'

'Yes, of course.'

The space between them hung heavy with apprehension and she knew they had to reaffirm that the remnants of their marriage were unsalvageable. The debris of their broken relationship had to be tidily packaged and disposed of before they could comfortably move on and work together as part of the smooth-running oncology machine.

'The sooner the better,' she said quietly, and was glad Richard appeared not to hear.

He began to stride towards the doorway leading out of the ward and Joanna found herself battling to keep up with his pace. When he reached the door, he waited for her to go through first. It was a gentlemanly gesture that reminded her again of the man she used to know.

'Well? Have you any suggestions of where we could go without the company of half the hospital?' He kept walking towards the lifts and stopped when he arrived, pressing the button to go down. 'We could buy something to take away.'

Joanna suddenly had no appetite as thoughts scuttled through her mind.

Was it wise? To spend time alone with him?

She'd thought she'd never see him again. Her life had been uncomplicated, her future predictable. But now...

She didn't have time to think of an excuse to back down, though.

'What about the courtyard behind the clinics? It used to be so neglected...in fact, very few people knew it was there,' Richard suggested, and smiled for the first time since they'd left the ward. 'When I was an intern, about a hundred years ago, we used to call it *lovers' lair.*'

'Yes, it's still there.' Joanna looked away and somehow managed to suppress the bitterness that rose like burning acid in her throat. She'd been so young when she'd fallen in love with Richard. In her third and final year of nursing training, she'd naively thought she was a woman of the world.

He'd been her first and only lover, though, and she'd never wanted to know about his past. Of course he would have had girlfriends before he'd met her and probably had spent more time than she wanted to think about in *lovers' lair*. The fact that he was eight years older than her and had the kind of eye-catching good looks that stood the test of time... He'd probably also had lots of girlfriends since they'd split up.

The secret garden was what she preferred to call the hidden patch of jungle tucked behind the outpatient block.

Yes it was still there but *she* used it as a place of peaceful solace. She would often take advantage of the solitude the secluded area provided when she needed to compose herself, usually after one of her charges had died. Fortunately life, and remission from the terrible disease, was the more common outcome for children with cancer these days, though the word 'cure' was still used cautiously.

'What's the matter?'

Richard's words broke her reverie at the same time as the lift arrived.

'Nothing,' she lied. She wasn't about to reveal to Richard that everything about being alone with him was the matter.

A slight upward tilt of his eyebrows was the only indication he didn't believe her.

'Okay, let's get some food and then we can talk.'

The stilted conversation came to a standstill as they travelled to the ground floor but it didn't seem to bother her companion. When they arrived at the canteen, it was full to overflowing with orderlies and domestics, fortifying themselves for the working day ahead. There was also a scattering of nurses and every table was taken so Richard's suggestion to find somewhere else made good sense.

They bought cartons of iced coffee and, despite Joanna's insistence she wasn't hungry, Richard loaded up with snacks.

'I haven't had any breakfast,' Richard said as the woman behind the counter packed a large paper bag with his purchases.

'Your appetite's still as hearty as ever.' Joanna regretted the words as soon as she'd uttered them. Already she'd noticed so many things about Richard that hadn't changed—the slight swagger of his hips when he slowed his usual brisk stride to a walking pace; the way his brow furrowed and the tip of his tongue protruded when he concentrated; the endearing dimple that appeared in his right cheek when he smiled, giving him the cutest lopsided expression.

But at least he didn't know how often he was in her mind.

He apparently read nothing more into her comment than a simple statement of fact.

'A bit too hearty at times. I've put on a couple of unwanted kilos during my stay overseas.' His tone was casual, as if he was discussing football scores with a mate. He didn't seem to expect a reply and continued, 'I need to get back into regular exercise.'

He paused as they arrived at the entrance to the canteen and waited for a group of chattering student nurses to come in then guided her out of the eating hall with a gentle hand on the small of her back. The simple gesture probably meant nothing to him. He'd always been free with those easy, tactile gestures that could set her heart racing.

He dropped his hand when they were through the doorway and set off at a slower pace she could keep up with.

'What was I talking about?' he said with a grin, and Joanna wondered if he'd been distracted by the group of giggling, nubile students who had cast blatantly flirty glances in his direction. A jolt of jealousy took her by surprise.

She had no hold on him, no right to be jealous, she reminded herself. They were about to discuss the best way to end a marriage that had floundered and failed dismally long ago, not have a friendly discussion about old times.

'Exercise,' she said in a voice barely above a whisper as they approached the clinic block.

'Exercise…that's right. I need to start swimming again, maybe join a gym. Do you know any decent ones around here that have a lap pool?'

She blushed, suddenly remembering all the weight *she'd* put on over the years since their separation. These days she never seemed to have any spare time for a disciplined fitness programme and her attempts at dieting had always been half-hearted; she liked food too much.

'Sorry, gym workouts aren't my thing.'

He hesitated. They'd arrived at their destination and it only lasted a few short moments but Joanna was acutely aware of her companion's head-to-toe appraisal. It was as though he'd stripped her completely bare.

'No, of course not,' he finally said with a smile. 'I imagine you get a decent workout with all the running around you do on the wards. Shall we go in?' He glanced at the entry to the garden.

Joanna's heart began to pound and her naked scalp prick-led as if each hair follicle had a direct connection with the emotions centre in her brain.

Why had she agreed to come?

But it was too late now to change her mind.

Joanna opened the vine-covered gate to the courtyard, which was indeed well hidden.

They sat on one of the bench seats in a corner. Richard handed her a drink and set the food between them, showing no indication he'd guessed how nervous she felt.

'Help yourself,' he said as he opened his carton of milk and took a long gulping drink. Joanna glanced at her watch. She definitely had no appetite.

'No, thanks.'

He raised one eyebrow as he peeled the paper casing off the muffin and popped a generous chunk into his mouth.

'Not on a diet, are you?' His eyes again wandered over her generously proportioned body but there was no sign of criticism in his tone. He had an unmistakeable twinkle in his eye, as if the statement was a challenge. Reminding herself she'd long ago stopped worrying about what people thought of how she looked, she refused to be unsettled by his question.

'Do you think I should be?' she said, rather more brusquely than she'd intended. She defiantly chose a Cellophane-wrapped portion of cheese and crackers from the selection of food, unwrapped it and began to eat.

'No, of course not. You're perfect just the way you are.'

Joanna nearly choked on an errant crumb. As she coughed to clear her throat, her eyes began watering and she felt a strong, warm hand first patting and then rubbing her back. It took all her self-control to stop herself from leaning into the blissful touch of his fingers on the exquisitely sensitive area between her shoulder blades.

She pulled away in alarm at the signals her body was sending. Fortunately Richard didn't seem to notice. His eyes were full of concern.

I am a good nurse, I love the children I care for and that's all that matters.

She repeated the affirmation in her head but it did little to divert her attention from the unsettling whole-body warmth she was experiencing in response to Richard's touch.

'Are you all right? Have something to drink.'

Clearing her throat, she tried to restore her self-control but Richard's eyes were firmly fixed on hers as if he had something important to say but was uncertain how to say it.

'I'm fine now.' She took a sip of the offered drink.

He put his carton of coffee down, ran long fingers through his mane of unruly hair and cleared his throat. He finally spoke.

'I guess it's time to talk…about you and me.'

'Yes,' she whispered, and fixed her gaze firmly on the ground.

'I saw you have your head shaved yesterday…' Richard hesitated. He was trying to break the ice by not launching into a discussion of their marriage as soon as they'd sat down. But the distressed look on Joanna's face left no doubt in his mind that he was being totally insensitive. She'd succumbed to a sacrifice most women wouldn't even consider, because of Sam. And probably because of every child with cancer that had been in her care.

'I'm sorry.'

Her eyes, which had been defiantly cast downward, found his and melted into a pool of heartache and exposed vulnerability. But it didn't last long. She slammed the door on her emotions and attempted a smile.

'What for?' Her expression was now as hard as steel.

'For…er…'

Why was it still so difficult to even mention the death of their son? He'd thought he'd regained some of his objectivity, but he should have realised that seeing Jo again would bring it all back.

She grasped his hand as if sensing his insecurity.

'We didn't come here to talk about Sam. He'll always have a special place in my heart and I'll never stop missing him but I can cope now. I'm no longer an emotional cripple and I've somehow managed to move on. It hasn't been easy but I've survived.'

From what he had initially thought of as Joanna's weak-

...ess had emerged a single-minded strength he envied. He was lost for words.

'We need to talk about our relationship,' she added.

She looked at him questioningly, expecting a reply.

'Yes.' Richard coughed to try and clear the stubborn lump in his throat but it refused to move. 'What do you want to do?'

He'd thought he'd worked through denial and regret and could finally deal with seeing Joanna again...for closure. But he still had strong feelings for her and was suddenly overwhelmed by the thought that he wanted to save his marriage; he was reluctant to mention what had been his initial intention—that they finally divorce.

It had seemed to be the logical solution to a problem that had been simmering in his mind ever since he'd made the decision to accept the position of head of the oncology department at Lady Lawler. But now he'd seen Joanna again, it wasn't that simple. He needed to find out if she still had any feelings for him.

'Do you want—?'

'A divorce?'

Apparently easy for her to say and there was no avoiding the issue. But the goalposts had moved. He needed time. They were both older and, he hoped, wiser. When they'd married, Joanna had been nineteen and pregnant with a child she expected she'd never have. The doctors had told her the scarring from a ruptured appendix three years previously had blocked her tubes and her only chance of bearing a child would be through microsurgery or IVF.

When she'd found out she was pregnant, they'd both been over the moon. Although they'd only known each other for a little over six months, they'd been insanely in love and the pregnancy had somehow validated that love. Maybe they'd jumped into marriage too quickly and for the wrong reasons. Many times he'd agonised over whether that was why their relationship hadn't been strong enough to survive the shattering stress of what had happened to their son.

Was it a bad thing to want to start over?

It had to be Jo's decision. She was the one who had suffered most and he didn't want to cause her any more heartache.

'Yes, I guess it comes down to that. We probably should have finalised things before I left for England, but—'

'I was an emotional vegetable and you couldn't bring yourself to add to my stress by going through a divorce.' She was actually smiling. 'I hated you for leaving me, you know. But I realise now that living with me at that time in our lives must have been a nightmare. Looking back, you certainly pulled out all the stops to try and bring me out of my depression. I don't blame you.' She sighed and then hesitated. 'I've moved on, Richard. I have a fulfilling life that doesn't involve a husband or children. Our marriage ended years ago and now it's time to formalise our separation.'

He cleared his throat but couldn't bring himself to say what he was thinking—he didn't deserve to be forgiven and it had been fanciful to even contemplate that she would give him another chance. Even if he hadn't gone away he had a feeling their paths would have diverged.

Why did he feel so gut-wrenchingly disappointed?

'I suppose so,' he finally said. 'Do you want me to get the wheels turning? I should have time to contact my lawyer some time in the next week.'

He couldn't go on. It all seemed so final, but Joanna was right. Why cling to the memory of something, no matter how beautiful, that could never be regained? They were different people from the young, naive nursing student and the indestructible, ambitious doctor who'd fallen in love more than a decade ago. Joanna had told him what he needed to know.

'That's fine by me. Let me know what I have to do.' She glanced at her watch, took a hurried sip of her drink and then stood up to leave. 'I have to go. I've got less than five minutes to get back to the ward and take over from Lynne.'

She paused a moment, as if waiting for his response, but looked anxious to leave. He needed a few moments to reprogramme his thoughts into work mode, though.

'Yes, of course you must go back. I have an appointment with someone called Jodie to discuss accommodation, so I might see you later, back on the ward.'

She nodded, then leaned forward and kissed him lightly on the cheek, as if he was one of her charges to whom she'd had to impart particularly bad news.

At that moment he knew the thread he'd been clinging to in the hope they might get together again was finally broken. She'd stopped loving him long ago, and she was right. He needed to get on with his life. They both did. So why did it hurt so much?

CHAPTER THREE

RICHARD wasn't sure what Jodie Francis's job description was, but he was grateful she'd contacted him the previous day to enquire if he needed assistance to find accommodation. He'd forgotten about the block of half a dozen terraces tucked away two streets from the hospital and used as temporary lodgings for 'homeless' employees. In the past they'd been leased to visiting, top-level professionals who had temporary appointments such as post-graduate fellowships or academic posts. At the moment he was living in a holiday apartment, about half an hour's drive from Lady Lawler, and he hadn't thought far enough ahead to consider more permanent housing. He was eager to find out what Jodie had to offer.

He knocked on the door of a small office in the administration wing.

'Come in,' the owner of the youthful voice sang out.

By the time he'd opened the door she was out of her seat and headed in his direction with her hand extended in greeting.

'Hello, I'm Jodie, and you must be Dr Howell.'

The woman, who Richard estimated to be in her late twenties, grasped his hand and beamed.

'That's right. You phoned and left a message on the ward yesterday.'

He waited for her to sit down before settling in the austere, grey-upholstered chair opposite her desk.

She thumbed through a folder of papers and extracted a single page, which she placed on the top of the pile. 'I understand you've been back in Western Australia for less than a week and, er…' It was the first time the confident young lady had shown any sign of hesitation and Richard second-guessed what she was trying to say.

'You assumed, since I'd been away for so long, I might be looking for somewhere to stay?'

'Exactly.' She paused again. 'And am I right to assume… um…that you're on your own?'

'Yes.'

His heart rate quickened as a painful memory of a bleak conversation with his wife popped into his mind. When he and Jo had parted, he'd fully expected the break to be purely down-time to allow wounds to heal and that they would eventually reconcile. Their dream home, purchased midway through Joanna's pregnancy and lovingly renovated and decorated to accommodate the needs of their expanding family, had been a symbol of his wife's vision of their future together.

When Sam had died, that vision had been irreconcilably shattered.

Before he'd departed for the U.K. he'd assured Joanna the house was hers as long as she wanted it, but six months after he'd left she'd sent him a matter-of-fact email stating she wanted to sell the house and move into something smaller. 'More suited to a single woman' had been her exact words. But he'd suspected what she'd really wanted to say was *without the memories*.

It had broken his heart, and his phone call to her had done nothing to reassure him Jo had been coping any better than when he'd left. She'd stated calmly, when he'd offered to return to Australia, that it would be a waste of time and she didn't want to see him.

It would upset her too much, he read between the transparent lines of her conversation.

He had a sudden thought that he didn't even have her current address.

'You were saying?' the ebullient Jodie cut into his reverie, and he frowned, trying to remember the last thread of their conversation.

'Ah, yes. I'm separated and in the process of getting a divorce.' The words were out of his mouth, like a confession, before he had a chance to stop them. She'd not asked for any information on his marital status but he'd felt the need to explain why a thirty-nine-year-old consultant didn't have the wife and family that were often expected of someone of his age and position.

Jodie looked embarrassed and busied herself rearranging the papers on her desk.

'So what do you have to offer?'

The girl blushed crimson and Richard suddenly realised what he'd said.

'I didn't mean... I'm not...' he stumbled, and then they both laughed.

'I know.'

'Shall we start again?'

Twenty minutes later, Richard had signed a lease, organised for the rent to be deducted from his salary and taken possession of a set of keys to number 6B Peppermint Mews, the second house in the row of quaint terraces that the hospital owned. He'd made the decision without even viewing the place, on the basis that it was the only empty house in the row at the present time. The fact that it was fully furnished, he had a three-month lease with the option of staying longer and he could move in straight away added to its attraction. There was a tiny light at the end of a very long dark tunnel, he thought as he said goodbye to Jodie and strode off towards the main part of the hospital.

Joanna was in Richard's thoughts for most of the day and into the evening as well. She was a remarkable woman, an amazingly dedicated nurse and she had stated, without hesitation, that she wanted to go ahead with the divorce as soon as possible. Before their private talk that morning he'd nursed the tiniest hope she might still have some feelings for him. He was not deluded, though, and didn't expect to recapture what they'd once had. He'd thought more in terms of the remnants of their former relationship being intact; a starting point; a foundation from which to rebuild.

It wasn't going to happen.

Joanna had changed, while he was stuck in the past.

So what he had to do was cast away any thoughts of rekindling a personal relationship with his wife and start over.

Today. Right now.

He returned to the ward after the meeting but his and Jo's paths didn't cross again. He focused his attention on his patients.

He spent an hour with an eight-year-old and his parents, explaining stem-cell transplants and answering their many questions. Then he'd been called to deal with a teenager who had developed a dread of her chemotherapy and, for the last two treatments, had started intractable vomiting the night before her three-weekly sessions, in anticipation. She was on the verge of refusing to continue despite an excellent response and it took a lot of persuading to get her to consider coming into the ward as an inpatient to tailor strategies to help her cope. There'd also been two new admissions he made a special effort to see before he left for a hurried, late lunch.

Joanna had been busy with her own duties and, though he'd been aware of her presence, they hadn't actually spoken again and Richard's afternoon had been a full on session in clinics.

Now he was heading home.

Home...

He'd stay in the apartment until at least the weekend, when he hoped he'd have time to shop for food and the essentials like bed linen that weren't provided as part of the package of his new home. He was looking forward to moving in.

Alone.

If only things had been different.

He drove into the underground car park and headed for the lifts. It wasn't long before he let himself into his apartment and faced the prospect of a long evening with the only company his own. He dumped his briefcase on the coffee table, opened the blinds, exposing a vast expanse of glass and an impressive view of the ocean opposite, and went to the fridge.

He knew exactly how Old Mother Hubbard felt.

There was enough milk left in the half-litre complimentary carton to make a cup of coffee—but he'd used all the coffee. A lonely bottle of mineral water stood next to two bottles of beer, the remains of a six-pack he'd bought on the weekend. Apart from a loaf of stale raisin bread his cupboard was indeed bare.

He reached for a beer, opened it and threw the cap into the bin, the bottle tilting as he did so and dribbling part of its contents onto his hand and the cuff of his shirt. He pulled a couple of tissues from the box on the kitchen counter at the same moment his phone rang.

'Hello, Richard Howell.' He gave the automatic greeting

'Hi, Dr Howell. It's Jodie.' She paused. 'Remember me? We met this morning.'

Richard's initial response was annoyance. He couldn't think of any reason a member of the administrative staff would ring him at home on his mobile.

'Yes, I remember. Is there a problem with the house?'

It was the only reason *he* could think of for her after-hours call.

'No, it's nothing to do with that.'

'What, then?'

He thought he could hear the rumbling of voices in the background and then she giggled. He had the fleeting thought it might be a prank and it was the last thing he needed at the end of a long day.

'I know you've only been back at work two days…'

It sounded like she was about to ask him a favour and he took a deep breath.

'Go on.'

'And you may not know that my dad is James Francis and he said he's known you since you were an RMO and that you used to be a member of the hospital jazz band.'

He heard her take a deep breath and tried to make sense of a conversation that was becoming increasingly vague and convoluted. So Jodie was the daughter of Mr Francis, the paediatric surgeon, and, yes, he'd known her father for a long time and they'd jammed together a few times. But when he'd commenced his specialist training at the Stirling then married Joanna within the year, Richard had found the commitment to regular band practice and the occasional charity performance hadn't fitted with the long hours and hectic schedule of a paediatric registrar with a pregnant wife. Most of the other band members had been either old enough to be grandparents or young and unattached. He'd given away music almost completely, although he still had his saxophone.

'And?'

'Um… There's a charity concert planned for the Easter weekend and the band is without a sax player. Dad suggested contacting you. I know it's over two months away but—'

'No. Thanks for thinking of me but I don't play any more. Even if I wanted to it's been so long and I doubt I'd have the time for regular practice. I was never any good.'

He'd first met Joanna through his music. She'd been in the Stratton University choir and he'd continued to play in what had jokingly been called the Lady Lawler Big Band—more to do with its size than the type of music they'd played, which could range from pop rock to classical as well as traditional jazz. The good old days…

The last thing he needed at the moment was to be reminded of a time in his life that was in his thoughts nearly every day. Playing the saxophone was a rare, solitary activity these days.

'That's not what Dad says. He reckons you're the best saxophone player the band has ever had. Are you doing anything Friday night?'

'Er…' Lord, this woman was pushy, just like her father. He tried to picture the oncology after-hours roster. 'I'm on call.' He was fairly certain Friday and Sunday were his rostered days.

'Perfect. We're having auditions in the B J Cohen Lecture Theatre so if you get a call you'll already be at the hospital.' He heard her clear her throat. 'Not that you need to audition, but it will give you a chance to meet the crew and assess the new talent. What do you say?'

The woman was wearing him down and the idea of getting back to his music had some appeal. Maybe it was meant to be, all part of his new start. There was also the possibility of rescuing his social life, which he'd thought he'd lost for ever.

'Okay. I'll come on Friday, but it doesn't mean I'm committing to playing.'

'Great. Seven-thirty, and bring your saxophone.'

Then she hung up, leaving Richard wondering how she'd managed to persuade him to do something that he really didn't want to do.

The next few days flew by in a blur of ward rounds, clinics, lectures and med-student tutorials. Richard's only contact with Joanna had been on the wards in her capacity as an extremely dedicated and efficient paediatric nurse. There was no doubt in his mind she had a special relationship with her patients and she gave so much more than expected from the job description.

He certainly hadn't had time to think about getting the ball rolling with their divorce but he would try and at least make a couple of phone calls, including one to his solicitor, on his afternoon off the following week.

He packed his briefcase with some paperwork he wanted to take home and then slung his stethoscope on the top before he clicked the case closed.

Friday already.

The reality of committing to even a brief appearance at the concert audition night had been intermittently interrupting his thoughts through the afternoon and now he longed for a quiet evening at home, with a glass of wine, listening to his favourite mood music...*with Joanna snuggled up beside him on the couch.*

An impossible dream.

He sighed as he walked out of Matilda Ward at the end of his first working week. In many ways it was good to be back in Australia; his only disappointment was that the grieving process was beginning again—this time not only for his son but for the demise of his marriage.

Joanna hated being late.

By the time she arrived, there were only a couple of stragglers in the foyer of the lecture theatre—a middle-aged man she didn't recognise who was carrying a cello case and one of the new intake of medical students dressed as an outrageously eccentric clown.

She laughed. The young student stopped and turned around. He'd only been working at Lady Lawler for a few weeks but already had a reputation for his cheeky sense of humour and the occasional practical joke.

'Guess what role I'm up for tonight?' he said in a ridiculously high-pitched voice, but managed a deadpan expression. He waited for her to catch up with him.

'Wow, that's a hard one.' She chuckled. 'It's a long shot but I am guessing it could be the stand-up comedian slot?'

His animated, black-painted lips drooped in an exaggerated expression of despondency as a bright blue tear trickled down one cheek. He whipped out a flamboyant bunch of daisies from somewhere in his baggy trousers and began waving them about as if he were conducting a full symphony orchestra.

'I was hoping for the job of choirmaster.'

Joanna burst into laughter again. He would make a wonderful kids' doctor. An off-beat sense of humour, as long as it was combined with sensitivity, made for ideal qualifications in an aspiring paediatrician.

'Seriously?'

His face lit up again with a grin.

'Seriously,' he repeated, as he made an overstated gesture

inviting her to enter the theatre before him. She walked in with a smile on her face, looked around and made her way over towards the section of stage with 'CHOIR' written in broad felt-tip pen on an upended cardboard box. It was part of a disparate set, which seemed to have done the job to guide the hopeful performers to different parts of the stage, depending on their abilities and aspirations.

She waved at the student as he headed towards the section designated 'MISCELLANEOUS'. He was obviously enjoying the attention.

'Good luck,' she called.

But then she stopped dead in her tracks.

She'd been aware of the discordant sound of the various band instruments tuning up but she picked up the strains of a saxophone playing ragtime out of the din. It was a popular Scott Joplin composition but she couldn't remember the name.

Oh, God!

The memories came flooding back.

Why was the saxophonist playing the song Richard had been playing when they'd first met? It must be simply a cruel twist of fate, she thought as she looked over to the crowded band section to see who it was. It certainly didn't sound like Steve, the hospital's long-time player. It wasn't his style.

She scanned the group, telling herself it was simply an unusual coincidence.

Then she saw him.

Richard's unruly hair flopped over his forehead but Joanna could see he had his eyes closed, concentrating fully on the music. He'd always had the ability to focus totally, blocking everything out but the sound of his own instrument. When he finished the lively tune, he stopped and took a deep breath before playing the soulful opening bars of an old traditional jazz ballad called 'Sunset of Sadness'. It was a melody with lyrics about aching hearts, broken promises and shattered dreams. She knew the song by heart. The hummed melody had been a lullaby for Sam during his illness when he'd had trouble getting to sleep. And then, after it had all ended, the song had been comfort for her and Richard when there'd been no other way to express their grief.

Joanna began to mouth the words and then something strange happened. One by one the other instruments silenced and the rumble of conversation gradually ceased until all that could be heard was the clear, poignant sound of Richard's saxophone. He seemed oblivious to what was happening around him, totally absorbed in the music.

But it was too much for Joanna. The memories stabbed at her heart and silent tears ran down her cheeks. She suddenly felt claustrophobic and had to leave. She stepped off the stage and, head down, walked quietly towards the exit.

But then, in her haste to leave, she stumbled. She grabbed hold of the nearest thing to steady herself. Unfortunately it was a fold-up chair—the top one in a stack leaning against the wall. She fell backwards, taking at least half a dozen metal framed chairs with her.

The music stopped.

The entire occupants of the theatre seemed to take a collective breath before…all hell let loose.

How humiliatingly embarrassing.

The first person to reach her was Richard, closely followed by the clown. At least a dozen concerned faces drifted in and out of her field of vision.

'What happened…?'

'Are you okay…?'

'You've cut your head…'

'Does it hurt anywhere?'

'Did you faint?'

Joanna knew they were well meaning but all she wanted to do at that moment was to escape to somewhere quiet, on her own.

'I'm sure she's okay and I'll take care of her.' Richard's authoritative voice silenced the curious and concerned. 'I think it's best you get back to the auditions.'

With a firm but gentle grip he lifted her to her feet, conveying the message with his eyes that he understood she needed time and space to regain her composure. It was her pride that was injured, not her body. To add insult to injury, she'd exposed her weakness in times of stress, not only to everyone in the lecture theatre but to Richard.

She sniffed, wiped her eyes on the back of her hand and untangled herself from Richard's protective grasp.

'I'm all right. You can go back now,' she said in a voice as unsteady as her wobbly legs.

'What are you going to do?' *His* voice was as steady as a rock.

'I can't stay.'

The expression in Richard's eyes told her he knew why.

'I'm sorry…'

She swallowed, clearing her throat of tears and the rawness of her emotions.

'Don't be. It wasn't your fault. You didn't even know I was there.'

'No,' he said quietly.

She wanted to go home and she also wanted Richard to go away and leave her alone. She felt the shell of her control coming dangerously close to cracking. The way she'd managed her grief and protected herself from painful memories had been to block them out. She couldn't return to that aching place full of sorrow and guilt that had imprisoned her for so long after Sam's death.

She hadn't thought Richard coming back would have this effect, though.

'I'm going home,' she said, reaching up to run her fingers through her hair—before she realised her scalp was covered in less than a week's stubble, and there was something sticky and warm near her ear. She quickly dropped her hand to her side, hoping Richard hadn't noticed. As she turned to leave, Richard grasped her wrist and pulled her around to face him.

'Where do you live? I don't think you should drive. And you need someone to deal with the cut on your head.'

She smiled. Feeling her confidence return, she realised she now had an out.

'I only live around the corner and I walked, so you don't need to worry,' she said defiantly.

'That solves the problem. I can walk with you.'

Maybe it was a culmination of a busy working week, restless nights or possibly a simmering resentment at how easily he'd been persuaded to go public again with his sax playing—whatever the reason, he had become so immersed in the music he hadn't even noticed Joanna arrive.

What on earth had come over him to result in him playing *that* song?

It was a personal and very private part of a past he'd shared with the woman he was certain he'd carelessly hurt badly. No wonder she'd attempted a hasty exit.

'It's not necessary. I told you I only live a street away. I'm quite capable of getting myself home in one piece.'

He wasn't about to be put off by Joanna's stubborn tone. Even if she hadn't stumbled and bumped her head, he firmly believed it wasn't wise for a woman, and certainly not his Joanna, to walk home alone after dark.

She'd already begun to stride ahead of him and he had to quicken his usual brisk pace to catch up. She was definitely a woman with a mission and her mission that night didn't include him.

'I'm only thinking of your safety,' he said tentatively when he caught up. Her protests morphed into a stony silence and he wasn't sure which tactic he liked least. But, thankfully, she wasn't physically pushing him away and the tears he'd noticed earlier had stopped.

They reached the road at the back of the hospital and stopped at the kerb to wait for traffic to pass. Richard reached out to touch her arm in a gesture he hoped indicated friendship but she shrugged him off.

'How could you?' she said softly as she set off to cross the road at a slow run.

He had no words to explain so he remained silent and several tense minutes later Joanna rounded the corner into a softly-lit street of an odd mix of ancient cottages and more modern multi-storey blocks of flats. He was relieved when she stopped at the gate of one of the cottages.

'This is where I live, so you can go now. I'm quite capable of letting myself in.'

He lingered, not sure how he was going to persuade her to at least let him dress the blood-encrusted wound on her exposed scalp. She'd probably have a decent-sized lump on the back of her head in the morning and she didn't have the luxury of a normal head of hair to disguise it.

'Yes, I know you are, Joanna,' he said with what he hoped she would interpret as compassion. 'But…' It was a difficult decision to make—whether or not to dive in head first and tell her exactly how he felt. He wanted to believe he had nothing to lose but deep down he realised how much was at stake. Joanna didn't hate him—he knew her well enough to be able to gauge the barometer of her feelings—but he understood how much of an upheaval it must have been to have him land back on her doorstep with little time to prepare herself for the disturbing roller-coaster ride he'd forced her to embark on. He decided to try and compromise.

'I can only try and understand how difficult it must be for you, me turning up out of the blue.'

'All the oncology staff were told who was going to take over from Dr Price a couple of weeks after he announced his retirement. It wasn't a total surprise.' Her expression softened and she took a sighing breath. 'I had plenty of time to adjust.'

'So can I at least be your friend?'

'It's not that easy," she said but he didn't want to push her.

'Can we talk inside?'

Richard purposely kept some physical distance between them and hoped Joanna understood he wasn't trying to encroach on her personal space. He didn't want to continue their conversation on the pavement, in the dark, though.

She didn't answer but opened the gate and headed for the pathway running along the side of the building. He began to follow and was relieved she didn't object.

'I live in the house on the back half of the block. It fronts a laneway but I come in this way at night.'

Richard took her comment as a sign she had no objection to him coming with her and continued along the path, a couple of steps behind. By the soft light of the remnants of dusk he could just make out the roofline of a small house tucked behind a two-metre-high fibro fence. Joanna made her way to a second gate and left it open once she had gone through as if she'd resigned herself to the fact that he was tagging along, no matter what she did. A light was on, illuminating the small back patio, and she proceeded to unlock the glass sliding door that led into the rear of her house.

Richard followed her in and glanced around the cluttered living room. There were books piled in a corner, spilling off overloaded shelves. A guitar in a soft case leaned up against the wall next to a music stand holding what looked like a couple of 'how to play' books. The homely furniture was comfortably worn in.

'Sorry about the mess,' Joanna said as she scooped up a basket of washing and stashed it in what he presumed was a laundry room.

'What mess?'

Her response to his attempt at humour was a hard-edged glare as she shifted her roomy shoulder-bag from the coffee table to the counter separating the main living area from a small kitchen.

'Would you like a cup of tea?'

She'd remembered he preferred tea to coffee. It was a small thing but it touched a chord in his heart. She hadn't blotted out all the memories of their past.

'I'd love one.' He paused, wondering if he could penetrate the stubborn resistance she'd demonstrated so far to any help he offered. He decided to take the hard line. 'But after we clean up that wound. There's a fair bit of blood and it's hard to know what's underneath. Have you got a first-aid kit?'

'I'm quite capable of doing it myself,' she said with a scowl.

The hard line hadn't worked so he thought he'd try the practical.

'Maybe if you had eyes in the back of your head. The blood is coming from behind your right ear, so you'd at least need someone to hold a mirror for you. Are you working tomorrow?' As a last resort he thought he'd try and appeal to her sense of vanity. Cosmetically he would certainly do a better job than her, particularly if there was a significant laceration.

She frowned.

They both stood awkwardly at opposite sides of the room as if it was a stand-off. If only she would relax and realise his sole motive was to help her. He'd do the same for a complete stranger. Well, sort of...

'At least go and look in the mirror.'

He began to walk towards her and she edged away like a frightened animal that had been cornered. Was she really so terrified of being alone with him she couldn't bear him to come near her?

'Okay, you win. I'll go and have a look.'

He managed to suppress a gasp as she headed off down a passage that he assumed led to the bedrooms and bathroom. She had a decent-sized haematoma, already an impressive purple colour, on the right side of her occiput and dried blood streaked down her neck. He assumed it would be easy enough to treat the wound but he doubted he could do much to conceal the damage.

He went into the kitchen and opened her freezer, hoping to find something he could improvise as an icepack. His plan was to clean the wound and then apply ice before he attempted any repair work.

'What exactly do you think you're doing?'

Joanna had returned.

He thought of saying something flippant, like he had a sudden craving for ice cream, but he knew better. Joanna wasn't in the mood for jokes.

'An icepack? Can we use the frozen peas?'

She was standing about two metres away, holding a damp, bloodstained face cloth to the back of her head.

'Oh...er...yes, okay.' It wasn't exactly an apology but a step in the right direction.

'What's the verdict? Am I allowed to touch you with my healing hands?'

A hint of a smile crossed her lips and Richard took it as a sign her tension was lessening a little, though he realised he had a long way to go before she'd trust him.

'You're right,' she said, looking everywhere but at his face. 'It's a lot worse than I thought and I doubt I could do a decent job on my own.'

Thank God for that. He had no idea what he would have done if she'd refused.

'Wise decision. To the bathroom, then.'

He followed her down the passage, past two closed doors he assumed were bedrooms to the bathroom. It was efficiently compact, like everything else in the small house, with room enough for a shower recess and vanity. Mirror tiles, topped with a small fluorescent tube, took up most of the wall above the basin. She flicked on the mirror light, laid a first-aid kit and a hospital dressing pack on the vanity.

'There's gauze in the dressing pack, chlorhexidine in a specimen jar and butterfly sutures in the first-aid kit.' The simmering tension ramped up a notch but fortunately wasn't directed at him. 'I just hope it doesn't need stitches,' she added.

'You're certainly well prepared,' he said with a smile, but she'd already turned away from him so he could do his healing work.

'You can take the face cloth off now.' He poured antiseptic into the plastic tray and used the disposable forceps to dab a square of gauze into the bright green liquid. 'Okay if I put a towel over your shoulders?'

Lord, she had beautiful shoulders. They were softly rounded, lightly tanned...

He checked his errant thoughts in double-quick time. There was no point in dwelling on Joanna's physical beauty when he'd been treated like an unpleasant though necessary evil as soon as they'd walked through her door.

She reached across for the hand towel next to the vanity and draped it across her upper back as if she'd suddenly become aware of the amount of skin exposed by her strappy singlet top. She was obviously keen for him to get on with the job in hand so she could reclaim her territory.

'Right, then. This might sting a little.' Richard rolled out the standard hospital-speak.

She remained silent but he could see her tension as he applied the cool liquid to clean the skin around the wound before discarding it. He doubted his ministrations would be painful so she was most likely responding to his touch. He disposed of the soiled gauze and began cleaning the wound with a fresh swab.

'It's only small,' he said, to reassure himself as much as Joanna. 'About a centimetre. One butterfly suture should be enough to close the wound and I expect it will be healed in three or four days.' He ran his fingers over the boggy skin covering the haematoma. 'The bruising will take longer, though.' He chuckled. 'It's quite a work of art.'

'Just get on with it.' Richard could feel her disapproval. 'Please,' she added quietly.

Oh, how Joanna wanted him to hurry up and finish so she could send him packing. The last thing she needed was to experience Richard Howell, one-time husband extraordinaire, up close and personal.

The problem was that her reaction to him had been totally unexpected.

She'd thought she was over him, but she had been wrong.

When she'd seen him at the auditions and then heard *that* song, the memories had been like a bunch of sharp needles pricking her head, trying to penetrate her brain. And she'd managed to ward them off, keep them at an acceptable distance, until Richard insisted he accompany her home.

It wasn't his fault either. He was just being the same caring, loving, gentle man he'd always been. She was the one who had changed. She'd spent the past three years making a new life for herself with a thickly drawn line separating it from her past. Seeing Richard again meant reliving the deep, unremitting pain of losing their darling son and the cruel way she'd rejected her husband during her grieving. She was the one who'd destroyed their marriage by shrouding herself in a cocoon of sorrow. Richard had done the right thing in leaving her and he deserved a new life too…without her. He had to move on, not live in the past, and for him to achieve some sort of closure she knew she mustn't let him get close to her.

'Ouch!'

She was brought back to reality by the sharp pain of strong fingers holding her wound together while the butterfly suture was carefully applied. Richard was leaning close and she could feel the comforting warmth of his steady breathing on her neck.

'I thought you were going to ice it first.'

'I changed my mind. The laceration's smaller than I thought.'

She turned around to face him, being careful not to put any tension on the wound. His eyes twinkled with amusement.

Dangerous.

He was making it difficult for her to maintain the distance

she desperately needed to… To what? To stop herself falling into his comforting arms? To stop the mesmerising look in his eyes from melting her resolve? To stop him from unravelling her tightly ordered world that didn't have room in it for a man, let alone a man who'd done everything he could to help her through the biggest tragedy in her life, the only thanks he'd had to be coldly rejected.

If there was still a tiny spark of attraction it was purely physical. He was a very good-looking, sexy man and she'd not shared her bed, in fact she'd not had a boyfriend, since Richard had left. Sex wasn't the basis of a long-term relationship, though. There had to be commitment, and that was asking the impossible of her. There was no denying her happiest days had been with Richard and Sam but she couldn't face the prospect of having to relive the anguish when things had gone wrong. She'd been so young. She'd had dreams of a perfect life. Now she knew there were no guarantees of happily ever after, but there were certain precautions she could take to minimise the possibility of being hurt.

She moved away from him.

'Thanks,' she said quietly as she collected the debris of the clean-up and placed it in the bin.

'My pleasure,' he said, still smiling. 'I'll go and make tea, shall I?'

I'll go and make tea.

The simple statement tripped a switch for Joanna. Tears rolled down her cheeks and she began to sob.

It had always been Richard's solution when the road had been rough or they'd had a disagreement—to make a cup of tea, sit down quietly and not make any decisions until they'd at least finished one cup. But she didn't need to be reminded.

She sniffed, but before she managed to bring her hand up to her eyes to wipe away the evidence of memories she'd tried to put behind her, Richard enfolded her in his arms. And she was powerless to resist. She felt the steady thud of his heartbeat, the gentle movement of his chest with each breath, the solid, reassuring strength of his arms around her, the feather touch of his lips on her forehead.

'No!'

No way. The stakes were too high. She couldn't bear even the slightest possibility of heartache all over again.

Richard dropped his arms as she pulled away.

'What's the matter, Jo?'

She wiped away the remains of her tears with a handful of tissues and blew her nose.

'Nothing's the matter. I'll be all right in a few minutes.' She took a deep breath to steady her voice. 'I don't want tea after all. I need to be on my own.'

The cold stare she sent him did the job and he gathered the jacket he'd shed before attending to her injury.

'Are you sure you're okay?'

'I'm fine,' she almost growled.

'Right. I'll see you at work next week, then.' He opened the sliding door, the lines on his face indicating a mixture of bewilderment and concern. At the last moment he turned. 'I'm sorry, I didn't mean to—'

'Just go,' she said, and closed the door firmly behind him.

CHAPTER FOUR

WHEN Richard arrived back at the hospital the auditions were in full swing. He couldn't face going back in, though. And he was too emotionally drained to even talk on the phone to James Francis. So he decided to leave a message at the switchboard, requesting them to contact his colleague and ask him if he could look after his saxophone until Monday.

Maybe by then he would be in a fit state to apologise and explain.

Maybe his busy weekend—shopping, moving into his new house, going through the motions of settling in—would take his mind off the disturbing thoughts of Joanna that wouldn't leave his head.

But it didn't.

He was still thinking of her when he arrived on the ward early Monday morning to do a quick check of the weekend admissions. When he found out Joanna wasn't starting until nine it was difficult to disguise his disappointment.

A busy morning in the long-term follow-up clinic at least cheered him up and gave him something outside himself and his inner confusion to concentrate on. The morning was taken up with seeing the happy, living evidence of all the hard work his team did in the early stages of diagnosing and treating childhood cancer.

It always gratified him to know more than eighty per cent of his charges survived their disease for longer than five years and the majority of those went on to live normal adult lives. All of the patients he saw that morning had done well: Jenna, who'd had a brain tumour removed as a baby, now a lively toddler; Jay and Tom, two young adults who'd been the same age when they'd developed osteogenic sarcomas affecting the tibia, a bone in the lower leg. Tom had needed amputation but Jay's leg had been saved. Though the boys lived in different parts of the state they'd stayed friends and always organised their clinic visits for the same time. And, of course, the majority of leukaemia victims did well.

When he waved the last patient out the door, Richard packed his things.

'See you next time,' Margaret, the sister in charge, called as he headed towards the door. 'Have a good afternoon.'

'I'll try,' he replied, feeling an unexpected jolt of nerves at the prospect of seeing Joanna again.

He had a quick lunch and headed for Matilda Ward for the first round of the week—a teaching round. He expected it to be demanding because it included the junior doctors as well as two or three medical students.

And Joanna would be there.

If his first working week was anything to go by, the ward rounds she attended always seemed to have an air of cheerfulness. She could be counted on to lighten the atmosphere if either staff or patients got bogged down in the sometimes daunting complexities of the diseases and their treatment.

If there was a bright side, she'd find it.

And there she was. He could see her through the glass partition enclosing the day ward, where procedures like outpatient chemotherapy, lumbar punctures and transfusions were performed. Her eyes were bright with encouragement as she assisted with supervision of three children having chemo. Though he couldn't hear what she was saying, one of her charges laughed and the others were smiling at her animated conversation.

He held up his hand in what could be interpreted as either a wave or a truce, but she ignored him and continued her jovial chat with the kids.

Did the woman have endless reserves of strength? he wondered as he swung into the nurses' station, almost colliding with Anita, the resident.

'Sorry, I was just coming to find you,' she said. She'd only been working on the unit a couple of weeks but Lynne had told him she'd already proved to be keen, competent and a quick learner.

'What can I do for you?'

She looked a little put out, as if she was about to ask for bus fare to the moon.

'I need supervision inserting a central line. Jack's in Theatre with Tilly Farmer and the plastics team.' Jack was one of the oncology registrars in his final year of specialist training, trying to learn everything he could and hoping for an overseas posting when he'd finished his exams. The young doctor took a long sighing breath. 'And this one will make up my quota so I can officially do them on my own.'

Richard glanced at his watch. He had twenty-five minutes before the round was due to start.

'Is it set up?'

'In the chemo suite. Joanna said she's available to help if I need her.'

Right.

Joanna was available.

Terrific. Wasn't it? Of course it was. She was the best nurse on the ward and he wouldn't let the unresolved issues he had with her distract him.

'And the patient?'

'Danny Sims.'

'He's an outpatient, isn't he? Pelvic Ewing's sarcoma.'

'That's right,' the resident doctor said as they walked towards the specially set-up suite of cubicles. 'Dr Price prescribed intensive initial therapy in view of the site and prognosis.'

The boy's diagnosis made working with Joanna even more difficult as Danny had the same type of cancer that had taken Sam's life. He wondered how Joanna would cope. Would she relive a little of the pain of Sam's illness every time she saw Danny?

Richard remembered seeing Alan Price's notes on the boy and the chemo regime he'd worked out. Though cures were increasingly common for the extremely rare but often fast-growing tumour of the connective tissue associated with bone, location in the pelvic area meant a much poorer prognosis.

'When's he due to start treatment?'

'Not until tomorrow but if we put in the catheter this afternoon, he should be able to start first thing in the morning. He's staying overnight.' She smiled as they entered the wash room where they scrubbed up. 'Of course Dr Price asked that you review him before we start. I was going to ask you to look at his notes this afternoon after the round and get Jack to supervise—'

'But he's in Theatre, for a long haul.'

'Probably all afternoon. And Pharmacy needs the okay today to make up his drug regime.'

'No problem. Let's go and say hello to Danny, then.'

Richard was pleased to find out the thirteen-year-old patient and his father, who looked more nervous than the boy, had been well prepared. Anita had explained exactly what would be done and Danny had been given a mild sedative by one of the nurses as soon as it was confirmed the procedure was to go ahead.

Richard introduced himself.

'I'm Dr Richard Howell, the specialist who will be looking after you from now on. Anita is going to put a tiny plastic tube into one of the large veins in your chest so you can have the amount and type of drugs you need without having to have a new line each time you come in.'

'Will it hurt?' Danny said drowsily.

'A little,' Anita answered with a smile. 'You'll feel the needle with the local anaesthetic like a pinprick, but that will make the skin go numb.'

Richard turned when he heard the curtains of the cubicle part.

'Hi, champ,' Joanna said cheerfully, as if she had known Danny for years. Richard's worries about any difficulties she might have coping were immediately allayed. 'And I checked up about…ahem.' Joanna made a theatrical show of clearing her throat. 'That very special person *is* coming to the ward on the day you have your second treatment, but you mustn't tell a soul I told you. It's supposed to be a big surprise,' she added with a wink, and Danny managed a grin.

'Our secret,' he said.

She nodded in the direction of Danny's father. 'Jenny's with the kids today, is she, Pete?'

He nodded and then paled, looking as if he was about to faint.

'It's getting a bit crowded in here. Why don't you go and make yourself a cuppa in the parents' room?' she said tactfully, glancing in Richard's direction for his approval to give Pete an excuse to leave. He nodded, aware that their young patient's anxiety level had definitely ebbed after Joanna had appeared. 'Okay, Danny?'

The teenager's eyes had drifted closed and he opened them briefly, managing the slightest smile. 'Yeah, you go, Dad, but you'll stay, won't you, Sister?'

She patted his leg. 'Of course. Someone has to keep an eye on these doctors. Is that okay with you guys?' she asked.

She was in total control, treating Richard like a consultant she was working with, behaving exactly as she should be. Maybe he'd blown out of proportion her almost hostile reaction to him on Friday night. She was certainly better at filing away the past than he was.

'Fine by me,' Richard said, trying to adopt the same attitude, which hovered somewhere between professional and friendly-casual.

'Good.'

Joanna peeled open another set of sterile surgical gloves and then tilted the bed head down to help fill Danny's chest and neck veins. She went off to wash her hands while Anita carefully swabbed the skin of the right side of the boy's torso.

'Feeling all right?' Anita asked, but Danny seemed to be drifting in and out of a light sleep, a sign of effective sedation. There was a good chance he wouldn't even remember the catheter insertion.

Joanna returned and slipped her hands into her gloves.

'I'll just watch and let me know if you want any help or advice,' Richard said as he moved back from the bed and stood where he had a good view of the two women at work.

Anita anaesthetised the skin just below the clavicle then made a small cut to locate the subclavian vein, which sits beneath the bone but in front of the artery. Joanna dabbed at the small wound and placed a finger in the notch at the top of the breastbone so that Anita could line up the needle at the correct angle. Insertion of the plastic tube into the vein and its tunnelling under the skin went smoothly, a good back flow of blood indicating it was likely to be in the correct position. A small cuff on the tube was inflated to help keep it in place under the skin and an X-ray would confirm it was in the right place and that no damage had been done to the underlying lung.

'Well done.' Richard checked the time. 'Can I leave you to suture, check Danny's chest and organise radiology? I'll speak to Danny's father before he leaves.'

'Yes. And thanks, Dr Howell.'

'I'll see you on the ward round when you've finished.'

Richard was only five minutes late to the round and Anita joined him and his group not long after, but he noticed Joanna's absence.

'Isn't Sister Raven joining us this afternoon?' he asked Lynne quietly when they were walking between patients.

'No, she's working in the chemo suite until the day cases finish. It's better she stays there. Is there a problem?' He chose to ignore the curious look in the charge sister's eyes.

'No, of course not. It's just that…'

'She brightens your day?'

Yes, that's exactly right, he thought. She's like a ray of sunshine generously shedding light and warmth wherever she goes.

'She brightens everyone's day,' he conceded to say with a pleasant but what he hoped was detached smile as they reached a grizzling toddler in a cot.

'Hello, Mrs Bryant.' The child's mother looked over-wrought and overtired. Now was not the time to enquire how she was coping and he made a mental note to call back and see her at the end of the round.

'Would you mind if Travis…' he indicated one of the medical students '…gently examines Taylor's tummy?'

The child had a Wilm's tumour, a cancer arising from the kidney, and often presented as an abdominal mass. She was undernourished and being fed by a nasogastric tube in order to try and improve her general condition prior to surgery the following week.

'All right,' Liz Bryant said with a sigh, but she moved protectively towards her daughter and began to stroke her head.

Travis completed the examination awkwardly, one of his hands big enough to span the child's abdomen from side to side.

'I'd like to come back and see you later on my own,' Richard said quietly.

She picked up her crying child and rocked Taylor in her arms. She nodded then turned her back on the group and walked to the window. Richard wished Joanna was available to comfort her and realised, after one short week back in Matilda Ward he had begun to take her bubbly, happy, caring presence for granted. He was coming to depend on her being there for her tireless ability to comfort and offer hope in the grimmest situations.

He missed her…

He wanted part of the joy she spread for himself.

'Come on,' he said with enthusiasm. 'Let's head for the tutorial room. Don't think you can get out of it. Alan told me he'd asked one of you to prepare a case presentation.'

There was a general chuckle from the group as they followed him down the corridor and out of the ward.

Richard wasn't like some of the other hospital consultants who would rather starve than go to the canteen, but sometimes, like this afternoon, he wanted solitude during his breaks. The couple of times he'd had lunch in the busy dining hall, hoping to see Joanna, he'd found himself bullied into sitting with a group of chattering nurses, at least one of whom would decide to flirt with him.

Not that there was anything wrong with nurses, or chattering, or flirting, but if it continued unremittingly he knew it would wear him down. If he'd been ten years younger he would have been flattered but he had matured and was past all that now.

So after the tutorial he'd headed for the public coffee shop, which he knew was rarely frequented by staff. He needed a few minutes time-out before he went back to Matilda to tidy up loose ends and leave his work in the ward in order for the evening staff. That had always been his way of coping with the stress of never seeming to have enough time in the day—pacing himself; not succumbing to time pressure or being hurried; not leaving a job half-done, hoping others would pick up the pieces.

It was close to closing time so he wasn't surprised to see he was the sole customer and ordered a flat white—it was the only place you could get a decent coffee in the hospital—and chose a quiet table hidden from the entrance but with a view of the passing parade going in and out of the main hospital block.

When he'd seen Joanna coming out of the nurses' amenities building and heading his way he'd assumed she was on her way home but Marnie—the woman had introduced herself the first time he'd visited the shop—must have seen him looking at her.

She'd set his drink down and said, 'She's one of the few who are brave enough to go all the way.'

He hadn't quite understood what she meant.

'Sorry?'

'The full shave.'

'Oh, I see what you mean.'

'She'll have a cappuccino. I'll put money on it.'

'If she comes in and asks for one, let me buy. I work with her and I wouldn't mind some company.'

The woman's eyes widened fractionally and then she smiled as if they were plotting a secret revolution together.

'Okay.' She sashayed back to the counter.

A few seconds later Joanna *did* come into the shop and although Richard couldn't see her he could hear the conversation. The muscles of his jaw tightened just a little and he unconsciously began tapping his saucer with his spoon. He seriously wanted to share a drink with Joanna, enjoy her smile and her honey-smooth voice. And if it was only work they talked about, that would be okay. He realised he'd be more than disappointed if she refused. So when Marnie started rambling on about secret admirers he felt he had to show himself. He'd set up the situation, and there was no room for second thoughts.

There were only a few kids Joanna came back to visit after-hours and she was careful not to give the impression she had any favourites. She knew how attached many of the sick and frightened children could become to a staff member who gave that little bit extra. She was lucky she had plenty to give but made sure she rationed her off-duty time and energy with care.

She couldn't help what she felt for young Danny Sims, though. It would take a miracle to cure him; she knew from firsthand experience the odds were stacked miserably against him.

When Sam had been diagnosed with Ewing's, Richard's knowledge of paediatrics hadn't been enough for her. She'd read everything she could get her hands on about the disease that had been threatening the life of her son, from scientific, evidence-based research to personal anecdotes on the internet. Even testimonials about farfetched miracle cures. She remembered one of the few times Richard had become frustrated with her emotional attempts to cling to increasingly fading hopes. He'd accused her of clutching at straws and it had probably been the first tiny step at the fork in the road—where she'd begun to reject him.

If she could turn back the clock… If she knew what she did now…

Richard had been trying to cope in his own way.

She'd seen only one case of Ewing's since she'd been working on Matilda and the boy, a couple of years older than Sam, who had just turned six when he passed away, had miraculously survived and was in remission.

But Danny Sims's case was different.

For a start, his chances of getting the disease in the first place were roughly the same as winning Lotto. And if you ticked the boxes of the features of the teenager's cancer that were associated with a poor prognosis, he would probably score a six or seven out of ten.

But Joanna's philosophy was that there was always hope, exceptions to those horribly inhuman statistics. Miracles did happen, and if they didn't, Joanna always tried her best to make the road less bumpy for the unfortunate few in her surrogate brood.

If she couldn't have children of her own, she'd decided, she'd devote that instinctive maternal part of herself to her job—caring for kids with cancer.

She had completed her nursing degree during her pregnancy and graduated a month before the baby was due. Then she'd put her career on hold while she'd been a full-time mum.

She'd planned to go back nursing when Sam started school, but it hadn't happened. Her son's illness had been diagnosed when Sam had been in pre-school and he'd survived only eleven heart-breaking months.

Making the decision to go back to work had been a turning point for her once she'd managed to control her grief and had been sure Richard wasn't coming back. It had been an easy decision to extend her nursing qualifications to include oncology. The last two years had been immensely satisfying.

And now Richard was back…well…there was no reason anything should change other than formalising their separation with a divorce.

I am a good nurse, I love the children I care for and that's all that matters.

'That's all that matters,' she repeated in a whisper to reinforce the words she'd found herself repeating several times over the weekend when troubling thoughts of her husband had kept steamrolling into the peaceful solitude of her days off.

Thank goodness it was Monday afternoon and she'd finished her shift. She planned to call back and see Danny and Taylor as well as Raymond, a new admission who'd looked scared to death when he'd come in but she hadn't had a chance to have a *proper* talk to him. Then she'd buy some take-away for dinner, head home and spend a quiet evening watching a DVD. Relaxing. Unwinding from her hectic day.

She changed into jeans and a T-shirt, slipped out of her sensible black lace-ups and into low-heeled sandals, deciding to head for the hospital shop. She might even treat herself to the luxury of a cappuccino in a real china cup before she hit the wards again. At least once a week she enjoyed checking out the magazines as well, so she knew what was stocked in-house if one of her patients who needed cheering up had a passion for soccer or horseriding or fashion. Small, personal things could make a big difference.

She breezed into the shop.

'Hi, Jo. Love the five-o'clock-shadow look,' Marnie, the woman in charge of the coffee shop cum newsagent cum florist said with a smile. Joanna was finally becoming used to her bald look but the comments still came in abundance, especially about the bump that at least now was reducing in size. She ran her palm across the stubble on the top of her head.

'Like it? Maybe I'll keep it this short. It's certainly easy to care for.'

'Don't you dare. You've got beautiful hair. Finished for the day?' she added.

'Yes, thank goodness. It's been a long one.' She wasn't about to tell Marnie that it was partly due to the trouble she'd had sleeping the last couple of nights.

'We all have those but in your job you probably get more than your fair share.'

'Mmm…'

Joanna began flipping through a magazine on home renovation. It had caught her eye because on the cover was a photo of a house that looked uncannily like the house she'd lived in with Richard and Sam; the house she'd loved and had had every intention of spending the rest of her days in.

The best-laid plans, she thought with more than a hint of world-weary cynicism.

'There's a special on cappuccino today.' Joanna could tell her friend was about to come out with a friendly jibe. If the shop was empty Marnie would sometimes give her a second cup free of charge. That was usually when she couldn't hide her tiredness or the fact she'd had a particularly difficult day. Perhaps the prison hairstyle made her look gaunt and contributed to the *poor me, I need some comfort* look. She hoped that she wasn't so transparent that even Marnie could see right through her.

'Oh, yeah?' she said with a grin as she placed the glossy on the counter. 'I'm going to treat myself. What was that about the coffee?'

'On the house, sort of. I've got instructions from a secret admirer.' The middle-aged woman giggled like a schoolgirl and Joanna wasn't sure she'd heard correctly.

'Pardon, what did you say?'

Marnie's gaze fixed on something behind her and Joanna turned to see, of all people, Richard emerge from behind a large display of dried flowers. If she hadn't been so surprised, she would have laughed. He and Marnie were looking at each other conspiratorially.

'What's all this about?' Joanna asked, with a sudden urge to turn around and head out the way she'd come in.

'I'll leave it to the doctor to explain. Coffee for two, I presume.'

'Thanks,' Richard said as he led Joanne to a table by a large window at the back of the shop.

She wondered if it was more than coincidence that she kept bumping into him at every turn.

'Richard…er…what a surprise,' Joanna said with a twinkle of what Richard assumed was amusement in her eyes. She was definitely more relaxed than the last time he'd seen her outside the workplace.

'Just needed a break and some real coffee for a change. I thought you'd finished for the day.'

She certainly looked different in her civvies. The clingy, watermelon-pink T-shirt, scooped low at the neckline, highlighted the delicious fact that she had generous curves but in all the right places. And she had gorgeous legs, snugly denim-clad and stretching right up to… She was as beautiful as the day he'd met her.

'Please sit down and join me.'

'Thanks.'

'I thought as soon as you downed tools you'd be heading off to relax.'

A wayward hand went up in the direction of her hair. Nervous? It was the only indication she gave. He smiled.

'Phantom hair?' He couldn't resist the jibe. The conversation was flowing smoothly and he didn't want the tone to change, not just yet.

'Pardon?' she said, obviously not understanding his light-hearted remark.

'You know, like a phantom leg. A person who's had an amputation can still experience sensations like itching or pain where the limb used to be.' He paused, waiting for a response, but her face was expressionless. 'You have phantom hair,' he repeated.

'Oh, I get it,' she conceded, but concentrated all her attention on making patterns with her spoon in the froth in her cup.

'So why aren't you heading off for some down-time?'

She looked up and stared straight into his eyes, as if deciding whether it was worth the effort to reply with the sort of explanation she assumed he wanted to hear, or take the simpler option of telling the truth.

'Sometimes I visit a particular child, or parent even, as a friend, when I'm off duty. It's not easy to spend the time with them they need if you've got dressings to do, medications to give. You know what I mean. I particularly wanted to see Danny.'

'Danny,' he repeated softly. Of course she'd want to do everything she could for Danny and his family. She would know that his chances of getting through the next year or two were slim. His cancer had already spread.

'He's staying overnight...but of course you know,' she added, flushing slightly.

'Yes.'

He wanted to ask her if she was okay, but he wouldn't. It wasn't the time or place. He guessed no one else in the hospital knew about her past, about Sam. And he had to respect that.

Marnie appeared with more coffee.

'Sorry I took so long,' she said with a grin. 'Everyone decided to come at once.' She glanced over at a table where a family of four sat with what looked like a mountain of sandwiches, cakes and bottled soft drinks. 'Can I get you anything else?'

Richard shook his head and glanced at his companion.

'Nothing for me,' she said.

He pushed his empty cup out of the way and began absently stirring his fresh one.

Joanna was silent. Uncomfortable maybe?

'I wanted to have a word with the Simses as well. And Taylor Bryant's mum seemed...' He stopped to think for a moment.

'Depressed?'

Not only was Joanna insightful but she really cared.

'That's what I thought too.'

'She told me she'd had postnatal depression after Taylor was born, and recovered. She'd been doing really well until...' She was much more comfortable talking about work.

'The books tell us that parents experience a process of grieving when their child is diagnosed with a chronic illness, and cancer is the worst scenario. But in the real world no case is the same.' Richard suddenly realised he was talking to someone who had gone through it all. And he'd been there with her. He'd shared the shock and denial, the anger and finally acceptance long after the diagnosis had been made. The knowledge he'd had as a paediatrician in training hadn't made it any easier. In fact, it had probably made it worse. And then they'd experienced it all again when Sam had died. He wished he'd kept his big mouth shut.

'Sorry,' he added.

She looked at him for a long moment, the pupils of her striking black-brown eyes dilating a fraction before she spoke.

'Don't be,' she finally said. 'I'm okay with it.' Her eyes moved to focus on a place in the distance before they returned to fix on his. 'I'll never get over it. I don't think any parent who has to cope with what I…*we*…did does. But we all heal in different ways. I'm sorry I made it so hard for you. I know you tried to be there for me but I just couldn't believe anyone, not even you, could understand. I needed to work through the whole process on my own.'

She'd been fiddling with her spoon, rotating it on the table, but she stopped and surprised him by reaching over and laying her hand on his.

'Like you said, people cope in different ways. And that was my way. Alone.' She paused to take a sighing breath. 'I've got a good but very different life now. And I wouldn't want it any other way.' She gave him the same sort of soothing smile she bestowed on grieving parents and confused kids.

'Look I didn't mean to—'

'We had to talk about it. I thought there might be problems with you worrying how I would deal with Danny. It needed to come out in the open. I'll cope.' Her hand went up to her head again. 'And you don't have to worry about my personal history interfering with my work. I make sure it doesn't.'

Richard wanted to talk some more on a different level, to

reassure her and tell her how brave she was and that there was no one in the world like her, but he knew anything he said would be a clichéd pat on the back and he wasn't sure how to open his heart without hurting her even more.

'I don't doubt it for a moment,' he finally said. 'I've been back long enough to see how you work and I've no complaints.'

Joanna sipped her coffee.

'I'm a bit of a cappuccino junkie. This is good, but I really must go.'

She stood, leaving half her drink.

'You're going to Maltilda?'

'That's right.'

'To see Danny and his dad?'

'Yeah.'

'Mind if I come with you?'

She smiled again and the warmth of it enveloped him like a curative hug. It was like the old days but he knew he'd have to work hard at keeping Joanna on his side.

'Of course not. We're playing on the same team after all.'

She was right. And for once in his life he believed winning was important, not just how you played the game.

CHAPTER FIVE

THEY visited Danny together and Richard learned a lot about his young patient and a little more about *the new, independent* Joanna. And what he discovered, he liked...a lot.

She seemed to have a natural rapport with teenagers by somehow tapping into that unique kind of humour that allowed them to stick a finger up at authority but at the same time laugh at themselves. The haircut definitely helped. He knew he was being selfish but an image of those stunning, lustrous locks haunted him as he put his signature to the last patient folder, filed it away and stood up to leave.

After he left the ward, picked up his saxophone from the receptionist in the department of surgery, bought enough food from the deli opposite the hospital to put together a light meal and headed for home.

Home?

It was a house full of someone else's furniture he didn't particularly like; a house decorated in sombre, neutral colours he would never have chosen himself; and, in a weird subliminal way, it reminded him of the hospital.

It was a comfortable two-storey terrace house that would fill the gap nicely until he found a place of his own, but nothing more. He doubted he would ever think of it as home.

He rinsed his plate under the tap and left it on the draining board, poured himself a glass of wine and settled on the sofa. Withdrawing his hand midway on its journey to the TV remote control, he sighed. He'd always believed that watching television was what you resorted to when you had neither the motivation nor energy to do anything else. He'd watched a lot of TV in England but he'd used the excuse that it was often late at night after working a twelve-hour day and a way of turning off his brain from the highs and lows of his job. He didn't want to get into that same rut and one of his New Year resolutions had been to *make time* in his hectic schedule for two things—exercise and socialising, preferably involving an activity that combined the two.

His first dalliance into meeting people—the concert auditions—had been a failure. During his first week at Lady Lawler, despite the abundance of eligible and attractive females, he'd not had the slightest inclination to ask a single one of them out. Even if he had fancied any of the hospital staff, he felt so out of practice when it came to dating, he doubted he'd have the courage to ask.

Knockbacks hurt.

He was in the process of wading through the result of the ultimate knockback—a divorce—and he didn't really want to visit that place again any time soon.

So that left exercise.

He got up, went to his bedroom and rummaged in the bag of new purchases, retrieving a large, fluffy, navy-blue bath towel. Then he found the chlorine-faded swimming trunks he'd taken with him to the U.K. but had hardly worn. He threw them both in a small backpack he used for hand luggage when travelling by plane, grabbed a handful of change, his car keys and headed outside.

Swimming was the most restful form of exercise Joanna knew. Up until Richard had mentioned joining a gym with a lap pool, she'd forgotten how soothing cutting through cool water, stroke by rhythmic stroke, could be. One of the things Richard had insisted on was that their son learn to swim at an early age.

'We live in a country surrounded completely by water. Australia has some of the most beautiful…and treacherous… beaches in the world.' Richard's words echoed in Joanna's mind. 'He doesn't have to be a champion swimmer, just fit and strong enough in the water to be safe. Or as safe as he can be.'

They'd started him in the baby classes at the local public pool and he'd taken to the water with the grace and playfulness of a dolphin. He'd loved swimming, just like his father. A month before his fifth birthday he'd been accepted into the Seals Squad with the distinction of being the youngest member of the group. Richard's heart had almost burst with pride. It had been a father-and-son activity and attending Sam's swimming meets had been something Richard had always seemed to be able to make time for.

Because of Richard's work commitments, Joanna had usually been the one to take Sam to training, though. One of the high points of her week had been the twenty minutes she spent with him simply having fun in the water before the formal session began.

Sam had endearingly called it his warm-up, probably so as not to lose face with his pint-sized mates by admitting he enjoyed mucking about in the pool with his mum.

As well as regular visits to the pool, on every warm Sunday Richard had had off work, they'd gone to the beach. They'd taken Sam to the beach the week before he'd died. It had been a heart-wrenching experience for Joanna to see her husband gently carry their fragile son to the water's edge and ease him into the calm sea of the bay until they had been waist deep. Over the many years they'd been coming to the coast, a pod of dolphins had appeared, probably half a dozen times. Miraculously the dolphins had come that day, swimming quietly and with unprecedented curiosity. They'd actually come close enough for Richard to guide his son's hand to touch one of them.

It had been the last time Joanna had seen her son laugh.

She'd been convinced they'd come to say goodbye.

And it had been the last time she and Richard had shared the raw emotion of the love they had for their precious child. Tears had been streaming down Richard's face when he'd emerged from the shallows. Tears that had dried up and been replaced by solid calm.

The memories flooded back.

They'd been the perfect family, living a perfect life.

She'd often thought Sam had been growing up too quickly. But then he'd had his childhood stolen from him...

At the age of six years and four months.

A tear trickled down her cheek as she smoothed the electric-blue one-piece swimsuit she'd chosen to wear in preference to the way-too-revealing ice-white bikini Richard had bought her for their fourth wedding anniversary—along with a wonderful romantic holiday to Coral Bay. She scrunched up the garments and jammed them back into the corner of her underwear drawer then opened the door of her wardrobe and looked in the full-length mirror. She straightened her back, pulled in her stomach and had fleeting second thoughts that she knew she mustn't let take hold.

'If I don't do it now, I never will,' she muttered as she pulled on shorts and a T-shirt, grabbed her bag and headed out the front door.

* * *

The pool was a couple of kilometres away from where she lived, far enough away for Joanna to take her car.

When she pulled into the parking area of the recreation centre Joanna could hear the booming music of an aerobic dance class and nearly collided with a family group tumbling out of a people-mover van that pulled up next to her.

'Sorry,' she said as she jammed herself flat against her car door to let the four children pass, and almost succumbed to an impulse to get back into her car and drive home.

'No, I can do it,' she whispered with new resolve. She needed the exercise, she loved swimming and coming back to where she had spent so many happy hours with Sam she hoped would be cathartic.

'What did you say? Were you talking to me?'

Joanna looked up to see a woman carrying a large bundle of towels and what appeared to be various floaties and pool toys suitable for pre-school-aged children. The driver who Joanna assumed was the children's father, was already halfway to the entrance of the recreation complex with three children of various ages and sizes following. The youngest straddled his shoulders.

The woman looked vaguely familiar.

Joanna smiled. 'No I'm just talking to myself.'

The woman was now out of the car and staring at her.

'Joanna? Joanna Howell? Your hair—I hardly recognised you.'

Joanna squinted, trying to make out the stranger's features in the half-light of the electric lamps illuminating the car park.

'Sorry, do I know you?'

'It's Teresa. Teresa Deleo. Angie and Sam used to swim together.' She chuckled. 'And your Richard and my Rick used to be way more competitive than the kids ever were. We

sed to get so embarrassed.' Her expression turned serious.
I wanted to contact you after…er…Sam passed away, but
Rick said it was too soon. That seeing our kids might upset
ou. And then we heard you'd gone overseas.'

Her friend had got it wrong but Joanna didn't have the en-
rgy to explain that it had only been Richard who had moved
way. That they'd separated. It was way too personal to go
nto the details in the leisure centre car park.

Suddenly Teresa's arms were around Joanna's shoulders,
mbracing her in a heartfelt hug. It felt so good—the unconditional hug of an old friend.

At the beginning, Joanna hadn't intentionally avoided the
riends she'd made through play group, then pre-school and
school. There hadn't seemed to be common ground any more.
t had been a time when she definitely couldn't have coped
with the well-meaning gestures of a group of mothers where
he glue of their friendship was their children. It had been
partly her fault. She'd shrugged off the phone calls and oc-
asional visits with the often brusque explanation that she
was coping as best she could, in her own way, and she didn't
need their help. After a few months they'd given up trying
o contact her.

At the time she'd wondered why Teresa hadn't got in touch.

Teresa dropped her hands and took a step back. Joanna
was suddenly aware of the chill of the night air and shivered.
Her companion noticed.

'Hey, let's go inside and then we can chat.'

Joanna felt oddly off balance as she obediently followed
Teresa through the car park to the entry of the large public
eisure centre and the pool area beyond. Her friend chatted
continuously, asking questions and not seeming to require
answers, but it had the effect of distracting Joanna from her

own demons, which had come close to sending her runnin home with her tail between her legs.

'Shall we go out to the play pools where the kids are?' Sh smiled. 'Or are you seriously into fitness?'

'I have to admit I haven't been here since…' Somehow sh couldn't finish the sentence with the painful truth. Teres paused and sensed her discomfort.

'Oh, I'm so sorry,' she said quietly. 'Of course, I shoul have kept my big mouth shut. How could I have been so in sensitive?'

In all the years Jo had known Teresa, she had never see her blush, but her cheeks were glowing crimson now. In roundabout way, her friend's discomfort helped Joanna re gain her own composure.

'There's no need to apologise. In fact, I'm glad we bumpe into each other. I was close to chickening out and going home

They'd reached the noisy area where twenty or so smal children were competing with each other to see who coul make the most noise. Interspersed were a half a dozen super vising adults, including Teresa's husband. He was a big, hir sute man with Mediterranean features and a face that seeme to naturally accommodate a permanent grin. When he spotte his wife he hitched a small boy of about two or three year old onto his hip and waved, gesturing with his free hand i a form of sign language that Teresa seemed to understan perfectly.

She glanced at Joanna.

'He wants me to take over with the littlies. Vince has tim trials in ten minutes and Rick wants to watch.'

'Vince?'

Teresa pointed to a sullen adolescent sitting on the edge o the 'big kids'' pool, making no attempt to disguise his preoc cupation with two giggling teenage girls.

'I know. It's hard to believe he turned twelve last birthday and started high school this year.' She took a sighing breath. 'And of course our youngest was born…er—'

'That's right, you'd just found out you were pregnant—'

'And I'd vowed to stop at three. I blamed Rick for not having the snip.'

Joanna laughed. It was just like old times. But before she had a chance to get maudlin, Teresa began peeling off her clothes. She hesitated a moment, as if she was gauging Joanna's mood, then she broke into a grin as broad as her husband's.

'Last one in's a rotten tomato.'

It didn't take Joanna long to be swept up in the moment and she wondered why she hadn't had the courage to venture to the pool before today. The combination of water, happy, energetic children and lots of noise was a potent enough antidote to the blues to be packaged and sold. She whipped off her shirt, stumbled out of her shorts and, ignoring her friend, plunged into the shallow water. It was truly therapeutic. When she surfaced for air she suddenly found herself in possession of a small child thrust at her by a large man who was making a hasty retreat. Teresa splashed up to her.

'Rick must remember you too.'

'He hasn't changed.'

'Hasn't he? He frets about losing his hair and finding a belly, like most men his age.'

The squirming child was trying to jump out of Joanna's arms onto a large, inflatable floating island. She let him go but before she could take a breath he had taken a flying leap back into her arms.

'That's Carlo. The spoilt baby of the family. As you've probably guessed.'

'He's delightful.' Joanna pulled a silly face and the child laughed before leaping from her arms again.

'Mmm… But a handful.' She grinned. 'If you want a break or actually want to seriously swim, just say the word.'

'I'm fine.' In fact, she hadn't enjoyed herself so much in longer than she could remember and spent the next twenty minutes doing a workout more strenuous than the most vigorous aqua-aerobics class.

Finally Teresa indicated she'd had enough. She glanced at the large clock suspended from the wall.

'I promised I'd watch at least part of Vince's trials and Angie is trying out for the intermediate squad so I might have to leave you to it.' She hesitated. 'Unless you want to come and watch too.'

Joanna was grateful Teresa had the sensitivity to realise she needed a little more time to be able to revisit an activity that she'd never done alone. Watching the Seals was part of her old life, a life that had included Sam and Richard. She vowed she would do it, but not tonight.

'No, thanks. But I hope to come back regularly.'

'Great, we'll look forward to seeing you.'

Joanna watched Teresa gather up the younger two of her brood and corral them into the supervised play area near the kiosk. She sighed and suddenly felt exhausted as she paddled to the side of the pool. It was definitely time to go home.

She glanced across to the adult pool, and noted how busy it was. Maybe next time she'd come straight from work or possibly on her days off and do some laps.

Then she saw him, hoisting himself out of the pool. The most obvious thing about him was his creamy white skin; skin that hadn't been exposed to the boundless Australian summer sun. But he had the same muscular torso, the same firm thighs, the same broad swimmer's shoulders, glistening and rippling. The sight of him, as close to naked as she was likely to see him, took her breath away.

She felt her own near-naked body react with alarming speed and intensity.

He still had the ability to do that to her!

She looked for a means of escape because he mustn't see her like this.

But she was too late.

He was looking directly at her and had an expression on his face that mirrored exactly how she felt. Uncomfortable was putting it mildly.

And now he was walking towards her.

'Joanna!' Richard was smiling but Joanna could tell it was forced. 'Fancy seeing you here. What an amazing coincidence.'

He seemed to be waiting for a reply but she could think of nothing to say. Her thoughts had suddenly entered lockdown mode but her silence didn't put him off.

'I suppose you come here often?'

He was standing uncomfortably close to her. Aware of every gleaming muscle of his body, it took a supreme effort to stop taking in its glory with a full body appraisal. She concentrated on fixing her eyes above shoulder level.

'No, it's the first time…' The words stuck in her throat for the second time that evening and she couldn't bring herself to finish the sentence. The look in his eyes softened. She wished he wasn't so finely tuned in to her emotions.

'I know,' he said. 'Seeing all these kids, the Seals—' As if on cue he was interrupted by a loud whistle coming from where she assumed training of the aspiring young competitors was taking place.

Joanna self-consciously shifted from one foot to the other not quite knowing how to extricate herself from an extremely uncomfortable situation. She was still in her costume and was aware the flimsy, time-worn Lycra did little to conceal every bump and bulge of her out-of-shape body. She wanted to get to the showers, change and go home. She cleared her throat before voicing her thoughts.

'I'm heading off to change and then going home,' she said.

He reached out to touch her arm, probably merely a gesture of friendship or uncomplicated comfort, but she pulled away.

'Can I buy you a cup of tea before you go? Or a cappuccino, if you'd prefer? I noticed the coffee shop on the mezzanine next to the gym is still there and they used to do a reasonable brew.'

His expression was a cross between little-boy pleading and fully-grown-man insistence and she couldn't think of any reasonable excuse to refuse. The thought of a lovely strong cup of tea had its attraction too.

'Okay, but I'm on an early tomorrow and I was hoping to get away soon.'

The twinkle in his lively blue eyes lasted a short second but there was no mistaking what he was thinking. She knew he was a gentleman and wouldn't act on his thoughts. Most women wouldn't have even noticed but she was so tuned to his body language, even now, after more than three years. Joanna took her towel from her shoulders and fixed it around her waist.

'Great. My things are over there on the seat. I won't be a minute.'

She stood at the side of the pool and watched him walk over to the benches. His trunks were still wet and clung to his perfect buttocks like a second skin. An image of a similar front-on view flashed into her mind. To her bewilderment, heat suffused her face and her body responded in a way that brought back downright sexy memories of a time in her life she'd believed she would never revisit. She was definitely glad Richard had his back to her.

This wasn't supposed to happen.

She was over this man and finally getting a divorce was well overdue. She had nothing to give him. Most of her love had dried up and what she had left she gave to the kids she cared for on Matilda. She knew Richard well enough to realise that children were a very important part of a marriage for him. And she didn't have the physical or emotional strength to go through the traumas of IVF, with no guarantees of success.

She banished any romantic thoughts of her husband from her mind.

'A quick cuppa, inconsequential small talk, and then home,' she muttered, wishing she'd had the assertiveness to say no to Richard's invitation in the first place.

Richard was ambling back looking as relaxed as a med student who'd just finished his final exams. He'd pulled on his T-shirt but it stuck to his damp skin and did little to hide the muscles beneath. She thought of her own exposed state, well aware that unlined wet Lycra probably made her look like she was trying out for a wet T-shirt competition. She doubted Richard would have more than a passing interest in her less than perfect body, though.

As if he was reading her mind, he said, 'If you want to change, I can meet you up at the coffee shop.'

'Yes, good idea,' she said, grateful for the opportunity to have a few minutes on her own in close proximity to a mirror. She cringed at the thought of what she looked like—shorn scalp with a double layer of transparent adhesive dressing pasted onto the back of her head, which was still decorated with a small wound and a large multicoloured bruise; a five-year-old swimsuit that only still fitted her because it had lost much of its elasticity with age; and a body that had folds and bulges she'd rather not think about and had also lost much of its elasticity with age…and pregnancy…and lack of time or motivation to keep in shape.

She had to admit she hadn't paid much attention to her appearance over the past few years—she'd had no need. Her *kids* didn't care what she looked like. They hadn't reached the age where the buzz words when it came to the opposite sex were that looking good was all that mattered. She rarely went out socially and if a male paid any attention to her she always managed to put them off in the first five minutes.

So why was what she looked like suddenly so important?

Of course she knew the answer.

She didn't want Richard to think she'd let herself go. Being attractive for *him* was suddenly taking on an importance that made her feel anxious and she certainly didn't need any more stress in her life.

Get a grip of yourself.

She was above all that flirty, sexy, look-at-me stuff that some women seemed to make a vocation of. If it mattered to Richard what she looked like, which she doubted, then he'd changed and it was another reason to get the divorce through as soon as they could.

When she reached the change rooms she untucked her towel from around her waist, dried herself and slipped off her bathers, deciding to leave her shower until she got home. She took care not to look in the direction of the mirrors, which seemed to have multiplied since she'd entered the room. She slipped on her knickers, shorts and T-shirt and finally glanced at the mirror as she attempted to finger-comb her hair.

Whoops!

What hair? She still hadn't gotten used to the bald look. She took the opportunity to do a full body assessment and decided she had definitely had bad hair days when she'd looked a lot worse.

Taking a deep breath, she gathered her things and headed off to the coffee shop to find Richard.

Richard decided if he couldn't avoid seeing Joanna, he'd make the most of their meeting. A cup of tea had seemed a good idea at the time. Neutral territory, the distraction of others as insurance against awkwardness, a view of the pool area.

His gaze settled on the splashing, yelling, exuberant clump of children in the water.

Happy children.

Healthy children.

Children who had their whole lives ahead of them.

He thought he'd prepared himself for the inevitable memories but the heart-rending emotion he felt took him by surprise. Maybe seeing all the kids either playing or seriously swimming wasn't such a good idea. He'd just have to wait and see.

He found a table that wasn't right on the edge of the mezzanine floor but close enough to get a good view of the pools. His attention drifted to the play pool and he recalled the many evenings he'd spent with Sam and Joanna. Sometimes, like now, he'd been content to just sit and watch the antics of the children and their parents. The youngsters were usually accompanying older sibs who were having more formal lessons and the thing he loved so much about watching them was their lack of inhibition. They were exuberantly happy most of the time but occasionally there'd be a disagreement about someone going ahead of their turn on the slide, or pinching another kid's beach ball. Simple things that usually resulted in all hell letting loose.

But, at times, the parents were even more entertaining.

Over the years of taking Sam to the pool and the beach he'd worked out there were three broad groups of parents. First there were the blustery, sergeant-major types—shouting orders no one took any notice of, trying to organise team games that were totally inappropriate for pre-school-aged children, and when the screaming started the aim of this type of parent was to yell at least twice as loud as the child or children to drown them out. Usually the pool attendant had to intervene by asking the parent to leave.

Second was the I-don't-want-to-be-here parent. They would sit on the benches, reading magazines, occasionally glancing up to make sure their child hadn't drowned but otherwise leaving the hapless youngster to their own devices. The poor kid was usually decked out in such an elaborate array of floating devices that he or she could hardly move, let alone protest, and if the child became involved in a mêlée the parent would intentionally ignore the fact their son or daughter was involved and leave someone else to sort it out.

And the third type of parent was…Joanna. Well, she was a perfect example. She came into the pool with a smile on her face that said she was glad to be alive and even more overjoyed to have a beautiful, happy, healthy child to share that joy. She was capable of totally shedding her inhibitions and *playing*, in the fullest sense of the word. That meant blowing disgustingly loud raspberries, splashing great spurts of water, not only at the kids but at often bewildered parents, throwing children high in the air, sorting out disagreements by distractions that always left both the aggressors and victims laughing.

He'd seen that natural love of the simple things in life when he'd observed Joanna playing with the toddlers on Matilda Ward. It cut a hole in his heart. Why had someone who loved children so much, who had such a natural affinity for nurturing and mothering, been deprived so cruelly?

He had spent many hours ruminating over this question during the course of Sam's illness but he still hadn't come up with an answer.

It was meant to be?

Every cloud has a silver lining?

What goes around comes around?

All glib clichés that lost their relevance in the brutal reality of life, he thought.

Joanna…

He watched her climb the stairs and wondered if he was falling in love with her all over again, for different, more enduring reasons.

There was no doubt she was still the full package in the looks department. He loved her new curves that she'd displayed so tantalisingly in that gorgeous almost see-through costume. The naked-but-not-quite-naked look had blood coursing through his veins at a speed he definitely wasn't used to. And not only was her body different but she was happy again.

She'd been stick thin and gaunt when he'd left to go overseas and she'd rarely smiled. Her GP had diagnosed depression and done all the right things. Referred her for grief counselling, suggested a support group and prescribed an antidepressant. But she'd not followed through with his recommendations and said she would get through in her own way and her own time. He'd felt so guilty when he'd left but Joanna had made it quite clear that his presence in her life was making her recovery more difficult. Her telling him that, over and over, had been like a series of body blows but it had probably been her way of trying to spare him the pain of experiencing her suffering.

No wonder she didn't want to get close to him again.

Her new life seemed to have left the past where it belonged. And good for her.

But—there was no other way of saying it—his heart still ached for her and he still wanted to be the one to be there for her, her significant other.

She stood at the top of the stairs, gazing around the shop, looking for him.

He waved and she manoeuvred her way through the scattered tables to where he sat.

'Hi, sit down. I haven't ordered yet. What would you like?'

'A white tea, thanks.'

'That's all? Nothing to eat?'

'No, thanks, just the tea.'

They were carrying on a conversation like wary strangers. Richard got up to get the drinks and came back with a packet of sandwiches and Joanna's favourite chocolate bar. He smiled sheepishly, expecting to be reprimanded.

'They had a special on chocolate and I thought we deserved an indulgence as a reward for our hard work in the pool.'

It was worth the risk—she actually rewarded him for his humour with a smile.

'I don't know whether I deserve any. I spent the best part of an hour playing with Teresa Deleo's youngest. Do you remember the Deleos?'

'How could I forget? If you dared to cheer louder than—was his name Rick?' Joanna nodded. 'For a child that wasn't his you'd risk life and limb.'

Joanna laughed and it was like the winter sun emerging from behind a dark cloud and lighting up the whole world with happiness. For a moment he was lost for words and just wanted to soak in the warmth of her.

'That's right. Do you remember Teresa was pregnant?'

'Not really. Men don't take much notice. That's my excuse, anyway.'

'You're forgiven. She was only a couple of months, I think. Their fourth. Little Carlo, the baby I had the pleasure of borrowing to play with, well, he's the result.'

Richard looked at Joanna for a moment, trying to gauge if there were any regrets, any resentment that she didn't have a child of her own. For a change, her face was open and easy to read. She had enjoyed her time with her friend's child and unless she hid it well, she had no bad feelings.

'You probably had a harder workout than me. You definitely deserve chocolate.'

She took the offered chocolate and carefully unwrapped it to expose a couple of triangles, which she snapped off, offering one to him.

'No, thanks, I'll start on the sandwiches.'

For some reason he expected she'd refuse the food and he interpreted her acceptance as a symbol of her acceptance of him. Not as a husband or potential lover but someone she was comfortable sitting with in a coffee shop, simply sharing a hot drink.

It was a start, if only a small step, and would make their work together easier.

He opened the sandwiches and offered the package to her but she shook her head, already sucking the chocolate, making it last as she always had.

They ate and drank in silence for a couple of minutes. Richard wanted to ask her so many questions, personal questions like what had finally brought her out of her depression? Had it been a difficult decision to embark on nursing children with cancer? How did she cope on her own? Did she still sing? *Had she had any lovers?*

But it was too soon and she would probably think it was

none of his business, so instead they talked about work and a little about his trip overseas and nothing about what really mattered. There was a film of tension hanging between them that they were both trying their hardest to pretend didn't exist.

When they finished it was close to nine-thirty, half an hour before the centre's closing time, and the staff of the coffee shop made it clear they were keen for their remaining customers to leave so they could get on with the cleaning up.

'Do you want a lift home?' Richard offered. He didn't know if she had a car.

'No, thanks, I've brought my car.'

'I'll walk you out to the car park, then.'

She shrugged as if she didn't have the energy to resist and he followed her down the stairs. They walked past the main pool in silence. The Seal Squad had disbanded and gone home and there were only a few stragglers in the play pool—certainly no sign of the Deleos, to Richard's relief.

'You don't have to walk me to the car,' Joanna said when they reached the foyer. 'It's just over there.'

He looked in the direction she was pointing and squinted at the few vehicles remaining in the car park.

'The truck or the hatchback? My guess is the truck.'

She laughed. 'Guess again.'

'Well, if it's the hatchback, it looks suspiciously like a limited model. Never mind the gentlemanly valour, my motive is to check out your wheels.'

She'd replaced the large family wagon she'd had when he'd left. The smaller car would be much more practical and the small but sporty model suited her perfectly. To his relief she didn't protest when he began to walk with her towards her car and when they got there she turned and hesitated.

'I'm glad I came tonight,' she said in a voice that trembled slightly.

'So am I. Maybe it's something we can do again?'

'Maybe.'

It was a *maybe* smile that hinted at possibilities, combined with the old sparkle in her eyes that he remembered so well, that suggested… He couldn't resist. He'd just have to find out.

He touched her lips with his fingertips—simply to give her the opportunity to refuse—before he kissed her.

But she didn't refuse.

The taste of her lips was a tantalising rediscovery of a sweet and tender place he'd thought he'd never experience again. Her skin was soft as fine oriental silk, her breath warm and laced with the slight scent of chocolate and Earl Grey tea. She exuded sensuality from every pore and he was certain she knew what effect she was having on his self-control. He couldn't stop.

He nibbled her lower lip and then teased her perfect teeth with his tongue until she opened up to him.

Her eyes were seductively closed and the corner of her left upper lid twitched slightly. She held her breath while he deepened his kiss and their bodies pressed so close, Richard could feel the fluttering of her heart and the faintest whole-body tremble that set his own muscles into a state of tension that could only be relieved in one way. His hands moved slickly down from to her shoulders to her back and then to her softly rounded buttocks.

He wanted her so much but he felt her tense as if she'd read his mind. Her eyes snapped open to reveal a dark, agitated sea of uncertainty. She pulled away and took a sharp breath.

'I can't do this, Richard. I'm sorry but you shouldn't even expect me to try. There's too much at stake. You don't know me any more. I don't know you…'

She fumbled for her keys and opened her car door.

'I...I shouldn't have...' Richard couldn't find the words to express how he felt.

Already in the driver's seat, Joanna looked close to tears and he couldn't think of anything he could do or say to reassure her, to explain his impulsive actions.

'Neither should I. Goodbye, Richard.' Her voice was now as hard as steel, emotionless, painfully like the many times when she'd closed off the part of herself he'd so much wanted to reach, to comfort, to *heal*.

She was right. It had been a mistake.

'Goodbye Jo,' he whispered, but she already had the engine running and, with a squeal of rubber on bitumen, drove away into the night.

CHAPTER SIX

OVER the next week both Joanna and Richard made a very good job of ignoring what had happened in the car park of the local leisure centre on Monday night. No one would ever suspect there was anything more to their relationship than that between consultant and dedicated nurse. When Friday came, Richard bowed out of band practice and was glad he was on call the whole weekend. Fortunately he had enough to keep him busy to take his mind off thinking about his wife, who he understood was about to start working nights the following Wednesday after two days off. Though he'd miss her on the ward they wouldn't have to keep up the pretence that their relationship was purely a professional one.

The fortnightly multi-disciplinary team meeting finished at about eleven and when Richard came into the ward, he didn't expect to see Joanna. It was her day off. She was in the chemo suite with Danny Sims and his father, Lynne, Tracey, Kerry, half a dozen kids who were well enough to move from their beds and a very tall young man Richard didn't recognise—who seemed to be the centre of their adoring attention. Richard poked his head in the door to say hello before he began his official rounds. He was curious to know what was going on.

'Hi, Danny.' He acknowledged the boy who was having

his second chemo session and looked remarkably relaxed and comfortable, considering the high doses of medication being delivered.

'Hi, Doc Howell.' He raised his hand in greeting and smiled as if it was his lucky day. 'You'll never guess who's here.'

'Someone pretty special?' Richard said. The boy's delight was written all over his face.

Danny chuckled. 'You're not wrong.'

The towering young visitor turned and grinned. He was wearing a polo shirt with the state basketball team logo on the pocket but Richard had no clue as to his identity. He didn't follow the sport and the fact that he'd been away meant he'd lost touch with a lot of the local news.

'Hi, I'm Bobby Masters.' He paused as if waiting for signs of recognition.

Richard offered his hand and Bobby shook it vigorously. 'I'm Dr Howell, Danny's doctor.'

The excited chatter that had filled the room a few moments ago suddenly stilled as if waiting for Richard's acknowledgement of the obvious celebrity status of Bobby Masters. Richard wondered if he should admit he had no idea who he was or alternatively make a polite excuse and leave. He was rescued from his dilemma by Joanna, who was smiling broadly. She reached for Danny's hand and gave it a squeeze.

'It's not every day you get to meet the captain of the Western Slammers, let alone be presented with a team jersey signed by all the players in last year's premiership side.'

The uninhibited rapture on Danny's face was impossible to ignore and his joy was contagious. He held up the basketball uniform covered in signatures and a photograph of Bobby, also signed.

'Wow, I'm impressed.' Though he didn't share the boy's obvious love of the sport, Richard *was* genuinely impressed.

'It's a privilege to meet you Bobby. And you've undoubtedly made young Danny's day,' Richard added, directing his comments to the basketball player.

'I reckon he deserves a bit of special attention.' Bobby then glanced at Joanna with a mix of admiration and youthful respect. 'But it wouldn't have happened without Joanna's…er… Well, let's say she can be extremely persuasive. She organised the whole thing.'

Joanna laughed. 'Just doing my job.'

At that moment a photographer appeared in the doorway and Richard took the opportunity to make his excuses and leave.

'I have to go now, Danny, but I'll see you later to check how you're going.'

'Thanks, Dr Howell.' It was Danny's father who spoke. 'Thanks for everything.' He shifted his gaze to Joanna and looked on the verge of tears.

Richard nodded and slipped quietly out of the room.

Half an hour later he bumped into Joanna coming from the direction of the chemo suite, which was now quiet. The photo session had finished and the celebrity guest appeared to have left.

'You knew this was happening?' He directed his question to Joanna.

Danny's father popped his head out of the parents' room with a bottle of juice in his hand.

'I heard a rumour she organised the whole thing,' Danny's father said, with a broad grin, rivalling his son's recent rapt expression.

'Really?'

Joanna seemed to have an endless supply of generosity

and goodwill when it came to looking after her young patients, which extended beyond her usual working hours. She answered him with a wink, not appearing to want any recognition or praise.

For the rest of the week he missed having her around on the ward and it was obvious other staff did as well without actually saying so. He'd hear them talk about her and leave messages in the notes for the night staff that were obviously meant for Joanna.

If he was early enough to catch her before her shift finished he found himself confiding in her about the day-to-day events on the ward. She missed a lot of the bread-and-butter happenings that were taken for granted by the staff working day shifts and seemed to relish information about things like how Rebecca's dance classes were going or what Liam's reaction was to having his whole year-two class come in for his birthday party.

There weren't enough hours in the day, Richard mused, and the thought occurred to him that the time he valued the most was the time he spent with Joanna.

'Come in, Richard. It's great to see you again. I heard you were coming back to our fair city but I wasn't sure when.' Adam Segal extended his lightly tanned, freshly manicured hand in greeting.

Richard hadn't been able to find any credible reason to procrastinate in initiating divorce proceedings and had made the appointment with his solicitor for late afternoon on his one half-day off for the week. It didn't seem right, though, and more than once he'd considered cancelling the appointment and came close to missing it that afternoon.

He arrived just in time.

Though he considered himself an optimist, on days like

today he believed there was a lot of truth in Murphy's Law. He'd predictably got caught up with work, having to deal with Liz and Phillip Bryant whose two-year-old daughter had finally been scheduled for surgery. She was to have the tumour, which was rapidly filling her abdominal cavity, removed the following day and he'd ordered a transfusion to boost her low red cells prior to her operation. Unfortunately she'd had a rare, unexpected reaction to the blood and had slipped into severe respiratory distress.

The crisis had been treated and her condition stabilised in the few short hours after her transfer to the intensive care unit but the drama had tipped the balance of Liz Bryant's already fragile mental state into what could be loosely described as borderline hysteria. He'd managed to calm her down but it had taken up most of his afternoon and the last thing he felt like doing was starting the onerous process of filing for divorce.

But it had to be done.

It wasn't fair on Joanna to delay any longer. She'd worked so hard to make a new life, she deserved to be free.

'Hello, Adam. It's good to see you again too.'

'Come through into my office.'

Richard followed the solicitor down a short corridor and into a spacious, tastefully decorated room with a huge window looking out on the Swan River.

Richard sat down on a leather-upholstered club chair while Adam Segal settled behind a highly polished, antique oak desk. He opened his laptop, pressed a few keys and then focused his attention on his client.

'So what brings you here? What can I do for you?'

Richard realised the best thing to do was get straight to the point.

'I want to divorce Jo.'

The elevation of the lawyer's brows was so slight Richard wondered if he'd imagined it, but realised it was part of the man's job to have the ability to turn body language on and off at will. He wrote something down in a ring-bound file and then looked up with the hint of a sympathetic smile on his face.

'You know my area of expertise is company law and financial advice, not family law.'

'Yes. I'm aware of that but I'd prefer if you could handle it.'

He'd known Adam for many years. They'd gone to uni together and Adam had met Joanna socially several times. He knew that shouldn't make any difference, but it did. It somehow made what he imagined would be a brutally impersonal procedure a little more tolerable.

'Mmm…' Adam rubbed his clean-shaven chin thoughtfully. 'I'd be happy to guide you through the process if it's clear cut. Are there any possible complications? Custody issues? Property issues where there might be some dispute?'

'No. No children and we sold the house not long after I left for the U.K. Joanna has her own, smaller home now and I agreed that she could do whatever she wanted with the proceeds of the sale of the Barclay Street place.'

The eyebrows definitely went up this time.

'Generous,' he said, and wrote some more in his file. 'As this is obviously all new to you I'll give you the family court booklet to read and the application papers. When you've been through those I'll see you again and we can complete the application and organise to serve the notice on your wife. After that it's relatively simple.'

Adam picked up the phone and pressed one of the buttons.

'Could you ask Marie if she can get me the divorce application paperwork and then bring it in?' He looked up apologetically. 'You understand this isn't my usual field.'

Richard felt a little guilty but then remembered his friend had never been shy of charging hefty fees.

'Thanks, Adam, I appreciate it.'

The meeting was effectively wound up when the receptionist, who had taken his details when he'd arrived, came in with a folder. The lawyer handed them over after doing a quick check of the contents.

'Perhaps you could make an appointment in about a week.' He hesitated. 'And I'm so sorry to hear about you and Joanna.'

I'm sorry too, Richard thought as he stood up and shook his friend's hand.

'I'll make an appointment when I check my schedule for next week.'

When Richard arrived home, he felt exhausted. He discarded the folder Adam had given him, vowing he would go through it on the weekend and make another appointment after that, without delay. He had the feeling the longer he postponed the process of actually signing the papers that finally struck the death knell for his marriage, the less likely he would go through with it.

But it was what Joanna wanted. She'd made that perfectly clear and he had no valid reason to persuade her to try again… other than that he still loved her. He knew that for certain now. Yes, she'd changed and she'd made a new life for herself but, in a peculiar way, her newfound independence endeared her to him even more. Any doubts he'd had while he'd been overseas had vanished after the first conversation they'd had together. The problem was, he could never tell her because she didn't need the added complication of dealing with his futile emotions.

The rest of the evening dragged painfully slowly and when he was just about to go to bed his phone rang. He glanced at the small screen on his cellphone and recognised the number of Lady Lawler.

'Hello, Richard Howell,' he said, now fully alert and wondering why the hospital was contacting him. He wasn't on call.

'Hi, Dr Howell. It's Barbara, charge nurse on Matilda Ward. I hope you don't mind me ringing.'

'Of course not. A problem with one of our patients?'

'Er...' The nurse hesitated and then cleared her throat. 'Not exactly. I just wanted to have a quick word with you about Joanna Raven.'

'Joanna?' His heart rate quickened and he swallowed the lump that had suddenly formed in his throat. Why on earth would she want to talk to him about Jo? At ten-thirty at night. Had something happened to her?

'Yes. I may be concerned unnecessarily but she spent over an hour this evening talking to Danny Sims's mother on the phone. When she finally finished, Jo seemed close to tears and without any explanation she took off for about fifteen minutes. She's never done anything like that before and if I stuck strictly to staff protocols I should report the incident to the director of nursing.'

'That seems harsh.'

'I know, and when she came back she was fine, perfectly composed. I just thought you should know and maybe have a word with her, if you have a moment. You've spent a lot of time with the Sims family and know them better than anyone. You and Jo seem to get on really well together as well. I know she holds you in high regard. She refused to admit anything was wrong to me. Said she just needed to go to the toilet in a hurry, but I've known her long enough to suspect there's more to it than that. In fact, she's been a bit edgy all week.'

'Okay, I'll speak to her tomorrow. Her shift finishes at seven?'

'That's right.'

'So she'll probably want to get some sleep during the day.' Much as he would have liked to jump in his car and drive to the hospital straight away, he realised he was overreacting. He'd try and call her some time during the following afternoon. 'I'll certainly have a quiet word with her tomorrow, if I can.'

'Thanks Dr Howell. I wasn't sure what else to do.'

'You did the right thing to ring me.'

Richard spent a restless night, drifting in and out of sleep in between thinking of Joanna and speculating about what it was concerning the Sims family that had upset her. If it was because Danny had the same tumour that had taken the life of their son he definitely needed to discuss the problem with her on a professional as well as a personal level.

The last time he looked at his bedside clock it was 5:00 a.m. and, after what only seemed like a few moments, the buzz of his alarm jolted him out of his slumbers.

The beginning of another day.

Despite the fact Joanna was so tired she could hardly put one foot in front of the other, she couldn't get to sleep. First, it was an uncomfortably humid day and a lukewarm shower did little to either cool her down or refresh her. Second, she seemed hyper-alert to every sound in her usually quiet neighbourhood that morning. First it was the garbage truck, then a mob of raucous laughing kookaburras and she finally gave up when the noise of chainsaws pruning street trees started at about eight-thirty. And, of course, this was all superimposed on the underlying unsettled feeling she'd had since Jenny Sims had phoned and asked her if she could explain some of the things she and her husband didn't understand about Danny's illness, including his prognosis.

Of course her answer had been that they should discuss any queries they had with the doctor, but then Jenny, with Pete in the background, had launched into a heart-wrenching account of how they blamed themselves for their son's illness. They should have known something was wrong when Danny had developed back pain after the school athletics carnival; they'd ignored the fact that he'd complained of tiredness, thinking it was purely due to a growth spurt and starting at a new school; when he'd seemed to lose his usually voracious appetite they'd assumed he was pigging out on junk food after school. Jenny also felt guilty about commencing full-time work at the beginning of the year when Danny had started high school, and they both believed their GP had waited too long before ordering X-rays.

Joanna had listened with the kind of understanding that came from having been in that same dark whirlpool of guilt, regret and blame. She knew the agony of going over and over in her mind what she hadn't done and not knowing whether it would have made any difference. She'd suffered the despair of a depression she couldn't shake when she'd realised Sam wouldn't survive. And she'd rejected her husband when he had tried so desperately to help her and had probably needed her more than she'd needed him.

Of course, she hadn't voiced any of her thoughts to the Simses but hoped just letting them express their concerns and pointing out they didn't have to shoulder the burden alone would help. They'd thanked her and seemed calmer when she'd hung up but it had taken its toll on her own peace of mind. She'd managed to hold herself together until she finally excused herself and finished the call.

Then she'd had to escape. It had only taken five therapeutic minutes in the nurses' locker room for the tears to wash away at least some of the anguish of her memories. They'd been so vivid. She'd thought time had done its healing work but she'd been wrong. Thankfully she'd had the distraction of work to get her through the long night and she'd managed to fob off Barbara's concerned enquiries about her wellbeing.

She was glad she had the weekend off—her next shift was Monday night—so if she didn't get any sleep that day she could always catch up on her days off.

After a light breakfast, a banana smoothie, and a tidy up of her house she finally drifted off to sleep at about lunchtime. She'd turned her phone off and hung the 'Quiet, Shift Worker Sleeping' sign on her front door and woke six hours later feeling refreshed…and restless. Usually she was quite content with her own company and had got used to living alone, but tonight she felt she needed people around her.

She looked at her watch and it was just after six. She had plenty of time to have a shower, a bite to eat and make it to choir practice with time to spare.

Richard called Joanna's number several times that afternoon but had been diverted to her message bank each time. He'd left several messages for her to contact him but, at five-thirty in the afternoon, she still hadn't got back to him.

He refused to imagine the worst. She was probably just sleeping. Although it had been a long time in the past, he still recalled how exhausting working nights could be. He made up his mind to call around to see her the following day if she still wasn't answering her phone and decided not to resist James Francis's pleas to make up the numbers at band practice that evening. It would take his mind off Joanna. Or that was the plan.

He drove the short distance to his house, microwaved a plate of yesterday's leftover ravioli and sat in his living room, eating his meal while watching the evening news. When he finished, leaving half the soggy remains of the pasta, he showered and changed into casual clothes, gathered his saxophone case and walked back to the hospital.

When he arrived he was greeted by the dozen or so members of the band as if he was a celebrity and he not only enjoyed playing in the band, but the time passed quickly.

'See you next week,' was the farewell comment from James.

'Yes, I'll try and make it,' he said, being careful not to commit himself. Unexpected demands often came up that he couldn't avoid and he had a clinical heads of department meeting the following Friday afternoon that he'd been told might continue into the early evening.

He strode out of the lecture theatre and set off along the walkway with a much lighter heart than when he'd arrived. Deep in thought in an endeavour to plan the best use of his time off on the weekend, he rounded a corner and nearly collided with…

'Joanna? Is that you?'

The question was redundant. He could easily tell who it was. She was wearing snug-fitting white cropped pants that accentuated the golden colour of her calves, topped by a sleeveless T-shirt with a scoop neck that revealed a glimpse of gorgeous cleavage. A white-peaked, Oliver Twist style cap shaded her eyes from the glow of the lamps that illuminated the path and made it impossible to assess her mood from the expression on her face.

She hesitated as if in some kind of dilemma about how to answer him.

'Are you all right?' he added as she lifted her head. Her eyes connected with his and now he could see she was annoyed.

'Why shouldn't I be?' Her tone wasn't exactly hostile but she obviously wasn't pleased to see him.

'Er…' How could he tactfully broach the fact that Barbara had been worried about her and asked him if he would follow up her concerns? Maybe the best tactic would be the truth. He'd never been good at hedging around issues. 'I wanted to talk to you, and planned to call around and see you tomorrow.'

Her eyes narrowed.

'About the divorce?'

In all honesty he'd managed to put all thoughts of the divorce to the back of his mind and hadn't yet made a follow-up appointment to see his lawyer friend.

'No, something else.' The static weight of his saxophone case was beginning to make his arm ache so he placed it on the paving between his feet. The diversion also served the purpose of giving him another couple of moments to decide what he was going to say. A young couple with a small child in tow walked past and looked at them curiously. It wasn't the best place for a gently probing conversation about issues that were close to both their hearts.

'It's a delicate matter,' he continued. 'And maybe we could go somewhere more private.'

Her brow furrowed in a frown.

'Where?'

'Are you walking?'

'Yes.'

'Can I walk with you? My place is in the same direction and maybe—'

'Okay. I'd rather we go back to *my* place, have a cuppa, if it's so important—this delicate matter.'

Richard sighed with relief. He'd been expecting the third degree.

'Yes. That would be perfect. It shouldn't take long. When's your next shift at the hospital?'

'I have the weekend and go back Monday night. I'll probably be awake most of the night because I slept this afternoon. That's the trouble with working nights, you have a couple of days off to get back into your normal diurnal rhythm and then it starts all over again.'

They talked little on the brief walk to Joanna's and the limited conversation they had was superficial small talk. Richard recognised the house at the front of the block and followed Joanna to her place at the back. She opened the sliding door and Richard followed her inside.

'Sit down,' she said, as if she were about to entertain the tax inspector.

He sat on the sofa and watched her walk into the kitchen. Yes, she looked decidedly uncomfortable, which was the last thing he wanted.

'How was choir practice?' The question was merely an extension of the conversation they'd started on the walk home when he'd rambled on about the band and the pieces they were rehearsing. It had simply been a strategy to break the silence.

'Okay.' She turned her back on him and reached up to a cupboard where several mugs were stacked. 'Someone suggested we could look into seeing if any of the kids wanted to be involved.'

'You mean patients?'

She turned to face him. 'And possibly members of their families or friends as well.'

He took a moment to process what she had just told him. Definitely a good idea from the viewpoint of morale but the practicalities of getting a group of sick and injured children together and transporting them to the town hall, the venue that had been booked for the concert, would make the project difficult to say the least.

'How would—?'

Joanna smiled. 'I know what you're going to say. The physical restraints imposed by half the performers being in wheelchairs or hospital beds or hooked up to IVs and various monitors would make a concert in the normal sense impossible.'

She had his curiosity aroused.

'Tea or coffee?' she asked as she turned off the bubbling kettle.

'Tea, thanks.'

She poured the drinks and brought them over to the low table near where he sat. Also on the tray was a small plate of home-made coconut slice, one of his favourites. He thought how touching it would be if Jo had made them especially for him, but of course she'd had no idea he was going to visit. As if reading his mind, she picked up the plate and offered him a piece. He took a bite.

'This is even better than I remember.'

Removing the tea bag, she stirred milk into her tea.

'It's probably my downfall. I still love baking.' She cast her eyes downwards. 'Although it's not the same…' Her voice trailed off.

'Delicious,' he said. 'I'm glad you still like to cook.'

He suddenly realised what a tactless thing that had been to say. He leaving her was no reason to stop cooking the things he'd always liked. In fact, talking to Joanna felt like walking on thin ice. He had no idea where the fragile areas lay and certainly didn't want a dunking. How much of the past was out of bounds?

'What were you saying about the concert?' Talking about the present was a much safer bet.

She leaned back in her chair and rested her tea on her knee, taking a measured breath.

'Well, if you're really interested…'

'I am. After all, I've been persuaded to perform so my reputation's at stake.'

She smiled. Richard was relieved she still showed traces of the sense of humour that he'd thought she'd lost.

'One of the nurses on General Surgical—I don't think you know her, Lorraine Henderson…' He shook his head and she continued. 'Her husband is a professional video photographer, does wedding DVDs and the like.' She took another breath and it was evident by the look on her face she was discussing the beginnings of an idea she was already passionate about. He let her go on without interruption. 'To cut a long story short, the whole concept is to create a movie of the kids without having to necessarily move them from their beds, let alone the hospital.'

She was beaming now, expectantly waiting for his comment. He certainly didn't want to put a damper on the suggestion before it had gone past the planning stage but he had his doubts.

'Sounds fabulous. Definitely original.' He hesitated a moment. 'Have you got a big enough pool of talent?'

Her eyes narrowed. She'd undoubtedly interpreted his comment as criticism rather than simple caution.

'You don't think it would work,' she said flatly. All her previous enthusiasm vanished.

'I didn't say that.'

She took another mouthful of tea and brushed some coconut off the table.

'Have another.' She offered him the plate again.

'No, thanks.'

The both sipped their drinks and it suddenly seemed the most difficult task in the world to broach the subject of her talk with Danny Sims's parents. Maybe he would leave it to another day but Joanna solved the dilemma for him.

'So what was so important you'd planned to visit me on my day off to discuss it?'

Right. *She'd* brought up the subject. And it needed to be discussed. He owed it to Barbara to at least try to find out what the problem had been.

'Barbara asked me to talk to you.'

She put her cup on the table and crossed her arms across her chest. He took it as a defensive gesture.

'Barbara? I don't understand. Why would Barb—?'

'She was worried about you.' He leaned across and put his hand on hers, relieved she didn't pull away.

'Worried about what?' He imagined the cogs of her brain turning but he had the feeling she knew what he was talking about.

'She said you were upset last night after talking to the Simses. I can guess at why—'

'You didn't tell her?' Joanna cut in sharply, and Richard felt her tension increase.

'You mean about us and Sam? Of course I didn't. That's our own private business.'

'Yes.' Her eyes connected with his and the look she conveyed was one of understanding, of the bond of a shared past.

'What did Jenny and Pete want to talk about?'

Joanna withdrew her hand and edged away from him. He

didn't want her to reject him and he felt partly responsible for any distress she was experiencing. Coming back and opening a window to a time that had been so traumatic for both of them wasn't something he'd planned.

She attempted a smile but it was unconvincing.

'They were suffering from information overload and started asking questions like "What are Danny's chances of pulling through? Will he suffer? What is the success rate of the treatment?"' She sighed. 'All things I'm sure you've told them already but they didn't want to believe the odds are so heavily stacked against their son.'

'And what did you tell them?'

'It's not my role to spout cold statistics. I told them to ask you.' She paused. 'I said you were a wonderful doctor...' she flushed and looked away '...and not to be worried about talking through things with you, no matter how long it takes.'

'And?' He wouldn't let her stop there. Her lower lip began to tremble.

'I said they're going through exactly the same emotions as just about every other parent of a child who is diagnosed with cancer.'

Richard knew there was more. He hadn't lived with and loved Joanna for over seven years without being able to tune in to her emotions. He didn't want to push her, though. So he waited for her to decide whether she would reveal that little extra. She looked up and her pupils dilated. A single tear escaped and coursed down her cheek. She sniffed.

'They wanted to know if I'd nursed any patients with Ewing's before or if Danny was the first.' Her tormented gaze was again fixed on his as if continuing the conversation was a challenge for her. The look in her eyes said she was determined not to break down. Why? Richard wondered. During the good times they'd had together they'd always been honest with each other, always been able to unburden their worries and share the load. He wanted so much for her to share with him now.

On impulse, without a care for the consequences, he moved to sit next to her. Draping his arm across her shoulders and drawing her towards him seemed a natural thing to do. Again she didn't resist and leaned into his embrace.

'What did you tell them?' he whispered as he reached across and began gently stroking her hair. She sighed and stilled his hand by grasping it with both of hers.

'I said Danny was the first. Which wasn't strictly true. I've seen one other case—a boy called Callum—but his tumour was picked up early and he survived. I didn't want to get their hopes up.' She turned her face to him and for the first time since Richard had been back she dropped her protective shield of guarded coolness and let him close to her.

'Danny reminds you of Sam?' Richard said gently.

'Yes, but Sam was our son and there's a world of difference... He was our son.'

He knew what he wanted to say but the words stuck in his throat. He wanted to tell Joanna that the pain of losing Sam was the worst thing he had ever experienced; that he'd hid the sadness and guilt because he'd wanted to be strong for his wife and child; that he'd never been able to share the dark depths of his emotions with anyone, not even her.

'You never cried for him.' Joanna looked away and began running her fingers back and forth along the back of his hand with a restlessness he recognised. She was still hiding something. He stilled her hand.

'I never let anyone *see* me cry.'

'But you were always a tower of strength, never lost control.'

And that was exactly what he had wanted her to believe.

One of them had had to stay at least outwardly strong, and he'd spent years as a doctor fine-tuning the skill of keeping his distance, of not getting emotionally involved. But if he'd known his intentional coolness would drive a wedge between him and his wife, he would have willingly shared the truth of how devastating that time had been for him. He hadn't wanted to be pitied, though. His job, in some ways, had made it worse. He could recite the statistics, he knew the odds, but he'd prayed every day for a miracle. And deep down he'd assumed he'd failed as both a father and a husband and nursed the irrational belief that he had been somehow to blame.

'It was a facade, Joanna. It was the only way I knew to help you through. I thought—'

'Oh, Richard. Why didn't you tell me? I was convinced you'd stopped caring. That you'd fallen out of love with me and I was a burden to you.'

He released her hand and drew her closer. He gently kissed her forehead as relief flooded his senses like the first rains after a brutal and unforgiving drought.

'I still love you, Joanna.' He could see the beginning of tears brimming in her eyes but he'd come this far and had to tell her. 'After I left to go to the U.K. I tried to stop loving you but...' Words suddenly seemed inadequate. He tilted her chin so he was looking straight into the depths of her dark, unfathomable eyes. 'It might sound like a cliché but there is no other way to tell you.' He attempted to swallow the lump in his throat but it stubbornly stayed put and made his voice rough and erratic. 'The years I shared with you and Sam... They were the best of my life.'

She reached up and placed her hands behind his head. Her touch was an exquisitely sensual caress. He wanted to hold her close in his arms, to rock away the years of hurt and misunderstanding. He wanted to kiss her but the most precious thing for him would be the gift of her love. He realised it was asking too much so soon. He imagined she was more confused than him. They had only touched the surface of a past full of misconceptions, misplaced untruths and delusions. Both their lives had changed and they needed to get to know each other all over again.

It was a start.

If Joanna was willing...

'What are you thinking?' she said.

He hesitated but wanted to start afresh and be perfectly honest with her.

'I was thinking how much we've both changed.'

She surprised him with a smile.

'For better or worse?' Joanna asked, but it wasn't a fair question and the answer fitted somewhere in between.

'Neither. Just different.'

'Because it's just you and me? No baby, no child to cement our relationship? You know, for such a long time I thought life would never be normal again. Sam was... Sam was our future...' She took a deep sighing breath. 'He was a gift... and I only had one shot at being a mother. I didn't expect it to be easy but I was prepared to give it my best and I blew it.'

Richard leaned forward and kissed her lightly on the mouth, with what he hoped was tenderness and reassurance. His lips moved to her forehead then her temple. Not only was she attractive on the outside but she had an inner beauty that she guarded like a precious jewel. She had been a wonderful mother and it hurt to hear her say she was to blame.

'You can't mean that.'

'I don't know...no...I didn't mean—' Her eyes were moist and brimming with sadness.

Richard cut short her answer by placing his index finger

on her mouth. He felt responsible for the anguish that accompanied their memories. He saw much more hope and joy in looking forward and he desperately wanted Joanna to be part of his future.

'I'm sorry I've made you unhappy. If there's anything I can do...'

She swallowed. The sadness left her eyes and was replaced by a dogged certainty. She'd made up her mind about something—something that had erased the negativity.

'Stay tonight.' The words were barely a whisper. He wondered if he'd heard correctly and battled to contain his surprise. He'd been expecting a rejection.

'Are you sure?'

'I've got nothing to lose, Richard.'

But he knew, in reality, how much they both could lose. Sleeping with Joanna now was a huge gamble but he didn't know how to say no. He wanted her with a powerful passion he'd thought he'd never feel again. He stood up, reached for Joanna's hand and she led him to the bedroom.

CHAPTER SEVEN

To ask Richard to stay, to share her bed and invite the inevitable consequences, wasn't a snap decision for Joanna. From the day she'd first seen him sitting in the canteen she'd known she still had feelings for him but couldn't even consider acting on them. *She'd* closed herself off from Richard and driven him away three years ago. Even if he forgave her, there was no way things could be the same. A divorce had seemed the logical solution; to cut the one remaining tie they had. She'd worked hard to make a satisfying life that didn't involve Richard. She'd thought his return would bring back the pain of the past. Of course it had, but talking with her husband, the only person who had truly known what her grieving had been like, was a release as well as a comfort.

And she wanted…needed physical comfort, to be cradled in his arms and desired as a sensual, attractive woman. Her mantra echoed in her mind.

I'm a good nurse. I love the children I care for and that's all that matters.

But it wasn't enough, it wasn't all that mattered.

She needed to be loved as well.

Richard had told her he still loved her and she was prepared to take the risk to find out if the sexual spark of their relationship was still alive. The last thing she needed was for

Richard to feel sorry for her. In fact, if he'd refused her invitation, that spark would have been extinguished once and for all.

She had nothing to lose, but so much to gain if…

They reached the bedroom door and hesitated before opening it.

'You're beautiful, Joanna,' Richard whispered as he cradled her face with both hands and leaned towards her.

The gentle, familiar touch of his lips on hers was an exquisite pleasure. He lingered, his mouth moving across her upper lip in tender possession. His eyes were open as he deepened his kiss and Joanna felt a swamping, pulsing heat she hadn't felt for a long time. Her heart quickened. She saw Richard's pupils dilate just before she closed her eyes and melted into his embrace.

'Not here.' Richard's husky voice brought her back to reality.

'No,' she said as he opened the door, but they lingered on the threshold as if unsure whether to take the next, life-changing step.

After only a moment's hesitation he drew her towards him, their arms entwined with every point of contact between their bodies alive with vibrant energy.

Joanna could tell Richard felt it too and they were both powerless to resist.

Her hands shook slightly as she began to explore and rediscover Richard's body and she now realised there was no turning back. The sizzle of sexual tension that they both knew was buzzing between them was like static electricity building up in air heavy with anticipation and humidity before a thunderous summer storm.

Her hands seemed to take on a life of their own but it was her mind that savoured every sensual touch. She dragged her fingers down the roughness of Richard's cheeks and then to his sleek, damp neck. His sweat smelled seductively masculine and she tasted it with the tip of her tongue.

'No,' he groaned, but she knew he meant yes. He guided her towards the bed and she showed no resistance as his hands worked their way under her top and up her back until he found the fastening of her bra. While he skilfully undressed her he sought out her errant tongue and devoured it. As the kiss progressed, Joanna felt she was losing herself in something wonderfully out of her control.

It felt so right and Joanna knew that whatever happened she would have no regrets.

Joanna, naked and aroused, was the most beautiful vision and the most sublime experience Richard had ever known. They had both matured since the frenzied love-making of their courtship and then the exhausting years of parenthood that had followed when sex had slipped close to the bottom of their priority list. It was like discovering each other all over again. He gently ran his finger tips over the mallow-soft skin of her breasts with their delicate web of veins; he yearned for the lush and secret darkness of her and he delighted in the perfect, smooth contours of her buttocks. There was no doubt she had a magnificent body.

But she was much more than skin and flesh and bone.

Up until now she'd kept her inner beauty locked away, showing only glimpses to those she felt needed it most.

Richard felt privileged she'd revealed her true self to him in their exciting and startling love-making.

He hadn't planned it but, as he skimmed his fingers across Joanna's belly and leaned over to kiss her cheek, he knew it was meant to be.

'Are you okay?' he said softly as he clasped her hand and

eased his head back on the pillow. He watched the slow rise and fall of her chest with each breath and marvelled at the perfection of the human form.

The gentle pressure from her hand was answer enough.

'I'm fine. It was good.' She opened her eyes and looked at him. 'Thank you, but you don't have to—'

'Shush.' He placed his fingers on her lips, not wanting to acknowledge that something so precious and uplifting could be transient. More than anything else in the world, he wanted to spend the rest of his days with Joanna.

'Let's think about tomorrow when it comes.'

She closed her eyes and brought his hand up to her lips, kissing his fingertips one by one.

'I don't think it's as easy as that.' She reached for the sheet, pulled it up to her waist and then rolled on her side to face him. She pressed his hand to her breast as if she wanted him to feel her heartbeat, to tune in to her life force.

'It's as easy or as difficult as you want to make it for yourself.' Richard knew from firsthand experience. It had been an agonising decision to leave Joanna but he'd believed it had been the best thing to do for both of them.

'But that's the problem.'

Her eyes were level with his but she was staring past him. She refocused with an intensity that was mesmerising.

'Problem?'

'We're still good together in bed—'

He smiled. 'I couldn't agree more.'

Her face was set and she wasn't in a joking mood so he refrained from saying anything else and waited for her to continue.

'Since you left I've really tried hard to keep my life as simple as I can make it.' She paused as if deciding whether she trusted him enough to go on. 'I've not let anyone get close to me since Sam died and…since you left. It's not worth it, all that heartache.' She took a deep sighing breath. 'I'm so sorry if I led you on, but I needed to know.'

She rolled onto her back again. Richard understood how the intimacy of their physical closeness could make what she was revealing difficult.

'To know?'

'Yes. To know if… How can I explain?'

'There's no need to explain. Me coming back, not knowing what to expect and having to decide whether to finally end our marriage. It must be—'

'Overwhelming. And I need to know that you are prepared to accept me for who I am now. I'm not the girl you married or the mixed-up woman who'd lost a child, a husband and a wonderful life with a future to look forward to—all in one fell swoop.'

She reached for his hand and gripped it with tense fingers.

'I know I said I wanted a divorce but I need time. All I know is that I still have feelings for you but I'm not sure if it could work, after all that's happened. If we try and start over we need to go very slowly.'

He appreciated the implications of what she was saying. And she'd opened herself to him. Given him something she held precious, and he realised he must be careful not to abuse her generosity.

'And you know it's unlikely I can have any more children.'

She said it as a simple statement of fact but he knew the words hung heavy with emotion. If anyone deserved a child—a truckload of children, in fact—it was Joanna.

He reached up and touched her cheek.

She pushed his hand away and folded her arms across her breasts.

'I'm sorry, Richard.'

'No.' He felt like shouting to make it clear to her there was no need to apologise. 'I'm the one who should be apologising.'

'Why?' She turned to face him again but held her body so they weren't touching. 'I have no regrets. About tonight, that is. It was wonderful.' She smiled and her whole face softened like a ripe peach on a warm day. 'Truly wonderful. But I don't want to start something I can't finish. I'm sorry.' She repeated the words softly.

They lay together without speaking for several long minutes.

'It doesn't matter to me whether I father children. It's you I care about.'

She sighed. 'You say that now but I know how much you loved Sam, and that you wanted more children—that I couldn't give you. You're capable of fathering as many as you want, but not with me. And your career choice... To do the job you do, you have to love kids.'

He knew that anything more he said to try and make her realise his life could be complete without children would fall on deaf ears.

'I agree, we both need time,' he said cautiously. 'And, whatever you decide, I'll go along with it. If you want to give it a go and it doesn't work out, then that's okay with me. If you need a few weeks, or months, just to think things through and you decide being married to me is not what you want then I'll go ahead and organise the divorce.' She seemed to be relaxing. He grinned, feeling the unexpected evidence of his physical desire return, and he was sure it hadn't gone unnoticed.

'And if you decided you wanted me to move in tomorrow I'd—'

She rewarded him with a twitch of her lips and a twinkle

n her eye. Her hands caressed, her eyes teased and her body
flushed a deliciously sexy shade of pink.

'Stop, I think you've made yourself perfectly clear,' she
said. 'And I think you're right. I'm not ready to make a decision.' Her hand strayed to below his waist. 'But for now let's
just seize the moment and let tomorrow take care of itself.

Joanna woke on Saturday morning alone and wondered if
the events of the previous night had been a dream. The late
summer sun streamed through her window as she basked in
the heady contentment she'd always felt on the morning after
satisfying love-making. But in the background was disappointment that Richard hadn't stayed. They'd both decided
it was for the best, though. It would give them time to think
things through.

He'd been right in suggesting they didn't rush into anything they'd regret and she certainly had no desire to launch
into something as scary as attempting to take up where they'd
left off. If they were to try to get to know each other again
the process had to be a gradual one.

One careful step at a time.

Although the love-making had been fabulous, better than
she remembered, she was certain that basing a relationship
purely on good sex was asking for failure. She knew the statistics. One in three marriages in Australia ended in divorce.

It was something she didn't want to think about that morning, though. She rolled over, deciding to indulge in the luxury
of staying in bed a little longer on her first day off in over a
week. She was beginning to doze when the phone rang and
jolted her back to full wakefulness. Grabbing her robe, she
hurried into the living room and picked up the handpiece.

'Hello,' she said, half hoping it would be Richard, telling

her he couldn't bear to be away from her, but it was a female voice.

'Hi, it's Lorraine. What are you doing this afternoon?'

A smile spread over Joanna's face. Lorraine Henderson was the sort of person who tackled life head-on and definitely wasn't one to mince words. She'd emailed Joanna a couple o days ago to say she'd received permission from the hospital' medical director to go ahead with her plans to film the children for the concert. Apparently the request had generated the usual hefty volume of paperwork—documents to be prepared explaining the how, why, when and where; consent forms to be filled out by patients' families; permission to be obtained from the senior staff of each ward involved; disclaimers, and so on.… Joanna thought it would take weeks to sort out.

Maybe she had underestimated her friend's ability to move things along. She couldn't think of any other reason Lorraine would ring her at ten o'clock on a Saturday morning.

'Nothing, and I bet I can guess why you're asking. Something to do with the concert?'

Her friend chuckled. 'How did you know?'

'It's consuming all your spare time, isn't it? What's happening today?'

Lorraine paused as if she needed a moment to organise her thoughts.

'Steve's got a free afternoon to give us a hand with the camera work and I've managed to get all the paperwork sorted to start on Matilda Ward.' She paused only long enough to take a breath. 'And since it's your patch, and you seemed pretty keen about the idea, I thought you might like to be involved in our maiden shoot.'

Joanna laughed. The woman's enthusiasm was contagious

'You've sussed out the talent, have you?'

'Sort of. Karen, your innovative play therapist, has alread

rganised the littlies who are well enough to sing a couple of ursery songs. She said she'd get some costumes together for he final shoot but she's coming in today and it would be an ideal trial run. And when we get there we'll see if any of the lder kids want to be involved.' She chuckled. 'If they don't vant to perform Steve said we could lure them with technology.'

'Technology?'

'As well as his state-of-the-art, high-tech camera, he's ringing a couple of smaller camcorders he's happy to lend, nder supervision of course. He also said if any of the older atients show interest or ability they could get involved in he editing later on. We've actually been given a tiny room in dmin. It has a desk and is lockable so it may come in handy or, at the very least, a storage area.'

'Wow, you've been working hard. And Steve's being amazngly generous. I'd love to come and help. What time?'

'Does around two o'clock sound all right? It's a time that vould cause the least disruption to the ward.'

'Yep, sounds great. I'll see you then.'

Lorraine's invitation to go to the hospital gave Joanna a ocus for her day and she was looking forward to the challenge of prising talent from the disparate group of small paients on Matilda Ward.

After breakfast she went to the nearest supermarket and tocked up with food and other essentials for the week ahead. On her way out she lingered at the newsagent and finally ought a fashion magazine. She then paused in front of a bouique displaying a new range of autumn clothing. The trend eemed to be feminine skirts, loosely flowing tops and lacy atterned knitwear in soft, warm colours. It had been a while ince she'd bought any clothes, and these days she spent most f her time when she wasn't working in jeans, or shorts and

T-shirts. A feminine outfit would make a change and seeme
to suit the cheerful mood she was in that day.

She decided to unload her shopping in her car and go bac
and have a closer look.

Half an hour later she emerged from the boutique with
bagful of purchases and headed off to seek out a shoe stor

When she got home she unloaded her groceries and the
spread the new clothes on her bed. After much vacillation, sh
still couldn't decide what to wear that afternoon. It someho
seemed important that she get it right. After all, she might t
on camera and it made a change from her everyday uniforn
She even considered wearing make-up.

After a late lunch and lengthy deliberation on what outf
to wear, she finally decided on a skirt with a subtle patter
in muted cream, ginger and peach and a simple sleevele:
cream top. By the time she'd changed, it was time to leav
for the hospital.

Richard heard the clapping and cheerful whooping befo
he entered the ward and paused in wonderment at the enc
less resourcefulness of the nursing staff. He'd had an ur
usual phone call that morning from the woman Joanna ha
mentioned was involved in producing the film segments f
the concert.

'I need your signature on some papers before we can g
ahead. Is that all right with you?' she'd asked. She was
woman not frightened of cutting to the chase and he imag
ined she would be a formidable rival if you found yourse
on a team opposing her.

'Yes, that's fine. Shall we make a time on Monday—?'

'Um… If we could somehow get it done today… You se
Steve is available this afternoon and I was hoping…'

'Steve? Should I know who he is?' Lorraine was comin

cross as used to getting her own way but he admired her
bility to get things done.

'He's my husband, our cameraman.' She paused but for
nly a moment. 'I could bring the documents to your house
f that's more convenient.'

'No, I can meet you at the hospital...' He checked his elec-
ronic organiser on his phone and noticed he had the whole
ay free.

'Lunchtime. We could meet in the canteen, or up on the
ard if you'd prefer.'

'I'd prefer the ward.'

'Right, Steve and I will see you at about one-thirty.'

He arrived at Matilda at twenty past and, as well as being
oisy, the playroom looked like the venue for an elaborate
hildren's party. Helium-filled balloons of all shapes and sizes
obbed and floated and a low table was loaded with rainbow-
oloured party food. Hand-made streamers looped and tum-
led around the windows. There was no indication that illness
ad had any effect to dampen the enthusiasm of about half a
ozen pint-sized, noisy dynamos. Lorraine, Karen, a nurse
ichard hadn't met and a tall, thin, bearded man he assumed
as Lorraine's husband were bustling around trying, unsuc-
essfully, to instil some kind of order into the joyful chaos.
arents were dotted around the room, chatting and smiling.

It was truly a wonderful sight.

After letting one of the ward sisters know he was there,
e made his way to the glass-walled playroom and lingered
n the doorway, and it wasn't long before he was spotted.

'Dotta Howl!' Leisha, aged three and a half and on
rutches, launched herself at him. She discarded her walk-
g aids and hugged his knee with the strength of a child twice
er age. She'd adapted amazingly well to her mid-thigh am-
utation and was due for discharge the following week.

He reached down to hug the girl and she managed to plan a sloppy kiss on his cheek before Karen whisked her away.

Then Lorraine saw him and greeted him with a broad grin.

'Thank you so much for coming. We all really appreciate it.' He looked around the room and acknowledged a few of the parents he recognised.

'No problem. Maybe we could go somewhere quieter to do the paperwork,' he said as Lorraine retrieved a folder from the top of a tall cupboard, safely out of reach of her small charges.

'Good idea,' she said.

Fifteen minutes later all the formalities were complete and Richard got up to leave the tutorial room. Suddenly, the thought of going home to a coldly impersonal, empty house held no attraction for him and he wanted to be involved in the rowdy pandemonium that was happening down the corridor.

'When do you actually start filming?' he said tentatively.

'If Steve can manage to find a space to set up his gear, hopefully in about half, maybe three quarters of an hour.' She smiled. 'You're welcome to stay and watch if you want. If you're hungry and don't mind fairy bread, peanut-butter pinwheels and fruit jelly for lunch...'

'I think I'll pass. I might go over to the doctors' dining room for something to eat and come back.'

'Wonderful. The more the merrier, but don't expect to stand on the sidelines. I'm sure we'll be able to find something for you to do.'

And with a flurry she was off, humming what he guessed was a slightly out-of-tune rendition of 'Raindrops Keep Falling on My Head'.

When he came back half an hour later, a little more order prevailed in the playroom. It was relatively quiet, though the numbers seemed to have swelled. In the few moments before Karen grabbed him and led him over to a group of parents who seemed to be involved in some sort of artwork, he gazed around the room. His eyes stopped and fixed on the gorgeous, dark-eyed woman with a toddler on her knee.

She was truly beautiful.

Centimetre-long, jet-black hair contrasted with the softly tanned skin of her face, reminding him of an olden-time porcelain doll. Her swirling full skirt fell below her knees and he could see her underwear—a lace-edged camisole—through her almost transparent blouse. The outfit left just enough to the imagination to make it tantalisingly seductive.

She looked like an angel cradling a cherub and the vision took his breath away.

All he wanted to do at that moment was scoop Joanna into his arms, hold her body close to his and pray she could find it in her heart to at least try to love him.

'Quiet, everyone.' Steve's clear, authoritative voice managed to still even the most boisterous child. 'Ready to go.' Lorraine then scissored her arms in the air, mimicking a clapper board and Joanna began to sing.

The toddler on her knee, the other patients, their parents and the staff were all mesmerised as Jo's clear, pure voice filled every corner of the room. Richard heard few of the words of the bouncy little song, though. The lyrics didn't seem to matter. What really mattered was that Joanna's total attention was focused on the child. The expression on her face, the look in her eyes were straight out of the past.

The memories flooded back to happier times and it was as if Sam was again snuggled up to her, as if she was pouring the deep love she had for their son into her song.

It was as if Sam was still alive.

The room began to close in on him, faces blurring, sounds

becoming fuzzy and indistinct. Richard cleared his throat, stood on shaky legs and did his utmost to quietly leave the room before Joanna noticed him. Once he was out of sight he slumped against the wall and wiped away a tear—the first tear he'd shed since his son had died.

When Joanna finished the song, she realised the occupants of the room, even the babies, were totally silent and their attention was focused on her. She felt the flush of embarrassment rush from her neck to her cheeks. She'd been so absorbed in the song, and the living, breathing bundle of life sitting on her lap, she'd blocked out everything else.

'That was *so* moving.' Karen came over and gave Joanna a hug and, to her relief, a buzz of conversation began again. She wasn't used to being the centre of attention and felt acutely uncomfortable. She released a nervous laugh.

'How can you say "The Easter Bunny Song" is moving?' Karen looked at her searchingly.

'Well, I reckon Dr Howell was touched.'

What on earth was Karen talking about? Richard had nothing to do with the song. An uneasy thought entered Joanna's mind that Karen knew…knew they were married or at least had some kind of personal relationship happening. Karen was still staring at her with a half-smile on her face.

'Dr Howell? What do you mean?'

Karen hoisted Leisha, who was grizzling quietly and was obviously tired, onto her hip. The little girl yawned.

'He was here a minute ago and left in a hurry. He looked as if he was…um…'

Several alarming thoughts skittered through Joanna's mind. What was Richard doing in the ward on the weekend in the first place? She knew he wasn't on call. Had he hinted at a relationship between them without realising the ramifications, particularly if they decided to go ahead with the divorce?

Had he let her down?

Now the conversation with Karen had got this far, though, she needed to know what was going through the play therapist's mind. She didn't want to be the topic of unsubstantiated gossip; she valued her privacy when it came to her life outside the workplace.

'How did he look?' Joanna surprised herself with the hard edge to her voice.

'If you want my honest opinion, I'd say he was close to tears.' There was nothing in Karen's tone of voice or the expression on her face to suggest she was joking. She looked deadly serious.

'And he left a few moments ago?'

'That's right.'

Leisha began grizzling again and Karen looked around the room to see if the girl's mother had returned from taking Leisha's twin brother to the toilet. She spotted her on the other side of the room, cuddling another unhappy pre-schooler.

'I'm going to have to leave you to it. I think it's time to get these over-excited kids back to their beds for a rest.'

Joanna welcomed the distraction of the now restless children and took the opportunity to slip away—she hoped, unnoticed. Karen's words kept repeating in her mind.

I'd say he was close to tears.

But Richard never cried.

She'd often wondered if their marriage would have had a second chance if they'd been able to cry together, to grieve together, to share the emotional devastation that had wreaked havoc in their lives nearly four long years ago.

Joanna thought she'd moved on, but had Richard?

Close to tears.

She knew him well enough to know what would bring up the pain of the past. There was no other reason she could think of for why he would become noticeably emotional—a man who could always keep his feelings in check. To break down in public would be the worst humiliation imaginable.

Joanna needed to see Richard, even if it meant paging him and saying it was an emergency.

She hurried out of the ward, ran to catch the lift before the door closed and tried to formulate in her mind what she would do, what she would say to him if...when she tracked him down.

She didn't need to ruminate for very long, though.

When the lift reached the ground floor and the doors opened, she almost collided with him as he strode through the entrance to the stairwell. His head was down and he seemed so determined to get out of the building he didn't notice her.

'Richard.' It was barely a whisper. She quickly swallowed the stubborn lump that had formed in her throat.

'Richard!' she shouted as she broke into a run.

He stopped and turned as the automatic doors began to close and was unable to contain the look of surprise on his face. Joanna could see no sign of tears but could tell he was upset. A shard of anger appeared in his eyes but was replaced by his normal control in the time it took him to blink.

Why was he angry?

She understood why he would be upset, but the anger confused her, and while she hesitated he backtracked and walked towards her.

'Joanna, what a coincidence. It's great to see you.'

He obviously had no idea she knew he'd been on Matilda Ward while she'd been singing.

She grasped his hand and pulled him close enough for him to hear her whisper.

'I need to talk to you, Richard.'

He lifted his eyebrows as if her request had taken him by surprise.

'Here? Now?'

'No, Richard.'

Somewhere private where tears won't cause loss of face.

'It's a…er…sensitive matter that I think needs privacy to discuss.'

He hesitated for a moment or two. 'Would you like to go back to my place, then?' he said, his smile erasing any remnants of distress. She refused to read anything between the lines of the invitation, though. It seemed a reasonable request.

'Yes, Richard. That would suit me fine.' She readjusted her bag on her shoulder and began to walk towards the doors. She'd heard he'd moved into one of the doctors' houses a couple of streets away. That suited her. It was on her way home and it meant she didn't have to depend on Richard for a lift.

'Did you walk?' she asked as they set off on one of the meandering pathways that ended up at the back of the hospital. Richard adjusted his usual long stride to her slower pace. He glanced in her direction.

'Yes, I moved into Peppermint Mews the weekend after I started at Lady Lawler. It's only five minutes away.' He paused. 'You'll be my first guest.'

Joanna wanted to spout a witty reply but she couldn't think of anything appropriate to say and they walked the rest of the way in edgy silence. Unfortunately it provided an opportunity for Joanna to think and she began wondering if she'd made a mistake. What would she say? Just come right out with it— that Karen told her she thought he had been on the verge of tears? Or skirt around the edge of the issue? Hope that he'd pick up on her concerns without having to spell it out?

But it was too late now to bail out.

They reached the block of terraces where Richard lived and he stopped at the gate of the house second from the end. It was identical to all of the others apart from the colour of the front door—his was a glossy navy blue—and the contents of the front garden. Richard's was crazy paved and decorated with a couple of terracotta pots containing a pair of struggling geraniums.

'This is it,' Richard said as he opened the gate for her.

'It doesn't suit you.' Her comment, though bold, was the truth.

'I know. You're absolutely right.' He ran his fingers through his hair. 'It's only temporary until I find something better.' He stepped into the tiny portico and unlocked the door. To Joanna's surprise he looked embarrassed. 'And I take no credit for the decorating.' In a roundabout way he was apologising for his humble, short-term lodgings, which surprised her. He'd never paid much attention to keeping up appearances.

'Come in and sit down,' he added, indicating a doorway, one of several opening off a central passage that led to what looked like a kitchen-dining area. She presumed the bedrooms were upstairs. 'Can I get you something to drink?'

'Just water for me, thanks.'

Joanna wasn't thirsty but wanted a minute or two to compose herself. Richard left the room and headed towards the back of the house. She took a couple of deep breaths and glanced around the room and her gaze froze when she saw the photos on the mantle above the fireplace—for all the world to see.

Oh, my God!

Her heart began to race.

She recognised both snapshots. They were displayed in a decorative, hinged silver frame and were the only homely touch in what Joanna viewed as a comfortable though boring room.

She picked up the frame and examined the photos more closely. The first was a head-and-shoulders portrait of her and Richard on their wedding day. It wasn't a professional shot but the photographer had captured the essence of their mood, which was a heady mix of joy, laughter, and unquestionable love for each other. Richard was gazing at her with a big goofy grin on his face and stars in his eyes. She, at twenty, looked so young and innocent but she was beaming with happiness and waving at the camera.

The second photo was at the beach. Joanna must have taken the picture but, although she remembered the day vividly, she didn't remember recording it on film. It showed Richard and Sam and it was also brimming with the joy of living. Richard was chest deep in the water and held his precious son in his arms. You could easily see that Sam was smiling as he reached out to touch the graceful dolphin gliding by. It was the last time they had taken their son to the beach—the last time before the cruel disease had taken his life. And it was as if the beautiful, intuitive creature knew Sam didn't have much time left and had come to say goodbye.

Joanna wiped a tear from her cheek and put the photos back at the same moment Richard walked into the room. She stood in front of the fireplace, not knowing what to do or say. Her visit that afternoon was supposed to be about trying to free Richard's cloistered emotions, but she was the one who couldn't hold back the tears. She sniffed and moved over to the couch where Richard had placed a tray.

'What's the matter?' His look was razor sharp and soft as duck down all at once. It cut through her defences and stripped her of the calm control she'd learned, from her husband, to wear like a suit of armour. 'Have you been crying?'

She shrugged. The question was unnecessary. He could easily see the tears smeared on her face.

'The...the photos...' she faltered.

'They are the only family shots I have.' He stood with his hands in the pockets of his jeans and looked past Joanna. His eyes lost focus and he swallowed.

'When I left, I thought I'd be coming back...to you. I needed a break and I thought time would heal at least some of the hurt.'

He sat down next to her, fixing his searching eyes on her face. He reached for her hand and she didn't resist his firm and consoling grasp. *He* had taken the role of comforter away from her and claimed it for himself. Jo knew that role usually came with unspoken permission to store his feelings in an inaccessible box; to do the job he'd been trained to do, regardless of whether it was at the expense of dealing with his own anguish. He could then concentrate on the task of healing and reassuring others...*covering old wounds with a veil of optimism*.

No, not this time.

Joanna was unable to contemplate a life with Richard if he couldn't be open with her. Trust and communication were two essential characteristics in any relationship. One of the reasons why she and Richard had parted had been that they had stopped communicating. Joanna realised, too late, that she'd been as much to blame as him.

But she hoped she'd learned from her mistakes. The opportunity to start over opened up the way to getting it right this time.

Or getting it very wrong.

Joanna couldn't afford to take that risk.

Sometimes love wasn't enough and she would rather spend the rest of her life alone than with a man who felt he had to be strong for her all the time.

She finally broke the silence.

'Those photos represent two of the most important turning points in our relationship.' Richard waited for her reply cloaked with an unreadable expression. 'The beginning of our marriage, our long-term commitment to each other and...' Jo knew what she wanted to say but the words stuck in her throat.

'And?'

'And the end of our marriage.' There, she'd said it. Their life together had fallen apart when they had lost their child. Sam had turned out to be the sustenance of their love and it was only when he'd gone that the full impact had struck. Neither of them had had the strength to do battle with their own demons, let alone share their grief. Joanna had cocooned herself in despair and Richard... She knew he'd tried his best but it hadn't been enough. In being the strong one, he'd buried part of himself. He'd buried his own guilt and pain and devastation. Joanna could see that now and was grateful for how hard he'd tried to help, but it hadn't made sense to her at the time.

She'd wanted him to cry therapeutic tears with her, to share the load so they could carry it forward, together. Not ignore their problems and maintain an outwardly happy face in the name of toughing it out.

Richard's thumb traced a pattern on the palm of her hand with warm, gentle pressure.

'I tried so hard—'

'I know. But maybe you tried too hard. You never broke down. You were always the tower of strength. But what I needed was to see that you were as vulnerable as me. In the end you seemed to almost stop being human.'

'It was the only way I knew to cope.' The dark pupils of his deep blue eyes dilated and Joanna thought she detected a slight tremor in his hand. It was the reassurance she needed. He was on the brink of sharing his feelings.

'But you still do it, Richard. I don't think you've…' But she couldn't say it. She didn't know how to tell her husband she thought he hadn't yet worked through the grieving process necessary to move on. She suspected it was the reason he'd stayed away so long; it had probably been an escape for him, to a life full of strangers and distractions and a full-on workload.

Richard opened his mouth to speak but closed it again.

'Do you want me to forget we had a son?' he finally said, his voice a husky whisper.

'No, of course I don't. There's not a day goes past that I don't think about Sam. He was an important part of our lives. Still is. But I realise it serves no purpose to let the memories overwhelm me. It's taken me a long time to realise that.' She took a deep breath in an effort to give herself the courage to continue. 'And my work in Oncology has helped.'

Richard reached across for the bottle of spring water he'd brought in on the tray. He opened it and half filled both glasses. He took one for himself and offered the other to Joanna but she refused. The dryness she felt in her throat wouldn't be relieved by water.

'Yes, I know.' Richard swallowed a mouthful of his drink. 'Anyone can see how much you care for the kids on Matilda.'

'It makes it easier when I know how difficult it would be to fall pregnant.'

Richard's gaze lowered and he rubbed the back of his neck as if to massage away a ball of tension. Then he looked up.

'So what do you want me to do, Joanna? I can't change who I am. I can't change the past.'

She looked at him for a long moment and realised the only answer she could give was the truth.

'I still love you, Richard. I want us to try again. But it won't work if we can't share the bad times as well as the good. I know the memory of Sam will always be there and I want...' She took a sip of water while Richard waited for her to continue. 'I want you to let yourself cry for Sam.'

He stood up and walked over to the window that faced the street. He leaned on the sill with his arms spread wide. At least he was thinking about what she'd said. He hadn't dismissed her words as being sentimental nonsense. The barrier hadn't gone up yet.

Finally he turned.

'I can't turn on tears for you, Jo.'

'I don't expect you to. I just want to know you are able to... How can I say it...? You're able to give yourself permission.'

He walked back to where she was sitting, leaned forward and kissed her gently on the forehead.

'I'm not sure I can do what you want, but I'm prepared to try.'

CHAPTER EIGHT

NIGHT shifts weren't usually a problem for Joanna but now she was nearing the end of her month-long stint the days were dragging. She was counting the shifts until she finished, looking forward to starting work in daylight hours and going to bed after sunset. She knew nursing involved around-the-clock care but the busy, hands-on day shifts suited her better than the usually quiet and uneventful nights.

And, of course, she would see more of Richard when her roster changed.

His attitude seemed more relaxed as they took the first tentative steps to get to know each other again. He'd said little about their heart-to-heart talk but she was perceptive enough to notice his attitude towards her had changed. The spark was still there but they'd both agreed to take things slowly.

The tongues of the hospital grapevine had already started to wag, though, which wasn't surprising because it was difficult to disguise the fact that their relationship went further than a straightforward professional association between nurse and consultant. She hadn't yet decided whether the gossip was a good or bad thing, but at least no one knew about their past. Joanna had enough to deal with without having to cope with the possibility of endless questions, probably associated with well-meant but unwelcome sympathy.

The combination of Joanna working night shifts and Richard's busy schedule meant they'd had little opportunity for one-to-one contact. He'd walked her home from choir rehearsals a couple of times but she'd been shy of asking him in. The closest they'd come to a date had been his invitation for her to come swimming with him after work. They'd also shared a meal with the 'film crew' the previous Saturday after helping Lorraine and Steve with the final shoot of the Matilda Ward segment for the concert. But that didn't count because they'd been part of a large, noisy and excited group and had barely spoken to each other.

The concert.

It was only two weeks away and preparations were going well. The performance was scheduled for Easter Saturday and Richard had promised to take Joanna out on a *proper date* on the following evening.

To celebrate, he'd said mysteriously.

To celebrate what?

Of course, the predicted success of the concert was cause for celebration but the look in his eye when he'd invited her suggested he had more than the hospital fundraiser on his mind.

He'd told her he'd already booked a table for two at a fancy, waterside restaurant but he wouldn't tell her where. She was looking forward to it and had bought a new dress in honour of the occasion.

She smiled as she walked back to the nurses' station after doing her 6:00 a.m. rounds. It was her last night shift for at least another three months and she was dog tired. The previous day she'd found it difficult to sleep and as a result had felt overtired and cranky before she'd even started her shift. This stint had taken its toll more than usual and in the last hour she'd resorted to watching the clock. She yawned and followed it up with a deep, sighing breath.

'What's up, Jo?' Barbara asked. The ward was quiet and they had time to share a cup of tea. She must have noticed the number of times Joanna had yawned that night. 'You look like the subject of a sleep deprivation experiment.'

Joanna managed a smile.

'Funny you should say it. That's just how I feel.'

'So what's going on with Matilda Ward's very own Miss Cheerfulness? What's caused you to lose some of your shine?'

Joanna tried to suppress another yawn but without success. She sipped her tea, hoping it would revive her. Although she appreciated the older woman's concern, she liked to keep her private life to herself.

'I'm fine. Just a bit tired. I've been lucky up until now, being able to sleep during the day. Quiet street, neighbours who work—'

Barbara was looking at her with a quizzical, motherly expression, but seemed happy with the answer. The supervisor went back to her work, checking that the medication doses and times had been filled in correctly. She checked and doublechecked. The hospital was currently cracking down on recordkeeping, particularly regarding medications, after a near fatal mistake in the emergency department.

'Anything else I can do?' Joanna said, suppressing another yawn.

The concerned look Barbara gave her said more than words.

'If you weren't at the end of your stint on nights, I'd recommend you take a couple of days' leave. Are you sure you're not coming down with something?'

'Really, Barbara...' She attempted to laugh off the fact

that she felt dead on her feet. 'Maybe I'm just starting to feel my age.'

'All right, but how about you go home early? It's only an hour and I can sign you off as being unwell. You're not much use to us in your state and the ward's really quiet. Tracey and I can hold the fort.'

'No, I'll be fine.' She could count the number of sick days she'd had over her entire nursing career on the fingers of one hand. She wasn't about to take time off because she'd had trouble sleeping. And it wasn't as if she didn't know the reason. 'And I assure you I won't let a couple of extra yawns interfere with my work,' she added.

Barbara was studying her intently.

'You look pale.'

'I'm okay, really I am.'

'Not feeling a bit queasy, are you?'

'No. Is there a bug going around that I don't know about?'

Barbara smiled, got up to replace the charts in the trolley and patted her on the shoulder.

'There's always a bug going around in this place. It's a hospital isn't it?'

'You're not wrong, Barb.' Another yawn threatened. Joanna picked up a magazine and began flipping through it. Barbara went over to the cooler and poured herself half a cup of water to swallow the blood-pressure tablet she always took at six o'clock. She stood silently for a minute or so, as if deep in thought.

'You're not pregnant, are you?' she finally asked.

Fat chance, in fact no chance at all.

It must have been her weariness, the culmination of a series of unusual events over the last week, and she knew she should be laughing at Barb's well-intentioned inquiry.

Joanna looked over at Barbara.

'No, I'm not pregnant.' She had to work hard at stopping her voice from shaking.

'How can you be sure?'

'Anatomically impossible, I'm afraid,' Joanna, the clinical, rational nurse managed to say in a rock-steady voice. 'My tubes are blocked. I had a ruptured appendix when I was sixteen…'

'Oh, Jo, I honestly didn't know.'

'Of course you didn't. I don't go broadcasting…' Then Joanna burst into tears and couldn't stop sobbing. Barbara wrapped her arms around her.

'You poor love. I insist you go home and I'll arrange a taxi. You can't stay here like this.'

Joanna didn't have the energy to protest.

A good, solid, uninterrupted nine hours' sleep made all the difference to how Joanna felt. It was as if she'd been born again and the events of the morning hadn't happened, or at least had diminished to a hazy, distant blur.

Her only problem was that she had slept so well during the day she was unlikely to sleep that night. She knew she should have set her alarm to help her inbuilt rhythm restore itself but with all that had happened, she'd forgotten—and it wasn't the end of the world.

She gathered clean underwear, the new peach-coloured towelling robe she'd treated herself to the previous week and headed to the bathroom. The cake of hand-made apple and almond soap she hadn't been able to resist at the market smelled delicious and almost edible. She felt she had not a care in the world.

It was a warm evening so, after her shower, she dressed in casual knee-length shorts and a T-shirt and actually ran a comb through her centimetre-long hair. It made little difference, though. Her hair refused to be persuaded to do anything but stick up at a right angle to her scalp.

After fortifying herself with a good strong cup of tea, she decided to go for a walk. She felt she needed an extra-strong dose of fresh air after a month of working nights and sleeping for three quarters of the day. She hoped an hour or so of exercise would help her sleep at least a few hours that night, although it usually took a couple of days for her normal diurnal rhythm to get back to normal. She also decided to pick up some take-away on the way back. Putting a twenty-dollar note in her pocket, she grabbed her broad-brimmed hat and strode out of her little house. She followed the quaint, brick-paved laneway that fronted the property to the main road and then headed for the park a couple of blocks away.

Joanna started off walking at a fairly brisk pace but began to tire by the time she reached the park so she slowed down. The sun was sinking lower and a gentle breeze cooled the early evening air. She enjoyed strolling along the path that circled a haphazard string of pools and small lakes. She smiled at a middle-aged man who was being dragged along by a boisterous young German shepherd, and stopped to chat briefly to a couple proudly pushing tiny twins in a contraption that looked like it was ready to take off for outer space.

'They're beautiful,' Joanna said as she leaned forward to take a closer look at the sleeping babies, both dressed in white. 'Are they boys, girls or one of each?'

'Girls, only a month old,' was all the beaming father managed to say before his wife interrupted.

'And they're not identical,' the young mum said.

'They look very similar.' In fact, it was difficult for Jo to tell them apart. Her heart swelled for the couple. 'What are their names?'

'Emily and Victoria, after their grandmothers.'

A tiny splinter of jealousy niggled in Joanna's mind but she dismissed the thought quickly. She'd long ago accepted that motherhood wasn't going to be part of her life again.

'I'll let you get on with your stroll.'

The woman linked her arm in her husband's. They set off in the opposite direction and, from that instant, Joanna's mood subtly changed. She couldn't help thinking of Richard and his declaration of love. Had he fully thought things through? If they *did* manage to resurrect their marriage, would there always be something missing? Richard was physically able to father a child but had told her it didn't matter to him if their future didn't include children. But Joanna couldn't help wondering if she'd feel guilty for depriving him of something she knew was important to him.

And she couldn't cope with IVF. Not now. The journey would be too painful for her and she knew the failure rate was relatively high.

And what if she did become pregnant? She wasn't sure she'd be able to go through a pregnancy that might end in a miscarriage or stillbirth or, even worse, result in a living, breathing perfect child that was taken from them…

She couldn't do it.

By the time she'd walked two circuits of the park she was tiring again. Her heart thudded in her chest, queasiness niggled in her stomach and she'd lost her appetite. She was now feeling tense halfway through a walk that was supposed to relax and energise her. Suddenly she felt light-headed and looked around for a seat. There was a park bench at the water's edge, a few metres away. When she reached it her legs felt like jelly as she sank onto the seat.

What was wrong? Was she having some kind of anxiety attack?

She'd never had one before.

She took a few slow, deep breaths but it didn't make much difference.

The only time in her life she'd felt anything like this had been when she'd been pregnant with Sam.

Pregnant with Sam...

Pregnant.

Could she be?

No, of course she couldn't. She'd had tests and she was infertile. She and Richard had never used contraception because there'd been no point.

But...

She'd managed to fall pregnant at age nineteen, against all the odds.

Her heart was now pounding and her head ached but she needed to start thinking rationally or her outlandish suppositions would consume her.

When was her last period? She never kept a record because there'd been no need but she knew her cycle was regular. And it had been a while, certainly before she'd started working nights. She racked her brain and then recalled her last period had been around the time Richard had started at Lady Lawler.

She did the calculations.

Oh, my God.

She and Richard had made love about two weeks later and she hadn't had a period since. Which had been well over a month ago.

'So if I'm pregnant, I'd be six or seven weeks,' she whispered, not quite believing what her mind and body were telling her.

But how unlikely was that?

The odds were stacked so heavily against her... A nervous laugh surfaced from somewhere deep in her throat.

More slow breaths.

She fingered the twenty-dollar note in her pocket. There was a late-opening pharmacy on her way home. If she was to get any sleep that night she had to know.

The pharmacist, the only person in attendance in the small shop, was a dark-skinned man, who looked several years younger than her. There were a number of people waiting to be served and an elderly couple, who were trying out walking sticks, took up most of the central aisle space. Joanna heard the young man explain to the woman at the head of the queue that his assistant had had a family emergency and had to leave. He was waiting for her replacement. He looked harassed and Joanna began to have second thoughts.

But she had to know.

As soon as was practically possible.

Once she'd confirmed that the test was negative she'd be able to relax and the troublesome symptoms of her uncertainty would go away.

She decided to wait and, after ten, long, agonising minutes, her turn came.

'Yes, what can I do for you?' To his credit the pharmacist attempted a smile.

'I want a home pregnancy test kit.'

'Dip or stream?'

'Pardon?' What on earth did he mean? Despite her nursing background, she had no idea what he was talking about.

He lowered his voice. 'Do you want to dip into a specimen cup or just pee on the stick?'

Joanna was acutely aware that the other occupants of the shop could hear every word. She felt the heat rise to her neck and was glad she hadn't removed her hat.

'Whichever is most accurate...' She had a quick thought.

She had no idea how much the tests cost. 'And costs less than twenty dollars.'

A look of sympathy crossed the man's face but it didn't change the fact he still looked about eighteen to Joanna.

The man glanced behind her as if reminding her there were other people waiting, but she'd got this far and she wasn't going to chicken out now.

'It depends on how far along you are.' The guy was assuming she *was* pregnant and it unsettled her even more.

'Um…' The conversation was turning into an ordeal. 'About six weeks, I think.'

'They're all between ninety-five and ninety-nine per cent accurate at that stage.' To her relief the inquisition stopped and he moved to scan a shelf to one side of the counter. He selected a couple of boxes.

'This is a popular one. Easy to use and to read. You can buy it in a single pack for seven ninety-five or in the double for fifteen dollars.

She handed him the money. 'I'll take the double.'

At that moment, a middle-aged woman in a pale blue uniform burst into the shop with a flurry.

'I can take over now, Ramesh. I'm sure you have some scripts to do.'

The pharmacist, looking relieved, nodded as the assistant took the twenty-dollar note from one hand and the test kit from the other. He made his way onto the platform overlooking the shop, where the prescriptions were made up. The woman glanced at the box and then at Joanna.

'Just this?'

'Yes, thanks.'

The woman completed the transaction, placed the purchase in a small paper bag and handed it to Joanna with her change.

Joanna nearly bowled over a wandering toddler as she left and had never been more relieved in her life to get out of a shop.

Twenty minutes later she was standing in her kitchen, ripping off the packaging of the pregnancy test kit. She unfolded the instructions and spread the single sheet of paper on the bench. Words blurred in and out of focus.

'Concentrate!' she muttered. 'You don't want to stuff this up.'

She read the instructions.

Absorbent tip pointing downward...

...urine stream for five seconds...

Wait three minutes before reading results...

TWO PINK LINES...

Her gaze shifted from the diagram that showed the two lines to the one next to it.

NOT PREGNANT, ONE PINK LINE.

That was the result she was expecting and the instructions seemed simple enough. She took the test stick into the bathroom and when she finally stopped shaking managed to pee on the stick.

The next three minutes were the longest three minutes of her life.

She sat on the toilet lid with the tester in her right hand and her eyes fixed on the second hand of her watch on the other wrist. She decided not to look at the result until the time was up because she felt sure she would imagine lines and confuse herself.

'Ten, nine, eight...' She began a countdown back to zero and when she reached five her hand began to shake. 'Zero.'

Her eyes moved to the results window as she tried to steady her hand.

Right.

She focused.

Two pink lines. Yes, definitely two, so if the test was accurate she was pregnant with Richard's child.

Tears of happiness filled her eyes and vibrant warmth suffused her whole body.

She was pregnant with Richard's child.

Oh, dear God, what was she going to do?

A moment later all her fears descended on her like a landslide and she began to weep.

Richard was looking forward to the Tuesday morning ward round because Joanna was back on day shift. He'd missed her smiling face, her common-sense suggestions and her ability to make even the most despondent child laugh. He'd tried to contact her a couple of times on the weekend, hoping to meet up, maybe go on a picnic, but she hadn't answered her phone. Although he'd been disappointed, he didn't want to be pushy. At the last concert rehearsal they'd attended together just over a week ago, she'd seemed exhausted and she'd probably wanted a peaceful weekend to get her energy back.

When he entered Matilda Ward at just after eight o'clock, there was no sign of Joanna. Lynne had the trolley with all the patient notes ready, but was on the phone. She waved and mouthed the words, 'Won't be long.'

Richard nodded and used the time by having a quick look at Danny Sims's latest scan. He smiled. The bulk of his tumour had reduced by roughly twenty per cent, which was more than anyone had hoped for in such a short time. If he continued to respond so well to his chemotherapy, there was a good chance his prognosis would improve. A full remission was too much to hope for at this stage but it at least put a positive outcome for his treatment in the realms of possibility.

Lynne hung up the phone and summoned the student nurse, Tracey, to the nurses' station.

'Good morning, Richard,' the charge nurse said with a cheerful smile. 'Do you mind if Tracey comes with us on the round this morning?'

'No, of course not.' Richard tried to hide his disappointment. 'Where's Joanna? I thought she was back today.'

Lynne's eyebrows elevated. Maybe he hadn't disguised his disappointment as well as he'd hoped.

'Yes, she is. But she said she felt a bit off colour on the weekend so she's been designated as our runner. I decided, just as a precaution, to reduce her patient contact today. Just in case she has a virus and is contagious.'

Richard wanted to cross-examine Lynne as to what exactly was the matter with Jo but decided to find out for himself later. He'd attempt to catch up with her at some stage during the day and if that didn't happen, he'd call by her house after work. Maybe take some food. Yes, that was what he would do.

Lynne looked at him expectantly. He tried to look interested but not overly concerned.

'Your runner?' The question was in neutral territory. Richard hadn't heard that term used to describe the duties of a nurse before and was genuinely interested.

'I guess we use the term in the same way "girl Friday" is used in an office. She runs messages, does odd jobs, that sort of thing. She's doing an inventory of our storeroom at the moment.'

'Oh.' He paused and Lynne looked at him questioningly. 'We'd better get on with the round, then.'

The ward round went smoothly but took a little longer than usual because Lynne spent extra time explaining certain things to Tracey. Richard only glimpsed Joanna in passing a couple of times and on both occasions she had her head down and appeared not to notice him. He couldn't help thinking something was wrong and he wondered if he was to blame.

After the round he had a couple of referrals from other wards to follow up, which he set off to do mid-morning, and when he finished close to lunchtime he headed for the canteen. He bought his lunch and stayed half an hour but there was no sign of Joanna. Of course, at five o'clock when his afternoon clinic wound up, her shift would have finished and he lamented the fact he'd not even said hello to Jo over the full duration of her working day.

It was after six when he completed his paperwork and was ready to go home. He realised how hungry he was when his stomach began to rumble so he walked home briskly to collect his car and drove to one of his favourite eateries, The Station Café, and emerged with a double serving of herbed lamb cutlets and three different kinds of salad. He hoped Joanna hadn't eaten already because he was looking forward to sharing a meal and part of the evening with her.

He parked in the street because he knew there was only space for one car in the short driveway off the lane. When he let himself in the gate he could see that Joanna was home because the television and lights were on. As he approached the back patio door he could see no sign of Joanna, though.

He knocked.

No answer.

He hammered on the door and called out but there was still no sign of life.

Maybe she'd gone out and left the television on.

As he turned to leave he heard movement, the noise of the TV silenced and Joanna appeared, damp and wrapped in a towelling robe. She eased the slider open just enough for her to talk to him but it looked like she had no intention of inviting him in.

He held up the bags of food as a peace offering.

'From The Station Café. I hope you're hungry.'

She still didn't open the door.

'I'm sorry, Richard, but I've already eaten and what I really need is an early night. I haven't been sleeping well over the last couple of nights.' She hesitated. 'I just need to be by myself.'

She definitely did look tired…and pale…and unwell.

'What's the matter, Jo? Are you sick?'

Her mouth set in a thin line and she shook her head.

'Really, I'm just tired and I…' She yawned and rubbed her reddened eyes. Had she been crying? Why had she suddenly closed herself off from him when he'd thought their relationship was beginning to blossom? She'd at least been friendly towards him during the few times they'd been together over the past couple of weeks. He'd been careful not to encroach too much on her personal space and he'd intentionally let her set the pace.

Which for him, at times, had been painfully slow.

Had she changed her mind?

'Maybe we can have dinner together another evening.' Her expression was unconvincing. 'If you let me know. Give me some notice.' She attempted a smile but didn't quite pull it off.

'I'm sorry.' She paled, her hand moved to her stomach and then she closed the door and walked away from him.

There was definitely something wrong but he knew how stubborn she could be. If she didn't want to talk about it, there was nothing he could do to help.

Joanna had felt queasy all day but she suspected it had nothing to do with her pregnancy and more to do with stress. She'd repeated the test that morning, this time staring defiantly at the little window that showed the result and the second line had started to appear after about thirty seconds. She'd also noticed her breasts had begun to tingle and she seemed to be peeing more often. And as for her mental state… She felt permanently on the verge of tears, totally confused as to whether she was pleased or distraught about her condition and coming to the conclusion it was a mix of both.

She needed to tell Richard, but she wasn't ready now. During her shift she'd intentionally avoided any contact with him and when he'd arrived on her doorstep she'd felt like pleading with him to simply go away and leave her alone. Although she'd not followed her impulse to turn him away, she suspected Richard knew she wasn't her normal, happy, cope-with-anything-and-everything self.

But she definitely wasn't ready.

She needed time to think things through.

'When all else fails, have a cup of tea,' she muttered as she boiled the kettle and made herself a strong, sweet brew. Then she turned the television onto a chat show she usually found both funny and entertaining. The regular music segment was on and this week it was a jazz band. The musicians were playing a foot-tapping contemporary number as backing for a beautiful, young female singer.

It reminded her how quickly the concert was approaching. The final rehearsal was less than a week away. Not long, but it would give her an incentive to try and sort out the turmoil in her mind.

She would tell Richard about her pregnancy on Easter Sunday. On their dinner date.

Yes, that's what she would do—tell him after the concert.

* * *

The concert was a sell-out and, strangely, Richard felt a little nervous. The show was scheduled to begin at seven-thirty and the performers had been told to arrive at least two hours early. Richard had offered to drive Joanna to the town hall and she'd been sitting next to him in his car for the last ten minutes, gazing out the window and biting her lip. He wondered if she was suffering pre-performance jitters as well. He pulled up at traffic lights as they changed to orange.

'How are you feeling?' he enquired.

'Okay.' She shifted her gaze briefly but then resumed looking out the window.

'You look great.'

Male members of the hospital staff who were performing had been instructed to wear black trousers and a white shirt and, for the women, their uniform for the night was a long black skirt and white top.

Joanna looked gorgeous. She was wearing a silky culotte-style, ankle-length skirt and a sheer long-sleeved blouse over a lacy white camisole that was clearly visible through the almost transparent fabric of her top. Since they'd not had a full dress rehearsal, the outfit was new to Richard—and the whole package took his breath away. She looked so feminine and elegant and sensual all at the same time.

'Thanks.'

She ran her fingers through her hair, which was now a couple of centimetres long and growing back thicker and darker than ever. Although the elfin style suited her, Richard was looking forward to longer locks that he could run his own fingers through.

In fact, he was full of hope that they would formalise a reconciliation when he took Jo out to dinner the following night. He hoped she'd be more relaxed by then and that the coolness that had descended like a sudden winter chill when he'd picked her up would dissipate when the mood of excited anticipation changed once the concert was behind them.

'You still okay for tomorrow night?'

The way she was behaving towards him at the moment made him wonder if she might have changed her mind.

She smiled but it looked forced.

'Yes, I'm looking forward to it.'

By that time they'd arrived at the venue of the concert and parked in an area designated for performers in the public reserve across the road.

Richard hoisted his saxophone out of the back, locked up the car and they headed towards the hall. In the foyer, they caught up with a group of chattering nurses from one of the general medical wards, which signalled the end of any chance of one-to-one conversation. Joanna seemed to disappear into the middle of the group and before Richard realised she was gone he was being corralled by Jodie Francis into the area on the stage designated for the band. With the twenty-voice female choir, the band was to stay on stage for the whole show. Individual performers would come and go and the poignant, happy-sad and sometimes funny video footage would be played in two blocks—one just before intermission and the other at the conclusion. Although he'd only seen parts of the film, Richard had been impressed. Lorraine and Steve had done an excellent job.

The next hour and a half dragged and, after two cups of tea, half a ham sandwich, a quick run through a number that had been included at the last minute and the interminable prattle of Jodie Francis, Richard was relieved when the call for silence was finally made. As the curtain gracefully rose, the silence was broken by a 'squeaky wheel' sound coming from the side of the stage.

'Daisy?'

A loud, clear voice, without an owner, added to the suspense.

'*Daisy!*' the voice boomed, as a clown zigzagged his way onto the stage on a rickety old tandem bicycle.

'Where are you, Daisy?'

A girl of about fourteen or fifteen, who Richard knew was a survivor of childhood leukaemia, heavily made up and wearing a Dorothy from *The Wizard of Oz* style dress sidled onto the stage.

That was the cue for the band to softly play the opening bars of 'Bicycle Built for Two'. The volume of the music gradually increased as the clown began to serenade the teenager and then the choir joined in for the chorus.

When the song finished the audience burst into rapturous applause and the mood was set for the rest of the evening—one of light-hearted, fun-filled family entertainment.

The next few hours flew by with a mix of music, song, laughs and film. From the audience response, one of the most popular segments was the video footage of the children in the hospital wards. The capacity crowd was rapt, from Karen's lively little group of toddlers, to a spectacular solo from Danny Sims, a segment of fragmentary 'knock-knock' jokes that Steve had somehow melded together perfectly and everything in between.

It was a brilliant performance from a cast of close to a hundred.

Just before the closing video segment, another song had been added to the programme that hadn't been rehearsed. It wasn't a melody that lent itself to sax playing so Richard had the luxury of sitting back and watching. He was curious to see who was to be the solo vocalist for the well-known John Lennon song.

He didn't have to wait very long.

Considerable ceremony was made of hauling an antique rocking chair onto the stage. A woman carrying a small child of about two or three walked, barefoot and draped in a lacy sunshine-yellow crocheted shawl, onto centre stage. She sat down and began to rock slowly, her total attention focused on the child.

A moment later the band began to play to the rhythm of the mesmerising movement and the woman began to sing.

The audience was totally silent as, in a pure, uplifting voice Joanna sang the simple, moving lullaby. It told about a father's love for his son; his impatience in wanting the boy to come of age; and his promise to guide the child through his life's journey, whatever happened.

He knew that Joanna was singing not only for the child sitting, enraptured, on her knee…but for him…and Sam, their *beautiful, beautiful boy*.

The words travelled like an arrow, straight to his heart, and he was almost certain, as the melody softly faded, that the last words Joanna sang in what was close to a whisper were 'darling Sam'.

Richard waited for the band to finish, and the final video segment to begin before he quietly got up from his seat and slipped away, off the stage and out of the hall into the cool night air.

And he walked…and walked…and walked.

Twenty minutes later, in a dark, quiet street, he began to cry. Silent tears at first, then uncontrollable sobs.

For Sam.

For the loss of a child he couldn't bring back.

For the gift of his own life that he would have willingly traded for his son's.

For the love of a woman he couldn't bear to lose.

The sense of relief was incredible.

Joanna had been right.

She had shown him something that had eluded him for the past three years—how to grieve for Sam.

How to cry.

CHAPTER NINE

EXCITEMENT was a strange feeling to be having at the prospect of taking Joanna out on a date, but there was no other way to describe it. During Richard's time in the U.K. he'd dated half a dozen women, enjoyed the company of a couple enough to want to go out with them more than once but they'd never *excited* him. And he'd not had the faintest desire to take any of them home and get tangled up in *strings*.

With Joanna it was different. He wanted *strings*. Desperately. With his heart, body and soul. He knew, if they started over, it would be on different turf. They had both changed but not to the point where they'd lost the connection that had led to their marriage in the first place.

He wanted to make their evening something truly special. He wanted to reaffirm their marriage and suggest they try living together again. He was willing but it all depended on Joanna, and over the last two weeks she'd done her best to avoid him.

So he decided he'd surprise her in more ways than one and he hoped he'd have the time to put his plans into place.

First he showered and shaved. He changed into freshly cleaned and pressed navy-blue casual trousers and a crisp white shirt with the faintest navy stripe. He pocketed his tie. Even the smartest restaurants rarely insisted on ties these days but he didn't want to be caught short. As an afterthought he grabbed a jacket but he doubted he'd need it as it was an exceptionally warm evening.

Then he got in his car and drove to the nearby weekend markets, already bustling with early evening trade.

His business in the markets didn't take long. He chose roses—a dozen long-stemmed, sunshine-yellow buds—from the busy florist. His next port of call was the chocolatier where he selected a simple clear-topped rectangular box of an exquisite, hand-made combination of dark and light confections, tied with a yellow ribbon. Lastly he went to the jeweller to pick up the pendant he'd ordered a fortnight ago.

He smiled as he placed the small box in his pocket and gently laid the rest of his purchases on the back seat of his car. By that time it was a quarter to seven so he decided to while away a pleasant half-hour across the road at the recently restored Premier Hotel. He rarely spent time drinking in pubs but when he did he usually enjoyed the rowdy cheerfulness of the patrons and the interactions of the young people playing out the public mating rituals that seemed to change little over the years.

His sojourn in the popular front bar, including one tall glass of iced mineral water, served its purpose. He was feeling relaxed and primed with pleasant anticipation as he left the hotel, crossed the road and walked down the pavement towards the traffic lights not far from where he'd parked his car.

Before he was able to register the speed of the motorbike accelerating to beat the red light, it braked, swerved onto the footpath, narrowly missing a woman with a pram, waiting to cross, and then bulldozed into a shopfront—right where he stood.

The pain in his side was excruciating; the blow to his head

transformed the scene to slow motion for what must only have been seconds before he blacked out.

Joanna had mixed feelings about her date with Richard. It was a big night for her and she had psyched herself up to tell him all—first that she was pregnant and, depending on how he reacted to that monumental piece of news, that she still loved him and was seriously prepared to try again. She knew if that happened there would be many hurdles but she felt strong enough to cope this time. Even if they lost the baby... She felt, with Richard's help, she now had the strength to survive.

She had plenty of time to get ready as she wanted to look her best. After a long, lingering shower, she towelled herself dry and automatically looked down at her belly. If her dates were right she'd be about two months pregnant, the baby growing inside her now fully formed and roughly the size of a broad bean. Approximately the same length as her two-centimetre-long hair.

She smiled and then grabbed her robe, walked through to the bedroom and stared at her face in the mirror. Grimacing at the pallor of her skin and the faint dark rings under her eyes, she opened her make-up drawer. Twenty minutes later she did a reappraisal and was happy with the result. It was amazing what a difference a soft beige foundation, some blusher and smear of deep crimson lipstick could do. She rarely wore eye make-up but completed the look with a light application of mascara.

Now the dress.

She slipped the shimmery black mini-dress over her head and stretched behind her to do up the zip. Glad of the kilo of weight she'd lost due to her unpredictable appetite, she smoothed the slightly flared skirt and adjusted her full breasts in what now seemed a skimpy and seductive bodice. The

V of the neckline was too revealing and the straps too narrow. She hadn't known she was pregnant when she'd bought the dress and hadn't expected to be at least a bra size bigger.

But she didn't have time to change. Instead she fastened a velvet choker around her neck and slipped a black lacy wrap around her shoulders

She glanced at her watch and noted, with alarm, she was running late. But so was Richard. It was twenty to eight already and he'd said they'd leave at seven-thirty. Not that she minded but it had been a long time since lunch and she was getting hungry.

Strange…

Where on earth was he?

Should she be worried?

No, of course not. He was a grown man, quite capable of looking after himself. But she couldn't help her concern. She was just deciding whether to be annoyed or apprehensive when the phone rang.

'That will be Richard,' she muttered as she padded into the living room in stockinged feet. 'He's been caught up with work.' *As inevitably happened to doctors on a public holiday weekend*, she added in her mind as she picked up the phone.

'Hello.'

There was a pause.

'Richard?' she said tentatively.

'Is that Joanna Raven?' It was a female voice she didn't recognise.

'Yes.'

'My name's Sue.'

'Sue?' The woman sounded as if Joanna should know who she was but she couldn't place her.

'Yes, Sue Tyler, RN in the emergency department of Perth

General. I may have spoken to you on the phone. You work in Oncology at Lady Lawler, don't you?'

She vaguely remembered the woman but wondered why she would be ringing her at home. Maybe it was something to do with the reason Richard had been delayed. There was a strong link between the oncology departments of both hospitals. Childhood cancer survivors grew into adults and at some stage were transferred. Information from and consultation with their paediatric specialists was often important.

'I'm ringing about Dr Howell.'

Now it made sense. He *had* been caught up in some sort of emergency and he couldn't get away.

'What's happened?' she said, assuming she'd end up having a sandwich for dinner and spend the rest of the evening watching TV.

'He's been involved in an accident—'

'What? What did you say?' The implications of what the nurse said suddenly hit home. 'What happened? What sort of accident? Is he hurt?'

'He's only just come in by ambulance and the boss, James Headland, and the team are with him now in the resuscitation room.'

Only the most seriously injured went straight to the resuscitation suite. It meant he was… She didn't want to imagine how bad he was. She needed to find out for herself.

The nurse was still speaking, though, attempting to answer her questions.

'He has a fracture of his left femur and a head injury. That's all I can tell you so far. He was unconscious when he arrived but regained consciousness for a few minutes and was asking for you so that's why I'm ringing. He insisted he wanted you and nobody else.'

'Okay, Sue. Thanks, I'll be there in fifteen minutes.'

Joanna slipped on her work shoes, grabbed her keys and ran out the door to her car. Richard had been in a serious accident and he could be dying! My God, she thought. How could this happen? Why did all the good things in her life have to be snatched away from her? What had Richard done—kind, gentle, wonderful Richard—to deserve this?

But she mustn't jump to conclusions, or imagine the worst, she reminded herself as she resisted the temptation to put the accelerator of her nippy little car to the floor.

He was being resuscitated!

She needed to stay calm and focused.

He had a broken leg and had bumped his head. He was probably being assessed in Resus to determine the extent of his injuries, to make sure he was stable before tests such as X-rays and scans were done to clarify how badly he was hurt. He was in good hands. He had the best doctors and nurses looking after him. He would get through this and she would be there to help him.

Worrying sick about him wasn't going to change the outcome. She needed to stay calm.

She parked in a drop-off-only bay near the entrance to the emergency department, knowing she would be longer than fifteen minutes but thinking that was the least of her problems at that moment.

She arrived at Reception in the busy casualty department, breathing hard, her heart thumping. Fortunately a message had been left that she could be shown straight in to the treatment areas. The first thing she noticed was that two resuscitation rooms were occupied and she knew she couldn't burst in on the important work being done. Then she saw a nurse coming towards her. She was smiling.

'Hi. You must be Joanna.'

'That's right. How's Richard?'

Joanna curtailed her impatience. She knew what it was like to work in a hospital. Protocols had to be adhered to, rules obeyed. No matter how much she wanted to demand to see Richard, to make sure he was alive, to tell him how much she loved him...

'He's okay. He's stable and is off for X-rays and a CT of his head any minute now.' The nurse grasped her hand and gave it a gentle squeeze.

'Is he awake?'

'Yes, though drowsy. He's got an impressive haematoma on his forehead, though.'

Joanna sighed with relief, although she still nursed a ball of tension that felt like a watermelon sitting in her stomach.

'Can I see him?'

'I'll just check with James. But there shouldn't be any problem with you sitting with him, at least until he goes off for scans.'

'Thank you,' she said as she was directed towards a seat.

She chose to stand and the next few minutes felt like an eternity.

Richard remembered the collision and the pain that had followed but nothing of the ambulance journey or his admission to the emergency department of the Perth General Hospital. When he regained consciousness—he knew he must have been unconscious as it was the only reasonable explanation for his memory lapse—the first thing he was aware of was the noise. It was a cacophony. Like being woken by a full symphony orchestra playing Beethoven's Fifth out of tune.

He opened his eyes briefly, but immediately closed them against the dazzle of an overhead light with the strength of a searchlight. He had a mask over his face so he decided not to even try to speak. In amongst at least half a dozen beeping sounds he heard an unfamiliar female voice so loud he wanted to cover his ears. But his hands felt bound, his arms heavy and he had a needle-like pain jabbing at his wrist.

What was all the fuss about? It sounded as if he was on the wrong side of a scenario being played out in a hospital TV soap.

'He's awake, James. Opened his eyes,' the woman shouted.

'BP stable, one ten over eighty,' someone else called out.

'Good, start the second bag of Haemaccel.'

A man, who smelled of coffee and mint, leaned close and again shouted. *Do they think I'm hard of hearing?* Richard wondered.

'Open your eyes, Richard.'

No please or thank you. An order barked in the voice of an army sergeant.

'Are you awake? Open your eyes.'

Richard had the feeling the man wasn't going to go away until he did his bidding, so he opened his eyes and said what he really wanted.

'Where's Joanna?'

The man with the coffee-mint breath loomed close. He wore green surgical scrubs and had the air of a man who was used to giving orders and having them obeyed without question. Richard assumed he was a doctor and someone fairly high in the pecking order. His fuddled mind was clearing a little.

'What did you say?'

'He said, "Where's Joanna?"'

At last, a voice soft with compassion. Unlike the others, she saw no need to shout. Someone he could talk to, knowing she would hear what he needed to say.

'Who is Joanna?' she said. 'Is she your wife?'

Someone had turned the light away from his face and he

could see the owner of the kind voice. She also wore green scrubs but he couldn't tell if she was a doctor or a nurse. He squinted at her name badge.

'Sue?'

'That's right. I'm a nurse. You had an accident outside the markets and you're in the emergency department of the General. Do you remember anything?'

The noise had gradually abated and there were only two people that he could see in the room now. The loud doctor had left him in the care of the quiet nurse but he expected him to be back.

'Yes.' He remembered buying roses and chocolates, having a quiet drink at the pub to pass some time. He'd had a date with Joanna and it had all gone wrong.

'Is Joanna your wife?'

'Yes,' he said without hesitation. 'But we're separated and she uses her maiden name, Raven. She's a nurse.'

The effort of speaking only a couple of sentences was taking its toll but he wasn't going to give up until someone contacted Joanna.

'I need to see her.'

'How can we contact her?'

'Her home number is in my mobile.'

He heard the nurse rummage somewhere below his feet and then he saw she had the standard blue plastic bag containing his possessions.

'You had your phone with you?'

'Yes.'

'Ah. Here it is. Looks like it came off better in the accident than you. Not a scratch on it. Is it okay if I look for her number?'

'Yes.'

'And tell her what we know so far.'

'And…er.' He was about to tell this person, Sue, to apologise on his behalf. To tell Joanna he was sorry for making such a mess of something that could have been wonderful. The acuteness of his pain and the fuzz around the edges of his mind were enough to make him realise there was morphine dripping into one of the IV lines in his arm. He also realised the only person who could explain those things to Joanna was him.

'Tell her I need to see her.'

'I will.'

Just then the doctor returned and he heard the sound of his voice, now quiet, muttering to Sue but not loud enough for him to hear, and he suddenly felt annoyed. His emotions seemed to be cascading out of control and he knew that some of what came into his head and threatened to come out of his mouth was out of character but he felt he had to tell Dr Coffee-mint there was no need to whisper.

Somehow his hand found his mouth and he pulled down the mask.

'I'd like to hear what you're saying about me. I'm a doctor and want the facts.'

The man smiled.

'I see you're getting better, then. Good to have you back, Dr Howell.' He moved nearer to the head of the bed and stood with both hands on the side rails. 'I'll need to examine you again now you can tell me where it hurts, though the analgesia should be working well by now. Where's your pain?'

'My left thigh, left ankle and left shoulder.' He could see the splint and presumed he had a fractured femur. 'I've got a generalised dull headache and an ache across my lower back.'

'No gut pains?'

'Just a bit of nausea.'

'Chest pains?'

'Not really.'

Unless you consider a whole body ache to include the sum of all the parts.

'Breathing problems?'

'No.' Richard tolerated the mask being put back over his mouth but couldn't help asking, 'How am I doing, then?'

'Remarkably well, considering…' The man's expression turned serious as his voice trailed off and then he added, 'In fact, you're a very lucky man. But you won't be doing any doctoring for a while.'

He went on to explain he had an obvious leg fracture, the nature of which needed to be confirmed by X-rays, but he was ninety per cent certain he would need surgery to fix it. He would also order X-rays of several other areas of his skeleton they suspected might be damaged. A CT scan of his head would be performed and after that he would be transferred to a general acute bed in the ED and await assessment by the orthopaedic surgeon and the neurologist.

The realisation of how close to being killed he had come suddenly struck Richard and he spoke quietly as the doctor was about to leave.

'Thank you for what you've done.'

'My pleasure.' The man turned and extended his hand. 'I'm James Headland. I don't think we've met, before tonight, that is. I'm one of the ED consultants.' As they shook hands he added, 'I've heard of the good work you do and I reckon your job's a lot harder than mine.'

At that moment Sue breezed in.

'You'll be off to Radiology in the next ten minutes or so.' Then she grinned. 'And your wife is here.'

'Richard?'

Joanna had a full thirty seconds standing behind the nurse

before Richard noticed she was there. During that time a dozen different emotions battled with each other for her attention.

Her first and most overwhelming feeling was fear. Lying battered and bruised on the ED trolley and hooked up to an alarming number of monitors as well as two IVs, Richard was almost unrecognisable. He peered through swollen eyelids and appeared to be battling to remove the oxygen mask the nurse insisted on repositioning.

His left leg was immobilised in an air splint and a blood-soaked dressing covered his upper arm.

'Richard,' she said, a little louder. She suppressed an almost irresistible urge to rush to him and embrace him, kiss his swollen face and offer comfort with whatever resources she could muster. But he would be hurting and she didn't want to make his pain any worse.

'Joanna, you came.' He suddenly noticed her and his initial attempt to smile turned into a grimace.

A mixture of relief and overpowering, all-consuming, gut wrenching love took over her fear—he was alive and at least trying, though not too successfully, for cheerfulness.

'I'll just replace this dressing,' Sue said as she donned gloves and replaced the sodden gauze and anchored it with a bandage. 'How is your pain?'

'Bearable,' Richard said with a frustrated edge to his voice.

'Out of ten?'

'Seven, maybe six.' His voice croaked and he frowned as he cleared his throat. Joanna's heart went out to him. She could imagine him playing down his injuries for her benefit and by the tortured look on his face it was probably pain keeping him from drifting into a morphine-induced sleep.

'Improving, then?'

'A little.'

'Okay. As long as your BP's stable and normal Dr Headland's ordered a bolus of painkiller before you have your X-rays. I'll just check your blood pressure and then leave you two until the orderly comes.'

There was a brief moment of awkwardness when the nurse left but it didn't take long before silent tears began running down Joanna's cheeks and she leaned forward and kissed Richard on his bruised forehead.

'I'm sorry...' he whispered.

Joanna pulled herself away and reached for his hand.

'No, how can you say that? You're apologising?'

'I wanted...' He managed to pull off the mask and his words were husky with emotion. 'I wanted to tell you...' He hesitated as if he was choosing his words carefully. 'I wanted tonight to be special.' He paused again and took a moment to look at her as well as catch his breath. 'Look at you. You're the most beautiful woman...'

He closed his eyes and Joanna tried to wipe away her tears but she couldn't stop them. Richard was lying in the resuscitation room, his body broken and no doubt facing a long and difficult road back to health, and all he was thinking about was her.

'Shush.' She laid a finger gently on his lips and was surprised at the coolness of his skin. 'You don't need to tell me this now. Save your energy.'

'But I need to tell you. Before I go... If I have surgery...'

She suddenly realised he was thinking of the possibility of not surviving and she couldn't bear it. She stopped crying and took a deep breath.

'Don't even think about it, Richard Howell. Not now or ever.'

He frowned and said quietly, 'I don't understand.'

'I've fallen in love with you all over again,' she whispered.

'And I'm not going to let you have the slightest thought that you might leave me.'

The tears began again and this time a single drop of moisture escaped from Richard's eye but he was smiling a devilishly crooked smile.

'That's just what I was trying to tell you.'

The door swung open and James Headland stood in the doorway with an orderly behind him.

'How are you now?' he asked as he grabbed the chart and nodded his approval.

'Much better.'

He sent a glance in Joanna's direction and she knew Richard would come through this. He was bracing himself for whatever it took and she was going to be there with him— all the way.

Joanna accompanied Richard to the X-ray department and then sat with him while he waited for the orthopaedic surgeon's assessment. She shared the news that he needed the fracture of his femur fixed with an intramedullary nail—the sooner the better—and then anxiously waited four long hours while he was in surgery. The time dragged and she was overwhelmed with the news, at just after two in the morning, that the operation had been a success.

'When can I see him?' she asked the surgeon when he emerged from the operating rooms looking as weary as Joanna felt.

'It will probably be another hour before he's ready for transfer to Intensive Care—'

'ICU! Is there something wrong?'

The surgeon must have read the look on her face as alarm He touched her arm.

'No, nothing's wrong. Everything went smoothly in

heatre. He's had a head injury, though, and lost a lot of
ood. It's just a precaution to watch him overnight, give him
other unit of blood, make sure he's stable before transfer-
ng him to the orthopaedic ward.'

Joanna still couldn't relax and wasn't going to leave until
e saw him, even if it meant staying at the hospital all night.

'So when can I see him?' she repeated. 'I need to know—'

The surgeon sighed. 'You're his wife, are you?'

'Yes.' Joanna was surprised how easy it was to slip into
at role.

'And a paediatric nurse?'

'That's right.' She tried her hardest not to sound impatient.

'If you put on a gown, mask and cap, you can pop into
ecovery. It's unlikely he'll be awake as he's on a fairly hefty
ose of morphine. In fact, the best thing you can do after you
ee him would be to go home and get some rest. He should
e well enough to have a visitor late this afternoon.'

What he was saying made sense and she was grateful for
e time the doctor had spent with her and the concession
e'd made in allowing her to go into the recovery ward.

'Thank you.' She held out her hand and he shook it briefly.

'The change rooms are down there.' He nodded in the di-
ction of the operating theatres just before he strode away.
hen he stopped and turned, smiling. 'He's lucky to have you
nd I'm as certain as I can be that he'll recover.'

Joanna knew that nothing was certain in medicine but
e accepted the reassurance and told herself something she
ften said to the distraught relatives of her own patients—
at wasting energy on worrying achieved nothing. But she
nly half convinced herself and her anxiety escalated when,
fter quickly changing, she arrived in the recovery room.

'You must be Mrs Howell?' The nurse looked up briefly

before glancing at the bag dripping blood into a vein
Richard's arm and writing something on his chart.

'Yes.' The word came out as a whisper. She felt herse
flushing.

From what she could see of Richard, he looked deathly pa
and seemed to be hooked up to even more monitoring equip
ment than in the emergency department. The nurse beckone
her to come closer.

'The anaesthetist has just taken his endotracheal tube ou
He's breathing well on his own and he even opened his eye
He'll probably be on the move within the next half-hour. He
doing really well.'

Joanna sidled up to the trolley and tucked her fingers in
the palm of one of his hands. He showed no sign of wakefu
ness at first but then slowly opened his eyes. His face, sti
swollen, had darkened with more bruising over the hours
had been in surgery.

'Richard?'

His eyes slowly closed, as if it had been a great effort
open them but, under the mask, she could tell he was tryi
to say something.

'Don't try and talk. I just needed to see you.' She didn
add that she'd wanted to make sure he was still alive, ar
that she was scared and confused, balanced on the edge of
bunch of emotions she hadn't fully come to grips with. He
grief at the prospect of losing him had been acute and ove
whelming.

She leaned over and kissed his cheek and in a husky whi
per Joanna could barely understand he said, 'I love you, J
I always have and I always will.' His eyes opened again ar
were full of passion. 'So much that it hurts more than...' F

squeezed her hand and then, before she had a chance to answer, he drifted off into a deep sleep. She could barely hold back the tears.

It must have been scarcely a minute or two that Joanna stood staring at the battered figure of the man she loved, but it seemed like an age. There was so much she wanted to tell him, so many words that had been left unsaid.

She turned as she felt a gentle hand on her shoulder.

'Mr Nichols said you could only have five minutes. I'm sorry…'

'I know. Thank you.'

She leaned close and kissed Richard again, whispering the same words he'd made such an effort to say to her a minute ago but knowing he wouldn't hear her.

'I'm sorry, but…' The nurse smiled.

'Yes, I know I must go.'

Joanna released Richard's hand and walked out of the ward, suddenly overcome with tiredness. She needed to go home to try and get some sleep.

Richard groaned.

The dull pain in his leg was unremitting but bearable, as long as he didn't move.

'What the hell…?' he muttered, then opened his eyes, glanced around him, and remembered.

He was in hospital. There'd been an accident—a nasty one—and he'd had an operation. He remembered a dream, so vivid it could almost have been real. He'd seen Joanna. His beautiful, caring, Joanna—and he'd told her he loved her.

The door of his room slowly opened and he was surprised at the ferocity of his desire for it to be her.

'Dr Howell, you're finally awake.'

Disappointment.

The middle-aged nurse bore no resemblance to his darling Jo.

Very perceptive of you to notice, he felt like saying, but simply nodded instead.

'Good.' She wheeled in the hardware required to do his obs. 'How is the pain?'

He flinched as she looked as if she was about to prod his heavily bandaged leg but instead pinched his big toe.

'Ouch.' He uttered the protest out of surprise more than genuine pain but the ache in his leg seemed to go up a notch. The nurse raised her black, pencilled eyebrows but thankfully didn't comment.

'Seven out of ten,' he finally said with a frown. He thought he had a reasonably high tolerance to pain, but he hadn't broken the biggest long-bone in his body before.

'I'll give you a bolus of morphine, then, and now you're awake I'll organise PCA. I assume you know what that means.'

'Yes.' He didn't have the energy to verify he was familiar with the system where he could give his own medication, the so-called *patient-controlled analgesia.*

The nurse checked his BP, temperature and oxygen saturation as well as his urine output. She jotted a note on his chart and told him she would be back in five or ten minutes with the morphine.

'And you have a visitor.'

It was then he noticed Joanna hovering in the doorway with a broad grin on her face. It lasted only a moment and then her brow furrowed in an expression he'd seen many times.

Something was wrong. What had upset her? He wasn't fooled by the smile and he was pretty sure his mind was clear, despite the cocktail of medications coursing through his veins.

'Come in, Joanna.' He went to stretch out his arms to give her a hug but got caught up in a tangle of tubes and wires. Before he had time to apologise she was at his bedside, her hands resting lightly on his shoulders, her soft, warm lips on his cheek. God, her touch was more therapeutic than any drugs.

'What time is it? I hope you haven't been here all night.' He glanced at the window, covered with Venetian blinds open just enough to see slivers of sky tinged with the orange-gold of a rising sun... Or was it setting?

'I left about half past two this morning, after your op, and when I phoned at lunchtime they said you were still out of it.' She ran gentle fingers over the back of his hand that wasn't connected to an IV tube. Her touch felt so good. 'It's nearly seven o'clock.'

He paused for a moment, taking in what she'd said. He'd lost an entire day.

'At night? And it's Monday?'

'That's right.'

She withdrew her hand and pulled a chair close to the bed but he still had the impression something was wrong. Had the operation not gone as well as he had been led to believe? Had he done something to upset her? He couldn't imagine what. He'd been unconscious for most of the day. Perhaps something had happened that had nothing to do with him. The thoughts began to spin in his head and he closed his eyes and took a couple of steadying breaths.

'There's something wrong, Jo. I can tell you're upset. I know you must have been to hell and back over the last twenty-four hours but—'

'There's nothing wrong.' She smiled with a return of the

old warmth that he knew so well. 'But, yes, it's been a strain. I'm not the one with a metal spike in my leg, though, and a face that bears an uncanny resemblance to a half-inflated soccer ball.'

He laughed. And his awareness of the pain in his leg increased, but he felt a little better.

At that moment the nurse came in with his analgesia. She glanced at Joanna, who stood and dragged the chair a little away from the bed to give the nurse access to the arm with the drip.

'Are you happy to stay while I set up the PCA?'

'If it's okay with you.'

'No problem.'

Richard felt the effect of the bolus of medication almost immediately. The throbbing in his leg eased and a swooning light-headedness made the room spin. He closed his eyes and that was the last thing he clearly remembered until he felt a gentle squeeze of his hand.

'I'm going now.'

He saw Joanna through a fuddled haze.

'So soon? You've only just arrived.'

'You've been asleep for…' she looked at her watch '…five hours. It's past midnight and I have to work tomorrow. I have an early. I'll come in and see you after work.' She grinned. 'And Mr Nichols made a brief appearance and said you're doing great.'

'Midnight? I'm sorry… Of course you must go… Come here.'

He kissed her hand, drew her close then kissed her lips.

He wanted to reaffirm that he loved her but she pulled away, patted his hand and left the room before he could even say goodbye.

His earlier worries came rolling back. Something was defi-

itely wrong. His heart did an uncomfortable somersault and
hen fell with a heavy thud and came to rest in the pit of his
tomach.

She'd stopped loving him. And he was somehow to blame.

oanna couldn't tell him. It was too soon after his opera-
ion and it wasn't fair to add her life-changing news when
e'd been through what she assumed was one of the biggest
raumas of his life.

She decided she'd leave it at least a few days, until he was
over the worst of his post-operative pain. She'd know when
he time was right. Or at least that's what she kept telling her-
elf, over and over.

She'd know when the time was right.

t was the fourth post-operative day and, apart from a nag-
ing pain in his left thigh when the physio cajoled him into
is daily exercises, Richard was feeling nearly normal. He had
tarted eating and actually enjoying the hospital food. One of
he IV lines and his urinary catheter had been removed the
previous day and the frequency of his morphine injections
vas decreasing and being replaced by tablets.

What had been his prime motivation to make as speedy
a recovery as he could was Joanna. She'd visited every day
and they'd managed to fill in an hour or two chatting about
he goings-on in Matilda Ward—how Alan Price had apparently welcomed a break in his retirement to return to work,
Karen's new boyfriend, the death of Barbara's elderly father
rom a heart attack, and a dozen other snippets of inconsequential gossip.

Joanna seemed to have developed an uncanny knack for
avoiding discussion of anything more personal than work,
hough.

So he was going to talk to her today. To explain that th
dinner that had never happened was all part of a surprise tha
he hoped she'd be pleased with.

She was due any minute and he felt strangely nervous.

Half an hour later she arrived, looking absolutely gorgeou
in a gauzy, floaty mini-dress that wasn't sheer enough to b
transparent but it certainly drew attention to Joanna's femi
nine attributes.

'You look fabulous,' he said with a grin. 'I love the dress

Her cheeks flushed. 'It's new. They had a fifty per cer
off sale at Jenny Lee's.'

'It really suits you.'

'Thanks.'

Small talk was all they'd managed over the last couple
days and Richard wondered if a serious talk would clear th
air and at least restore their relationship to where it had bee
before the accident. Perhaps the drama of his injuries ha
swept them up in the *idea* that they loved each other but no
she was having second thoughts.

Second thoughts? Was it possible?

He knew he still loved Joanna and he'd believed what she
said on the night of the accident—that she loved him. But no
he was beginning to have doubts of his own and was confuse
about whether the feeling was still reciprocated. Or perhap
she had told him in the heat of the moment.

Joanna rummaged in her bag and brought out a packet
photographs.

'Lynne organised these. She said it might help you realis
how much the staff and the kids all miss you.' Her smile wa
one of genuine affection, most likely for her young charge
whose smiles lit each snapshot.

'They're fabulous. Can you make sure you thank Lynn
for me?'

'Perhaps you can tell her yourself. She said she'd come and visit on the weekend.'

'With her camera, no doubt.'

'Of course.'

The conversation dried up and Joanna began fiddling with the photos. He took them from her, put them away in the drawer of his bedside cabinet and grasped both her hands in his.

'We need to talk.'

'Yes,' she said in a quiet voice. Then she presented him with a heart-melting look and added, 'About our future.'

'That's right.'

Richard was about to continue: to try and explain how much he wanted the marriage to work again; to tell her he couldn't imagine spending the rest of his life with anyone else.

But she spoke first in a trembling voice so quiet he didn't quite hear what she said. At first he thought she'd said, 'I'm pregnant,' but he knew that was impossible.

'Pardon?'

She cleared her throat and reached for his hand.

'I'm pregnant.'

There was no mistaking the words this time. He beamed, not quite believing that she was telling the truth but thinking there was no reason for her to lie.

'Pregnant?'

She nodded, a smile spreading across her face.

'But—'

'We didn't believe it was possible, but we've been given another chance, Richard, another chance to bring a child into this world.' She took a deep breath and the tears began to trickle down her cheeks. 'And I'm scared to death.'

He spread his arms and reached out to her and she dissolved in his embrace.

'We're in this together, my darling Jo,' he managed to say, before tears started streaming down his own face.

They were tears of happiness.

It appeared all his dreams were coming true.

CHAPTER TEN

THE next month turned out to be an ordeal for both Richard and Joanna. Despite the pain and frustration of what seemed to be a never-ending struggle to get Richard back on his feet, an unfailing light shone bright to keep them both moving forward with hope and optimism.

That light was their love for each other, which was fuelled by the knowledge of the new life they had created. That love survived and sustained them through those awful early days of tests and surgery and not knowing.

Fortunately Richard's only broken bone had been his femur, which had apparently taken the full impact of the motorbike and snapped in two. Its repair had involved surgery to insert an intramedullary nail to hold the broken ends in place over the many months it would take the fracture to heal. Joanna still cringed at the thought of a massive nail being hammered through the top of the femur at the hip down the hollow part inside the main bone of the leg.

His other injuries had been relatively minor—concussion with no sign of long-term brain injury, a dislocated shoulder, a badly bruised ankle and various cuts, abrasions and bruises.

'I'm beginning to hate the physio sessions,' he said on the Monday of the third week when Joanna called to see him at the rehabilitation hospital. He'd been transferred from Perth

General the previous week, keen to at least learn the basics of day-to-day living so he could be discharged. He sat on a chair next to his bed. It was the first day she had seen him dressed in day clothes, the clothes he had insisted she bring when he had been moved. He looked even more handsome than usual.

She leaned across and kissed him, at first a light touch of her lips on his but he captured her face in his warm, strong hands and kissed her long and thoroughly until she had to pull away to catch her breath.

She laughed.

'You're feeling better, then?' she said.

'When can you take me away from all this, my wonderful fairy godmother?'

'You know they say doctors make the worst patients. Have you forgotten already what it's like, dealing with those stubborn souls who think they know best and don't do what they're told?'

He looked wistful for a moment.

'No, of course I haven't. That's why I want to get out of here. As soon as I can manage getting around on my own for longer than the regulation half-hour in this place, I should be able to at least touch base with work.'

Joanna chose to ignore his comment. She realised it would be a while before Richard was strutting the boards of Matilda Ward again but she had no doubt he would.

'You've had two days of rehab and you think you're ready to go back to work?'

He grinned sheepishly.

'No, not really.'

'Good, you're not as pig-headed as you pretend to be. And Alan Price is quite happy to interrupt his retirement. He actually said he'd become bored with golf.'

'Not too happy, I hope,' he said with a grin, and then added, 'Patience is something I've had to learn quickly here to stop me going insane.'

'Mmm.'

They sat in comfortable silence for a minute or two, holding hands. Richard had a single room on the second floor, overlooking an expanse of garden crisscrossed by several meandering, wheelchair-friendly paths. Joanna was impatient for the day they could walk together through the gardens and hoped it wouldn't be too long.

Richard had been told by his surgeon that early intervention following surgery focused on immediate weight bearing and then progression to strengthening exercises. She'd been amazed at his progress and suspected in those early post-op days he'd made a heroic effort to work though his pain without complaint.

Richard and Joanna decided to reaffirm their vows in the second week of spring to allow Richard's bones to heal and to give them plenty of time to make sure the day was as wonderful as it could possibly be. Joanna would be nearly six months pregnant by then. They decided on a small morning ceremony in one of their favourite places followed by a lunch for a group of close family and friends in the recently renovated and landscaped garden of their spacious new home. On a Saturday in mid-September it dawned an ideal day for a wonderful wedding and by mid-morning the small group of guests had assembled.

Joanna held a bouquet of yellow, perfectly formed, sweet-smelling rosebuds, which complemented the delicately feminine, cream silk dress that was softly gathered below the bust to accommodate her now very obvious pregnancy. Richard looked elegant and sexy and gorgeous all at the same time in a tailored black suit, the palest lemon-yellow shirt and a silver-grey tie.

The second-time bride hesitated as she reached up to tame a feral lock escaped from her dark glossy cap, still a long way from reaching her pale, bare shoulders. His smile reached out to her like the first sunlit rays of a delicate spring dawn and her husband made her feel so special in an amazing way she'd always dreamed he would...again.

They stood at the makeshift altar in the secret courtyard garden of Lady Lawler Children's Hospital amongst a crowd of beaming children. Some were on crutches; others were in wheelchairs hooked up to IVs and portable oxygen cylinders; many were bald and had the round faces of chemotherapy— but every single child was brimming over with happiness for the couple about to endorse their love and commitment.

Richard and Joanna recited their vows of love and caring to an audience hushed with anticipation, and then the clear, sweet voice of a boy soprano rang out in the crisp air of a perfect spring day. Danny Sims sang 'The Rose'.

Then a tiny girl in a long white dress toddled forward and presented the bride with a small posy of sweet-smelling freesias to add to her bouquet.

'From all us kids,' she said grandly.

Joanna bent forward and kissed the child's cheek.

'Thank you, Taylor,' Joanna whispered a moment before the little girl ran back to the protective arms of her smiling mother.

Richard squeezed his wife's hand.

'And I'd like to thank everyone here today for sharing our happiness. Though I'm afraid we can't put it off any longer: what you've all been waiting for; what started this whole thing with Joanna and I.'

The guests chuckled and then began to clap as Jessie and

Cassie brought out a chair, Karen following close behind carrying a small case and what looked like a Spiderman cape slung across her arm.

Lynne and Barbara came next with sombre expressions on their faces.

With the theatrics of a circus ringmaster, Lynne led Richard to the chair. He sat down and Karen draped him in the cape while the noise of the clapping gradually increased to a crescendo.

Barbara raised her hands.

'Quiet, everyone.'

She beckoned Joanna to come across and handed her a set of battery-operated shears.

'Since Dr Howell…er…your husband is making this sacrifice for you and for all of us too, would you like to perform the first cut?'

Joanna laughed. 'No, I think I'll let you do the honours,' she said, as she bent to kiss her apprehensive husband.

'Are you sure you want to do this?' she added.

'Definitely. I've never been surer of anything in my entire life.'

And as the first locks began to fall Danny again began to sing…the opening verse of 'Wind Beneath My Wings'.

* * * * *

A sneaky peek at next month...

Medical Romance™

CAPTIVATING MEDICAL DRAMA—WITH HEART

My wish list for next month's titles...

In stores from 2nd December 2011:

❏ New Doc in Town & Orphan Under the Christmas Tree
  — Meredith Webber

❏ The Night Before Christmas — Alison Roberts

& Once a Good Girl... — Wendy S. Marcus

❏ Surgeon in a Wedding Dress — Sue MacKay

❏ The Boy Who Made Them Love Again — Scarlet Wilson

Available at WHSmith, Tesco, Asda, Eason, Amazon and Apple

Just can't wait?

Have Your Say

You've just finished your book.
So what did you think?

We'd love to hear your thoughts on our
'Have your say' online panel
www.millsandboon.co.uk/haveyoursay

- 🌹 Easy to use
- 🌹 Short questionnaire
- 🌹 Chance to win Mills & Boon®
  goodies